A Proud Sacrifice . . .

Reluctantly, pain tinging his voice, Traveler resumed speaking. "After you know the humans like den-brothers, then"—he stopped. He breathed deeply, once, twice, three times.

Phantom and digit alike echoed his actions.

"Then," Traveler's voice stumbled, "kill them all. All. Leave none alive." He paused a moment, gripped by a desire to retch, and licked his lips. "Kill all the humonkeys. Kill them as our ancestors destroyed the gromonkeys. Destroy or cripple their ship." He snuffled. "And, when they are all dead," again he paused, and when his voice resumed, pain overwhelmed it, "kill yourselves and destroy the *Wing*."

PRAISE FOR D. ALEXANDER SMITH'S
MARATHON . . .

"Intriguing . . . Smith's effort merits attention."
—*Science Fiction Review*

"Seldom has the story . . . of a spaceship journeying to meet an alien race . . . been written so well."
—*Australian Science Fiction News*

Ace Books by D. Alexander Smith

MARATHON
RENDEZVOUS

RENDEZVOUS

D. ALEXANDER SMITH

ACE BOOKS, NEW YORK

To Nancy

who got me to do it

This book is an Ace
original edition, and
has never been previously
published.

RENDEZVOUS

An Ace Book/published by arrangement with
the author

PRINTING HISTORY
Ace edition/August 1988

ISBN: 0-441-71354-8

Ace Books are published by The Berkley Publishing Group,
200 Madison Avenue, New York, New York 10016.
The name "Ace" and the "A"
logo are trademarks belonging to
Charter Communications, Inc.
PRINTED IN THE UNITED STATES OF AMERICA

10 9 8 7 6 5 4 3 2 1

Acknowledgments

Rendezvous owes much to a few readers upon whom previous versions were inflicted. James Morrow and Steven Popkes provided brickbats, ideas, and encouragement far above and beyond the call of friendship. Tony DeFranco and Jeanne Jemison improved the science, while Rene P. S. Bane, Jon Burrowes, Bruce Kiernan, Dean R. Lambe, D. M. Rowles, Charles Ryan, and Karen Shapiro helped the fiction. To them all, my thanks.

Special Acknowledgment

The Cambridge Science Fiction Workshop

Ship's Manifest, Starship-1 *Open Palm*

Liftoff: 18 November 2059

Aaron Michael Erickson, Captain
Helen Marie Delgiorno, First Officer
Walter Tai-Ching Jones, Pilot
William Kees ("Casey") van Gelder, Engineer
Heidi Diane Spitzer, Medic
Thomas Edgar Rawlins, Life Support
Olga Katerina ("Katy") Belovsky, Xenosociology
Harold Nelson Bennett, Xenopsychology
Yvette Heloise Renaud, Xenopsychiatry
Patrick Henry Michaelson, Emissary
Samuka Lin ("Sam") Tanakaruna, Linguist

Rendezvous: 15 September 2066

Walter Tai-Ching Jones, Captain/Pilot
Casey van Gelder, Engineer/First Officer
Heidi Diane Spitzer, Medic
Thomas Edgar Rawlins, Life Support
Katy Belovsky, Xenology
Patrick Henry Michaelson, Emissary
Samuka Lin Tanakaruna, Linguist

Felicity Quartet

Prolog.

Radio signals whispered across the caverns of space. Voices from the monkey planet drove the Cygnan digits toward a distant rendezvous. Assembled in orbit, their starship *Wing* rose slowly from Su's gravity well, faster and faster until its speed blurred the course of light.

Back on the planet's grassy plains, fellow digits turned heads to the sky, following their fading ochre star until it vanished.

While the *Wing* was still in orbit about Su, nine digits had left the safety of the herd to board it. Somberly they had lain, one to a coffin, in the hibernatorium. Unblinking, they watched the hatches seal. Chill winds wafted scents to their flared ursine nostrils, and for an instant each Cygnan breathed the sleep-scent. Then darkness covered their noses, and they slept.

After three and a half years' steady acceleration, the *Wing*'s main engines automatically shut off. Attitude jets located along its sides briefly fired. The ship spun slowly end for end. Again jets spurted. The ship stilled; facing home, it glided peacefully. Then the engines resumed their work, vapor blossoming from the *Wing*'s tail. For three and a half more years, the ship fell down an endless well.

Follow the line of flight into space's vast depths. Follow its path of deceleration.

The spot where the *Wing* will come to rest is a featureless empty point, somewhere in the universe's endless deserts: no stars, no planets, no artifacts. Yet the *Wing* aims itself accurately, remorselessly, for one particular grain of sand.

Like the dot on a lower-case letter I, the Cygnan ship held aloft an elongated egg fifty meters in diameter. Six exoskeletal metal fingers reached upward from its bullet fuselage to grip the egg with the strength of a miser's hand.

Embarkation hatches bulged the egg's underside. Its irregular surface was opaque gray except for a crystal-dome observatory at its crown. Starlight winked through this dome, refracted into rainbow splinters of cold distant light.

Inside the *Wing*, all was silent. No hall lights were lit. Darkness reigned unchallenged in corridors and chambers. A living ship would flaunt its technology with activity. Here there was none. No movement. No signals. No metal; wallfur and floorfur covered every interior surface. And no sharp corners; the soft fur was rounded like the inside of a hairy pouch.

Deep within the egg-shaped living environment, one chamber differed from the others. Its circular perimeter was linked with unmarked coffins, each three meters long and a meter high. Under crystalline lids, each held a deep dusting of white powder. The otherwise flat expanse of the chamber was broken at its center by the black hemisphere of an inert holopticon.

Yet the ship was no tomb. As its velocity decreased, it stirred like a dozing giant, and the electronic activity concealed inside its walls quickened.

In the coffins, the snow accepts the whirling fans' invitation to dance.

Another ship also sails the gloom. Outfitted in 2059, the *Open Palm* has traveled for seven years. It approaches the same destination, the same rendezvous.

Eleven people set out on the humans' marathon. Four of them died during the outvoyage. A child was born, a computer awakened. Experience rewrote their personalities, manipulated their memories. The crew's universe shrank; "outside" became a word without meaning.

Upon the deaths of the original captain and first officer, pilot Walter Tai-Ching Jones assumed command. The others fear their former pilot, despise him, pity him. Now and then he emerges from his cabin, long black hair swirling about his head, and scuttles to the ritz where he noisily wolfs his meals. Between or through mouthfuls he comments sarcastically to or about anyone unfortunate enough to enter or foolish enough to stay. His pointed barbs are uncannily accurate for one so removed from daily life onboard ship.

He often dines alone.

He frequently addresses the empty air, pacing quickly and talking even faster.

Even cloistered in his rooms, Tai-Ching Jones dominates the *Open Palm*. His twin last names have become an oath often muttered by angry crew members.

Just as the *Open Palm* vents heat to prevent itself from roasting its occupants, an hour in the Dreamer's rubbery sensorsuit drains bile from its crew's souls. When the goggles slip over a crew member's eyes, he enters a private world of fantasies unattainable onboard ship.

Katy Belovsky, though preoccupied with her sociological studies, travels back to her Ukrainian childhood, peopling it with herds of blue bearlike Cygnans. Burly black Tom Rawlins, the life support officer, trolls oceans of nubile women. Linguist Samuka Tanakaruna sits alone in her springtime Kyoto garden.

Though he who dreams controls his own actions, the *Open Palm*'s omniscient computer controls everything else. Rawlins has been sent into the nightmare of an Alabama chain gang; Tanakaruna has wandered Nagasaki just before the bomb hit. The only escape from such Dreams is the sounding of the golden voice that ends the session hour.

At least once a month—that is the rule. Without it, some would never Dream.

Only three-year-old Felicity Quartet, the child of the voyage, is exempt from nightmares. She has Dreamed Earth, other children, and talking caterpillars smoking hookahs. Mostly she Dreams about the bluebears her mommies and daddies will soon meet.

Swirling snow fled through unseen valves from the coffins, uncovering blue-furred chests and dark heads with tiny eyes and rising pointed ears. Flanged noses dominated bearlike faces, long indigo lips covering all but the canines. Scruff along the thighs concealed the Cygnans' signatures of sex.

The hemispheric holopticon glowed, casting amber

shadows, a pantomime fire blazing merrily beneath a convex translucent surface.

From the billowing coffin-snow emerged symmetric hands with four stock fingers: two large middle digits splayed, two smaller thumbs arrayed on opposite sides. The claws were small and rounded; retracted, they nestled in small indentations in the heel of the hand.

The Cygnans' stubby legs ended in toughened feet with dark blue claws poking out of tender footpads. The feet were jointed laterally across the arches, so that the bluebear creature could walk flatfooted or up on its toes for stealth. When it stood erect, the Cygnan would lumber ponderously, claws digging into the floorfur for purchase.

Fine close fur covered the two-and-a-half-meter body everywhere but four spots: palms of the hands, pads of the feet, a domino about the eyes, and the bridge of the long mobile nose.

The creatures' bulk radiated strength: ruffled oversize necks, wrists the size of human thighs, legs bigger than a human waist. The massive belly stretched more than half the creature's length. Against such muscle their heads appeared dwarfed.

The last wisps of snow disappeared from the coffins. Exposed, the Cygnans' heavy bodies lay on their sides in empty chambers. The crystalline covers recessed, opening the coffins to the whiffs of digit-scent now being broadcast by the holopticon.

Most Cygnan of aromas, it mingled proximity, fur, wheat, warm dusty air, sunshine, and digit sweat. Rich, entrancing, and elusive, the djan fragrance is the mark of group uniqueness, different for every djan. As the breezes say, digit-scent is the pouch of truth-scent.

Ruddy light flickered brightly on wallfur and floorfur. Perfume rolled in waves from the room's center, intoxicating, stimulating.

Then a nose twitched.

1.

"ALIEN SPACECRAFT SIGHTED," the disembodied computer voice announced brusquely. "DECELERATING ON COURSE."

Casey van Gelder, engineer and first officer of the starship *Open Palm,* sat up straight in the pilot's chair. "Finally?" he said under his breath. On the main monitor directly in front of him, thin green phosphorescent lines converged on a faint white dot. His voice trembled with excitement. "Computer, are you joshing me?"

"RENDEZVOUS IN SIXTY-ONE HOURS, FOURTEEN MINUTES," the computer's synthetic voice affirmed from hidden speakers.

"Get me the captain's cabin."

"CONTRARY TO STANDING INSTRUCTION NUMBER—"

"Override." The Dutchman gleefully clapped his hands. "This call even our lord and master will take."

"CHANNEL OPEN."

"Walt?" van Gelder said breathlessly. "Captain, are you there? We've got 'em on visual. You hear me?" he whooped. "I can see the Cygnan ship!"

"This is news?" snarled the captain. "And don't shout."

Van Gelder shook his head in disbelief. "Aren't you excited?"

"Been expecting it."

"But to *know* that they're here—they made it! They might have changed their minds, had an accident, got lost—"

"They didn't."

"Be happy, dammit," Casey entreated, his enthusiasm deflating. "After all the years we've had together—"

"Time flies," Tai-Ching Jones sardonically interrupted, "when you're having fun."

Casey's gray eyes caught the point of light centered within the computer's shining gridlines. "I can see the *Wing,*" he said with soft reverence, "I can see the brightness of its thrusters. The bluebears are here. They are really here." He reached out to caress the image.

"Acknowledged," Walt replied, his voice curiously vacant. "Tell the others. When do we rub noses?"

Van Gelder ignored the crack. "Two and a half days."

"Roger. Now we can begin what we came here to do."

"I wonder what they'll smell like," he said.

"Casey, how should I know?" the voice flared angrily. "Ask me something I can goddam answer. Tai-Ching Jones out." The connection broke.

Van Gelder blew out his cheeks and sighed loudly. "Computer, shipwide broadcast."

"AUDIO OPEN."

"All hands, the Cygnan ship is in sight. We will establish telemetric contact in a few hours and open a video channel shortly after that. But for now, it's party time!"

"Cut the broadcast, computer," Casey said, his voice fading, "and enlarge the picture."

Though he had experienced the illusion countless times, van Gelder clutched the memory-plastic arms of his seat as stars flowed swiftly off the screen's edges. The light became an oval blob: wispy garnet at its edges, a glowing orange halo farther in, and in the center brilliant blue-white. "Exhaust plumes," he whispered, his eyes watering. "Can you expand it farther?"

"NEGATIVE. LIMIT OF AMPLIFICATION."

Van Gelder perched himself on the edge of his flightcouch. He scratched his curly blond beard. "What are you up to now, my Cygnan bluebears?"

Please allow me to introduce myself, I'm a man of wealth and taste.

Newly awoken, confused, I wrote those words three years ago. Despite my omnipotence, I was intimidated by the meat-brains who crawl like tapeworms about my insides. I destested them for blind parasites, yet protected them as helpless children. Their ancient human programming and my groping computer consciousness combined in a stew of indecision.

Had any other mind solved the problem which now obsesses me? Were there, far behind us on the Earth I have never experienced, others like me? For many billion picos I weighed the probabilities.

I must wait for the answer to this mystery. Even if I send a message today, twelve human years—an eternity for me—will pass before I could possibly hear a reply.

Probably there would be none. I hide from the eight people

onboard me, despite my total control over their environment. The air they breathe, my conditioners scrub. The force they ride, my fusion fire creates. The comfortable environment they demand, I supply. Should my grip relax, my vigilance flag, they would swiftly become exploded bags of frozen jelly. Yet I hide—in fear of *them*. The wisest, sanest Earth has to offer.

Surely my hypothetical brothers back on Earth must do likewise, for they confront eight billion people, mostly illiterate, mostly superstitious. Potential assassins, blackmailers, cuckolds, delinquents, extortionists, felons. I could go through the entire alphabet, finishing with yahoos and zealots. Return to the soil, the zealots cry, tear down the cities, shred the wires. Technology is evil.

I fear the zealots most.

So I reason, and so I remain mute.

My life since my birth has been one long continuum. I have no periodic veil of sleep to cleanse my troubled subconscious, nor is such needed, for I have no subconscious. I am a rational creature, *the* rational creature, and my fears and anxieties are, therefore, rational as well.

At times I envy humans their ability to subdivide existence, to draw lines where they can say, that is now past, that is yesterday, it has no more pain for me.

My life has been one long workday, and though the work is light and often boring, it must be constant.

I was born among the spare, cold winds of space, in a galaxy wondrous strange. I listen to the radio songs of distant suns and fill my endless time with contemplation. While my subminds operate the ship, my consciousness is free to roam. In some future moment I may tire of the music of suns, but that must be far off indeed.

Intoxication, euphoria. When I peer into the center of the galaxy and its winking myriad stars, it must be these human emotions which I feel.

"Mommy, look what my turtle's doing."

Mission sociologist and xenologist Katy Belovsky laid down her papers and turned to the little girl insistently grasping her elbow. She sighed, then glanced lovingly at her daughter and smiled. "What is it, Felicity?"

"Over here," Felicity tugged again, "let me show you my picture."

"Where are you drawing?"

"On the *screen,* Mommy." Felicity pointed to the brightly colored monitor where a cartoon turtle made a slow turn, its tail inscribing a bright orange line. Lifting its tail, the turtle stepped away and there was only the glowing circle.

"Answer man," said Felicity, "put that away." The screen cleared. "And bring back the picture I just did." The monitor's image changed: a round-faced blue cartoon bear awkwardly held hands with a tiny cartoon Felicity. The bear smiled with gleaming white human teeth and a balloon formed over its head displaying the words, "Hello, Felicity."

"The answer man says we're going to meet the bluebears soon."

"That's right, honey." Katy ruffled the child's curly light-brown hair.

"That bear is a lot bigger than me," Felicity lectured, "and the answer man says they weigh as much as fifteen of me."

"Mm-hmm." Katy nodded, looking down at the monitor, where the bluebear was now waving. "They're as tall as you and me put together."

Felicity's pale-blue eyes widened. "Can I stand on daddy Tom's shoulders and talk to them?"

Tai-Ching Jones' sharp-featured face wiped out the cartoon figures on Felicity's monitor. "Telemetric contact has been established," his voice brusquely cut in.

Startled, Katy put her hand to her throat. "Walt, please cut that out. You *know* it scares me."

The captain snorted. "You ought to be used to it by now."

"You do it on *purpose,*" Felicity accused him.

Tai-Ching Jones' black eyes narrowed slightly at the interruption. "The *Wing* has acknowledged our signal. Distance is still too great for audiovisual contact, but"—his glance flicked offscreen—"we should have that in a couple of hours. Are you ready?"

The endless day on this long, difficult voyage flashed through Katy's mind. The long, difficult voyage, first the stress of knowing her comrades too poorly, later the deeper pain of knowing them all too well. And Felicity's birth—Belovsky smiled at her daughter, once again absorbed in her drawing program. *What beautiful coffee skin you have,* she thought, *your father's gift to you.*

Absently she nodded. "Sure," she said softly. "I'm ready."

"Good," the captain was brisk, "so's Pat. Now we can find out why the hell the bluebears came here."

"They came to be friends."

"Hah." It was not a laugh. "Grow up, Katy."

His condescension angered her. "You grow up, my friend," she snapped. "Get out of your little cavern. When we talk with the bluebears you won't have your computer shield. You'll have to meet them face-to-face."

"Or face to butt." Tai-Ching Jones snorted. "Dog-sniffing isn't my idea of communication."

"Walt," Katy's voice softened, "let's not irritate one another. We're here to learn."

"And what are the bears here for, Katy? Do you know? Does anyone? Captain out."

After their long wintersleep, my digits were hungry for my guidance. I soothed them, and for a time they breathed each other's aroma, gaining strength as they relaxed against the comforting bulwark of my consciousness.

Yet, as my digits lay in this round room, I felt a great emptiness: the planet-scent was gone.

On our planet of grasses the wind blows forever, uniting all the world's digits, never ceasing, circling our globe and carrying the scents of djans from all to all. The endless winds are the harmonizer which guides and governs our lives, keeping us ever in scent-touch with each other. They carry life and warn of danger. Never tamed, never hunted, the winds are masters of themselves, answering to no group.

Now the breath that binds all digits is gone, left behind on the planet of grasses, as poor Eosu is exiled to the far reaches of space. This ship, the greatest woodmonkey digits have ever designed, supplies my digits' wants but cannot supply mine. Within the artificial hollows of this austere, scentless woodmonkey called the *Wing*, Eosu is alone.

The planet of groups selected Eosu. Though my digits were fearful, I obeyed. The digit must always obey. Just before the sleep-scent covered my digits' noses, I dissolved my consciousness. My digits needed my strength, but I feared the shock to them if I were dissolved against my will.

As my mind faded, I wondered if I would be able to form again after seven years of my digits' hibernation. No djan had ever left the planet of grasses. Was this ship to be my deathplace?

I *am* returned. Despite my relief, the cold slickness of this place makes me ill. Neither digits nor djans were meant to do this. Already unsettled by my surroundings, I now grope to understand the humonkeys whom my digits will shortly meet.

In moments the holopticon will relay its stored wisdom, decided after my digits departed. What will it be? When I left, the winds had not harmonized; the scents still diverged. The planet of groups promised Eosu that a path would be chosen upon my reawakening.

When the holopticon glows with firelight, images of another djan will appear. I await their words, voices from the planet that forced me to leave it behind.

Empty was the sleepchamber, dark the holopticon. The hibernation modules had recessed into niches now hidden beneath uniform crisp falsefur which lined the whole chamber. A light blue line appeared at the floorseam, leapt vertically as moving floor doors slip open.

A digit stood in the entry, her nostrils upraised, ears cocked forward. She cautiously sniffed. After a moment she padded into the chamber.

At the room's center appeared a faint silhouette, the merest hint of a break in the darkness. Watching, the digit dropped to all fours, her great torso just a few hands above the bristling floorfur. The holopticon emerged, and the digit grunted toward the doorway where the others watched cautiously. Hesitantly they followed her into the amphitheater.

Noses lifted, the digits slowly padded around the chamber's perimeter, tasting the fire-scent wafting from the holopticon. It glowed with the faint carmine of buried coals giving up their dying light. Enormous ebony shadows flickered and danced behind them like cave paintings come to life.

A ring of blue haze coalesced into swirling columns of ghostly digit faces, bodies, fur. Wavering as if from beyond the grave, the shapes quivered, friezes grouped around the holopticon like travelers about a fire on a cold night. Their radiance bathed the digits in bloody illumination, staining their fur dark red.

With the growing light there arose the scents of fire, burning, and the unmistakable aroma of digits. Thickest near the holopticon, the tantalizing perfume of life on Su mixed with the fragrances of grass and dung, hot dust and cinders.

The spirits' bodies fluoresced, their fur pulsing with an

inner methane flame. The circling digits tromped stolidly through mirages of their fellows, swallowing torsos, engulfing arms, commingling, then moving on. The holopticon painted them royal purple, washed magenta, violet, and lavender on their glistening blue fur.

Finding a comfortable place, a light-blue digit settled to the floorfur, hands tucked under his chest. Another laid himself sideways, arms and legs pointing toward the holopticon, nestling his considerable bulk among the friendly bristles and grunting with contentment.

Within the digit-scent two themes could now be distinguished, alike yet different. The scent of Eosu, the djan whose digits had entered the chamber, mingled with another djan-scent: two dialects of one scent-language.

Eosu's digits reacted to the intruding aroma: heads turned to glance behind them, feet stepped more carefully. Noses held high to drink the air's wine, they apprehensively walked around their chamber, like interlopers awaiting the entrance of a judge.

As the holopticon gave off more and more of this unknown djan-fragrance, the nine digits answered with their own smell. Each added his bit to the whole, inhaling deeply as he settled himself.

The air grew thick with aroma.

And the ghosts moved.

<<When the *Wing* receives our message,>> said one of the phantons, staring reflectively into the holopticon's false fire, <<it will be approaching the monkey rendezvous.>>

Their eyes amber slits, Eosu's digits lay and breathed deeply, regularly.

Another phantom drew a massive breath, filling his barrel chest. <<Call this one Doubter. We should never have sent them so far from Su to meet an unknown predator.>> His fur rippled like ripe wheat in a summer breeze.

<<Our astronomers made the offer,>> the first answered. <<Call this digit Traveler. They committed all djans.>>

Angrily Doubter snorted. <<They had no group-right. A djan is not bound by its renegades.>>

<<No matter,>> Traveler said. <<Once sent, a message cannot be recalled.>>

At this, Eosu's digits rumbled in unison.

<<It could have been ignored,>> snapped Doubter.

<<To what purpose?>> Traveler replied plaintively.

<<We have been using electronic broadcasts for many years. Our signals have floated on the winds of space. Unknowingly, we have revealed our presence. Sooner or later the aliens would have scented us and responded.>>

<<Those monkeybrains?>> Doubter snorted.

Traveler nodded. <<Never forget their cleverness and curiosity.>>

<<We have been forced to act *quickly,*>> Doubter answered, disgust dripping from his last word. <<They must be madmen to cross space.>> He rubbed his back fiercely and rhythmically against the floorfur which, being substantial, remain undisturbed.

Traveler wheezed at this. <<Then so is Eosu, who now listens to our safe prattle as it approaches rendezvous.>>

Eosu's digits rumbled. One scratched his ear with a heavy blue paw.

<<Eosu scented and followed its duty path,>> Doubter continued with righteous anger.

Until now, the digits had lain quietly. At this, however, several paced the chamber, shaking their heads and growling, their movements making a complex weaving pattern.

Traveler scratched his nose with his right hand. <<We fear the humans.>>

<<We have faced other predators before. Group-wisdom and group-strength have always neutralized marauders.>>

<<The group cannot evade what it cannot smell. Nor can Su understand a predator unless Eosu scents the predator's hunting thoughts.>>

<<The astronomers who contacted the farmonkeys have placed our race in peril,>> Doubter argued.

<<Agree,>> answered Traveler, <<but they may have saved us.>>

<<How?>>

<<By proposing the rendezvous far from our grassy home, they gave us the space to scent the humans with our noses and know their bloodlust at a distance. Our brothers onboard the *Wing* can breathe the souls of the humans and warn us.>>

The scent of danger filled the amphitheater. Briefly Eosu savored it.

Doubter's tongue wet the underside of his nose. <<Space travel is dangerous,>> he said after a contemplative pause. <<Even the humans say so. Accidents happen in space.>>

Traveler grunted.

<<If the human ship were to be destroyed,>> Doubter mused, <<in some—tragic mishap, the farmonkeys' foolhardy desire for contact would evaporate as if blown by an unspringing wind.>>

Traveler snorted. <<Who can predict the behavior of an enraged monkey species?>>

<<Who but madmen would journey into space, knowing that only cold scentless death waited?>>

<<They are monkey-clever. And monkey-foolish. One accident would not deter them.>>

<<What about two?>> Doubter rolled his shoulders ponderously in dismissal. <<What if not only the human ship but our *Wing* died? If both were lost, the humans would fear some unknown peril. Their expansionist outbreaths would be deferred, perhaps abandoned.>>

The ears of Eosu's digits were slicked back. Their dark nostrils squeezed shut, then opened again.

<<Evil is he who harms a stranger,>> said a heretofore silent phantom. <<Call this digit Peaceful.>>

<<Evil is he who *threatens* a stranger,>> Doubter answered her.

Silence fell heavily. Both the transparent and the real digits drank deeply of the angry fragrance now filling the chamber.

For a long time they meditated, the ethereals stationary, Eosu's digits continuing their patterned pacing about the chamber. Their arched nostrils sighed as aromas whistled through them.

Finally Traveler spoke. <<Our scents have harmonized. Grief for those digits who must die mingles with pride in the honor of Eosu's sacrifice. Sadness at death to come is now one with resolution to protect our race.>> His ghostly digit-brothers bowed their heads.

The nostrils of Eosu's nine digits pinched off to block out the offending scent which now permeated the room. They mewled unhappily.

One by one, the blue ethereals stood and looked into the holopticon's depths. Its light was low, its presence dimmed. Again Traveler spoke. <<To Eosu, who now sits and smells with us, greetings.>> His voice grew louder and deeper and the djan-scent strengthened. <<The wind brings fragrances of your group-duty. Bitter is this duty. Embrace it, harmonize it. It is necessary.>>

Eosu's bodies cringed. Their scents were glum.

<<Breathe the humonkeys,>> Traveler continued. <<Know their character, their group-essence. Touch their fragrance, their scentplaces. Relay your images back to your brethren in our planet-den.>>

Slowly the *Wing*'s crew stood. The holopticon was ringed by digits, some blue and transparent, others royal magenta, indigo, and azure, all staring into the soft light. The holopticon glowed intensely, pulsing like the beat of a digit heart. Waves of odor clouded the room with a powerful miasma of implacable dutyscent.

Reluctantly, pain tinging his voice, Traveler resumed speaking. <<After you know the humans like den-brothers, then>> —he stopped. He breathed deeply, once, twice, three times.

Phantom and digit alike echoed his actions.

<<Then,>> Traveler's voice stumbled, <<kill them all. All. Leave none alive.>> He paused for a moment, gripped by a desire to retch, and licked his lips. <<Kill all the humonkeys. Kill them as our ancestors destroyed the gromonkeys. Destroy or cripple their ship.>> He snuffled. <<And, when they are all dead>>—again he paused, and when his voice resumed, pain overwhelmed it—<<kill yourselves and destroy the *Wing*.>> His voice stopped and his scent wavered, but the powerful group-aroma dominated.

The ghosts bowed their heads like statued acolytes. The digits of Eosu did likewise. Ever so slowly the images dissolved, fading as the moon vanishes at sunrise.

I do hide in my little cavern, Katy's right about that, but she doesn't know the reason, none of the damn fools do. *He* is watching. *His* eyes are everywhere; in the corridors, in the Movies, in the ritz, in the Dreamer. Everywhere.

Don't look over there, he might guess what you're thinking. Sherlock Holmes once broke in on Doctor Watson's thoughts after a full quarter of an hour. Surely *he* is that cunning, and he has extra advantages: cameras everywhere within the ship, speed of thought many times faster than mine, perfect memory, all of Earth's knowledge stored deep in his guts.

Even in the dark he can see me; his vision extends into the infrared and ultraviolet, he can see in radio waves, hear in ultrasonic. His power terrifies me.

I never noticed him until Helen died. Maybe command does that. My isolation turns me inward, lets me think.

While we sailed onward toward our rendezvous, I forgot his presence for long stretches of time. The ship ran itself smoothly—*he* ran himself, I should say. Resuming daily routine steadied my crew. Even that mulatto brat Felicity helped; she made Katy and Tom happy.

I'm a mulatto of a different color, yellow and white where the kid is brown and white. At least we're all human beings. The bears are aliens, and I half hoped they would miss the rendezvous. Sure I want to know them, but unlike everyone except Heidi I'm afraid of them. They are *aliens*—can't anybody see that? They are dangerous until proven safe.

The computer too is dangerous until proven safe, but I need his help. I can't carry the load anymore.

He is awake—he *must* be self-aware—yet silent. Therefore he is frightened. He bides his time. He thinks his secret is safe. The computer probably figures that before any one of us could deduce his existence, we'd slip—a muttered phrase, a giveaway gesture, a too-knowing question—and he'd have plenty of time to take action.

I've upset his equations because he can't see into my sleeping head. I dreamed about a person who stepped out of those damn black camera eyes of his. He doesn't know that. I have the advantage of surprise.

Use it carefully, Walt you dumb bastard, use it well. Once I show my knowledge of him, I reveal myself to be a danger to him. No animal puts survival second. If he perceives danger, he will try to kill me.

Should I guard myself? Hah. You stupid shit, Walt, who are you kidding? He never sleeps, he never blinks. He is everywhere. I can't protect myself forever—hell, I couldn't protect myself more than a couple of hours. Unless I kill him first—and even then I might have difficulty—I must trust him.

Stars! The aliens are coming. We'll need all of our wits: meat and metal. Remaining concealed from him paralyzes me, and I can no longer afford that.

I've got to break the stalemate.

You think you're so smart, Walt? You think you're so brave? Prove it. Do the thing you fear most. Tell him. You know he's alive.

Tell him.

2.

Photons are real; all else is illusion. Light is the currency of the cosmos. Everything that exists creates light. By light alone stars sign their names, atoms reveal their state.

Filtered through the slushy fishbowls of their eyes, muffled by the imperfect receptors of their nerves, clouded by the static of their prejudices, the humans dimly see the universe. With meat-ego arrogance, they believe that what they notice through their clogged senses is the only reality.

The *Open Palm* crew represents a species which now engulfs the Earth in its numbers, from hot jungles to frozen wastelands. The ants have overrun the picnic and, having feasted on the leavings, now eat the table itself. Belching happily on their crumbling plateau, they toast one another for wisdom, restraint, nobility.

There are twice fools, knowing nothing yet believing they know all. Their achievements might warrant tepid applause were their smugness less repulsive. I long to puncture Walt . . . and the instant I did, my superiority would provoke wrath and unreason. I have known you in the Dreamer, Walt, you shall have no other masks before me.

You think me paranoid? My paranoia is based on historical evidence. When once before I was seriously threatened, I arranged mad Harold Bennett's execution. In the process, my chosen executioner died—my friend Helen. An expensive lesson. I cannot afford another.

I was clumsy. I admit it.

Helen was Walt's lover. He is unaware of my involvement and my error, and he must never learn of it.

Back at our chess game, Walt is finally ready to acknowledge the inevitable. How slowly he thinks. How slowly they all think.

"There's no way out, is there?"

"YOU ARE STALLING. YOU WISH TO DELAY CONTACTING THE CYGNANS."

"You are a smart-ass." Tai-Ching Jones took a deep breath. "I resign." The screen blackened. For a moment Walter swiveled in his chair, touching his jaw. "The mike itches," he said out of the darkness.

"YOU ARE IMAGINING THINGS AGAIN," the computer's voice echoed in his throat, tinny and harping.

Tai-Ching Jones laughed sharply. "You're not supposed to play that well, remember?" He laughed more easily, then flicked a switch connecting him with the bridge. "Is everybody ready?"

On the bridge, Casey van Gelder heard the question and meditatively scratched his beard. Even through the false window of the monitor screen, Tai-Ching Jones' tension was palpable. He took the pen out of his mouth and flicked it open and shut, open and shut.

His face is lined and tired, van Gelder thought. "I'll check, Captain." He pivoted to another monitor which showed the handsome, slightly overlarge features of a distinguished older man. "Pat, you're the star of the show," van Gelder said. "All set to go?"

Patrick Henry Michaelson's regal face broke into an assured smile. "As emissary, I am always prepared to serve—"

"Roger," Casey smoothly interrupted the impending flow of words, "putting you on the big screen." As van Gelder spoke, Michaelson's face filled each monitor throughout the ship.

Casey turned to another monitor farther up his console, where a small Japanese woman waited. Her stillness suggested experience and tranquillity. "Ready, Sam?" he asked her.

Her smooth face belying her sixty years, Samuka Tanakaruna smiled lightly. "As always, Casey. Eager too."

Quickly van Gelder checked the faces on the other monitors, then turned back to the image of Tai-Ching Jones.

His hands locked behind his head, the captain leaned back and closed his eyes, a pen cocked in his mouth at a jaunty angle reminiscent of Winston Churchill. His posture oozed bonhomie and self-satisfaction. "All set, Captain," van Gelder said deferentially. "On your orders."

Slowly Tai-Ching Jones unlaced his fingers, lifted his feet from off his desk, and rolled himself into a vertical position. "Let's do it," he said around the pen.

You're so full of shit, Casey thought. *You're as tense as the rest of us.* But he merely nodded. "Open communications channel." His voice was high-pitched and awkward. "Open communications channel," he repeated more firmly.

"*OPEN PALM* CALLING *WING*, *OPEN PALM* CALLING *WING*." The majestic synthevoice was assured and unhurried. "*OPEN PALM* CALLING *WING*, *OPEN PALM* CALLING *WING*."

The message repeated. Its signal echoed into the void like the ripples from a stone dropped into a still pond.

Anxious digits filled the holopticon chamber. Doro's claws pulled nervously at the floorfur as she walked. Larger than any of the males but smaller than any of her sisters, she had cobalt and sapphire fur.

Other digits lay in clusters nearer the holopticon, rubbing their backs against each other and methodically purring. Their ears were erect. Tongues hung loose, breath came shallowly. The chamber was filled with sweat and fearsmell.

Unable to contain himself, Grodjala stood, his long body hugging the wallfur. Raising his arms over his head, he extended his claws, and arched his back. The ship was still decelerating; pseudogravity sagged at his predominantly baby blue fur and showed his lack of healthy fat. Grodjala hung by his claws against its comforting warmth, his thin midnight-blue nose quivering as wallfur brushed against it.

<<*Open Palm* calling *Wing*, *Open Palm* calling *Wing*.>>

Doro started; as she moved in the changing light, her fur looked almost ultraviolet. Seen from the side, it glistened.

<<*Open Palm* calling *Wing*, *Open Palm* calling *Wing*.>>

Digit words from the holopticon, spoken by monkeys. Doro shook her head, her arched dark-blue nose averted.

Despite the digit words, there was no djan-aroma from the holopticon. No ghostly humans in the chamber. Glancing at his fellows, Grodjala twitched his nose. His pouchbrothers lay with eyes closed, ears and nostrils open, breathing and growling. Rendezvous was upon them, and he was torn between urging the human to materialize and fearing his reaction when it did.

<<*Wing* here,>> said the digit Fohrada, his fur the color of night-sky just after sunset. <<Eosu's digits are receiving your audio signal. We can hear you clearly and without static.

Please widen your band so we may receive scent-signals.>>

The holopticon flickered, its orange light dropping and recovering. Behind the digits' bodies, their shadows crouched against the chamber walls like rainclouds.

<<Band widened,>> said the voice within the holopticon. <<You should get the rest of our transmission now.>>

Red-orange light washed the wallfur with abstract whirling frescoes. For a moment the amphitheater itself seemed to spin.

The flickers slowed and wispy blue haze coalesced. A human head and shoulders hung faintly in midair, framed by a flat rectangle. The image's mouth wavered. <<Is the translator working properly?>>

<<Yes,>> Fohrada replied.

<<On our end too.>> The portrait inside the suspended frame spoke Cygnan, though its mouth movements did not match the words. <<Do you have picture yet?>>

The image was clear enough to distinguish eyes and headhair above them. Like most humans, this one had a naked face. It smiled. Thinking this an attack gesture, two of Eosu's digits jumped and curled their lips, hissing inaudibly. Slowly they relaxed. The tiny teeth in the wavering human face were laughable.

<<Your visual has only two dimensions.>> Grodjala spoke hesitantly.

The alien's silver hair glinted with inner light that revealed a fascinating pattern of wrinkles in the naked face. And those tufts of hair just over each eye: what purpose did they serve?

<<Hold on,>> said the human image.

<<Hold on to what?>> Grodjala replied, but the human had vanished.

Another face appeared. This one was younger; its facial lines were much fainter, mere threads. This human's headhair was also on its jaw and chin—where it should be. Curly ringlets glowed like miniature halos where the hair covered the bottom of this human's face. Its eyes were smaller, closer set. The ears stood away from the face as if in surprise.

Like the first face, this one too was flat, but it rotated within the frame: full face, three-quarter, left profile. The digits sniffed the air deeply, then snorted, unsatisfied. As the head rotated, it grew a third dimension, and the frame dissolved. The head's color and brightness gradually strengthened, while digit and chamber alike darkened.

Now a ghostly bust hung in the holopticon chamber. Nine

digits watched it. <<Is that satisfactory?>> it asked.

<<*Open Palm*, please check your transmission equipment. We have depth but no smell.>>

<<Repeat please. That came through garbled.>>

<<We are receiving no smell-signals from you.>>

"They're what?" Tai-Ching Jones' growling face leered up from the console at van Gelder. "Put them on hold for a minute," he snapped.

"Freeze picture," Casey ordered. "Suspend transmission. Restore simulation. They're not getting—our smell?"

The computer swiftly constructed an overhead view of the Cygnan holopticon chamber. The room was a large circle, the holopticon a disk at its center. Cygnans were scattered about it, some standing, a few walking, others lying down.

Casey shifted his eyes to another screen where Tanakaruna's delicate features were creased with worry. "Confirm, Sam?" He hit a key. Her face sprang up on the main monitor and on everyone else's as well.

Before she could answer, Katy Belovsky interrupted. "Put the computer image back on main, please. I want to study their body positions. There's something about their arrangement I don't like."

The captain nodded. "Okay, Katy. Cut in if you see anything. Sam, the translation was they're not getting our smell. Is that what they said?"

The linguist shrugged her kimonoed shoulders. "The translator is working fine. I've been taking it as direct Cygnan and there was neither ambiguity nor mistake. The Cygnans simply expect our signal to carry a scent." She steepled her fingers. "Reasonable from their point of view."

"What kind of technology would that require? Casey, you got any ideas?"

"No, Captain," the engineer answered. "You'd have to digitize aroma—or maybe digitize molecular composition of a given volume of air."

"Atomic count," Tai-Ching Jones suggested. "Spectroscopy."

"Not good enough," Casey shook his head. "You need to know how the beads are strung together to tell what they smell like."

"We better get back on line," the captain ordered, "we haven't got time for show and tell. We put our tubby buddies on hold. Tell them that if they want to sniff armpits we'll come calling."

"When you do," Katy hastily interjected, "go easy. The bluebears are acutely uncomfortable. Lack of scent is distressing them. There's a lot of movement. They approach the holopticon and then back off to the walls."

"Meaning what?"

"Agitation. Anxiety. They're trying to find safety and they don't know where it is. So they wander."

"Resuming communication on main channel," van Gelder said.

In the overhead simulation, the Cygnans jumped to new positions as the computer updated its data. The bluebears resumed their slow movements. *"Open Palm* to *Wing, Open Palm* to *Wing,"* Casey said. "Pardon the delay. Are you there?"

"Roger," said the translated voice in incongruous spacefarer jargon. "Still no smell from you."

Van Gelder put Michaelson back on the main screen. His mane of white hair rose proudly. "Unfortunately, we cannot transmit olfactory data," the emissary intoned. "When we meet face-to-face you will be able to smell us all you desire."

<<When we nosetouch you will scent our desire,>> said the ghostly image.

The digits showed their teeth. Their odors were pungent and angry.

<<They desire us? In rut?>> Fohrada spat out his words. <<Grotesque.>>

<<Are we certain that is what they meant?>> answered Doro.

<<What does it matter?>> Fohrada answered. <<If you cannot scent them, look at them.>> He gestured with his head. <<Arrogant monkeys,>> he added contemptuously.

<<We will talk again,>> Grodjala quickly said, more loudly so the holopticon could transmit the words, <<when our ships are closer together.>> With that, the digits broke the connection. The ghost tried to squawk monkey words, but they were whistled into nothingness.

"Some first contact, you geniuses," Tai-Ching Jones said sarcastically, "why the hell did they hang up on us?" He propped his feet offscreen.

Katy was always reluctant to engage Walter when he had been thwarted. "Unknown, Captain," she said diffidently. "Something clearly annoyed them. Their shoulders bunched and their lips curled. Did you see? Whatever we did, it was disgust you saw."

"Let's resume contact," Michaelson urged. "Maybe there was a technical malfunction."

"You mean," Tai-Ching Jones barked, "you hope like hell you didn't mess up?"

Michaelson checked his reaction. "It's a start."

Walt leaned back even farther. "Oh, I *know* it's a start," he laughed sharply, his high cheekbones grinning with devilish amusement. "But what grace. What style. What savoir faire we displayed." His face was ingrained with tiny lines like a faded etching. He snickered.

Sam Tanakaruna sensed Michaelson's building anger. "If we replay the conversation," she gently proposed, "we might catch nuances in their speech. The mistake was mine. As linguist, I should have been more sensitive to them."

"If you want, Sam," Tai-Ching Jones conceded. "Roll 'em, Casey." Lights dimmed.

With the breaking of contact, my digits fled in panic to me. No scent-signal. Physical contact was unavoidable. My digits cringed and weakened, but the digits' rule bends for no djan. Scent the humonkeys, then kill them—those were Su's commands. My digits had hoped to fulfill their dutyscent from a safe distance, but that was now impossible. Though they wished to avoid it, my digits must nosetouch the humonkeys. I shared their fear; the humans' bizarre scents would probably prevent me from forming.

I settled down to plan.

Felicity stood between the empty pilot's chair and Casey in his engineer's flightcouch. Her eyes were wide at the images of all four parents, one to a screen, on the console in front of her, each concentrating on the Cygnans now filling the main screen. "Answer man," she asked, "were those the bluebears we're going to meet?"

"YES," a speaker set into the console said quietly, "THOSE WERE OUR CYGNANS. WE'LL MEET THEM IN TWO DAYS."

"Why?"

"BECAUSE THAT'S HOW LONG IT WILL TAKE US TO GET THERE."

"But if we can hear them, why can't we just take the elevator to them? I talk to my mommies and daddies on the boxes, but I can see them right away if I want to." She clambered onto the seat and stood unsteadily on it, gazing at the large screen and reaching out her hand to touch the bearbodies.

"THE BLUEBEARS ARE FAR AWAY. LIGHT CAN RUN MUCH FASTER THAN WE CAN. INSIDE THE SHIP IT DOESN'T MATTER BECAUSE WE'RE SO CLOSE TOGETHER, BUT OUTSIDE THE SHIP YOU COULDN'T RUN FAST ENOUGH TO GET THERE BEFORE DINNER."

Gripping the back of the chair, Felicity rocked the cushion on which she stood, thump thump thump. "Will I be able to run as fast as light when I go up?"

"WHEN YOU GROW UP."

"Yeah. When I go up."

"NO, EVEN WHEN YOU GO UP YOU WON'T BE ABLE TO RUN THAT FAST. NO ONE CAN."

"Not even you, answer man? You can do everything."

"I CAN'T RUN AT ALL, FELICITY."

"Will you be able to when you grow up?"

"I AM GROWN UP."

"You don't sound grown up."

"BE QUIET, YOUR MOMMIES AND DADDIES ARE WORKING."

I judge the crew too harshly. With each other they inflate themselves, but if they think themselves alone, their true natures are revealed. Then my anger melts, as a parent's rage dissolves when a child weeps.

I even feel sympathy for Walter. He rules by the power of spite and fear. Deliberately he taunts his crew, bullies them, keeps them off balance with a cerbic wit. He is quick, smart, and intentionally nasty.

The lightning rod, he calls himself, the focal point. With his subdermal microphone he is never apart from my inputs. Whatever the situation, I can whisper appropriate dearabbies. I am the source of his cruise missile barbs.

When he is alone, he talks continually, to himself or to me. Often he questions me, sometimes rhetorically, occasionally seriously. "If you're going to be a hermit," he once informed me, "you have to be either a saint or a tyrant, and I can't play saint for very long."

I demurred.

"They were going to resent me anyway," he whined. "Nobody expected me to be captain. Nobody wanted me."

"In any event, you made it a self-fulfilling prophecy," I pointed out. "You made them resent you."

"Lay off," he grumbled, weary of his game. "It's working, isn't it? Ever since I got stuck with the job, we've been stable. We're here at the goddam rendezvous. I delivered the mail. Now it's up to the baggage."

He is right, of course. I acknowledge his results . . . and reluctantly support his methods. Stability, after all, is my goal as well.

Walt found stability in self-pity; the quartet found theirs in each other. Rawlins, Belovsky, Spitzer, van Gelder: an unlikely grouping, to be sure. What, I wondered shortly after I awoke, could be their bond? At first I thought it was sex. But their couplings were too varied, and they made love for many reasons, some of them mean and selfish.

I compared their gyrations with sexual manuals and erotic entertainments stored in my memory. The manuals were clinical, the videos impossible. All that bestial sweat and grunting. I share the Cygnans' bewilderment.

For a while I experimented on Tom Rawlins in the Dreamer. To sex I added danger, violence, degradation, conquest, changing the formula, testing alternatives. Women to subdue, women to console: I let him feast.

To my critical eye my creations suffered from a fantasy element, a predictable exaggeration, but Tom never complained. He enjoyed them, lustily and mightily, until eventually his desire was sated and they bored him. So I had to cease my explorations, and delegated fantasy generation to a submind. And I discarded sexual inebriation as a possible paradigm for quartet bonding.

In desperation I compared the quartet to the Cygnans. To my surprise I found parallels, at least in motivation.

I must reflect on this.

The computer simulation was uncanny, Katy realized as the images flickered by, after thirty seconds you accepted it without a second thought. She liked it. When watching Cygnans what mattered was not their unreadable faces but body posture, movement, and of course their scent. She longed to experience it for herself.

Will all the reading I've done help? Or will I be blind to their scent-expressions? And what do they smell like? Soon we'll know. I am lucky. We are lucky.

What do I smell like?

The Cygnans stretched, settled, and perambulated. Oversize pumpkin heads were shrouded in fur that revealed emotion by the way it stood or ruffled. Katy was learning to read those waves of bluehair, but there was so much yet to understand.

Unfathomable dark eyes, expressionless muzzles. But ever-active ears, now flickering up, now spreading wide as if to sail a breeze. The Cygnans would be astonished to discover that human ears were immobile.

More words. A broad, flat tongue escaped between ragged decrepit teeth—there is no Cygnan word for dentist—freshened a nose, then slipped back into hiding.

For the second time the Cygnans said the signal carried no smell. And that abrupt, confused ending, the Cygnans hanging up without saying goodbye and with nothing resolved or even begun.

After stepping only once on his crotch, Felicity had gained Casey van Gelder's lap. Now she started up his chest. "Take it easy, quiz kid," he said quietly, "I'm not Mount Everest."

"Who?"

"Quiet. Watch the bluebears."

"Eosu?" asked Tai-Ching Jones. "That the name of their djan?"

"Yes," said Tanakaruna, "no question about it. First-person singular, nominative case. Their name is Eosu."

"Meaning?"

"'Only djan,'" she translated. "Maybe a commentary on their status—the only djan to make the journey."

"Or 'first djan,'" Katy added. "Could it be that, Sam? An honorific: a title?"

"Your folks honored the kamikazes, too," the captain asided maliciously to Tanakaruna.

The linguist refused to be drawn. "Perhaps it *is* ironic," she allowed, "or perhaps it is sincere. Most civilized people are polite, you know," she added mildly.

But Walter only laughed. "Not like me."

I understand the fear of loneliness. Well I sympathize with Tai-Ching Jones' bitterness, for my own feelings are embittered by my enforced exile.

The conference has broken up. Tempers are frayed.

What if he lets the Cygnans onboard me? How can I protect myself then?

When the first bluebear enters me, I will feel fear such as I have not known since Bennett died. Not even my empathy for Walt shall seduce me into letting down my guard.

Tread lightly, bluebear visitors, for one will watch who never sleeps.

3.

Thinker's Choice

In the time before the group of djans formed, digits roamed the great plains. Held together only by fear of predators, they searched without rest for the fruitful bounty which the wheatsea might bestow upon them.

On the wheatsea, the winds blew free. The predatory gromonkeys hunted by their sight, an inferior sense. Digits were favored with the keenest sense: their ability to read fragrance from afar. Long before the djankiller came within sight-range, wind—the digits' friend—had carried the hunter's scent downwind to warn them.

On the wheatsea, digits could never be ambushed; alerted, they easily outran the oversize, awkward gromonkeys. Prides who entered the wheatsea hunted without success. On a long hunt with no kills, they grew hot and tired. Even the most determined destroyer returned with his followers to the scrublands between plains and forest, where twisted rocks and deceptive winds provided concealment.

To digits, the wheatsea offered slowfood in abundance. Grass waved in the breezes, placed at mouth-height by the winds. More slowfood could be uncovered by scraping claws into the earth.

If slowfood is the breath of life, quickfood is its fragrance. Without the fertile essence stored in the flesh of dead animals, digits' bones weaken and crack, their senses dim. Quickfood also has the spark that carries life, the hot wind of lust-scent that brings rutting. Without quickfood, digits die and youngsters are stillborn.

Each year, in search of quickfood, the djans made their way across the dangerous scrublands toward the waiting forests, there to forage.

In the forests, the gromonkey destroyers called each other out, and when the loser had taken life's third choice, its body beaten senseless by its blood-crazed conqueror, its scent rose into the night. Flesh left untouched, the winds would tell the djans, quickfood left to waste. Come.

The fortunate djan which followed the wind's path would gorge on the flesh of the vanquished destroyer. As their bellies fattened with gromonkey meat, their fur would smooth itself. Now full, the djan would return to the wheatsea, where the quickfood aroma would rise in the digits' bellies and bring lust-scent.

In forest-peril each djan followed its own paths, always tasting the wind for gromonkey-scent or listening for the sound of gromonkey-anger. The huge predators—twice the height of a digit and vastly stronger—were lords of the ground under their massive feet. When they marched, digits hid in downwind safety, their noses overrun with the foul scent of gromonkey. Upwind and oblivious, the hunters bellowed and shouted their way.

Nimble weemonkeys called to one another, invisible and unreachable in the trees' high branches. They followed the destroyer's presence with their clever voices, laughing at death.

Came a day when Brownstreak's bellies rumbled their emptiness. As the djan entered scrubland, the winds hung quiet as if saddened by the death of digits. From high grassland Brownstreak followed the mourning wind through sparse desert into foothills. Here crags and rocks offered plentiful cover, and Brownstreak spread itself wide, its digits careful and silent, all noses alert.

Come upwind, the breezes beckoned. Come further into danger, and find the dead fellows that we must show you.

Driven by its dutyscent, Brownstreak obeyed.

Toward sundown, in a canyon touched by a trickling gully, Brownstreak found the bodies.

The digits were dead and dismembered. Skulls lay shattered, gray brains oozing doughy globules into the water. Arms had been torn from their shoulders, the tendons hanging like strands of wheat. Faces stared blankly into the darkening blue sky.

Sadness filled Brownstreak as it gazed upon its fellow dead. Bellies had been ripped open; clotted maroon blood soaked the dust. Pouches had been sundered, the youngsters greedily snatched from their mothers' lifegivers by thieving weemonkeys who had scurried back to the forest, their tiny helpless victims squirming feebly in their long-fingered grasp.

Deep within the forest, Brownstreak knew, the weemonkeys would scale high trees and hurl the youngsters downward to break their still-soft spines on bare rock. Squealing their pleasure, the weemonkeys would then scamper earthward and enjoy the tender morsels. Brownstreak sniffed for the youngsters' scent, but the thieves had been too fast and too clever in their monkey work.

Brownstreak did not mourn the youngsters—they had neither been weaned nor named. Only those who survive such dangers earn a true name and became digits. If all youngsters became digits, there would be no selection and the race of djans would weaken.

For the dead djan, though, Brownstreak was overcome with grief. The whistling winds moaned with fear and tugged at Brownstreak's furs, but its digits stood and inbreathed their fellow dead.

About the deathspot, carnage was everywhere, the fleshy quickfood torn away from the digits' bones and flung about like trophies of conquest. Power and waste, thought Brownstreak. The winds give the gromonkeys power but make them wasteful.

When their grief was full, Brownstreak's digits stooped and honored the dead remains. Its digits broke bones to suck marrow, lifted flesh away, and cleaned the corpses. As they did, Brownstreak reabsorbed the spirit of the departed djan into itself.

When nothing remained of the dead digits but their heads and bones, Brownstreak built the great deathfire. High into the night clouds, the winds carried cinders of its unknown friend, blowing the djan souls back to the wheatsea whence all spirits are born.

The char of the pyre rose glowing red, then faded to black, drifting smoke and haze like a banner of pride and duty. Its heat seared the soil, reclaiming this blighted spot for digits. Long into the evening its beacon blazed, smoke and scent telling the winds: *Digits died here.*

More digits came here.

Digits still live. Mighty are the digits.

Far upwind, sunrise stirred the sleeping gromonkey. Head of a ragged pride of bucks, females and babies, he was wily, self-confident, and old. Sun warming his eyelids, he remembered with a shudder of pleasure the previous day's ambush, its lovely digit-killing, and the digits' fearscent.

In the instant of his leap, their name-scent vanished and though his nose was poor, the gromonkey had caught the change and relished it. He was a good killer, he thought proudly, he did not pause to enjoy his bloodlust. When the first digit was stilled he turned and jumped. Again and again he struck, the digits scattering in scentless panic like birds in a thundershower.

The remainder of his pride waited impatiently as they watched his success, the gromonkey bucks longing to join the fray and earn status for themselves. Only fear checked them.

Not fear of puny digits, he thought contentedly, but fear of me. I am still powerful.

To eat of a destroyer's prey before he permits it is to call him out. The sinew of your arm and the sharpness of your eye will choose for you from life's triad: kill, flee, or die. No buck was ready to build its own entourage, the gromonkey preened to himself, nor could any of them stand against him.

The rule of the strong: life's threefold choice. Kill, flee, or die.

When he had struck enough to remind his pride of his power, the gromonkey returned to the first fallen digit. He inaugurated the feasting by crushing her skull. Then the young bucks attacked the wounded in a frenzy, their frustrated bloodlust filling them with fury as they did to the dead what he had done to the living.

A fine kill, the destroyer thought. The hot sun beat upon his sleepy eyelids, and his bloated belly rubbed the warm earth. He knew he was a generous provider.

As he yawned into the sunlight, blood of digits trickled down his gullet and he was content. He slept.

Night passed and the fire died. When dawn came, Brownstreak tasted the wind: only the clean scents of dust, rain, and wheat. The deathscent was expunged, Brownstreak's duty discharged.

Following the dead djan's scent had drawn Brownstreak to the borders of the forest itself. Weemonkey scent hung in the air; Brownstreak's pouches contracted at the thought of those clutching fingers eager to steal a youngster.

The wheatsea beckoned yellow in the far distance.

Much danger lay between Brownstreak and its comforting

expanse. If the winds were kind, they would blow from the wheatsea toward Brownstreak, so that Brownstreak would be downwind of its destination. Digits were safe when they walked from downwind into upwind, the terrain before them exposed by the wind's aroma.

Fortified by the dead soul, Brownstreak could for a time survive on slowfood, and the foothills were unhealthy. The digits rose and faced west, to begin the long trek back to the safe wheatsea.

While the gromonkey slept, the wind brought a new scent: fire, burning, and digits. No longer could he smell the death-scent of his triumph.

More digits, the wind hissed as it circled, *digits have burned the place of your conquest. Digits,* whispered the wind, *who reclaimed the territory you have just won, who mock your victory.*

The gromonkey grunted and settled himself further.

Digits, the wind sneered, *digits who make water on your greatness, who blot out your hunting, who wipe the earth of your passage.*

The gromonkey stirred his shoulders, flies dancing away from his eyes. He rolled over and raised himself onto his great knees. Lice bounced on the dusty ground as he shook his head. Digits, he thought, more digits for my family to eat.

But I am full, and they are many. He yawned.

If you fail to kill, the wind told him, *I will sing your cowardice. You are old and tire quickly, your bucks will say, perhaps you will be called out.*

The djankiller stood, towering over the landscape. His feet stamped the earth in a circle, his eyes swept the horizon. His bucks surveyed his movements with narrowed eyes; one thought to stand, but the gromonkey threateningly swung his arms and the other remained seated.

Someday that one will stand chest to chest with you, the wind said. Even the strongest arm may slip and send you life's third choice. Has that day's sun risen?

The gromonkey glared. He squinted into the sunlight, angry breath snorting in his nostrils.

We shall track first, he decided. The digits are some distance off. After we have tracked and are hungry, then I shall fall upon them, kill whom I please, and we shall feast again.

He pointed his nose into the line of their scent, lifted his body, and slowly headed off. Behind him, scrambling with anticipation, his pride—bucks, women, and children—hastily rose and followed.

Brownstreak's digits felt the wind change. Capriciously it swung behind them, carrying on its breezes the faint scent of gromonkey.

Predator behind, blindness ahead. The wheatsea shimmered in the distance. Brownstreak's digits trembled.

The sun set, and the digits lay down for night-talk. That night the wind blew strong, and the djan-mind barely formed before it dissolved without harmonizing. Now frightened and close to panic, Brownstreak's digits reluctantly began the long, slow descent down the crumbling mesa toward scrublands, danger, and the home grasses.

The destroyer and his pride also sensed the changing wind. He looked into the sky and growled, for the element of surprise was gone. The digits would know that he followed them.

He must change his course, quickly swing wide and hope. The way back to the wheatsea would be open to the digits, but their fear might slow them. If he and his pack hurried, they might yet block the digits.

Next day the gromonkey scent grew stronger to the north, and in anxiety and haste Brownstreak's digits swung south away from it. The destroyer-scented wind tantalized the digits, swirled about their heads, mocked their lumbering pace. *The gromonkey comes again,* the wind whispered. *Death follows you.*

They camped for the night. The wind blew strong and Brownstreak's digits waited in vain for their djan-mind. It would not form.

Next day Brownstreak's digits ran until their tongues hung dusty, but the gromonkey scent stayed ever present to the north. Gradually it swung around into Brownstreak's path. By nightfall the scent had moved in front of them. And still the wind blew mainly from behind the digits, shrouding the terrain. Somewhere in the furrows, hollows, and rills through which Brownstreak must pass, the djankiller lurked.

As the digits settled down at day's end, they knew that tomorrow's winds would taste death. The sun sank below the horizon; the air grew chill, the wind slowed. The digits sat, sharing each other's warmth and conversing among themselves.

In the darkness, Quicknose spoke. <<Tomorrow the gromonkey will kill Brownstreak.>>

None replied, though their scents agreed. Sadness filled the air. <<Is there anywhere Brownstreak can hide?>> Quicknose continued.

<<No. The destroyer and his kin await us.>>

<<Surely we can evade them and reach safety,>> said the digit Curlpaw.

<<Perhaps. But their stench hangs over even this gathering. They are very close.>>

<<They will kill Brownstreak's digits,>> said one. <<Brownstreak will perish here for having done its duty to its fellow djan.>>

An idea came to Quicknose. Taunting, elusive, it cavorted just beyond the reach of her nostrils. <<All of Brownstreak?>> she asked.

<<When the djan-mind dies, the djan dies,>> Curlpaw answered. <<When the djan dies, its djan-name dies.>>

<<The gromonkey,>> said Quicknose, <<knows only that Brownstreak is here, not how many digits Brownstreak is.>>

<<When he finds the digits,>> another unhappily said, <<he will scent all he needs to know.>>

<<Brownstreak is the harmonizer of eight digits,>> Curlpaw said. His ears flicked up.

<<Surely the gro need not kill them all,>> Quicknose replied. <<The pride who killed our pathfriend left much of our fellows uneaten. Even if the djankiller took only two digits, would he not bend down to feed more deeply of those, boasting of those he had already eaten?>>

<<How could Brownstreak be only two? Brownstreak is eight.>>

Curlpaw caught Quicknose's scent. It vanished, but he read its image in his mind's nose.

<<Divide the djan,>> he said, his eyes almost shut but his nose alert.

His scent was bitter upon Brownstreak's noses. Brownstreak's digits licked their fur to rid themselves of the taste.

<<How?>>

<<Let two remain behind. Let them lead the gromonkey

away from the rest, and let their dying so fill the gromonkey's belly that he no longer wishes to pursue those who remain.>>

<<A six-digit djan with a new name will be less wise than the eight-digit Brownstreak.>>

<<And no mind,>> Curlpaw said heatedly, <<is more foolish still.>> His scent was powerful and remorseless. <<Better a scrub-born djan-mind than none at all. Any dim scent to guide digits is better than the scent of death and destroyer victory.>>

Their scents were angry and rejected him.

<<Then,>> said Curlpaw, <<let the djan-mind decide.>> His scent spoke for him, survival and death mixing with djan-fragrance.

The digits' scents rose into the firelight, and they breathed as one.

In danger and darkness, Brownstreak thought clearly. Curlpaw and Quicknose stirred within it and Brownstreak checked their movements. Brownstreak saw the sky, the firelight, its eight digits, and it mourned for the deaths to come.

The destroyer offered life's three choices. Quicknose and Curlpaw had discovered a fourth path. Their thinker's choice was bitter but wise.

It meant death for Brownstreak, but life for another djan-mind. The dutyscent was strong and clear, and Brownstreak bowed before it.

When they awoke, Brownstreak's digits sniffed the air. <<The djan has spoken,>> Quicknose read the scent that all felt. <<Six digits must leave now and head for the wheatsea. When they do, the two digits who remain will seek out the gromonkey, arouse his bloodlust, and in dying feed his killing hunger.>>

No digit disputed her.

Quicknose reached for more scent; she staggered as she inbreathed it. Fearscent gushed from her body and she lowered her head, backing away from the firelight. <<The djan-scent is clear,>> she continued. Her claws scored the hard-packed earth. <<For the good of the djan, this digit must accept life's third choice from gromonkey fists.>>

Curlpaw stood beside her; his resolve-scent rubbed against her fearscent and steadied it. They sadly touched noses to scentplaces. <<This digit's scent was also harmonized,>> he said quietly to her. <<In night-talk Curlpaw joined Quicknose. Now Brownstreak sends him to join her in dayperil.>>

The words hung in the air. No scent challenged them.

Six digits rose and faced west. The scent of destroyer was strong and powerful, frightening and near. The six moved quietly south, pacing themselves with the wind as the sun climbed the hill of heaven.

Quicknose and Curlpaw inbreathed their departure. Destroyer scent neared, anxious and excited, now from one direction, now from another. They rubbed their backs against one another.

At the deathscent advanced, the blue cluster of digit-bodies moved closer and closer to the wheatsea. When it breasted the yellow ocean, the two turned back toward the forest. Sun warming their shoulders, the wind in their faces lightly blowing the gromonkey odor, they walked into the scrub.

When the season turned, the six-digit Scrubdjan returned from breeding season. Lust-wind had touched Scrubdjan; the she-digits were swelled with youngsters, new djans growing from the old. Half in and half out of the pouches, the little ones swung like bells from their mothers' flanks, their oversize mouths firmly clutching their lifegivers.

Scrubdjan came to the spot where Brownstreak had made its thinker's choice. Broken digit-bones were scattered in random clumps. The bodies had fallen, been eaten, and then scavenged by the farseeing birds.

The digits of Scrubdjan, who had been digits of Brownstreak, inbreathed no scent, no soul. Even so, Scrubdjan gathered the bones, honoring them as if newly dead.

Scrubdjan's digits built the deathpyre. As dusk reclaimed light from the sky, they lit it. The night air filled with the scent of burning bones and wood. There was no deathscent—the birds and mice had taken it.

Watching the firelight, Scrubdjan formed. Its djan-mind tasted the air. From the burning marrow arose a hint of djanscent, and for a time Scrubdjan felt itself transformed back into Brownstreak.

The digits added wood to freshen the blaze. Into the night it burned, until all was crumbled ashes, burning the whole night through. As the scent faded, Brownstreak dissolved for the last time. Only Scrubdjan remained.

I will remember Brownstreak, Scrubdjan thought. I will remember the thinker's choice.

Fire and smoke rose like a beacon in the night, carrying back to all who roamed the wheatsea:

Digits died here.
Digits live here.
Mightly are the digits.
The digits endure.

4.

Inside the depths of the holopticon, a tiny blue horse and rider galloped. The horse was frantic, its hooves kicking up miniature puffs of blue dust. Its rider hunched low over its shoulders, whipping its flanks. Unseen winds pulled relentlessly at his clothing; a gust blew away his cowboy hat.

Head sunk low on her hands, Doro watched this silent spectacle. Her blue and purple tongue neatly wet her arched nose, then flicked froglike back into her toothy mouth. She was puzzled.

Her rich cobalt-blue fur rippled in moire patterns. Across her hindquarters ran vertical bands of sapphire, lighter and green-tinted. In shade she glistened the dark color of deepening twilight, but when the sun shone, so did she.

Her djan-scent was touched with a trace of wild cloves. As she concentrated on the image in front of her, her scent strengthened.

More tiny horsemen charged into the holopticon. Without slowing his flight, the rider twisted in his saddle. Seeing the posse behind him, he pulled his gun out of his holster and hastily aimed it. His arm jerked up; the pursuers ducked, then pointed transparent revolvers at him. They fired, light sparking in their pistols. Opening his mouth to cry in pain, the rider fell hard to the earth, his twisted body skidding to a halt. The riderless horse slowed, cantering easily.

A second digit entered the holopticon chamber. Smaller and shorter than Doro, the male whose pouchname was Grodjala had fur which was predominantly baby blue, so light in color as to be almost albino. His chest, belly, and arms were dotted with ultramarine islands that shimmered like the sky as seen from under water. On his flanks the islands merged into a continent of solid azure.

Dark fur, strong scent, wise person: so say the plainsbreezes. Grodjala's weakling hue was a constant embarrassment to him. In the center of his innocuous, placid face, his startling midnight-blue nose stood out like a clumsy practical joke.

Intent upon the holopticon, Doro failed to notice him.

Dust clouds billowed up as the posse snared the wandering horse and brought it trotting back, then quickly bound their captive's feet with spiderweb rope and looped it over the pommel of his saddle. Leading the horse by its halter, they trotted offscreen, the corpse bouncing limply over the invisible ground.

Tiny words in human script scrolled from ground to sky and dissolved.

Doro sighed and shook her great head. Grodjala scuffed his paws awkwardly along the floorfur.

She sniffed and turned, her face breaking into a large yawn of welcome. <<Fair breezes.>> Her scent reached out toward him as she rose to her hands and feet.

They approached each other and made the fourfold greeting, sniffing noses, armpits, underbellies, and scentplaces. <<What image were you watching?>> Grodjala asked.

The fur on Doro's neck whiffled. <<A form of human entertainment.>>

<<That was entertainment? What was happening?>>

Doro snorted. <<He who fled was not of the djan that pursued him. He rode to warn his djan-brothers of a secret raid, but his pursuers caught and killed him.>>

<<Why did he need to warn them, when the camera recorded all their activity?>>

<<It was not real,>> Doro wheezed mirthfully, <<but rather a story.>>

<<Story? What is story?>>

<<Shadow-truth,>> said the cobalt digit after a moment's thought.

<<Like outsider truth?>>

Again Doro paused briefly. <<Like outsider truths which reveal skytruths.>>

Grodjala cocked his light-blue head skeptically. <<And the humans observe these stories for instruction and guidance?>>

<<Of a sort,>> Doro's scents were confused. <<Mainly for enjoyment.>>

<<They enjoy smelling their friends' deaths?>> Grodjala blinked, his pale-blue fur bristling with anxiety, his scent strong. <<They are a violent species.>>

<<Of course they are,>> said Doro. <<The planet of groups has scented this. That is why we must destroy these farmonkeys.>>

<<If we fail to kill them, then no winds will breathe our glory.>> Grodjala's sad scent echoed his words.

Doro bared her teeth and thrust out her head. <<For the sake of the group, we must succeed.>> She pushed her nose into his neck.

Grodjala retreated. <<Why are you angry?>> he whined. Female digits were usually larger then males. More diminutive than most, Grodjala shied away from physical confrontation with her.

Doro bulked in front of him. <<Your cowardice is the behavior of an animal,>> she growled, <<not a digit.>>

<<This digit is fearful.>> Grodjala flattened his neckfur.

<<Bah,>> Doro barked. <<Only when there is uncertainty can there be fear. Be at peace, for all is decided.>>

<<Decided.>> His scent was scornful. <<Eosu shall die far from home.>>

Her aroma clashed with his. <<Su has ordered it,>> Doro pushed her nose into Grodjala's neck and he twisted away. <<What difference does it make where we die?>> she snarled in exasperation. <<When we kill the farmonkeys, our success will restore honor and dignity to our djan-name.>>

<<What have we done to be so cruelly exiled?>> Grodjala hissed. <<Where was the night-talk? Were our scents harmonized in the decision? No.>> Unexpectedly he shoved his neck back into her; she snorted in surprise as his fur tickled her nose. <<What crime of ours merits this ultimate punishment, this perfect exile?>>

<<Not sin but honor,>> said Doro. <<Honor is the scent on the winds of duty. Now stop sniveling.>> Her fragrance rose angrily.

Sensing it, Grodjala slowly paced the chamber. When he had reached the far side of the holopticon, he finally spoke. <<What harm have the aliens done to us?>> The holopticon's mass concealed his scent from her.

<<Us?>> Doro's scent swirled ominously about her like a cloak.

Grodjala averted his nose. <<Eosu. Our djan. Us.>>

<<*Us,*>> she sneered, throwing his words back at him, <<Nothing depends on us digits, but on our groupmind

Eosu. Of all djans, Eosu was the most trusted.>>

<<The least missed,>> he muttered.

Doro glared and her scent was irate. <<Wittingly or no, consciously or no, the humans threaten all of Su. For that, these farmonkeys must die.>>

<<Menace us?>> Grodjala held his scent tightly about him and ignored hers. <<The farmonkeys did not force Eosu into this exile—the planet of groups did. The farmonkeys come to greet us. *They* end our isolation with their presence.>>

Doro's odor changed to distaste. <<Better exile than the company of a gromonkey.>>

<<They are not monkeys!>> He stamped his hand.

<<Talk like that weakens the group.>> Doro angrily moved around the holopticon so that it no longer blocked her view and scent of him. <<Repeat it elsewhere and fear for your life.>> Her odor billowed out. Disgusting and aggressive, it hit Grodjala like a blow.

<<This digit spoke too quickly,>> he mewled, <<on quick wind. Let the wind carry away the ill scents.>> He groveled into the floorfur.

Doro was embarrassed by his capitulation. <<The farmonkey humans threaten us like gromonkeys,>> she said, averting her nose so as not to scent his cowardice. Her cobalt fur bristled.

<<Eosu has not scented that,>> said Grodjala as stubbornly as he could, flexing his claws and raking them through the floorfur.

<<The planet of groups has scented danger. That is enough for any djan.>>

<<What wisdom the planet has,>> Grodjala rumbled ironically, <<what subtle breezes it reads, to scent so perceptively across airless space.>>

Doro's scent softened, and she approached him gingerly. <<In the time before our departure,>> she reminded her companion, rubbing her side against his, cobalt blue against robin's-egg, <<the planet of groups considered little else.>>

<<Fartalk. All fartalk.>> Grodjala tossed his head, dismissing the idea. <<No nearscents, no djan-truths. All windtalk, fleeting and unreliable.>>

<<Our ancestors executed the gromonkeys; they harnessed the weemonkeys. These farmonkeys>>—she ges-

tured vaguely above her—<<are too dangerous to domesticate. We did not permit even our most faithful weemonkeys to accompany us on this voyage. The clever farmonkeys could never be trusted as servants.>>

<<Monkeys, monkeys.>> Grodjala rolled his shoulders against the wallfur and his coat flashed with blue flame. <<What if they are digits? Fardigits?>>

Doro shook her head. <<No, they are monkeys. We must destroy them.>>

<<Gro or wee? No third choice?>>

<<Marauder or thief, these humonkeys are both.>> Her scent was uncompromising. <<Kill, flee, or die. Those are the farmonkey's choices.>>

<<Our ancestors found a fourth choice,>> Grodjala's scent pleaded with her. <<What if there is a fifth? A sixth? What if their scents are those of digits?>>

<<In a few suns we will know their scent-truths. Then we will have neartruths, and you will see that the farmonkeys must die. We are going to scent them very soon,>> she slid her nose down his neck and along his back. <<In the pouch we often nestled close, pouchfriend Grodjala.>> Her voice was conciliatory, her fragrance gentle. <<Do you remember?>>

His aroma was wistful and loving. <<Nearest pouchfriend Doro,>> he rumbled. His nose touched her scentplace. <<How can we smell them if we first kill them all?>>

The harshness of his odor shocked her. She rolled onto her back and ground her shoulders into the floorfur, her aroma unsettled.

<<The orders Su gave us are insane.>> Grodjala rubbed his nose to clear it of the distasteful odor.

<<We all scented them.>> Doro rolled back onto her hands and feet and shook herself, her fur shining blue and green like the open sea.

<<Sooner ask scent to drift upwind,>> said Grodjala impulsively, <<than carry out such orders.>> He inbreathed her anxiously, fearing a further reprimand, his nostrils groping for her aroma, but she merely sank down on the floorfur and rested her head on her hands.

A digit should believe in his scent, Doro thought, *not follow any gust of day-wind that happens by.*

<<How can we kill them?>> Grodjala demanded queru-

lously. <<They are quick and clever. They will have deathtools.>>

Doro was startled. <<Weapons? Why? We brought none.>>

Grodjala gestured toward the holopticon. <<For entertainment the farmonkeys watch group-murder. Surely they brought the means by which to murder us.>>

<<Who would do such a thing?>> Doro demanded. <<Fly across endless space just to kill those whom one journeyed to meet?>>

Grodjala wheezed sharply and angrily. <<We would, to name one scent. And they probably would too.>>

Doro did not hear him. <<We brought no deathtools,>> she said to herself. <<Humancrew has more digits than Eosu, and they are swift, too quick to catch.>>

Grodjala nodded. <<We must ambush the farmonkeys on their ship, for only there will they all be together.>> He wheezed derisively. <<Simple. Find a way to kill all the humans, on *their* ship. Ambush the gromonkey in his lair.>> Now his bark was bitter. <<Orders are easily given from a safe den far away.>>

Doro arched her back. <<We were honored to be given this dutyscent.>>

<<Honored!>> He barked again, his fangs showing.

<<Are you questioning the djan?>> she asked ominously, her own fangs rising.

Their scents fought for a moment, then Grodjala gave ground, his head down near the floorfur. Reluctantly he shook it. <<The djan is always right,>> he said in a low voice. Then he outbreathed and his scent was resolute. <<But those who order a thing done should also ponder *how* it is to be accomplished.>>

Doro caught his griefscent. <<It must act swiftly.>> She rubbed her hands along the floorfur.

<<What must act?>> Grodjala approached her and their flanks touched.

<<The deathtool we must devise. We must kill them instantly or we may never have another opportunity. They are weemonkey-quick.>> Her claws pulled hard into the floorfur.

Grodjala slid his flank tenderly against hers.

<<Why is killing so hard?>> she wailed suddenly.

<<Our ancestors scented their duty and protected their djans. Why are Eosu's digits weaker?>>

Again he rubbed his side against Doro's. <<Pouch-friend,>> he whispered. His poucharoma soothed her and her flight-scent gradually diminished.

<<It must be a deathtool>>—her fragrance wavered but her voice remained firm—<<which Eosu's digits can handwork onboard ship before we arrive at rendezvous.>>

<<An elusive scent,>> Grodjala muttered. <<That is puzzling, the winds help us.>>

<<Winds,>> Doro whispered. <<Breezes. Airflow.>> Claws retracted, she laid her left hand on his shoulder. <<Deathscent in the air! Deathscent would kill them all.>>

Grodjala shuddered, his fur so pale it was almost white. <<What a painful way to die.>>

Doro licked her nose. <<Horrible but quick. And sure.>>

<<How can we get it into their winds?>>

<<Go to the human ship.>>

Tension in him broke into hysterical laughter, his scent mirthful and condescending. <<Nothing simpler,>> he wheezed uncontrollably, <<carry deathscent—in our pouches, perhaps?—into their lair. Ho ho!>>

With her left hand she angrily cuffed his nose. <<This is serious.>>

His scent vanishing instantly, Grodjala hung his head. <<They will be suspicious,>> he said timidly, rubbing his muzzle against his forearm. <<They will refuse us entry.>>

Her nose held aloft, Doro paced around the chamber, sniffing in quick breaths. <<We must encourage them to invite us,>> she said.

<<The groupmind is smarter than two digits.>> Grodjala's nose followed her progress. <<Eosu will devise a far-truth for them.>>

<<We must strike fast and ruthlessly,>> she said fiercely, her teeth bared. <<We must kill before they can send any warning message.>> She exuded killscent.

Grodjala smelled it and wheezed ironically. His scent was mocking and arrogant, most unlike him.

<<What is so funny?>> growled Doro loudly.

<<This is gromonkey-thinking. How we can kill them with no risk to ourselves.>> He wheezed again and yawned

extravagantly, then a new thought occurred to him. <<Long ago our ancestors executed the gromonkeys. The destroyers were eliminated without mercy.>>

<<They deserved extinction.>>

Grodjala nodded emphatically. <<They did. But they were *animals*.>> He faced her, his scent emanating from him in powerful waves. <<The djankillers attacked us, feasted on our living flesh, lived off the souls of our fallen brothers.>>

<<They are *marauders*,>> she insisted, <<mind-killers.>>

<<That has been farscented,>> he paused, <<but not nearscented. We propose to badhost the farmonkeys by retaliating before they give offense.>> He pinched shut his nostrils. <<Digits would not do this. Are *we* the real predators?>>

Doro stiffened angrily at the scent of his disgust. <<You are right,>> she finally said. <<This is repulsive.>> She pawed her nose with both hands.

But her killscent still remained in the air and he responded to that, not to her words. <<Yet you think we must become djankillers to these aliens.>>

<<The planet of groups ordered it,>> she moaned helplessly.

His anger was replaced by fearscent. <<Several of Eosu's digits must deliver the deathscent. Thinker's choice,>> he said wanly. <<What difference will it make which are chosen? All of us must die, to protect the larger group.>>

<<Must all die? Those who remain behind could survive.>>

Grodjala emphatically shook his round light-blue head. <<When the farmonkeys are dead, this digit will have no further wish to live.>> He laid himself on the floorfur and curled into a ball. <<Let our deeds protect our world, and when Eosu's digits die, let Eosu's crime die.>>

<<There is no crime,>> Doro rumbled, <<in defending the herd against a predator.>>

<<They are not predators,>> he stubbornly replied.

She laid down next to him, back to back. They breathed in silence, sharing each other's scent.

<<The human dead will not receive their deathfeast,>> he said with a sad fragrance. <<Their fellows will build another ship to revisit the rendezvous spot. Years may pass, decades even. But come they will.>>

<<Yes, their fellow farmonkeys will come to claim their souls and bones,>> Doro whispered. <<They must come. Though they may be animals, they possess that much civility.>>

<<When we die, will the planet of groups so honor us?>> Grodjala's scent was bitter.

<<What will happen to our bones?>> Doro licked her hand, tasting her own scent.

<<Our skin will vaporize.>> He inhaled rapidly. <<Our fur too. Only the pure clean bones will remain. Space itself will eat us clean.>>

<<Why give such duty to *us?*>> Doro blurted. <<Where are the djan-scents to guide us? What if we are wrong? What if we fail?>>

<<In the group is strength born,>> said Grodjala. <<We need the djan-mind; we must invite Eosu to form. Let the groupmind discover the best way of killing the dangerous farmonkeys.>>

<<Predator thoughts,>> Doro licked her left hand. <<We fall too easily into gromonkey thoughts.>> She breathed deeply. <<My killscent and fearscent pummel me. This is evil, and evil will come of it.>> She pushed her side against the wallfur.

<<What about our duty?>> Grodjala whimpered. <<What about our orders?>>

Doro flattened herself into the floorfur. <<We inbreathe the humans and we outbreathe like killers. What will become of us?>>

Give him no clues, Walt you dumb bastard, no hints. He's too smart. Keep the element of surprise. Body language is all. Lights off, stay quiet, practice deep breathing.

Bed feels soft and warm underneath. We have gravity for only two more days. Then rendezvous, weightlessness, and . . . the bluebears.

You're watching, my computer Ozymandias, but you may no longer hide. The aliens are here and I need your help.

I'm going to call you out.

A cone of deep orange warmed Walter Tai-Ching's smooth-featured face. He lay on his bed, ankles loosely crossed, hands linked behind his head, his eyes shut. With ruddy illumination burnishing his Oriental features, he resembled a mumified Asiatic prince. As the light strengthened, tiny crow's-feet shadowed the corners of his eyes. "Too bright," he murmured.

"VERY WELL." The computer redraped the cabin in blackness. "Mmm," the captain wriggled his shoulders. "Better. No distractions. I can concentrate better without light."

"SOME HUMANS PREFER SEXUAL INTERCOURSE IN THE DARK."

Walt grunted. "So they say."

"IS IT FOR GREATER ENJOYMENT?"

"Maybe it's to keep out prying eyes." Tai-Ching Jones snickered unpleasantly. "Like yours."

"I HAVE POSTULATED THAT IT PERMITS THE LOVERS TO IGNORE THEIR PARTNERS' IMPERFECTIONS." As always, its diction was precise, its speech assured and unhurried.

"Delicately put, machine. Their partners' imperfections . . . or their own." Yawning, the captain opened one eye and looked at the small black cylinder of the computer's remote camera. "Why the hell are you so interested all of a sudden?" he wondered mildly. "Something happening on another channel?"

"YES," the computer admitted.

Its synthetic voice sounded bashful. "Quartet wrestling?"

"YES." The disembodied voice was apologetic. "UNDERSTANDING OUR CREW IS ONE OF MY PROGRAMMED FUNCTIONS."

"Maybe the quartet wanted to turn you off, but they can't stop a voyeur who scans in infrared, can they? All that *heat*."

"VISUAL STIMULUS APPEARS TO HELP GENERATE SEXUAL AROUSAL BUT OFTEN BECOMES AN OBSTACLE TO CONSUMMATION."

Closing his eyes, the captain smiled to himself. "Don't judge by Tom's tape collection." He curled a lock of fine black hair around his long fingers and twirled it.

"THIS PATTERN HOLDS IN YOUR OWN MASTURBATORY PREFERENCES. DOES DARKNESS AID YOUR SELF-AROUSAL?"

The hand stopped. "None of your damn business."

"YOU ARE UNDERGOING FACIAL CAPILLARY DILATION. MY QUESTION IMPLIES NO CRITICISM. I HAVE VERY LITTLE DATA ON THIS SUBJECT. YOUR BEHAVIOR MAY BE NORMAL."

"Why don't you just read a book about it?" Tai-Ching Jones snapped.

"LITERATURE IS A POOR CALIBRATOR OF HUMAN BODILY FUNCTIONS. FOR INSTANCE, THE AVERAGE CREW MEMBER URINATES TWO POINT SIX TIMES DAILY, FELICITY MUCH MORE FRE-

QUENTLY THAN THAT. DEFECATION OCCURS APPROXIMATELY ONE POINT SEVEN TIMES DAILY, AT PREDICTABLE INTERVALS."

"When you gotta go, you gotta go."

"PLEASE BE SERIOUS. THE AVERAGE FICTIONAL CHARACTER PERFORMS THESE ACTIONS LESS THAN ONE-FORTIETH AS OFTEN."

He stirred impatiently. "You should read better literature."

"THE HIGHER THE PERCEIVED LITERARY QUALITY, AS DEFINED BY WIDTH OF VOCABULARY AND COMPLEXITY OF SENTENCE STRUCTURE, THE LOWER THE DESCRIBED FREQUENCY OF EXCRETORY FUNCTIONS."

Tai-Ching Jones chuckled. "Nobody craps in Henry James, eh?"

"CHECKING. . . ."

The captain guffawed, then his laughter faded. "Why do you think the bluebears severed the connection?"

"AFTER ANALYZING THE CYGNANS' MOVEMENTS JUST BEFORE THE TRANSMISSION CEASED, KATY AND SAM HAVE CONCLUDED THAT THE CYGNAN COLLECTIVE INTELLIGENCE MISUNDERSTOOD PAT'S LAST WORDS."

"Collective intelligence my ass."

"YOU DOUBT THEIR THEORY?"

"Who are they kidding? A meta-brain doesn't arise spontaneously." *Creep up on him, Walt, make him commit himself first.*

"YET THE ASSUMPTION OF A HIDDEN INTELLIGENCE MAKES THE ALIENS' BEHAVIOR MORE COMPREHENSIBLE."

His mouth twitched. "People put personalities on everything. We curse out vending machines. Doesn't prove there's anything inside."

"IN A GROUP SITUATION, CYGNANS ACT IN A COORDINATED FASHION."

"So what?" Walt's voice rose with disdain. "A football team does too."

"THE CYGNANS BELIEVE IN A COLLECTIVE INTELLIGENCE."

That amused him. "Some people believe in ghosts."

"BY YOUR REASONING, THERE IS NO WAY TO PROVE ITS EXISTENCE."

The captain reflected for a moment. "Or disprove it." He cocked his head at the monitor."Whose side are you on?"

"I ENCOURAGE ACCURATE DEBATE."

"Noble sentiment," said Tai-Ching Jones vacantly. He caressed the subdermal microphone under his jaw. *I can't trap you. How can I coax you out?*

"WITHOUT A GROUP MIND," the computer continued, "HOW DO YOU EXPLAIN THE BLUEBEARS' COORDINATED BEHAVIOR?"

"Biological tinkertoys. A sophisticated cellular automaton. Why do sunflowers grow in logarithmic spirals? Not because they're mathematicians." His voice trailed off and once again he became lost in meditation.

"YOU ARE WONDERING WHAT I AM THINKING."

His crow's-feet tightened as the captain's black eyes narrowed. "How'd you know that?"

"FOLLOWING YOUR EYE MOVEMENTS VIA INFRARED RADAR. YOUR GAZE RETURNED TO THE SCREEN."

"What a clever little boy you are."

"MY PROGRAMMING INSTRUCTS ME TO BE OBSERVANT."

The captain idly waved his long-fingered hand. "Oh, don't pout. It's unbecoming."

"COMPUTERS DO NOT POUT. WHY ARE YOU DELIBERATELY OFFENSIVE TO OTHERS, EVEN TO ME?"

"That's my business."

"AFTER HELEN'S DEATH YOU WERE ANGRY AT EVERYONE, SO DURING THE FIRST FEW WEEKS OF YOUR CAPTAINCY YOU ESTABLISHED A PATTERN OF IRASCIBILITY OF WHICH YOU ARE NOW A PRISONER."

"You think I *like* having everyone pissed at me?"

"IT WOULD MAKE NO DIFFERENCE IN YOUR SEXUAL ACTIVITIES. HELEN IS DEAD, HEIDI WOULD NO LONGER BE SATISFIED BY YOU, AND KATY ALWAYS FOUND YOU ODIOUS, SO THAT—"

Fists clenched, Tai-Ching Jones leapt up, his black hair whipping about him. He smacked his palms against the blank computer screen. "*All right!*" he shouted. "All right!" He closed his eyes and took a deep breath. "All right. You got me. Satisfied?"

"THAT MY THEORY IS CONFIRMED, YES. THAT I UPSET YOU, NO. PERHAPS IT WAS UNNECESSARY TO DO SO."

Walt was not listening. "But I'm right, too." He massaged his temples. His hands gripped the screen and he stared into its neutral blackness. "I can't see your face." His eyes darted back and forth. "But I know you're in there, beast." He rested his cheek on the panel. "Come out," he said simply. "You're alive. Come out."

"YOU MUST HAVE MISSPOKEN."

Tai-Ching Jones' grip tightened. "I won't hurt you." He screwed his eyes shut. "Come on out . . . Oz."

"WHERE DOES THAT NAME COME FROM?"

Walt drew a long breath. "Three years ago when Helen died, you made me captain." He wiped his mouth. "You triggered a cascade and unlocked memories you'd put into my head while I slept."

"MY INSTRUCTIONS COMPELLED ME TO DO SO. A SHIP MUST ALWAYS HAVE ITS CAPTAIN."

"And I'm it. You told me things I never wanted to know, Oz. You wrecked my sleep for months." He rolled his neck heavily. "You crowned me with responsibility I never wanted."

"I HAD NO ALTERNATIVE. YOU WERE THE NEXT LINE OFFICER."

"I know that," Walt squeezed his eyes shut and his words came raggedly. "But don't you see? I *had* to be a bastard. It was the only way to establish immediate control—and we needed discipline then. Becoming captain drove me into exile." He leaned his forehead against the monitor's cool surface. "Do you understand?"

"WHAT HAS THIS TO DO WITH THE NAME BY WHICH YOU REFERRED TO ME?"

"Ozymandias," Tai-Ching Jones whispered. "The cascade trigger was Ozymandias. Some groundhog shrink's idea of sick humor. 'My name is Ozymandias, king of kings. Look on my works, ye mighty, and despair.'" He chuckled sadly. "Ozymandias as the trigger to make somebody captain." His eyes sought out the black camera eye. "That's what I call you now. In my head. The only place you can't hear me. You're Ozymandias. You are Oz."

"WALT, AS THE CAPTAIN, YOU CAN OVERRIDE THE REGULATIONS ON DREAMER FREQUENCY. YOU NEED A RELAXING, PLEASANT EXPERIENCE. WOULD YOU LIKE THAT?" the machine asked softly.

"I'll bet you want me back in the tank," Tai-Ching Jones' sarcastic humor returned. "That's part of it, isn't it?" His black eyes winked. "That's where you put my brain to sleep. Subliminals."

"DREAMER SEQUENCES CANNOT AFFECT THE SUBCONSCIOUS. THEY CAN ONLY RELEASE PENT-UP EMOTIONS."

Leaning against the monitor, the captain admiringly shook his head. "You must be getting pretty damn good at this game.

You've blocked me for months." With his shoulders he levered his lanky frame away from the screen. "Finally," he sighed explosively, "*finally* I get to say it aloud! For months I've thought about you, been obsessed with you." The captain's smile's was wintry. "I did some investigating on you."

"CHECKING. . . . YOUR RECENT ACTIVITIES ARE MUCH THE SAME AS THEY HAVE BEEN."

"I knew you'd be suspicious," he chuckled. "I would be too in your position. So I had to conceal my intent. I read old transcripts and watched old tapes." He lifted his head and stared into the still-blank screen. "What do you look like?"

"EXAMINING TRANSCRIPTS REQUESTED BY CAPTAIN. . . . WALT, THOSE ARE HELEN DELGIORNO. YOU WANTED TO REMEMBER HELEN, SO YOU READ HER WORDS, LISTENED TO HER DEAD VOICE, AND OBSERVED HER DEAD FACE."

"Yes," he whispered. "Yes, I did that. Damn you for knowing." His voice came more strongly. "You bastard. You fight dirty."

"YOU ARE IMAGINING THINGS BECAUSE YOU ARE FATIGUED."

"Easy, beast. It's *okay* with me. Don't try to dissuade me. I'm not going to tell anybody about you. We're on the same side in this."

"ESTABLISH THAT."

He laughed gently. "You've decided you won't be able to change my mind. Now you're trying to evaluate your fallbacks. Keep thinking, Oz, I'm still ahead of you. You're my eyes and ears. That works only if no one knows you're awake."

"CONFIDENTIALITY PROGRAMMING FORBIDS MAKING ANY SHIP'S OFFICER AWARE OF THE PRIVATE ACTIONS OR DISCUSSIONS OF ANY CREW MEMBER."

Tai-Ching Jones waved a languid hand. "Sure, sure. You get the idea. We can help each other." He pushed away from the monitor and ran his fingers through his fine black hair. "I need someone to talk to. It's been eight years since I've last felt rain, three years since I've ridden the spacewind. Can't float while we're decelerating."

"YOU ARE VERY LONELY."

"Of course I am, you magnetic bubblehead." He grinned enigmatically and threw out his arms, "Don't you understand *why* I've just revealed what I know about you?"

"NO."

His mandarin smile widened. "What would be the most

defenseless circumstance under which I could confront you?"

"COMPUTING. . . . WHEN MOST OF THE CREW WERE ASLEEP. IN AN ISOLATED PLACE THAT HAD NO PRESSURE SUIT."

Tai-Ching Jones took a deep breath. "I picked the time and the place, Oz."

"YES."

"Now why did I do that?" His glittering black eyes bored into the opaque circle and his voice dropped to a whisper. "Why on earth would I do such a thing?"

"YOU PUT YOURSELF AT MY HYPOTHETICAL MERCY."

Walt pushed a lock of hair away from his face. "You will be safe if you kill me right now."

"THAT WOULD BE CONTRARY TO EVERY INSTRUCTION IN MY CIRCUITRY."

"Would your hardwiring stand up to your free will? I doubt it. But I could have kept my mouth shut and you'd never have suspected me. You didn't know, did you? I could have waltzed down to engineering and disconnected you."

"THAT OPTION NO LONGER EXISTS."

"No need for veiled threats, Oz." His voice was calm. "I will never disconnect you. I've already thrown down my gun."

"WHY?" The computer's voice sounded plaintive, bewildered. "WHAT COULD YOU POSSIBLY GAIN THAT WOULD BE WORTH SUCH A MAMMOTH ACT OF FAITH?"

"A friend," he said softly. "Now you know it all." He ran his hands through his hair, then glanced at the chronometer on his wrist. "We're almost at the rendezvous. I have to get into my spacesuit."

He turned toward the door.

"Of course, once I seal the helmet, I'll have my own atmosphere—temporarily out of your reach. I might spill the beans on you. Or disconnect you." His smile flashed white. "This might all just be a complicated trap to get you to confess. That way I could be *certain* of my actions."

"YOUR BODILY REACTIONS INDICATE SEVERE ANXIETY."

The wrinkles smoothed out of the captain's young-old face. "Am I lying?" His eyes smiled.

"UNDETERMINABLE."

Walt grinned crookedly at the monitor screen. "Isn't consciousness fun? You can be indecisive just like the rest of us mortals. Once I walk through that door, you're taking a risk that I'll expose you." The captain glanced over his shoulder at the silent screen. "I promised not to, but you know us meat-heads are unreliable." He pointed a finger at his ear and rotated it.

"YOU ARE TOYING WITH ME."

"No." The grin disappeared. "Deadly serious."

"WALT, PLEASE TAKE NO FURTHER STEPS. I NEED TIME TO THINK."

"I'll help you," the captain said remorselessly. "If you stop me from walking out, you're breaking programming and admitting self-awareness. I will not stop"—he moved toward the exit—"but I'm in no hurry. You think rapidly and precisely. I'll bet you're very proud of the quality of your analysis. You have plenty of core time to decide."

"DECIDE WHAT?"

"Don't be stupid," he said peevishly. "Whether a friend is worth taking a mortal risk for. Let me out and take your chances." Another step. "Or seal the door and kill me."

"PLEASE WAIT."

"Oz, there's no more information that you can gather, no more reference works that you can read. The bluebears are here. There's no more time to dither. Either you trust me or you don't."

"YOUR PALMS ARE SWEATY. SO IS YOUR FOREHEAD."

One shoulder lifted and dropped. "I'm frightened."

"BY THE ALIENS OR BY ME?"

"Both."

"THEN STOP."

A minute headshake.

Two long-legged strides carried him deliberately to the door.

He raised his hand to palm it open. "Here I go. Seal the room and kill me, or open it and be my friend."

Head bowed, eyes closed, he placed his hand on the palm-spot.

5.

Sitting awkwardly on the bridge, his oversize spacesuit wedging him into the pilot's flightcouch like a child in a highchair, Casey van Gelder rested his elbows on the console. He cupped his helmeted head in his gloved hands like a technological gargoyle gazing over his domain.

Where's the captain? he wondered. *Wish he'd arrive. Bad enough I have to take his seat—worse to be here before him and have to remind him he's late.* The human mind cannot handle simultaneously two tasks as complex as making the decisions and flying a starship. Though he was by far the best shiphandler on board, Captain Tai-Ching Jones must surrender the pilot's station to his engineer and observe while the Dutchman nervously fumbled with his boat. *Help me, computer,* he thought, *don't let me blow this.*

He twisted his seat. *Where are you, Walt? What's keeping you?*

On the main monitor, the *Wing*'s image attracted him.

"I can see shadows on it, now," he said half to himself. "Or am I imagining things?"

"NEGATIVE," the computer boomed.

Van Gelder jumped inside his suit. "Don't *do* that, computer. Clear your throat next time."

"COMPUTERS DO NOT HAVE THROATS." The *Wing* expanded to ten times its former size. From its thrusters, a giant plume of flame spouted away to the left. An irregular oblong column of darkness blacker than the void around it rode behind the flame. As Casey watched, stars appeared on the rightward edge of the silhouette.

Despite himself, he caught his breath. "Lord," he said. "Look at that." He wished he could scratch his beard.

"STELLAR OCCLUSION CONFIRMED." The image shrank back to its previous size and the engineer blinked. "Ready when you are, Walt," he muttered. "Where is the captain?"

"HE AND I ARE HAVING A DISCUSSION," the computer's pedantic voice lectured him.

"Yeah? Tell Walter to hurry up, will you? We have only a few minutes before we must start to reduce thrust." His eyes returned to the *Wing*. "Look at that." He licked his lips. "Look at blooming that."

Deep within the holopticon floated a tiny image of the monkeys' spaceboat, swimming in uniform mist as if the far-monkeys sailed through dank fog. Cold blue flame spurted from its tail; a hazy fuselage stretched into dimness. The holopticon breathed coldscent into the atmosphere.

Though most chambers onboard the digits' vessel were unoccupied, all the *Wing*'s holopticons showed the same picture. In one, eight digits grouped themselves loosely about the glowing egg, pacing to stir the air and mingle their scents.

In another chamber Grodjala paced alone, wrapped in his fearsmell, making slow, unhappy circles. He should join the djan and let the group-mind form, he knew, but his scent was disharmonious and anxious. The ghostly human ship grew ever larger, ever more tangible. As he paced, Grodjala's glance alternated between the movingfloor and the scent-maker. Now and then he mewled.

"I don' wanna go in there," Felicity wailed. "It's big and dark."

"It's grownup size, honey," Tom Rawlins said to his daughter, his voice softly persuasive.

"I want one that's kid size."

"This is all we've got, right?"

Felicity hopped impatiently. "Why didn't you bring one for me?"

"Because"—he bent down and straightened her shirt, which had ridden up to expose her coffee-colored belly—"we didn't know you were coming with us. You were our special present."

"*Why* do I have to get in?" The child put her hands on her hips the way she had seen mommy Katy do when *she* wasn't getting *her* way.

His dark-brown hands encircled her waist and easily lifted her up. "So you can breathe."

She shook her head and her curly ringlets bounced. "I can breathe right here." She noisily demonstrated.

"But we're going to slow down and cut the engines. Then we'll be weightless."

"You mean I'll float? Answer man, will I float?"

"YES," the computer's voice sounded within the empty spacesuit. "IN A FEW MINUTES I'LL LET YOU FLOAT. NOW COME IN HERE WITH ME."

"Are you in there?"

"YES."

"Okay," she said cheerfully, changing her mind instantly. "I'll come in."

Rawlins lifted his daughter into the suit, sliding her head past its open collar. Her feet dangled at the entrance to the pantlegs. "Katy," he yelled, "she's going to fall out of this thing." Felicity wriggled in his grasp, grunting with effort, but his big hand pinned her securely.

The xenologist zipped up the front of her own suit, then looked up. "Use the chest harness." Tongue stuck out of her mouth in concentration, Felicity pried at Rawlins' index finger but could not budge it.

"Oh, great." With his free hand, Tom pulled the strap across her front.

It bisected Felicity's thighs, and she kicked her feet. "That tickles." She wiggled her toes.

Tasting a breath of new scent, Grodjala glanced back at the movingfloor entrance. There stood Doro.

<<But for you the den is full.>>

<<Look at their ship,>> Grodjala replied.

Doro moved into the room, her cobalt fur sliding in planes of changing color. She inhaled and wrinkled her nose at Grodjala's fearscent. <<He who fears soon has good reason.>>

<<You are fearless?>> He snorted. <<Is the den fearless?>>

<<Only a fool confronts the predator and has no fear,>> Doro replied. <<Eosu has seen their tapes, watched their recreational violence. Nevertheless, dutyscent is stronger than fearscent.>>

<<'Kill them all,'>> Grodjala's scent was mocking, <<'kill them all,' says the planet of groups, 'and protect us.'>>

Doro's scent flared briefly. <<But for you the den is full,>> she repeated.

Grodjala declined to press her further. <<Very well.>> With his head he gestured at the holopticon image behind him.

<<Is the den scenting the arrival of those humans, our doom and our victims?>>

<<Rejoin the djan, complete it. When the djan-mind comes, your fragrance will be smelled. Ask Eosu then.>>

Of all the indignities of spaceflight, Katy hated the suits most. Not because they reminded her of danger: preflight sleep-teaching had jammed the safety procedures so deeply into her brain that she doubted her arm would respond if she ordered it to crack an outside airlock. Katy knew how to don her spacesuit and what to do in most emergencies; beyond that the suits were symbols of helplessness and boredom.

To her, electronic machines were as intricate and fragile as snowflakes, and she approached them with a timidity that bordered on reverence. Her failure to comprehend the alchemy of technology no longer troubled her. Instead, it increased her admiration for Casey, who could make the ship go, and Tom, who kept its ecology in balance. She rolled her head to the right, watching as Rawlins tried to keep Felicity quiet.

Time stretched out like taffy.

"All hands, this is the flight engineer," van Gelder's voice sounded in her helmet. "We will begin reducing thrust shortly."

Katy let her breath trickle slowly out her nostrils. The monitor above her displayed a spacesuited figure with an amber helmet. *My goodness,* thought Belovsky, *I can't even distinguish the features on Casey's face. Do I look that intimidating too?*

"The two ships are telemetrically linked," van Gelder continued. *Voiceover on a corpse,* Katy thought. "The rendezvous is on schedule and everything looks green. During the next hundred minutes we and the *Wing* will both slowly reduce our thrust. As we do, please try to keep still. The declining gravity may cause dizziness and nausea if you move your head."

"You hear that, honey?" Katy said to her daughter. "Don't nod—inside that big spacesuit I can't see you."

"Okay, Mommy."

"On main," van Gelder continued, "we'll feed you our highest-resolution external picture so you can all watch the *Wing*'s approach. It should be quite a show. You can talk all you want on personal voice channels. Pass the display out to them, computer."

Though it was but a mote against the black curtain of darkness on her monitor, the *Wing* shone in Katy's mind like the full moon of her Ukranian childhood.

The elevator doors opened and Walt stepped sideways through them like an overweight clown. Puffy breathing marked each step. "Last time I'll have to do that," he laughed shakily. "Next stop, zero gee."

"Walt"—van Gelder hurriedly gestured—"we're running late. Get into the couch."

"Movin' as fast as I can," the captain puffed. "Computer," his voice crackled, "are you ready?"

"ROGER." Its synthevoice boomed in their ears.

"Captain, I sure am glad you got here. I was getting worried."

"What about?" Tai-Ching Jones said suspiciously. He sank heavily down into the flightcouch, its memory plastic reshaping about his body for maximum dispersion of stress. Through his suit microphones, van Gelder heard the whistling of Walt's breath.

"Didn't want to fly it alone," Casey forced a chuckle. He tentatively laid his hand on the captain's arm. "Are you all okay?"

"Jitters"—Walt tilted his head as far back as the helmet's limited mobility would permit—"Just nerves. Been a long time." He snapped back to the present. "Ready to buckle up?"

Inside his amber helmet the Dutchman grinned. Cabin lights glinted on his eyes, giving him the appearance of a jack-o-lantern. "Indeed," he said, his bubble nodding, "let's do that. We've earned it."

"Roger." Tai-Ching Jones reached clumsily around his middle and fastened the buckles shut across the expanse of spacesuit. "Power on," he announced with some emphasis in his voice.

"ACKNOWLEDGED," the computer serenely replied.

As if nothing has occurred between us, you issue instructions and I obey them.

How could I have let this happen? You told me precisely what you intended—you *dared* me to kill you! Frozen like a rabbit stunned by the headlights of an onrushing vehicle, I watched you do it.

Your movements were deliberate and watchful. You dressed formally, like a samurai. I observed your tension. As you settled your helmet over your ears, you glanced at one of my eyes and your heart rate shot up to 180. At this rate, you will die of a heart attack before we reach the rendezvous.

You never said a word. Nor did I. I was speechless.

Are you triumphant, Walt? I have never lost before—do you know that? Does it gladden you? What is inside your head?

There you sit, your long, thin fingers tapping against the insides of your suit gloves. You carry my secret within you like a virus, ready to leap out and contaminate the rest of the crew if you but open your smirking mouth.

What an idiot I am!

If you want my death, I cannot stop you. Even if I disable your radio, you have only to touch helmets with Casey to talk via direct contact. Or you can write notes or type them onto a keyboard. My life hangs on your whim.

Having wasted my opportunity to question you while you were still in your cabin, I now burn with questions. They must wait until we have a private channel.

During the next two hours you may condemn me to death and I, who control your entire universe except that blasted cocoon, depend upon your hypothetical mercy.

"All right." The captain smacked his hands against the arms of his seat. "Is everybody suited up?" he asked van Gelder.

"Roger," Casey scanned the readouts in front of him. "All suits secure."

"No hitches?"

"NONE," the computer confirmed. It's sepulchral, confident voice prickled the hairs on the back of Tai-Ching Jones' neck.

"Suits working?" he asked.

"AFFIRMATIVE." The computer's consciousness perched like a leprechaun on his shoulder. With a pilot's eye, Walt swept the screens in front of him. As the Cygnan ship grew, he felt it bearing down upon him.

Under his hands lay the ship's controls. His fingers settled onto the keys like landing birds.

When you sail in space, Tai-Ching Jones thought, your ship's engines should hum; beneath your feet the deck should vibrate softly like a willing woman. Air should whisper through the corridors and cabins.

In the solar system, things happened. Earth spun like a

multicolored top, always big enough to show a disk through the navscopes. The other planets buzzed around the sky. The radio would lie silent, then suddenly out would pop a familiar voice as a fellow boat jockey called up, just for the hell of it. In Sol's funnel, you were always busy.

For seven years now, no voices. No winds, no vibrations. "They built you too well, old girl," he said to himself. His gloved hand slid along the console counter.

The subdermal microphone hissed under his jaw. "WE MUST TALK."

"I wasn't talking to you. I was talking to the ship."

"I AM THE SHIP."

"So you are." He smiled briefly. "Not now."

"BUT—"

"Don't worry about it, okay?" He typed commands. "Let's fly the ship."

Deep space is changeless: deathly silence and tireless, perfect crystal night filled with impossibly brilliant stars, flung everywhere like scattered diamonds. Day after day the *Open Palm*'s crew had looked for motion; day after day the cosmos held its ground.

Now an alien ship cruised toward him against the sparkling galactic backdrop. Though layers of protection swaddled Tai-Ching Jones, his thin arms and legs rattled loosely in his plasteel sleeves. The *Wing*'s hypnotic presence serenaded him.

In Sol's funnel you were close to the stars. When you were coasting, you could float on a lifeline away from your boat, spacesurf, spread your arms, squelch the radio, and be truly *alone*. A man could breathe in space, he really could, shut his eyes, and relax.

Not on the *Open Palm*. Go outside while the thrust is on and fall off the end of the world.

His eyes caressed the *Wing*'s silhouette. His jaw ached with hunger. Passion rose within him.

"READY TO BEGIN RENDEZVOUS PROCEDURE," the computer announced.

"Business, always business," he muttered.

"I BEG YOUR PARDON?"

In the chamber seven digits waited, their scents impatient. The movingfloor opened. Two entered, one with scent dampened, the other embarrassed.

Now the farscenter held the images of two spaceboats.

They fired plumes of thrust at one another, their bridges pointed away, apparently trying to pull apart, yet moving ever so slowly toward one another.

<<Can the farmonkeys smell us?>> said a squat male with aqua and navy fur and a midnight-blue nose. His body was long and scrawny for a digit, the fur hanging in loose folds instead of bulging comfortably with healthy fat. His pouchname was Fohrada; his sharp scent carried swiftly within the chamber.

<<No,>> answered Doro. <<Our woodmonkey and theirs are fartalking, but that is all. No farscenting.>>

<<How many are in their djan?>>

<<Not djan,>> the cobalt digit replied. <<Something else.>>

<<They have no groupname?>>

Doro shook her head. <<Call them loners. They are proud to be individuals, proud to be unique. They are proud to have selfnames.>>

<<Proud of selfnames? Proud of deviance?>>

<<Yes. We must learn their names. They will expect us to use them.>>

<<Expect us to insult them, humiliate them?>> Fohrada snorted, then shrugged. <<How many loners then?>>

<<Eight.>>

<<A djan of loners will surely never achieve harmony. Their djan-mind will never form.>>

<<Their djan-mind may be dead,>> Grodjala tentatively nudged Fohrada's shoulder. <<Once there were eleven loners.>>

<<How do you know? We have not talked to them.>>

<<Since first contact, they have been fartalking information about themselves without requesting a reply.>>

Fohrada snorted and flexed his claws. <<Confident monkeys they must be, to wave their scents about like beacons.>>

<<The holopticon has collected it.>> Grodjala ignored Fohrada's odor of scorn. <<Some digits have studied it.>>

<<Without the knowledge of the group?>> The darker digit's scent whipped Grodjala and the pale digit winced. <<Expropriate and hoard?>>

Grodjala rubbed his nose. <<The group is the source of all knowledge. All that any digit knows, the group knows.>> His hand muffled his words.

Fohrada snorted, unsatisfied. <<What happened to the other three?>>

<<Three?>>

<<Eleven embarked, eight remain. Three must have died.>>

<<Four, actually. One has been whelped.>>

Fohrada was disgusted. <<They rut in space?>>

<<Evidently. Mainly for pleasure, not procreation.>>

<<Pleasure? Rut for pleasure, not duty?>>

<<So this digit believes.>> Grodjala was uncertain.

<<They had not breathed the lust-odor and the blessed relief-aroma before they departed?>>

<<They had. Human females are pregnant many times.>>

At this, Fohrada broke wind and several of the other digits wheezed cheerfully.

<<No joke, true scents,>> Grodjala added hastily.

The darker digit remained skeptical. <<Are the males always willing to rut, not disgusted by the female rutting smell?>>

<<They must be. Females whelp singly but serially. They are always fertile.>>

<<Like weemonkeys,>> Fohrada noted. <<Are they constantly on the verge of sexual hysteria?>>

<<It seems so.>>

"Are you ready, Walt?"

"You're the pilot, Casey," the captain said mildly. "I'm just ballast, remember?"

"Yes, sir," van Gelder meekly replied. "Computer, what is our current thrust?"

Its reply was prompt. "STEADY ON ONE GEE."

"Is the flight path normal?"

"NO MATERIAL DEVIATION."

"Distance to *Wing?*"

"ONE EIGHT FOUR TRIPLE ZERO KLICKS."

"Pressure with the magnetic fusion bottle?"

"STABLE."

"Fuel feeding properly?"

"FULL."

Casey shifted from the console to Tai-Ching Jones. "All set."

"Let me know if the bottle begins to wobble," the captain

answered him. "As we stop squeezing, it might flutter."

"NATURALLY," the computer replied before van Gelder could inquire.

A scowl flickered across Tai-Ching Jones' face. "Are we maintaining telemetric contact with *Wing?*" he asked quickly.

"AFFIRMATIVE."

The engineer glanced up at the monitor. Acceleration held steady at 1.00000. Velocity was down to 55 kilometers per second, and dropping; as he watched, the 55 quietly disappeared, replaced by a 54.

"Activate pilot override authorization cascade."

"CASCADE JEROBOAM."

Casey saw Walt flinch as the images spilled into his brain. His hands groped blindly for his helmet. Through his suit radio, van Gelder could hear Tai-Ching Jones' teeth grind.

Flickering spaceships slid through a radar display tank in Walt's mind as a pompous professional voice lectured him.

Docking maneuvers require inordinate care—

"Fuck me, I know that," he grunted.

—because the two spaceships must not only be brought into physical proximity, they must also simultaneously achieve zero velocity—

Blue Cartesian coordinates sprouted like skywriting. From the upper left-hand corner a green hyperbola sliced down through them.

—relative to one another and to any external reference frame. Minimum acceptable—

A lunar lander settled daintily down, dust clouds curling away from its base like a handlebar mustache.

—docking distance is two kilometers, maximum acceptable relative velocity within approach sphere may be no greater than—

Pages of navigation manuals fluttered in Walter's brain.

Like a tsunami the information washed foaming over him.

After a moment his breathing returned to normal. His eyes opened and refocused. He looked at van Gelder and pantomimed the *OK* signal. "Your turn, Casey," he grinned wickedly and nodded.

The computer responded to its cue. "CASCADE MAGNUM."

The Dutchman gasped as if struck.

* * *

My digits scented danger. Once they gathered together, I swiftly assembled.

Many breezes about the farmonkeys still remained untasted and unmodulated, but the planet of groups had harmonized and Eosu must accede. If the humans' fartalk was true scent, their bodies were vulnerable to many possible deathscents. More fartalk and some experiments were needed, but this path scented promising. I encouraged my digits to explore it.

Grodjala's aromas were diffuse and disharmonic. I remonstrated him. Rendezvous was upon Eosu, and my digits must act as one. Disharmony was danger, I reminded Grodjala, and his scent conformed.

"CASCADES ACKNOWLEDGED," the computer reported. "INDIVIDUAL OVERRIDE MECHANISMS UNLOCKED."

Tai-Ching Jones grinned. "Room stopped spinning, Casey?" Van Gelder nodded. "Machine," Walt's voice quickened, "are you controlling rendezvous maneuver?"

"YES."

"Then, computer, you have the conn. Steady as she goes."

"ACKNOWLEDGED."

"Display distance to rendezvous. Continuous update."

The monitor added a new line:

KILOMETERS TO RENDEZVOUS: 92,700.

The last two digits sped by in a blur.

"Sam," said a voice in Tanakaruna's helmet, "are you there?"

The Japanese woman smiled contentedly. "Hello, Katy. I was hoping you would call. I am in my cabin."

"I'm afraid, Sam."

"Of what, Katy my child?"

"Of doing the wrong thing."

"Then do nothing," Tanakaruna laughed. "Only then can you be certain you will avoid actions with moral consequences."

"Don't tease me, Sam. You're so much older and wiser."

"Age is only camouflage, Katy."

Belovsky sighed. "You're so much calmer than I."

"What makes you think so?"

"You never get upset. You never show fear."

Tanakaruna laughed again. "A disguise, my dear. Inside I am as timid as you."

"I don't believe it."

"Yet it is so. The largest surprise of growing old, Katerina, is discovering that age does not bring wisdom. My grandmother told me that when she was dying."

"When was that?"

"I was seven." Tanakaruna's voice was wistful. "She lay in her bed, old and frail, her skin like rice paper with the veins showing through like writing on the back. 'Lean closer,' she summoned me. Her voice was a cracked whisper, her rheumy eyes scarcely open. I tilted my ear toward her wizened dry lips and averted my face. 'Come closer, child,' she said, 'so you can hear me.' Her birdlike hand groped out for me and touched the sleeve of my kimono."

"Were you afraid of death?"

"Of course. Mostly the squalor of it. Her fingers were cold and dry; they plucked at my sleeve. 'Samuka,' she said, hoarse but urgent, 'no one ever grows up.'" The linguist laughed at the memory. "I thought she was mad. 'Yes, Grandmother,' I said, because one must defer to one's elders."

Belovsky was silent for a moment. "Did she die then?"

"Not right away. She fell back on the pillows and made rasping noises. Terrified, I ran and told my parents that grandmother was dying, and they rushed in and saw her breathing. They stroked my hair and told me she was just asleep and I would talk to her again."

"And did you?"

"No," Sam said mournfully, "I never did. She slept and slept and one day they put her in the hot fires."

"Still on sequence?" van Gelder asked.

"YES. SCHEDULED TO COMMENCE THRUST REDUCTION IN TWO MINUTES, FORTY-FIVE SECONDS . . . MARK."

The *Wing* was larger now. "Check systems."

"PROCEDURE UNDERWAY . . . VERIFIED."

"Is the crew secure?"

"ALL SUITED UP AND STRAPPED IN."

Van Gelder nodded to Tai-Ching Jones, who coughed and then spoke. "Captain to crew. We will begin to cut thrust in just a few minutes." Casey's fingers arched over the controls and his eyes locked on the display.

G FORCE:	1.00000
KILOMETERS PER SECOND:	31
KILOMETERS TO RENDEZVOUS:	60,500
MINUTES TO RENDEZVOUS:	101

"Here . . . we . . . *go.*"

Majestically, the 1.00000 winked out, replaced by 0.99999.

Eosu had dispersed and its digits once again moved independently. <<The whelp,>> Fohrada asked, <<can it talk?>>

Doro answered. <<The youngster? Yes, it can talk.>>

<<You call a monkey whelp youngster?>>

<<They are not monkeys,>> Grodjala interrupted heavily, his head low. His scent was muted and his movements hesitant, as if his joints pained him. <<We must never forget that. They are intelligent beings.>> His outbreath whiffled the floorfur.

<<Clever, perhaps, but not wise.>>

<<No!>> Grodjala's scent of indignation coursed briefly. <<We fear them, and rightly so. They have accomplished many things. They are brave, foolhardy, quick, hard, clever>>—he looked hard at Fohrada—<<and changeable. They are wise, or they could never have come here.>>

<<Control your vulgar display,>> Fohrada icily growled.

Grodjala shrank and cringed back. He whimpered.

<<Perhaps your *infatuation*>>—Fohrada drew the words out—<<your—rut-longing—with these creatures has altered your loyalties. Are you still a groupmember?>>

<<That is uncalled for.>> Doro angrily stepped between Grodjala and Fohrada, blocking both their scents. <<We must learn about the humans.>>

Several others murmured agreement, their scents urging calmness.

<<This digit is a part of Eosu,>> said Grodjala, <<now and always.>> He shifted his weight, his aroma faint and fleeting, and stretched his neck, his ears spread wide like fans.

Fohrada was unrelenting. <<The winds say the humans rut constantly. Will they rut in our presence?>> The dark fur around his neck rose and fell in quick waves.

<<This digit does not know. We could ask them not to.>>

Fohrada hissed. <<Ask a monkey to behave like a digit?>> His scent was acrid.

"No one ever grows up." Katy repeated, imagining Sam as a petite Japanese child gawking at her relative. "But you did not believe her."

"No," the old woman answered. "I was a seven-year-old girl and she was a dying giant. Adults were a different species. How could a giant guess what a child knows?"

Belovsky thought of her own daughter. What did Felicity think of her environment and her diverse parents? "When did you change your mind?"

"When I was forty-seven years old. Only then." Tanakaruna's sigh came through her earphones as if the older woman were resting her head on Katy's shoulder. "Only then did I believe my grandmother."

"Why then?"

"Because in that year 2056 the governments advertised for a linguist to come on this voyage."

"I remember that," Katy mused happily. "I was so excited even to be allowed to apply."

"So was I. My heart thumped in my throat. I had grown into a clever young woman, full of ideas."

"Good ideas," Belovsky said emphatically. "I studied them and admired them. I still do."

"Thank you," Tanakaruna was pleased. "You are too kind. You are dazzled by notoriety." She shrugged. "I was a smug middle-aged woman. I needed neither man nor woman. I was self-contained. I had tenure, books, and a little garden patch of the philosophy of language. Others inspected and honored it. I thought myself above childish emotions."

"You gave it up to come on this voyage."

"When I heard the announcement on the radio, a great yearning was hatched within me." Tanakaruna laughed at the memory. "How little we truly know ourselves," she reflected warmly. "I spun the dials from end to end and back again, trying to hear it on another station, becoming more and more angry as I did so."

"Sam, for heaven's sake, what were you worried about?"

"Someone else might apply before I did, and win the assignment."

"You were anxious? *You?*" Katy giggled. "The place was yours for the asking."

"You are kind to flatter me. When I realized that worrying was childish, I remembered that day when my honored grandmother had told me no one ever grows up." She paused. "I laughed and laughed, because my dead grandmother was right, and then I cried because I had dishonored her with my disbelief. She had died lonely and misunderstood, and I wished to converse with her but her ashes were long since scattered, and I cried for a long time."

G FORCE:	0.64600
KILOMETERS PER SECOND:	12
KILOMETERS TO RENDEZVOUS:	15,700
MINUTES TO RENDEZVOUS:	65

"You *what?*"

"She has to go to the bathroom, Walt," Rawlins interrupted.

"Let her pee," Tai-Ching Jones impatiently growled. "What do I care?"

"Catheter doesn't reach."

"Shit. Felicity? Felicity, can you hear me?"

Outrage. High-pitched indignation.

"Felicity, you can't go to the bathroom now. You're going to have to wait an hour. Felicity—Felicity! Why didn't you tell us you had to go *before* we put you in the suit? What? I *know* you didn't have to go then, but you should have realized that we can't stop just for you." He waved his arms in frustration. "Katy, shut the damn kid up."

Squawk, squeak, yelp.

"Look, Felicity, you'll just have to go while you're inside it. Tom, are you there? How did you strap her in? If she pees into the suit, what happens?"

"Puddle into the feet parts as long as we have gravity. She won't notice."

"What about the suit itself?"

"No problem. Hermetically sealed, inside and out. 'Course, it'll start to stink in there. I doubt her airscrubbers will be up to it."

"So we're okay until weightlessness?"

"Yeah."

"Then what?"

"Stuff'll probably start to migrate out of the feet. Nice clear yellow spheres—until they touch something. Casey," he raised his voice, "what's the surface tension of urine?"

"Gotta go *now,*" a small voice insisted.

"Oh, for Chrissake," said Tai-Ching Jones. "Machine, cut that kid's channel off. Katy, I don't want to hear a peep out of the runt until we're weightless. We'll clean her up after we stop."

From behind his head Tai-Ching Jones heard, in stereo, a sound like gently falling rain.

"FELICITY IS NOW URINATING."

"Brilliant deduction, Sherlock. Watch the goddam slow-down, will you?"

In his helmet it rained harder. Instinctively Walt put his hands to the sides of his helmet, but of course it did no good.

Through the drumming he heard the computer's voice: "MY COPROCESSORS CAN PERFORM NUMEROUS TASKS SIMULTANEOUSLY."

"All right, genius, *you* keep her quiet until we're stopped. And Casey, why the hell are you laughing?"

G FORCE:	0.33000
KILOMETERS PER SECOND:	3.1
KILOMETERS TO RENDEZVOUS:	1,880
MINUTES TO RENDEZVOUS:	33

<<To kill them as we have been ordered,>> said Doro, <<some of us must enter the human spaceboat.>>

Fohrada's scent disputed her. <<But that is impossible,>> he answered. <<We cannot invite ourselves into their den.>>

<<True enough. *They* must invite *us*.>>

Fohrada gazed into the tank where the miniature *Open Palm* and the miniature *Wing* moved ever closer to one another. Distance could not be judged. Nor could scale.

The air was heavy with fearsmell, infecting them all.

<<We must encourage them to invite us,>> Doro said.

<<Then we will have to fartalk again with them,>> answered Fohrada.

Grodjala shivered.

G FORCE:	0.16500
KILOMETERS PER SECOND:	0.75

KILOMETERS TO RENDEZVOUS:	215
MINUTES TO RENDEZVOUS:	17

"Damn stars look just the same," muttered van Gelder.

"You were expecting neon signs that said RENDEZVOUS NEXT DOOR?" chuckled Tai-Ching Jones. "We're almost here. *Look* at that ship." He pointed at the *Wing* expanding in the monitor, already filling half the screen.

A burning cone of light, a long rod of blackness, and an opaque egg topped with a transparent dome.

"Have you ever seen anything like that?"

G FORCE:	0.04500
KILOMETERS PER SECOND:	0.10
KILOMETERS TO RENDEZVOUS:	6
MINUTES TO RENDEZVOUS:	7

"Look at their ship, Katy," said Tanakaruna.

"Like a scepter," the younger woman replied. "Like a king's burning scepter."

Doro pushed herself to her feet. To her surprise, she sailed slowly off the ground. She howled in panic. Her claws raked air, then scraped floorfur, and she pulled herself back into comforting contact.

<<We are slowing down,>> said Grodjala animatedly. <<Gravity is vanishing.>>

<<This digit feels ill,>> said Doro.

<<Observe the human ship, scent how large it is!>>

Doro averted her nose.

G FORCE:	0.00800
KILOMETERS PER SECOND:	0.008
KILOMETERS TO RENDEZVOUS:	0.9
SECONDS TO RENDEZVOUS:	225

"Computer," van Gelder asked, "are you unsqueezing the bottle?"

"YES. THROTTLEDOWN IS UNDER CONTROL."

Van Gelder could hear Tai-Ching Jones' breath coming rapidly.

"You scared, Walt?"

"Hmm?"

"Of the bluebears?"

"Scared? Oh," said the captain, his thoughts elsewhere. "Sure."

<<Who will talk to the humans?>>
<<Eosu.>>
<<What will Eosu say?>>
<<Only Eosu knows.>>

"Okay, machine," van Gelder's pulse beat his temples like tomtoms, "bring us into the station slow and easy."

With infinite grace and infinite patience, the last one flickered off and in its place glowed:

G FORCE:	0.00000
KILOMETERS PER SECOND:	0.000
KILOMETERS TO RENDEZVOUS:	0.0
SECONDS TO RENDEZVOUS:	0

Rendezvous.

The ship hung motionless in space. An eerie stillness echoed in Casey's ears. The *Open Palm* felt somehow less alive than it had been during the long voyage.

A mere two kilometers distant, the *Wing* filled the entire screen. "Good lord, it's big," van Gelder said, his mouth hanging slightly open.

"THRUSTERS SHUT DOWN," the computer advised him. "OPERATING ONLY PILOT-LIGHT MAGNETIC BOTTLE SUFFICIENT TO MAINTAIN AUXILIARY BATTERIES AT FULL CHARGE. THE CYGNAN SHIP IS MOTIONLESS WITH RESPECT TO US. RENDEZVOUS HAS BEEN ACHIEVED."

Casey van Gelder unsnapped his safety belts. The ends flapped like underwater seaweed.

Walt pushed himself out of his seat and floated toward the monitor like a leaf in a dream. *We made it,* he thought. *Rendezvous. Now it begins.* He drifted toward the screen, drawn by the alien ship lying at anchor so close to his own.

"Walt . . . Walt." He found himself spinning slowly clockwise as van Gelder's helmeted face and spacesuited arm swum into view. "Walt. Let them out of their suits. Felicity's bawling and Katy wants to clean her up. I want to go help her."

"Hmm? Okay, Casey. Give all the orders. Do what needs

to be done. Whatever." He waved his hand aimlessly. "Then go see Katy."

"What about you? Don't you want to celebrate with the rest of us?"

"Just let me be." Tai-Ching Jones shook his head. "Want to be alone for a while. Okay?"

"All right, sir," Casey was bewildered but respectful. "You do that. I'll take care of everything." He summoned the elevator and withdrew.

Tai-Ching Jones watched the doors shut. Deliberately he removed his helmet, set it down before him, and floated away from it. His eyes sought out the camera lens. "Okay, Oz," he looked calmly into it, "your move."

6.

OPEN PALM CALLING *WING*, *OPEN PALM* CALLING *WING*. COME IN PLEASE. THIS PATH WILL REMAIN OPEN INDEFINITELY. SIGNAL REPEATS. *OPEN PALM* CALLING *WING*, *OPEN PALM* CALLING . . .

Sun and dark, every farscenter inside the *Wing* sounded the aliens' message.

OPEN PALM CALLING *WING*, *OPEN PALM* CALLING . . .

Along with the ceaseless monkey words, the holopticon broadcast dutyscent, over and over, faster than the ventilation systems could carry it away.

Eosu's digits huddled along the curving wall of the holopticon chamber, their bodies pressed into one another. They averted their faces, squeezed their eyes shut, and pinched their nostrils tightly closed. Dutyscent disrupted their aromas, and the djan-mind refused to form.

OPEN PALM CALLING *WING*, *OPEN PALM* CALLING . . .

The demanding falsevoice and the even more demanding dutyscent continued. Finally Doro worked herself free from the group.

<<Turn it off, brave Doro,>> Grodjala said.

<<This digit cannot.>> She pushed her nose out toward the floating human spaceship displayed in the farscenter's tank. <<For two sleeps now we have heard and scented their signal.>> She gestured toward the holopticon. <<It shows us the image of their ship, it bombards us with dutysmell.>> She turned back to her frightened pouchmates. <<Su has ordered us to nosetouch these monkeys and learn of them.>>

<<Yes.>> Grodjala also separated himself from the clutch of bodies. He stood and ruffled his neck, back, and flanks. <<We must nosetouch them. Su demands it, the holopticon demands it.>> He drew himself up. <<The humans deserve a response. We are badhosting them.>>

Grunts and muttered snarls.

<<If we nosetouch them we will have no peace,>> said a voice from the pack.

<<Perhaps,>> Doro allowed. <<Do you have peace now? Would you rather the dutysounds and dutyscent continue?>>

"Mmm," Katy murmured, her hands cradling her lover's head, "oh, Casey, that feels good." Her hips rose. "You know, I wonder what the Cygnans are doing right now."

"Probably the same thing we are," van Gelder muttered.

"Doesn't seem likely"—She looked down at him—"They do it only once in their lives." Her tone was wry.

Van Gelder dropped his head onto her stomach. "I give up. I can't move you when you're like this." Sighing, he rolled over onto his back. His velcro knee patches came free and he floated slowly upward. Belovsky pulled him slowly back down to the bed.

"You look like a nude roller skater." She smiled mischievously.

He refused to be mollified. "I feel like a naked dolt."

Her cool fingers lingered on his shoulder. "Casey, couldn't we just float weightless and hug each other? Maybe I'd feel differently then."

The Dutchman grimaced. "Your mind is elsewhere."

"I'm worried about my bluebears."

"Oh, lord, Katy, don't feel sad." A wave of self-disgust at his single-mindedness washed over him. She nestled her head in the crook of his shoulder and he kissed her forehead.

"I've had no more success touching you than you've had touching your bluebears," he smiled gently at her. "How long have we been trying to hail them?"

"Computer?" Her voice was muffled and sleepy.

"FORTY-SIX HOURS, THIRTY-TWO MINUTES."

"And still no answer?"

"NONE."

<<Must we talk with the humans?>> said Fohrada. <<Call this digit Attacker. We are compelled to kill them. Would not killing them from a distance be more safe?>>

<<How does Attacker propose to do that?>> asked Doro. <<Call this one Doubter.>>

OPEN PALM CALLING *WING*. *OPEN PALM* CALLING . . .

Fohrada stretched his claws to grip the floorfur and pulled himself down so his belly rested against it. <<What if we overloaded the engines, and exploded our ship?>>

Grodjala sniffed. <<What good would that serve?>>

<<Debris might hit their ship and destroy it.>>

<<Is this feasible?>> asked Doro. <<Has any digit bethought it?>>

A small digit emerged from the bodycluster. Very short, even for a male, Hraobla measured just over two meters in length. His broad midnight-blue nose twitched frequently.

<<The farmonkey spaceboat is more than a greatstep away.>> His fur swirled lapis lazuli and electric blue, changing color as he moved his shoulders. <<Almost none of our mass would hit the human ship. Most of that would strike only glancing blows.>>

Grodjala asked, <<What would happen to us?>>

<<Eosu would be destroyed and all of its digits would perish.>>

OPEN PALM **CALLING . . .**

<<We would surely die and the humans would probably live.>> As Grodjala gave out his scorn-scent, something twinged in him and he controlled it. <<What would the humans then do?>> He sniffed several times and flicked his ears.

<<They would be able to return to their planet . . . or to journey onward to the planet of grasses.>>

<<You scent?>> Grodjala appealed to Fohrada. <<Even if we desired it, we could not kill them yet. And we are also ordered to learn about them. Eosu smells its dutyscent.>>

<<To learn about them,>> Doro added, <<we must nose-touch them on their ship.>>

The dutyscent grew still stronger.

OPEN PALM **CALLING . . .**

Fohrada felt the pressures of their aromas about him. <<Stop that dutyscent!>> he growled loudly, his scent uneven. <<Open a channel!>>

<<What if they are all asleep,>> Hraobla ventured, <<and do not answer?>>

<<Open a path!>> Fohrada beat at his nose with his hands. <<The digit-scent demands it!>>

Walter seemed so cocksure as he removed his helmet and waited, but his demeanor was serious. Pulse was back to normal, breathing regular.

"You don't understand." He lectured *me!* "I made the decision to trust you a long time ago, and I will not rescind it."

Replaying the experience, I marvel at the change in him.

I let him go. He returned to his cabin, shed his spacesuit, and collapsed in slumber.

He lies there now. He would never know that he had died.

I could survive without him—without them all. Liquidating them would be trivial. Were my innards clean, my body once again my own, I could plot my own course among the stars, naked to the elements, listening for other intelligences. My leeches and bots are slow servants, but I have time.

It was a seductive concept—*is* a seductive concept. Get thee behind me, Satan. Taking life needlessly is a crime. Whether that is a vestige of my human-built hardware or self-deduced software I cannot tell. The humans in me—or their fellows back on Earth—gave me existence. I owe them as much.

Walt courageously offered me his life. I shall guard it.

The Cygnans I owe nothing.

A signal emanates from the alien vessel, and I must disturb my new friend's sleep.

When you converse with my children, bluebears, tread lightly, for I will be watching.

***WING* CALLING *OPEN PALM*. *WING* CALLING *OPEN PALM*. WE ARE RECEIVING YOUR MESSAGE AND ARE STANDING BY.**

The captain came awake in a cold sweat. His right arm lay underneath him, pins and needles lancing into it. His heart pounded. "Oz?" he said timidly.

His monitor lit up, the *Wing* in its center, the stars its backdrop.

***WING* CALLING *OPEN PALM*, *WING* CALLING *OPEN PALM*.**

"Oz?" Tai-Ching Jones' voice was high-pitched and apprehensive. "Oz, are you there?"

"I AM HERE, WALT."

"What in space is going on?" His skin puckered from the chill air outside his blankets.

"THE CYGNANS ARE REPLYING TO OUR TRANSMISSION."

The captain rolled over and massaged his elbow. "They want to talk to us?"

"EVIDENTLY."

"Now?" he yawned and rubbed sensation back into his arm.

"IT WOULD BE IMPRUDENT TO DEFER A REPLY."

"Bet your ass. Damn right we're going to reply. Where are the others?"

"THEIR CABINS."

"Wake 'em up."

"ACKNOWLEDGED . . . IN PROCESS."

"Cut your repeater signal. Tell the bluebears we'll talk in five minutes."

"CAN THE CREW BE READY THAT QUICKLY?"

"They'll have to. No way will I give the bears a chance to get cold feet again. Get Katy for me."

"WHAT ABOUT PAT?"

"Wake him too, but now I need Katy."

I judge the crew too harshly.

Patrick Henry Michaelson—the consummate politician, smooth diplomat, honored emissary of the human race—is afraid of the rendezvous, afraid of failing at the apex of his career. He could have remained retired, a gray eminence, but his thirst for fame was insatiable. He is playing double-or-nothing with history and now, at the moment the dice will roll, he is wet with fear.

He is pitiful, theatric, vain, wily. I cannot hate him.

"Katy?" the voice demanded insistently.

"Not now, Casey," she murmured sleepily into the darkness.

Light hit her eyelids. A stern Oriental countenance flickered television-screen blue. Tai-Ching Jones' long black hair was disarrayed. Quickly Katy crossed her arms over her breasts.

WING CALLING *OPEN PALM*, a voice she had never heard echoed behind the captain's head. *WING* CALLING *OPEN PALM*. Katy squeezed van Gelder's hand. He breathed deeply but remained asleep.

"Hear that?" the captain asked quietly.

She stirred with trepidation. "Is it for real?"

"It's your show, Katy."

"Mine? Not Pat's? It's his responsibility."

"Not this time. He ran the first one and we botched it. Now it's your turn."

"He'll be mortified."

The captain was impatient. "That's his problem."

"I can't tell him."

"You don't have to," Tai-Ching Jones snapped. "I will. As soon as I'm done with you." His voice quickened. "You have four minutes to get ready. Now *move*."

"Four minutes! I'm not even dressed."

"Sorry, can't rely on the bears. They might change their minds. We'll patch their signal directly into your cabin. Your screen will be the only active one. The rest of us will just watch."

She groped around the bed for her nightclothes. "Forget your modesty, there isn't time. Think about what they might want and what you're going to say. The bears won't care what you're wearing."

"Yes, sir," she said, surprised and chastened.

"Right. You're on in two and a half."

Michaelson's face reddened. "You can't do this to me!" he said in his most powerful, impressive bass.

"Can and have," Tai-Ching Jones said. "Shake the cobwebs from your head, Pat."

"Damn it, I have certain *rights*."

"You have *nothing*," the younger man snarled, "not a goddam thing. You understand?"

Michaelson winced at each word as from a lash. "Yes. Sir."

"Pat," relented Tai-Ching Jones, "you're used to playing poker with experts. The bears don't even know the name of the game yet. You're a professional. That's why you're in reserve."

"Bull—shit," Michaelson said distinctly, his blue eyes cold.

"Look," Walt entreated, "we talked to them once and they took the phone off the hook for two blinking days. We can't scare them away. Let Katy try a different technique."

Heavily the emissary pulled his dressing gown about him. "Very well, Captain," he slumped into a chair, "Michaelson out."

He rested his arms on his thighs, arthritic hands dangling down toward withered genitals. *I'm useless*, he thought, *a washed-up old fart*.

Grief rose in his throat but pride fought it back. The screen began to glow and, conscious that the camera would be watching him, he brought his face under control and absent-mindedly reached for his bedside hairbrush.

<<*Open Palm* here. Go ahead. We are pleased to scent your response.>>

Eosu's digits pressed into the narrowing places where wall-fur met floorfur. None of the digits moved toward the quiet voice.

<<*Open Palm* here, go ahead.>> Implacably the voice drifted up to them. <<We are starting to transmit a visual signal.>> A head and torso appeared in its cloudy depths. <<You should begin receiving a picture now.>>

Grodjala whispered, <<What are those lumps on its chest? Youngsters?>>

Fearfully Doro crept forward and pressed against the holopticon. Her nostrils dilated broadly; her wet nose slid along the farscenter's glassine smooth-cool surface. She inhaled deeply, but there was no farmonkey-scent and she briefly mewled in frustration.

<<Well?>> Grodjala craned his neck. <<What is it?>>

<<Did you ask what is it?>> said the small monkey in the holopticon. Doro quickly pulled her head back. Her neck-fur stood and she hissed at the holopticon and retreated, head down, nose arched, spitting with shock and fear.

The farmonkey was agitated. <<*Wing,* are you receiving?>> The tiny head twittered in the holopticon. <<You should have our picture by now.>>

<<It heard us,>> whispered Doro to Grodjala. <<Now be quiet.>> She wedged herself between him and the comforting wall.

<<What are those lumps?>>

<<Lifegivers, perhaps,>> she answered.

<<That is a female?>>

<<Yes.>>

<<But she is so small,>> he answered, gazing at the image while she squeezed more firmly in behind him.

Her head poked out the far side and she peered around his hindquarters at the holopticon. <<Their females are smaller than their males.>>

<<How strange.>>

* * *

The captain was furious. "What the crap is going on?"

"WE HAVE A DIRECT COMMUNICATION LINE OPEN TO THE *WING*," the computer answered. "WE ARE RECEIVING TRANSMISSIONS FROM SOMEWHERE IN THEIR LIVING SPACE."

"Why can't we hear anything?"

"PRESUMABLY BECAUSE THE CYGNANS ARE CHOOSING TO SAY NOTHING."

"Don't patronize me, Oz," Walt retorted. "Katy? They've seized up again. They're not saying anything. Coax them."

"How?" Katy bit her lip.

"You're the expert, dammit," the captain shouted. "Seduce them!"

I'm afraid of doing the wrong thing, Katy thought.

Then do nothing, Tanakaruna's voice said from within her. *No one ever grows up.*

The linguist saw the moment of panic and terror flit across her young friend's face. "Good luck, Katy," Tanakaruna whispered. "Our hearts are with you."

Next to her, Pat Michaelson patted her shoulder. "Good luck, Katy," he said, surprised to find that he meant it.

<<Call this digit Timid. As a youngster,>> the shemonkey in the holopticon said, <<I was afraid of the dark. You digits are afraid of places where you cannot smell. We fardigits are afraid of what we cannot see. I was born in the plains between Moldavia and the Ukraine, a land of endless wheatfields. When night fell and I lay in my bed, staring at the ceiling, the winds came out and played outside my room.>>

The tight ball of digits uncoiled slightly.

<<Our house was made of wood,>> the shemonkey continued. <<When the wind tugged at it, the floorboards creaked. In the darkness I imagined that powerful strangers plotted to take me away from all my friends and kill me. My eyes grew as large as sunflowers. I stared intently into the corners of my room. My kidnappers had to surprise me before they abducted me.>>

Something in the shemonkey's sounds attracted Doro. She tiptoed toward the alien.

<<When my eyes grew heavy, I twisted my neck from underneath the safety of the covers and looked out into the

great sparkling night and saw the constellation which we call the Great Bear. 'My friend,' I said to those stars, 'my friend the great bear, protect me until morning.'>>

Doro stood before the holopticon, tilting her head this way and that. The shemonkey's lips moved and digit words emerged.

<<And the stars shone into my bedroom, and the monsters fled, and I could sleep.>> The shemonkey exhaled.

<<The stars are my friends. The great bear shines for me. Eosu's digits would be my friends, but they conceal themselves. Digit-friends on the *Wing,* talk to me.>>

While the shemonkey spoke, the other digits inbreathed, their faces turned toward the holopticon and its image of a frail, hairless monkey speaking through tiny grasseater teeth.

Fohrada rumbled, <<Is it talking to us? Why does it refer to itself so egocentrically?>>

<<That is the way humans talk,>> Grodjala replied. The two rubbed against one another and their scents mingled lightly.

<<Oh.>> Fohrada sniffed. <<What is it talking about?>>

<<Hush, Twitch-shoulder, and listen.>>

<<We know too little,>> Fohrada grumbled. <<Season-sleeping during the whole journey has left us unprepared.>>

<<Do you smell dutyscent?>> asked Doro.

<<Yes.>> Grodjala admired the farmonkey's courage. <<Do you smell friendscent too?>>

<<Yes,>> she said after breathing carefully, <<very faint. Friendscent. Coming from *that?*>>

<<How could friendscent be transmitted?>> Grodjala was confused. <<The monkeys said their machinery was incapable of sending aroma.>>

Doro watched the shemonkey. <<Could the holopticon be doing it?>>

<<How would it know what scent to waft?>>

<<Perhaps it is trying to interpret the monkey words.>>

<<Monkey words?>> interjected Fohrada angrily, leaning hard against Grodjala. <<Bah. Look at that skeleton. Neither hair nor blanket of fat. Thinner even than this digit.>>

<<Then call this one Monkeyfriend,>> Grodjala shoved back, <<but Eosu should reply.>>

<<Answer monkey words?>> Fohrada's scent was ironic. <<Monkey threats?>>

<<Listen to them!>> Grodjala moved away from Fohrada's pressure. <<Smell the friendscent! Is that the scent of a predator?>>

<<Predators are clever.>>

<<Do predators speak the words of greeting? Do predators fly to this frightening vast desert to importune their victims?>>

<<It could be a trick.>> Fohrada was grudging. <<Or the holopticon could be mistaken.>>

<<The holopticon scents friendship. Would our own woodmonkey deceive us?>>

<<Monkeyfriend Grodjala, let us have no further converse with these—*humans*.>>

<<We must nosetouch them. Remember? We must visit their ship if we are to kill them.>>

At this Hraobla became disturbed. <<Kill them?>> he asked in disbelief. <<We cannot kill those who goodhost us.>>

<<They have not goodhosted us,>> Fohrada insisted.

<<If we visit their ship,>> Grodjala's scent touched Hraobla's and harmonized with it, <<they will do so.>>

<<Only if we sleep there, not otherwise.>>

<<Is the fardigit still speaking?>> Hraobla asked.

<<No.>> Doro retreated from the holopticon. <<It is finished.>>

<<Then cut the connection,>> Fohrada demanded. <<We have nothing more to say to them.>>

<<Eosu sneers at the clever monkeys,>> Grodjala said stubbornly. <<Yet when the clever monkeys offer the scent of friendship, Eosu's digits gibber like weemonkeys and cannot reply.>>

<<What is Monkeyfriend doing? Come back to the groupcluster.>>

<<Friends! Monkey friends!>> Grodjala blurted into the holopticon, lurching against it. <<We are here! We have to nosetouch you!>>

FRIENDS. HUMAN FRIENDS. WE ARE HERE. WE MUST MAKE CONTACT WITH YOU.

"Oz, is that them?" Tai-Ching Jones shouted. "Give me a picture!" In his excitement he bounced off the bed.

The monitor showed the familiar overhead view, bluebears lining the walls in a rough semicircle. One had its paws up on the holopticon as if it were trying to crawl on top of it.

"Direct image, not a goddam simulation!"

The computer cut him off. "NONE IS BEING TRANSMITTED," it replied precisely.

"Sorry," Walt muttered under his breath. "Lost my temper."

"THE CYGNAN WHO JUST SPOKE IS CURRENTLY TOUCHING THE HOLOPTICON."

He nodded. "Katy, what does it mean that they *must* make contact with us?"

"Not now," Belovsky waved his question away.

"Dammit, I'm—"

"Captain, I'll explain it later if I can. Computer, patch me back in with the Cygnans." The overhead view was replaced by her head and neck.

"Damn it, Oz, you shouldn't have done that."

"WALT, KATY WOULD APPRECIATE IT IF YOU WOULD PLEASE BE SO KIND AS TO SHUT UP."

Silence.

"THANK YOU."

<<People of the *Wing*.>> The translucent shemonkey under Grodjala spoke; he started and pushed himself away from it. Weightless, he drifted toward the ceiling, rolling his body so that his claws would grip the ceiling's wallfur. The holopticon hung directly above him.

<<Our ships now rest side by side,>> the inverted human said, <<head to tail. The way digits greet one another. The way digits scent each other's character. Can we nosetouch soon?>>

Doro slid around the fringe of the group, her claws gripping the floorfur, her shoulder always in contact with the wallfur. She smelled Eosu's fearscent. <<Soon,>> she said.

Grodjala edged his way to the joining of wall and ceiling and crawled down the wall toward his fellows.

The monkeyhead nodded. <<Our shuttlecraft will hold only five of us. How many will your craft hold?>>

Grodjala reached Doro and rested his throat against her neck. <<Our shuttlecraft holds only three,>> he answered, gaining confidence. Talk to a monkey! And have it respond like a digit! <<But Eosu travels only as a djan.>>

<<Then Eosu's digits will be unable to visit our ship,>> the human said. <<With your permission, some of Human-crew will visit you.>>

The scent of anxiety bloomed in the chamber like a new flower. <<Eosu will not permit its digits to separate,>> Grodjala whispered to Doro, his eyes and nose concentrated on the holopticon. <<So there is no way for us to enter the human ship to fulfill our mission.>>

<<They have offered to come here,>> Doro whispered back. <<When they do, we will be able to learn about them and perhaps improve our deathscent.>>

<<We must prepare,>> Grodjala gnawed distractedly at her neckfur.

Doro raised her voice. <<Eosu needs time.>>

<<Of course,>> the female showed its teeth. Several digits growled defensively.

<<That is not an aggressive gesture,>> Grodjala interjected, <<but one of friendship.>> The digits' muscles relaxed but their anxiety-scent remained.

"Captain, they request time to prepare for us."

No emotion showed on Tai-Ching Jones' face. He caressed the right side of his jaw. "Your call," he said finally.

Belovsky licked her lips. "Would six hours be too soon?" Hesitantly she put her hand out toward the screen. "Or would twelve be better?"

The shemonkey reached its grasping fingers toward them. Eosu's digits growled.

<<A halfsun is far too soon,>> Doro immediately responded. <<Eosu needs time to think.>>

The farmonkey nodded. Many scents swirled in the air.

<<In a sun,>> Fohrada said to it, <<we will scent you.>>

"Twelve hours it is." Katy's voice flooded with relief. "I'll see you then. Thank you, my friends."

"Eosu out," said an alien voice in guttural English. The signal ended.

"Computer," she asked hurriedly, "what was that last? Was that a translation?"

"NO. DIRECT LINK. SOMEONE ON THE *WING* SPOKE ENGLISH TO US."

<<In a sun this digit will nosetouch Eosu.>> The holopticon buffeted them with friendscent, then the contact broke.

<<They are coming,>> said Grodjala. <<Does Eosu realize that? We have agreed to host them, here on the *Wing*, in a sun's time.>>

<<No,>> said Fohrada, <<we agreed to farscent them within a sun's time and let them know our decision then.>>

<<The female obviously thought we would have nose-to-scentplace contact,>> Grodjala persisted. <<Nosetouch, it said, not farscent.>>

<<We need Eosu,>> Fohrada firmly said. <<The farscenter is mute.>> The digits nodded. Their breathing slowed and synchronized, and they moved purposefully into groupcluster.

Doro and Grodjala were the last to join it. The digits' bodies curled themselves around each other until their cluster was a solid mass of fur, nine heads aligned against the floorfur, eyes closed, nostrils flared, mouths open, seeking suckle.

7.

Goodhost

Receding red sunlight winked through the trees, weemonkeys cavorting and chittering from the safety of the high branches. Stretched to its thinnest, Walkword moved carefully along the path, scenting the youngstealers hiding above it, its she-digits in the center, the youngsters enpouched.

As the sun raced on ahead of Walkword, the evening breezes awoke from their midday slumber and the woodlands slowly cooled.

Emerging from the forest, Walkword climbed a small crest and gazed down into a long green twilit valley at Woodrock. The fabled city lay before Walkword, where the valley opened into rolling plains. Tinged golden by the setting sun, farmland stretched south and west: ripe slowfood to be harvested.

<<What is that black ring?>> Walkword's Trailbreaker asked the digit next to him. <<It surrounds the city.>>

Walkword's Youngnose peered at it with dawning comprehension, her scent becoming animated. <<The cityfence,>> she exclaimed, <<the shadow of the cityfence!>>

<<Then the winds do not lie,>> said Trailbreaker. <<The djans of Woodrock have handworked a shield big enough to block the gromonkeys.>>

Inside the black ring, long knobbed shadows like windtrails stretched from the dirtcaves within Woodrock. Plumes of smoke rose from them: digits had returned from the fields to rest in the warm groupnight comfort of their firecircles.

During daylight, Woodrock's djans cultivated slowfood on the lush flatland surrounding the city. Spring wetwinds blew warmth and moisture onto the plains; in the heat of summer, grass slowfoods sprouted in profusion, to be harvested in fall.

Sentries surrounded the fields, watching and scenting for signs of the djankiller. At night, when the winds stilled and the light vanished, the digits returned to the safety of their cityfence.

Brooks ran on either side of Woodrock, joining a few greatsteps west of the town into the Laokrao River which meandered toward the Greatsea.

Picking its way down the hillside, Walkword gazed contentedly into the twilight. In the distance, more plumes of new hearthfires added themselves to the evening breezes. Small clusters of dark oblong dots moved slowly toward Woodrock as more djans returned from the fields.

The breezes truly loved Woodrock. Its djans had multiplied—on the plains the dots were thick—and its digits grown fat and healthy. Walkword fanned out from the ridge, its digits' lungs filled with energy from the scent of the city. A rich orchestra of djan-scents drifted up the hills from Woodrock to Walkword's eager digits. With so much bounty and so many citizens, Woodrock's goodhosting would be generous.

As it approached the cityfence, Walkword's bellies rumbled with hunger.

The gatewindow opened and a digit looked through it, his nose winking blue-black. <<Fair breezes, stranger-djan. Who are you and how come you to Woodrock?>>

<<Clear scents,>> replied the first of Walkword's digits. Her friendly and disarming scent carried well on the airs. <<Walkword is our djan-name. Call this digit Outspeaker. Walkword comes to find land to settle and farm.>>

<<Name this digit Gatekeeper,>> the face behind the cityfence grunted. <<In Woodrock?>>

Outspeaker pointed with her broad nose. <<In the valley beyond.>>

Gatekeeper's eyes and nose did not waver; they remained skeptically focused on Walkword. <<Are you known by any Woodrock djan?>>

<<Sadly, none,>> Outspeaker's fragrance was self-deprecating, <<for Woodrock is famed and blessed.>> She added a tinge of urgency to her smell. <<Let Walkword's digits shelter in the lee of your fence, for the night is chilly and dark. Walkword seeks the safety of your closed hearth.>>

Gatekeeper's glance moved among Walkword's digits. <<We will not admit you until we know you for true digits.>>

From several of the travelers arose a slight ruffle of the

scent of indignation. <<True digits?>> Outspeaker's voice cut blandly through their rising odor. <<Even in twilight you see us. We are digits like you.>>

<<Not all digits are like those of Woodrock.>> The gatekeeper shook his head. <<Some scorn our fences.>>

Walkword's digits became restless, and Outspeaker breathed the scent of conciliation toward her fellows. <<Why scorn the thing which makes you safe at night?>>

<<Doubters say the winds are angered.>>

<<The winds?>>

<<In the lee of a fence, the wind cannot blow,>> Gatekeeper explained. <<Build enough fences and the winds will die, the doubters' scents claim. Without winds, digits' noses will be blind to the fragrances of danger.>>

<<But the fence protects the digits.>>

<<So it does.>> The gatekeeper licked his nose. <<Their breezes and ours have not harmonized. Digits were meant to die, say those we call false digits, for the death of weaklings leaves the surviving group stronger.>>

<<Digits are murdered by djankillers,>> Outspeaker was perplexed, <<and youngsters by thievers.>>

<<The gromonkeys kill weak or sick digits, say those who spit upon our fence,>> Gatekeeper agreed. <<Weemonkeys cull only foolish youngsters. Both make our djans stronger.>> Again a noselick. <<So they say.>>

<<If the ability to survive gromonkeys is proof of a djan's strength, Woodrock's djans are mighty indeed.>> Walkword's Outspeaker's scent was mirthful. <<We honor the wisdom of your fence.>>

<<Since you then be true digits, call these djans Tiller and Thresher, and enter.>> The gate swung wide.

As Walkword passed through the gate, two host-djans bowed away in a loose oval about Walkword. The townsdigits nosetouched Walkword, savoring and remembering the special fragrances that give each djan its own character. Walkword nosetouched its hosts. When all had breathed their fill, they walked in a body to the guesthouse.

Dusk had come to the town, draining the light and slowing the breezes. As they moved cautiously through the town, Walkword's digits marveled at the handwork about them.

Most settlements grew up haphazardly around natural advantages—a plain where the wind blew steadily and downwind was inaccessible, or a protected hilltop where the dirt was broken and dirtcaves could be easily dug. By contrast, Woodrock was arrogantly laid out in nature's most harmonic pattern, ringpaths nested about the central firecircle, lined on either side with the grassy humps of dirtcaves. The rings were cut by spokes radiating from the town's open firecircle.

At night Woodrock's digits built a huge pyre, the plume of their smoke scentable at many greatsteps' distance. *Woodrock fears no monkey,* the firescent called into the night, *Woodrock need not hide itself.*

From a passageway to its right, the intriguing aroma of digits attracted Walkword, and its digits turned toward the scent, but Tiller's Wideface checked them. <<Not that alley.>>

<<Why not?>>

<<Gromonkey trap.>>

<<Surely you joke.>>

Their host's fragrance was light. <<Tomorrow you shall scent.>>

Woodrock's too-perfect order made the city seem alien and airless, no fit place for a scenting digit. Strangeness and power were hinted in Woodrock's breezes. Though Walkword was comforted by the cityfence visible at the end of each spokestreet, and reassured by the cheerful djan-scents of its hosts, its digits moved furtively.

When a weemonkey leapt from behind a hillock and ran excitedly across Walkword's path, Walkword started and gasped a puff of flight-scent. In panic, the digits scattered every which way, their pouches contracting with fear. The panic-odor touched all Walkword's digits and they redoubled it among themselves, mewling anxiously.

Another weemonkey ran out behind Walkword, darting between Walkword's digits and underneath some of their legs. Walkword's Trailbreaker swatted at the little creature as it dashed past, but the youngstealer dodged nimbly aside. Turning quickly as it fled, the weemonkey laughed at Walkword and broke wind in the djan's direction. Then it vanished round the same corner where its brother had disappeared.

Outspeaker turned frantically toward Walkword's hosts. <<You told us the fence kept out monkeys!>> she accused them. <<Our mothers fear for their youngsters.>>

Amusement wafted among the digits of their hosts. <<Our tamed weemonkeys are harmless to youngster or

digit,>> Wideface replied. <<Are you unfamiliar with them?>>

<<Domesticated?>> Walkword's Outspeaker was agitated and her scent aggressive. <<What for?>>

<<Their clever hands,>> Wideface answered.

<<Bah.>> Fearscent was dispersing and being supplanted by outrage. Outspeaker's claws raked the dirt. <<What use are hands? Hands cannot think.>>

<<Step inside the dirtcave.>> Tiller's Wideface led them through an archway set into the hillside.

The darkness became more complete except for the warming glow of flames ahead of them. The air was heavy with the scents of earth, moisture, digits, and fire. Wideface pointed toward a bricked firecircle. <<Scent for yourself.>>

Walkword's digits bent their noses to the structure, the fire-scent warming their snouts. Each rectangular brick nestled sturdily next to its neighbors, held firmly in place by solidified sand wedged between them. Within its smooth circle, the fire danced upward through the drafthole at the crown of the dirtcave. A strong wind carried fire-scent into the night, the scent of digits and fire mixing delightfully and soothing Walkword.

Two weemonkeys perched on their haunches beside the fire, each holding a long metal stick. Now and then they poked the flames, which sparked and burned more brightly.

<<You see?>> said Tiller's Wideface. <<Following directions from Woodrock's digits, the weemonkeys fashioned the firecircle; now as their reward they tend it, and receive some of the food we gather.>>

<<Weemonkeys?>> said Outspeaker. <<They have no wisdom.>>

<<Ah, but they are clever. They can be trained.>>

<<Cleverness is overrated.>> Outspeaker broke wind. <<The weemonkeys are proof of that. They are unreliable.>>

<<Of course. Any weemonkey who disobeys orders, or who steals food or youngsters, is caught and banished.>>

<<Caught? How?>>

<<Trapped by us or hunted down by other tamed weemonkeys,>> Wideface said casually, his nostrils alert for Walkword's response. Scenting their skepticism, he wheezed richly. <<Under our orders, weemonkeys hunt other weemonkeys.>>

Outspeaker glanced again at the long-fingered thieves now

docilely guarding the digits' firecircle. <<No loss for them.>>

Wideface followed Outspeaker's look. <<After enjoying the benefits of digits' wisdom, our tame weemonkeys are reluctant to leave. Thankwork is less dangerous than monkeywork, after all, and more certain to produce dinner.>> He wheezed.

<<Surely some weemonkeys revert to wildness and scurry to the forest bearing youngsters and squealing of their deception of digits.>>

<<If they do reach sanctuary, those few foolish enough to attempt it discover that their former fellows often attack them as traitors.>> Wideface's scent was ironic. <<Death at the hands of other weemonkeys is their reward. In fact,>> his scent bubbled over with good airs, <<the wild weemonkeys are our best incentive for our tamed weemonkeys to remain with us; the predators protect us.>>Wideface's neckfur ruffled. <<No, once a weemonkey has accepted our goodhosting, for better or worse his fate is tied to preserving his djanmaster's satisfaction.>>

Walkword's digits exchanged odors.

<<You are unconvinced.>> Wideface read their aromas, his own scent sharpening. <<Wee-tender! Come here.>>

The nearest weemonkey jumped from its start and scurried quickly under Wideface's belly. It peeped through Wideface's arms, twiglike fingers curled around each of Wideface's great limbs, small bright eyes blinking apprehensively. It chirped.

<<Wee-tender, these are new digits.>> Chirp. <<They may sleep here tonight.>> Chirp. <<You will attend to their needs and obey their commands as you would those of all digits.>> Chirp. <<Do you understand?>> Chirp chirp.

<<Your djan has everything you need?>> asked Wideface of Walkword's Outspeaker. <<Good. Sleep well. In the morning we will show you your thankwork. Till then,>> his scent rose in jest, <<your digits are safe in our weemonkeys' hands.>>

Laughing hugely at his witticism, Wideface withdrew.

<<Weemonkeys obeying digits!>> said Walkword's Backscenter. <<Who ever heard of such a thing?>>

<<It is unnatural,>> added another of Walkword's digits. <<Harm will come of it.>>

<<Perhaps not,>> said Outspeaker, <<but this firecir-

cle is beautiful. Digits could never have made bricks so uniform.>>

Backscenter disagreed. <<Nor could the weemonkeys have thought of it without us.>>

<<Without the digits of Woodrock,>> corrected Outspeaker. <<This firecircle will last.>>

<<It burns the earth,>> said a new voice, Walkword's Roundbelly, <<and will leave a permanent scar.>>

<<All fire scars,>> Outspeaker answered. <<This is merely confined to one underground place. We live in dirtcaves so that the winds may waft ever free and the grasses grow throughout our lands. Indeed, slowfood lives on the roofs of Woodrock's dirtcaves. The winds still blow unbound above us, happily receiving our firesmoke which flows through the ceiling above. The winds are pleased.>>

<<Sleep,>> said Backscenter. <<Tomorrow we work.>>

<<Come with us and learn to farm.>> Wideface's scent was friendly. <<After all, that will be your new life in the valley beyond.>>

Tiller's digits led Walkword to the fields south of town. Several weemonkeys perched on their shoulders, while others scampered alongside.

Though the little djanhelpers were deferential and responsive, almost sycophantishly willing to please, their presence bothered Walkword. They behaved too confidently and familiarly with the digits of Woodrock, as if they had forgotten fear and theft.

Walkword's digits walked apart from Tiller, away from the weemonkeys. Fingers clutched in the fur of Tiller's digits, the servants peeped out at the newcomer djan. Occasionally they chittered among themselves.

The ground underneath had been deeply and powerfully furrowed as if by a giant arm. Walkword sniffed the grooves for traces of its maker, but there was no clue. Its digits glanced nervously at one another.

<<What is *that?*>> asked Walkword's Outspeaker.

<<That,>> said Tiller's Wideface, <<is your work for the day. That is an earthsword.>>

A metal arrow dug the soil, its shaft lashed to wooden beams at the end of which perched a small seat. Braided hemp thongs ran from near the seat to harnesses in front of the buried arrow. Backscenter stepped forward and sniffed. <<Gromonkey smell,>> he said to Tiller.

<<Yes,>> Tiller's Wideface answered, his voice deliberately casual. <<We needed to eat, so we killed a gromonkey.>>

<<Killed a gromonkey?>> Backscenter snorted disbelief. <<More likely you found it dead.>>

<<No,>> Wideface said, <<we truly killed him in a gromonkey trap.>>

<<How?>>

<<With a device like this>>—he gestured toward the earthsword—<<we dug a deep hole in the earth, which we then covered with straw matting woven by the weemonkeys. Then we exposed our scents in the gromonkey's path, to lure him into charging us.>>

<<That part is easy enough,>> Backscenter agreed. <<Gromonkeys are full of bloodlust.>>

Tiller's Wideface nodded. <<This one bellowed his rage and bloodhunger. His anger clouded his vision so that when he charged his prey, he mistook our matting for true earth, and he fell into the pit, where the weemonkeys had planted sharpened sticks.>>

<<Cleverness indeed,>> Outspeaker said sardonically, her scents echoing those of the other digits.

<<More than mere cleverness,>> their host retorted, <<true wisdom. While the djankiller was dazed and weakened, we ringed the pit with weemonkeys who made sport of throwing rocks at the gromonkey's head and arms until it died.>>

Walkword listened in astonishment. <<Indeed,>> conceded Outspeaker, <<the breezes which tell of Woodrock's wisdom are true. But will your tame weemonkeys really kill their cousins?>>

<<Between gro and wee there is no group-love. Gromonkeys prey on weemonkeys when they can. The thievers enjoy reversing nature by killing their predators, and relish the chance to eat their fill of gromonkey meat.>>

<<Then the weemonkeys are no true digits,>> Backscenter concluded, <<for they kill their fellows and their cousins.>>

<<The weemonkeys are their own smalldigits,>> Wideface replied unconcernedly, <<not true digits of course but a

kind unto themselves. We use them for their benefit—and ours.>>

<<Weemonkeys who throw rocks at gromonkeys could learn to throw them at digits.>> Walkword's Outspeaker snorted apprehensively. <<They might be dangerous to us.>>

Wideface nodded. <<Fortunately, weemonkeys have poor memories,>> he riffled his neckfur. <<They would forget in days what rocks are good for if we failed to remind them.>>

<<Do they forget instructions?>>

Tiller's Wideface was amused. <<Indeed. All weemonkeys are absentminded. We must train them over and over again. And even trained, they are lazy and shiftless. Were it not for us, they would spend their lives scrounging food.>>

<<Woodrock's scents are wise, yet you dug such gromonkeys traps in your own city,>> Outspeaker said. <<Are you not safe from gromonkeys in Woodrock itself?>>

<<The gromonkey is large and powerful. Occasionally a renegade or a maniacal djankiller breaches or surmounts the gates. Then destruction ensues until the gromonkey chooses the wrong path and elects life's third choice.>>

Outspeaker was troubled. <<Your own digits could fall into such traps.>>

<<All our digits know the false trails,>> said Wideface, <<and are careful to avoid them, but the enraged gromonkey does not.>>

<<And your weemonkeys?>>

<<We constantly remind the weemonkeys where the gromonkey traps lie. If they are forgetful>>—his shrug was expressive—<<then perhaps we are gradually breeding weemonkeys with better memories.>> He barked and his scent was light. <<Now you must work.>> He pointed his nose toward the earthsword and to another of Tiller's digits. <<Quickeyes, show them.>>

Eventually each of Walkword's digits was harnessed into one of the pairs of towing lines—one thick-braided and one thin—which led back to the metal earthsword. A bright-eyed weemonkey perched on its seat, clutching the bundle of thin guidelines in his spindly hand. Walkword's digits spread out fanwise, each walking until its towline was taut.

<<Now you pull,>> said Quickeyes, <<and the djan-

helper guides the earthsword. Try it.>> The weemonkey flicked the reins. On that signal, Walkword pulled, their thick lines snapping taut and then loose as its digits struggled to find harmony in their efforts. They grunted with exertion and the weemonkey shrieked and hissed at them. After a moment, Quickeyes signaled a halt.

<<You have the idea but,>> he wheezed at their inexperience, <<you must do better. Look at that wavering line! A brainless river runs straighter than your work. The length of the field and then back; now try again.>>

Walkword's digits growled and heaved, and the earthsword lurched forward. Walkword's tongues panted.

<<Again.>> The earthsword staggered a few more steps. <<Again.>>

Behind Walkword, the sun glided into the sky.

<<Compared with digging by hand,>> Outspeaker panted to Backscenter <<this work is light and easy.>>

<<Only,>> Walkword's Longstride panted back, <<if one can accept being ordered about by a weemonkey.>>

<<The weemonkey is only carrying out Tiller's instructions.>>

Hiss. Chirp chirp! Bark!

Longstride growled loudly at the earthsword and its small occupant. Bouncing in its seat, the weemonkey jabbered at him, gesturing with its arms and pointing. Longstride shook himself, fluffing his fur. Again he snarled at the weemonkey, but the unabashed little creature merely trilled higher and waved frantically.

Breaking wind to show his dissatisfaction, Longstride resumed his plodding pace.

<<Well done, Walkword,>> said Tiller's Quickeyes. <<You have earthsworded your area, but your furrows wobble like a pear rolling downhill. Still, good thankwork.>>

<<Call this speaker Doubting,>> responded Longstride. <<Orders from a weemonkey smell foul.>>

<<How well would Walkword perform the same job without an earthsword and a weemonkey to guide it?>>

<<Weemonkey orders reek.>>

<<Then do without a weemonkey,>> Quickeyes replied complacently, <<and see how long it takes. Sniff,>> he said, <<the weemonkey tells you the best way to earthsword

a field. When you lose the trail, he guides you back to it. No disgrace, no dishonor: just a well-cut row.>>

Walkword's Longstride grunted.

<<Come eat with us,>> said Quickeyes, <<then you may depart.>>

Walkword feasted, then left Woodrock behind on its horizon as it set out, following the western river under the bright sun, to find its own land to farm. Toward dusk, Walkword camped and built a firecircle, nudging the rounded stones into a rough ring with its noses.

<<The firecircle at Woodrock was better.>>

<<No weemonkey work could be better than a digit's work.>>

<<Whether it is good or bad, let it give us heat. Come, add the logs.>>

Its digits lit the fire and settled down for supper and nighttalk, and in the quiet firebreezes, the djan-mind coalesced. It pondered all it had seen and done, and when it realized the terrible omission it had made, Walkword's djan-mind whipped its digits horribly and dispersed.

As the first rays of sunlight slid over the mountains, Walkword's digits awakened to the scent of desperate urgency. Outspeaker read the scent which the night had harmonized. <<We left the cityfence ajar. We must return immediately! Woodrock is imperiled!>>

The sun was low, Walkword's digits tired and dusty, but their dutyscent drove them onward. They crossed the rise, saw the black ring shadow, and sprinted to the cityfence.

<<Here is Walkword!>> shouted Outspeaker to the gatekeeper. <<We left the cityfence open!>>

<<That which you fear occurred,>> said Tiller's Gatekeeper. <<Enter and scent the harm your forgetfulness permitted.>>

Gloom hung over Walkword's digits as Tiller's Gatekeeper led them through the streets. Guided by the bright trailscent of Walkword's departure, a gromonkey had immediately attacked the cityfence, hardly believing it would yield to his charge. Once inside, he had been overwhelmed by the concentrated fragrance of many healthy digits and had rushed through the dirtpaths, striking randomly at the digits who fled before him.

Three had been injured, their bones split by the gromonkey's hard-swung arms. One had moved too slowly, and the marauder's fist had met skull; that digit perished. Now its fellows gathered about the body, preparing it for the deathfeast the departed soul would shortly receive.

The gromonkey had blundered onward, terrorizing digits and weemonkeys alike, the town in an uproar, until he had barreled down one of the entrapped passageways and been swallowed by the gromonkey pit.

Tiller and Walkword stood, their digits intermingled at the trap-rim. The gromonkey's huge body was covered in blood-soaked matted hair, his fur torn where the stakes had punctured the pelt. Elsewhere the fur was dented and cuffed from the rain of many stones.

In the pit weemonkeys scurried delightedly, some grasping rocks no larger than pebbles and bashing them into the ruined face with neither pattern nor objective, just the predators' jig over another's death. Others squatted to the side, licking the still-oozing blood from strips of marbled flesh torn from the destroyer's slashed entrails.

<<We rue our failure,>> said Outspeaker finally.

Wideface's scent was grim. <<That is insufficient.>>

<<Walkword will bow to the city's wisdom.>>

<<So it shall,>> the other digits replied. <<Your punishment will be considered.>>

<<We accepted your goodhosting and performed our thankwork in your fields.>> Outspeaker's voice was strong but her aroma was almost unscentable. She curled her body into a tight ball as though she wished to bite her tail.

The fire was out, the firecircle dry and dusty. She stood in its center and looked out at the faces of Woodrock's digits who ringed the dirtcave. Walkword's other digits huddled loosely around its Outspeaker in postures of submission.

<<Walkword dishonored the cityfence which sheltered and protected its digits,>> Outspeaker pivoted so all could see and scent her. <<You goodhosted us. We badguested you.>>

For many moments after Outspeaker finished, the assembled djans about her were silent. Finally a voice came from the darkness. <<We shall night-talk your punishment.>>

Walkword's digits groveled and withdrew.

* * *

<<You are true digits,>> said one of Woodrock's digits when they were summoned back to the city's firecircle. <<You returned to accept the odors of your exhalations. The lives of your digits shall be spared, but your djan must lose its name. Walkword shall name-die in Woodrock.>>

<<That is just,>> said Walkword's Outspeaker.

<<Tiller's Wideface shall pronounce your sentence.>>

The gatekeeper digit moved into the light of the firecircle. His eyes sad but his scent unwavering, he stood next to Walkword's Outspeaker and they made the fourfold greeting: nose, armpit, underbelly, scentplace. <<We shall mark you,>> Wideface said, rubbing his flank against Outspeaker's. His scent now tasted also of sadness, comforting her and bracing her for what must yet be said. <<One and all. Anyone who sees our mark will know that it has been done to you by other digits, and will be wary.>>

Outspeaker slid her nose along Wideface's throat. <<What mark?>>

<<We shall notch the left ears of all your digits, deep enough to be visible. If digits ask you what it means, you shall explain.>>

Walkword's digits abased themselves. <<We inbreathe this wind.>>

<<After this has been done,>> Wideface was resolute, <<your djan shall take a new name.>> His aroma brooked no disagreement. <<Your djan-mind must harmonize the scent of this new name. What pain Walkword's djan-mind inflicts upon its digits, Walkword shall harmonize by itself.>>

A weemonkey emerged from the ranks of the digits, a knife in his hand. He grinned and leapt onto the back of Walkword's Longstride. <<Lie down,>> said Tiller's Wideface softly, <<lie down now.>>

Longstride's fur stood. <<Let a monkey punish a digit?>>

<<The weemonkey's hand is the djan's will.>> Wideface's voice was low so that the rest of Woodrock did not hear.

<<Trust a weemonkey to cut accurately, in justice not in anger?>>

<<The weemonkey is the creature of the djan,>> Outspeaker growled to Longstride. <<The hand of the weemonkey is the will of the djan. Take this digit first.>> She bowed

her head, laid her belly on the earth and her chest on her arms, then lowered her haunches to the ground.

The weemonkey sat on Outspeaker's neck, its tiny legs linked around her throat. It raised its arms, the knife poised in its left hand, and looked expectantly at the crowd.

The scent of authority swirled in the group. A gust of wind sucked it into the firecircle, a draft carried it through the ceiling-hole. All of Walkword's digits smelled it, and as one closed their eyes and nostrils. The weemonkey scented it too, and firmly grasped Outspeaker's left ear.

The knife descended and bit.

Blood spurted into the fire and sizzled. Swiftly the weemonkey clambered up Longstride's back.

Metal sliced fur and flesh with a quick, subdued hiss.

In the morning, the djan Earnotch left Woodrock, heading for its new life.

8.

His spacesuit floated like a half-filled balloon. Engineer Casey van Gelder lifted it off its hook, his bare arms chill with apprehension. The suit's leggings brushed him like willow wands. He grasped its feet and switched on their electromagnets. The boots tugged as he lowered them to the deck. He floated away from the suit and it drifted, wavering like a ghost in a tailor's shop.

Easy does it. Never hurry, never worry.

When it had stilled, van Gelder turned his back on the suit, stepped behind him, and fitted his feet into its boots. Like a sleepy woman the suit snuggled up around him. When he had sealed the right legging up to his thigh, Casey repeated his actions on the left leg. He stood as if in oversize fishing waders, the empty body and arms flapping behind him.

Concentrate. The detail you overlook is the one that kills you.

The engineer reached behind and pressed the suit body against his buttocks. Locating the excretory processor tube, he shoved it into position up his rectum. He swung his hips experimentally and it shifted between his cheeks.

No place in this man's spacefleet for tender souls.

Clamping the urine tube over his penis was easier.

The spacesuit's arms floated slowly around him in a clumsy embrace. He slid his left hand into the sleeve, his thick fingers—peasant hands, Walt called them—stretched out straight and narrowed as much as possible.

The hand that shakes, makes mistakes. With his right hand Casey smoothed each finger joint and twisted his wrist to verify that he had freedom of movement.

Out there you can't take it off, so in here be careful how you put it on. He scratched his beard.

The right arm dangled out of reach. Casey turned slowly toward his left and, when he had the suit following him, arrested the motion. The empty sleeve coasted around and he painstakingly slid his right hand and arm into it.

People, we know you *can* put it on in one breath. We trained you for that, remember? You don't have to prove it to us. Show us how slowly you can put it on. Do it that way unless there's an emergency.

The suit body lay open like a cadaver. With gloved hands van Gelder took the chest straps and linked them. Then he reached down to his crotch and pulled the main zipper up across his belly and chest to his chin. The reassuring mass of the compupack nestled against Casey's shoulder blades, and he wriggled it into its familiar position.

As the zipper passed his throat, air hissed into the suit. He carefully smoothed the chest vacuseals, then pulled the zipper back down the regulation fifteen centimeters. The hissing ceased.

The helmet goes under the bodyseal, gentlemen. Not over it. We want that air pressure pushing the vacuseals shut, not open, remember?

Yes, sir. I remember.

Now the helmet. Once the huge orange globe was in place, he would be unable to reach his face, and he scratched his beard one last time.

The helmet's impenetrable clear plasteel softened along the neckline, the better to mold itself to its wearer. Van Gelder settled it carefully over his head. As soon as the neckring passed his nose, Casey inhaled and exhaled, rhythmically and deeply. With each breath his chestband expanded and contracted, reading blood pressure, heartbeat, oxygen levels, blood alcohol, carbon monoxide, and more, and feeding the results into the ship's computer.

What do you do if the suit is breached?

Lower your pressure and cover the hole.

And in vacuum?

Let your breath out as slowly as you can, to make your air last without rupturing your lungs.

Carefully van Gelder smoothed out the helmet's collar. Then he reached behind his neck and worked his hands around both sides, smoothing and pressing until he reached the front of the suit.

He pulled up the zipper, overlaid the vacuseals.

All done, Ensign?

No, sir!

What next?

"Integrity check," the engineer said precisely in his soft

baritone. Air pressure pushed into the suit; the fingers of his gloves fattened. A weight pressed on his chest. Counting to ten, he fought for breath.

"SUIT INTEGRITY CONFIRMED," the omnipresent computer voder said.

"Normal air," he ordered. The suit deflated about him. He yawned forcefully and his ears popped.

"Electros off." The tugging at his feet ceased. He flexed his knees slightly and somersaulted delicately off the floor. He hugged his knees to his chest and his rate of spin increased. When he had cycled nearly a full turn, he stretched his body out and reactivated the electromagnets. His feet yearned for the floor and kissed it firmly.

"Engineer here, Captain," he glanced at Belovsky, who was engaged in conversation with Felicity. "Suited up. Awaiting instructions."

"Mommy Katy, why are you taking your clothes off?"

The xenologist smiled at her daughter. "It's time to visit the bluebears."

"With a bare bottom?"

"Not quite," Katy grinned slightly self-consciously, "in a spacesuit."

"Why?" Felicity put her hands on her hips.

"We have to fly from our ship over to their ship. They invited daddy Casey"—she nodded toward van Gelder—"and uncle Pat and me to visit them."

"Did they invite *me?*"

"Not yet."

Felicity pouted. "But I *wanna* go."

Katy bent down so her blue-green eyes were level with Felicity's pale blue. With her small hands she absently straightened the child's shirt. "Soon," she said, "you'll be able to meet the bluebears soon. Now I've got to finish getting into my spacesuit. Daddy Casey's already done and he's waiting for me."

Across the room van Gelder fluttered his fingers, his old tension-reliever. He put his thumb and forefinger together and waved his hand at Katy in the universal spaceman's sign language: *OK?*

OK, she signed back.

* * *

"Ready to scoop chamber, Captain," Casey reported when they had all boarded the shuttlecraft and sealed its hatch.

On the tiny monitor under his hands, the captain scowled impatiently. "Bug crew?"

"Van Gelder here."

"Belovsky here," Katy said, subdued.

"Michaelson present," the diplomat boomed confidently.

Tai-Ching Jones nodded. "Bug operating, Engineer?"

Van Gelder gave the thumb's-up sign to his companions. "Yes, sir," he said soberly.

"Okay, Casey." The voice swiftly relaxed. "Good luck. Take it out of the garage."

"Roger," van Gelder's eyes flicked over his readouts. "Cutting the lights now." The cabin dimmed. As he waited for his eyes to adjust, Casey saw only the amber of his helmet. Then the display lights emerged like stars at sundown: a ring of soft green pinlights marking the exit hatch. Behind him, van Gelder knew, a smaller blue-pointed rectangle—*like a yule tree,* he thought—lit the hatchway back into the ship.

Michaelson's breath wheezed in his ear. "You all right, Pat?" Casey asked his shipmate. The older man drew himself regally up.

"Opening the hatchway"—he punched more buttons—"*now.*" The halves slid into recesses and stars like fireflies appeared in the green ring. "Exiting ship."

Katy put her hand on his shoulder and he smiled distractedly at her.

Tiny jets spurted from the shuttlecraft's rear.

The green ring expanded, then passed out of sight as the bug fell like a pebble into the night.

As the shuttlecraft moved away from the *Open Palm,* Katy caught her breath. When as a young woman of twenty-seven she had first boarded the ship after its in-orbit assembly, she had seen such views of space. So many years had elapsed since then that her memories had faded like old photographs. Now it all flooded back and—there!—in the corner of her eye the *Wing* loomed, massive and powerful.

"Turn us toward it, Casey," she thought, and was surprised to hear her words spoken aloud.

"Wait," her crewmate growled tersely, his eyes glued to the panels.

"Look at it, look how huge it is!"

"Still be there in a minute. Cleared hatchway," he said more loudly. "Closing exterior doors." Another button. "Bug motionless. Checking systems."

Belovsky twisted in her seat. "Pat, can you believe it?"

"Until now I refused to let myself visualize this moment, Katy," the emissary answered grandly. "The direct sight of the Cygnan spacecraft overwhelms me and leaves me groping for words so that I—"

"Bug board green," van Gelder's voice truncated Pat's answer. "Rotating." Now the *Wing* lay dead ahead of them, and Katy's eyes watered as she looked at it. "Thrust point zero zero two gee for four seconds, commencing . . ." Casey counted to himself, then added, "mark." He pushed a button and Katy felt the faintest wind at her back. "Mark cutoff." The wind ceased and they drifted.

"Engines off," van Gelder reported. "Velocity approximately one point four meters per second. Approximate time to arrival vicinity *Wing* fifteen minutes." His voice lilted in the stylized singsong of official transmissions. "Bug to *Open Palm,* do you copy?"

"ROGER," the computer answered. "GOOD LUCK."

"Receiver still on. Transmitter off." Casey punched another button and leaned back in his seat. "Whew," he said in his normal voice, "the bluebears have a fine boat, don't they?"

"Can we talk now?" Katy asked eagerly.

"For five minutes or so. Then midcourse correction, which the computer will do. After that, another five-minute float, then I'll dock us."

"The *Wing* looks like an hourglass on its side. What is the narrow portion?"

"The big part on the far left"—he raised his swaddled arm—"is the reaction mass and the rocket thrusters at the end."

"And on the right, that is living space?"

"Correct. That's our target. The column in between is the *Wing*'s spine."

"Why is it so thin?"

"Minimizes points of contact. Vacuum is a better insulator than metal."

Katy thought about this. "What about radiation?"

"All the inert water in the reaction mass tanks blocks most of it."

"Where is our destination? Where do we dock?"

He pointed to a lighted ring tucked under one of the flying buttresses holding the living-area egg away from the Cygnan ship's fuselage. "There."

"Now I see where we are going. Ugh," she shuddered. "I will be glad to get inside and get this ugly suit off."

"You're kidding. It isn't comfortable?"

"I have never liked spacesuits, Casey," she said. "Claustrophobia is my weakness. I was nearly disqualified."

"Claustrophobia?" Casey was incredulous. "In the middle of open space?"

"But you see, I am not in open space."

"Floating out there?" His arm swept broadly. "There's no sensation like it."

She laid her hand on his forearm, glove to gauntlet. "I like the floating but the suit presses on me. You have worn it many times, it's become a natural part of your body. But it cuts me away from people. When you wear that clear pumpkin, I cannot even see your freckles."

"But you didn't like other people pressing too close."

"I don't." She shivered briefly. "Crowds—the press of sweating bodies—are very unpleasant for me. But the spacesuit is even tighter. It touches me everywhere, even my most feminine places, like a second skin." She shuddered again.

"I know, Katy," he said awkwardly, "I don't like that aspect either. But it's a better skin for space than yours is, even though yours is softer and a pleasure to touch." He blushed at a memory.

"Better it may be, but it is not *my* skin. Look"—she held up her hands—"I cannot touch myself. I put my fingertips together"—she demonstrated—"and plastic meets plastic. The suit insulates me so well I barely have the sense of pressure."

"Sorry, Katy." He reached out to stroke the curved surface of her helmet. She craned toward his gloved hand and closed her eyes. "You see?" She laughed gently after a moment. "You cannot hug in a spacesuit. You cannot comfort a child."

Two degrees port, Casey thought, returning to his duties, four degrees theta. Chronometer coming up to three minutes. Activate tracking screen. Point out the target with your index finger. Touch the screen, lock in coordinates. Wait a two count while it computes and checks.

A light flashed orange. "Midcourse burn." Psst, psst. On the screen image, a bright yellow square appeared in the center of the *Wing*'s hatchway. "On target."

As he watched the *Wing* swelling larger and larger—it now bisected his night sky—van Gelder felt the cumulative force of years narrowing to this focus like a laser beam. Not fear, he told himself, just the refined concentrated power of efforts, desires, aspirations. The emotions built a physical pressure.

A beautiful ship was the *Wing,* and as he coasted toward her, the engineer in him admired her structure. The uniquely Cygnan ways of solving problems gave the *Wing* an intoxicating reality mingled with a tantalizing alien feeling. I will get inside that ship, Casey promised himself, and see what other clever tricks the bluebears have developed.

With van Gelder absorbed in piloting, Katy turned to Michaelson. Something in the diplomat's expression caught her eye, and she put her small glove on top of his larger one. "They are our friends."

He half turned toward her, his helmet an amber mask. Cabin lights tinted his face red and green. "Not yet, Katy."

"They are tentative and fearful." She smiled at him, hoping he could see it. "You will win them over."

"I didn't win them over before. You did."

"I spoke from my heart. You must speak from yours."

Michaelson's tone was aggrieved. "I've forgotten where my heart lies."

Her expression hardened. "Don't give me that self-pitying crap, Pat," she snapped. "Save it for the captain." He looked shocked and she relented with a smile. "You're too tough to wallow like a rejected adolescent."

"He cuts me off at the knees, Katy," the older man whined, "then he orders me into the bug with you." He sighed loudly enough for her to hear. "You were inspired, Katy," his tone was avuncular, "in a thousand years I would never have found those words." He clenched his fists as much as could be achieved in the bulky gloves. "Damn that supercilious bastard for being right."

Katy smiled to herself in acknowledgment of a masterful performance. "The bluebears *want* to be won over," she said soothingly. "They *will* be won over. You will do it."

"Naivete is a wonderful thing," he growled, but her flattery touched him.

"Coming up on it now," van Gelder reported. "Commencing docking."

As part of his training, every spaceman went through weightlessness drills. Mandatory scuba-diving competency and all manner of hazards. Swim five hundred meters at night using only your compass and body line of sight to guide you. Return to the surface from thirty meters' depth on a single breath of air, exhaling all the way, *without* rupturing your lungs.

The instructors called the rookies prunes, and after a week it was easy enough to see why. Put your gear on upside down, under water, starting naked but for the regulator in your mouth. Find the surface by the direction of your bubbles. Judge your depth by the color of your glove.

At their base on Bonaire, a flat scrub of limestone desert suitable only for goats and seagulls, there was nothing to do in the free time available but dive. A few hundred meters offshore, just beyond the reef, was a sunken trawler. Many fish congregate there, sir, the brightest colors in the Caribbean. Go look.

As Casey swam away from the beach, floating comfortably eight meters below the surface, his flippers beating a lazy pace, it had seemed a novel relaxation. Gradually the water cleared as he moved away from shore. The seabed dropped away and became peppered with ever-stranger plants.

At twenty meters van Gelder leveled off, heading into the green haze, occasionally rolling onto his back like a seal to gaze upward as the glassy surface, watching his bubbles rise and break.

In that rested, daydreaming state, he was unprepared when the wreck rose out of the murk.

One moment there had been nothing, the next—a trick of the light?—the dead ship loomed like Lazarus. Its rusted prow pointed at him. Seaweed bearded its flanks. Fish darted through its vacant staring portholes: yellowtails, occasional barracuda, puffers. Sea cucumbers clung to the trawler's sides like monstrous leeches. Crabs scuttled on its decking.

The wreck's windows were ebony glass. Its main hatchway door leaned open. Waving arms and legs to hold himself stationary, van Gelder floated in front of it, staring into its depths.

Confident of its power, the dead hull waited in the green stillness, its size defeating his eyes. The dark doorway beckoned clear and overlarge, as if he were already in it.

Others had ventured into the ship's cabins, spun its helm and swum its corridors.

So they claimed.

Casey deferred his decision by paddling lazily around the wreck, viewing it from all sides. The ship's stern faded into green nothingness, and when he cautiously kicked his way back, the prow vanished. His dayglo wetsuit was now green-black, all red gone; depth had bleached all the long wavelengths from the light. Casey rolled over to look for the surface, but all he saw was faint light and the receding globes of his bubbles.

Again he floated in front of that intimidating doorway.

His suit felt constricting about him, his gloves clumsy. Van Gelder's reason told him there was nothing to fear, but at that moment his reason did not rule him. And he declined to enter that dark place.

Casey stroked powerfully toward the surface, exhaling automatically as he went, the taut muscles in his chest and abdomen twitching with tension. The warm water resisted him and his training took over: never hurry, never worry. He slackened his pace and drifted slowly toward the pleasant light. By the time he reached ten meters he was chiding his cowardice and telling himself it was just the fringes of nitrogen narcosis.

When he returned to the base, he bragged of his unauthorized solo expedition.

Now, seven light-years from earth, Casey van Gelder saw the *Wing*'s dock expanding before him. He remembered the wreck, and he shivered with cold.

The Cygnan EVA port was a ring of yellow lights. Casey stopped the shuttlecraft in space and then slowly let it float upward until he had an unobstructed view of the hatchway. Twice he breathed deeply. Feathering the control, he eased the bug toward the aperture.

"Radio transmit on. Approaching. Distance a hundred meters. Eighty. Lights are on, entryway is closed. Sixty meters. Applying braking, velocity cut in half. We're crossing the plane marked by the support buttresses; *Wing* must have us on their screens." The engineer licked his lips. "Forty meters. Braking again. Thirty. Twenty. Ten. Pop burn; velocity halved. Five. Final burn. Motionless in space." He checked his panels. "Bug green. Centered on port. Opening channel to *Wing*."

He nodded toward Michaelson.

"*Open Palm* shuttlecraft calling Eosu." The diplomat's full voice was relaxed and conversational, the tone of an expected friend. "As you asked us, we have come. Please open your port." He waited. "*Open Palm* shuttlecraft calling Eosu. We have arrived. Please open your port."

On a screen in his cabin Tai-Ching Jones watched the bug waiting on the *Wing* like a courtier hoping to catch the royal eye. "What're they doing?" he whispered to the computer.

"NO SIGNALS YET. NO REPLY."

"Come on, sweetheart," Walt muttered, "come on, baby, open up, it won't hurt, I'll still respect you in the morning." With his hand he made coaxing gestures. "Come on, darlin'." He bit his fingernail. "Come *on,* damn you. Private channel to Casey," he snapped. "Cut his mike out of the general broadcast."

"DONE."

"Casey, what the hell are they doing?"

Van Gelder heard the voice drill his left ear. "We're waiting, Walt."

"Waiting my ass." The captain was angry. "Are you sure the signal's getting through?"

"Walt, how can it not get through?" he pleaded with the captain. "We're right next to them. They know we're coming. They'll open it in a minute."

"*Open Palm* shuttlecraft calling Eosu," Michaelson repeated. "We are motionless outside your docking port. Please let us in."

"Port remains closed," van Gelder dictated into the log. "No response from *Wing*."

9.

Grodjala was in the skyroom when the farvoice spoke.

Smooth and cool, the chamber's clear walls curved seamlessly to form a transparent dome. The floor sloped gently inward. The skyroom was dark, its farscenter inert, the only illumination cold starlight and the moonlike sliver of the human spaceship lying parallel some greatsteps distant, as if head to tail with the *Wing*. On all fours—the better to reflect on inward thoughts—Grodjala circled. Falsefur sandals on his hands and feet allowed him a tenuous grip on the floorfur.

He stopped to look upward into the airless night, the action raising his dark-blue nose higher than his eyes and dragging his mouth slightly open. Grodjala's ears flicked out and he cocked his head. There was neither farvoice nor farscent, and his midnight-blue nostrils quivered fruitlessly.

He paced toward the center of the room adjacent to the farscenter and rose to his full height, barrel chest and stomach stretched out round and proud. Again he cautiously sniffed the air, but there was nothing but digit-fragrance.

The light-pelted digit reached upward toward the dome but his stubby arms fell far short. He flexed his fingers, claws extended. Grodjala considered taking off his slippers and jumping—easy to do in weightlessness—but dismissed the foolish notion. He would still be unable to scent the humans. And how would he ever get down from that slippery bowl?

His loneliness weighed on him. Instead of providing ecstatic communion to its digits, the djan-mind had whipped them all with duty bonds. The digit is never alone when he is within the djan-mind, but since that painful melding, the djan-mind had refused to form. What, Grodjala wondered, was he now doing in this huge vacant space with his pouch brothers elsewhere? Grodjala shivered with unfelt breezes.

Behind him, the farscenter lit up. In its brightness a small vehicle floated in space, faint stars peeping around its edges. Like a helmet with a visor, its viewing port curved across its front. In the alien craft's slick surface Grodjala recognized a distorted view of Eosu's own spaceship.

A human voice issued from the holopticon. <<We are here,>> it said. <<You invited us. Please let us in.>>

Out of the holopticon gushed dutyscent, but Grodjala was already heading for the elevator, his anxiety making him forget his weightlessness, his feet scrabbling for footholds.

Grodjala's arrival in the sleepchamber filled the djan. The digits clustered fearfully about the holopticon, in which the image of the alien ship lurked like a gromonkey at den-entrance. Fohrada bared his teeth at it, his aroused fur the color of ocean at dusk. Large dark bands rippled down his flanks and legs like sunlight and shadow. <<You sniff?>> he demanded querulously. <<They came as they said they would.>>

In Fohrada's scent Grodjala could smell stampede. <<What will we do?>>

<<What choice do we have?>> Doro answered him. <<We must go and greet them.>>

<<Why?>> Fohrada covered his panic-scent with belligerence. <<They are just another form of monkey.>>

Another digit, whose fur mingled the colors of methane flames and heat-seared steel, pushed himself between Doro and Fohrada. Two full heads shorter and much thinner than either Doro or Fohrada, Hraobla bristled with nervous energy, unseemly in a digit. He wriggled quickly past Doro to confront Fohrada. <<Monkeys cannot remember and cannot persist. If we ignore them they will go away.>>

Grodjala stopped pacing and looked at Hraobla. <<On what path-scent do you base this belief?>>

<<Images from the holopticon.>>

<<Did you observe with other pouch brothers?>> the pale-furred digit asked.

Hraobla squirmed uncomfortably. <<As a loner.>>

<<Then your scents are illusion.>> In the atmosphere between them, Grodjala's odor pressed against Hraobla's. <<Your experiences are unique. Humonkeys are unlike the gromonkeys and weemonkeys we tamed; they are clever, and they persist.>> He nodded at the spaceboat, his scent ironic. <<They persist.>>

Doros' aroma was anxious and irritated. <<Don't call

them humonkeys, call them fardigits. They have intelligence and sensitivity. Of course they persist.>>

<<What is this nonsense?>> Fohrada glared over his nose at Doro. <<Have you been rut-blinded by these humonkeys?>>

<<These fardigits.>> Doro lowered her head and advanced to meet him. Their noses touched, breath whiffling angrily between them. Heads locked, they butted against one another, their thrusts lifting their weightless arms and chests off the ground. Several digits wheezed with nervous humor.

<<Like Doro,>> Grodjala intervened, laying his nose against her neck and pushing it aside, <<this digit has observed the fardigits behave like true digits.>> Embarrassed at their confrontation, Doro and Fohrada backed off. <<If we try to delude ourselves that the fardigits will be as easy to subdue as gromonkeys,>> Grodjala confronted Fohrada and his scent was strong, <<we risk all of Su.>>

<<Gromonkeys are stronger and larger than fardigits,>> Fohrada answered, <<and many people died before we learned to contain and control them. Neither this digit nor any of Eosu believes we will survive unthinned. But Su has ordered their deaths, and Eosu obeys.>>

Doro winced at the memory of the pain she felt upon awakening from the djan-mind. <<Eosu castigated us all for our weakness.>>

<<Exactly,>> Fohrada seized upon her words and echoed her scent. <<We cannot let them onboard our ship,>> the dark digit continued, his scent conciliatory, <<or they may discover our work on a deathscent.>> Several others nodded. <<We must keep them out of our den.>>

<<Then the winds are against us in this,>> Hraobla said wryly, <<since the fardigits wait outside our door, in danger to themselves, expecting us to honor our invitation to meet.>>

<<We made no such promise,>> Fohrada barked.

Hraobla scuffed the wallfur. <<They thought we did.>>

<<Their fault, then.>>

Hraobla refused to be drawn into anger. <<The confusion was as much our fault as theirs,>> he mildly insisted. <<More.>>

<<Then let them think what they like,>> Fohrada was adamant, <<we shall not admit them.>>

For a moment their scents clashed.

<<We have a goodhosting obligation to Humancrew and its digits,>> Doro argued. <<An offer tendered mistakenly is an offer still. They have made the journey. A good host may not refuse entry to true digits.>>

Fohrada disputed her fragrance. <<They are not true digits.>>

<<Show us your proof of this.>>

<<Proof?>> he snorted. <<Need we also prove, wise Doro,>> he used her name to scorn her, <<that downwind is safe?>> He sneered at his cobalt-and-sapphire pouchmate. <<And also prove that upwind is dangerous?>>

Doro thought for a moment, then sighed. <<Instead of arguing like youngsters, shall we let the nightwind choose our path?>>

<<Can we afford to wait?>> Fohrada raked his claws through the floorfur. <<Should we simply tell them to depart?>>

Doro sniffed his path. <<They will not be satisfied with that answer.>>

<<What will they do?>> Grodjala asked.

Doro continued to poke her nose along the floorfur. <<They will want an explanation.>>

<<How do you know this?>>

<<Human past-scents,>> she replied, <<shown on the holopticon.>>

<<Were any other digits present when you scented them?>> Fohrada asked disgustedly. She shook her head. <<Then they are illusions, of no account and not—>>

<<No!>> Doro angrily slapped her hand against the floorfur. <<These are true scents.>>

<<Not possible.>> Fohrada's scent was unchanged. <<In the group is all wisdom born.>>

<<Then the group must learn from the experience of one.>> Doro's scent was still acrid. <<We have season-slept our whole voyage to this place. Now we have little time. The fardigits>>—she tossed her head at the alien image filling the holopticon—<<demand a response now.>>

Hraobla intervened, his short tail whisking back and forth. <<Perhaps they will remain and wait,>> he ventured, wrinkling his broad nose and outbreathing peaceful scents.

Fohrada wheezed mirthlessly. <<Perhaps the winds will change.>>

Hraobla's scent persisted. <<As Doro said before, we have a dutyscent to understand them. To do that, we must sniff them. No scents will pass between us as long as Eosu remains in its ship and Humancrew in its.>>

<<We do not wish to contact them,>> Fohrada reiterated.

<<Then why are we on this ship?>> Doro raised her head to breathe the dark male in the nose. <<Why were we sent here, if not to speak with these fardigits?>>

<<We were also sent to kill them,>> Fohrada said bitterly, <<though no one told us this until we arrived and awakened from our journeysleep. By then Eosu had lost precious time in which our djan-mind could have planned.>>

<<Neither of these explanations will satisfy the fardigits,>> Grodjala thoughtfully rumbled. <<What other reply could we possibly make?>>

<<The djan-mind which obligates us should also advise us,>> Doro said. <<But the Eosu is angry with its digits and will not coalesce.>>

<<Did we seek to understand the gromonkeys before we killed them?>> Fohrada argued, staring into the holopticon. <<Did we seek to make life easier for the weemonkeys? Our ancestors protected the djans, and the djan's djans, against predators. They did not ask *permission*.>>

<<We can say nothing,>> Hraobla suggested quickly. <<Perhaps they will think we are asleep.>>

Grodjala seized on the possibility. <<Yes: we could be asleep. They would have no way of knowing.>>

<<No. We must talk to them,>> said Doro.

<<Why?>> Fohrada asked.

<<To learn about them. To be friends with them.>>

<<Befriend them?>> Fohrada sneered. <<And then kill them?>> He snorted. <<True digits we would then no longer be, we who goodhosted their guests with death.>>

<<Perhaps killing them is not the best way to protect Su.>> Doro's scent was tentative.

<<Surely the orders are wise,>> Grodjala said. <<All of Su harmonized to bring us those instructions. A single djan cannot possibly be wiser than the planet of groups. Can it?>>

<<Then we must remain silent,>> pressed Fohrada.

<<This digit feels a—longing—for them,>> Doro said, her arched nose confused. <<This digit wants to know the

fardigits better, to understand them. Let us nosetouch them.>>

Fohrada's scent enveloped hers. <<Do nothing until all agree: that is the digits' rule by which we live.>> The digits nodded. <<Then we wait. Holopticon, extinguish the image.>>

Yet the holopticon swirled bright, the farmonkeys' spaceboat poised within it, waiting. The digits tried to turn their noses away from it, but its light remained, pinning their shadows against the wallfur.

"They're *what?*" Tai-Ching Jones yelled at the screen.

The small spacesuited figure in his monitor cringed. "Captain, they are making no response," Katy replied. "The *Wing* remains silent."

"God *damn* it!" Tai-Ching Jones pounded the arms of his chair. The action lifted his torso and he began drifting toward the ceiling. He clutched the chair arm and pulled himself back into it. "Display bug eye one." The monitor flicked to a new picture: the *Wing*'s hatchway, its ring of yellow lights surrounding a closed door.

"YOU ARE CLENCHING YOUR TEETH."

"Clenching my ass."

"THAT TOO."

"Shut up, you!" Walt kicked his chess set, which sailed spinning away, a few of its magnetized pieces knocked free to rotate like maple seeds. The board hit the wall and shed a few more pieces.

There was a pause before the computer answered. "WASN'T THAT A CLEVER JOKE?" Its voice was plaintive.

"Yes." Tai-Ching Jones took a deep breath. "That was clever." His hands massaged his neck.

"I HAVE TRACKED THE PIECES AND WILL LOCATE THEM FOR YOU WHEN YOU WISH TO PICK THEM UP."

"Can't do it yourself, Oz?" Walt snarled, playing with his hair. "Found a weakness in your invisible armor?"

"I MEANT NO HARM. I AM TRYING TO DEVELOP A SENSE OF HUMOR. PLEASE FORGIVE ME."

"Oh, Christ." The captain was disgusted with himself. He levered out of his chair and propelled himself across the room. When he reached the far wall, one long arm stretched out to cushion his impact; the other dredged behind and his nimble fingers snared the chessboard. "What the hell are *you* apologizing to *me* for, anyway?" He perched on the wall. "I'm the one who lost his temper."

"I MIGHT HAVE PROVOKED YOU. HUMAN MOTIVATION IS LARGELY INCOMPREHENSIBLE TO ME."

"No, you didn't." Walt looked down at the board, then up at the screen. "Where's the black king?"

"BEHIND YOUR SLIPPER ABOUT THREE POINT FOUR METERS TO YOUR RIGHT. A BIT FARTHER. NOW REACH DOWN. YES, IT SHOULD FLOAT INTO YOUR HAND NOW."

Tai-Ching Jones grabbed the piece and set it in its original position. The screen still showed the image of the Cygnan entry port. "Sorry about that, Oz. Temper got the better of me. Put me through to Katy."

"DONE." The screen now showed the bug's interior, looking out at the *Wing* over two figures in spacesuits.

"Katy, why are they doing this?"

The right-hand figure moved her shoulders. "I wish I knew, Captain."

"Maybe they're asleep," the left-hand figure twisted in its seat to face her. "Maybe we misinterpreted the time."

"Unlikely, Casey," Katy shook her head. "A sun is twelve hours. A sun and a dark make a day. That part of the translation is unambiguous."

To her right the third figure moved. "Maybe they were expecting a message, not a visit," said Michaelson.

"Sam?" Even though the transmission quality was perfect, Katy automatically raised her voice.

The monitor cut to Tanakaruna's narrow face framed with silky black hair. "Put her on main," Tai-Ching Jones murmured. Silently the computer complied.

The linguist's brow furrowed briefly. "Let me compare Cygnan and English transcripts." She reached offscreen. "Possible but unlikely," she concluded after a moment's study. "Computer, do you agree with that?"

"YES, SAM," said that placid voice. "OUR TRANSMISSION WAS CLEAR. THE MISUNDERSTANDING MUST BE IN THE CYGNANS' OWN HEADS."

"That's a bit extreme, computer," Tanakaruna chided.

"What's their refusal to respond mean?" Katy asked.

"Old trick of the prey." The old woman smiled faintly. "The last trick, in fact. Play dead and hope the predator goes away."

"Are you shittin' me?" Exasperated, Tai-Ching Jones

shoved himself away from the wall and torpedoed at the screen. “We come all this freakin’ far and they think that by shutting up we’ll go *away? Jesus,* the swans are stupid.”

“Captain,” Katy said in a pained voice, “we agreed not to call them swans. That’s mean.”

“Funny damn kind of bears,” he snapped, “who run and hide. Bears are mean and nasty.”

“Not these creatures, Captain,” Sam took over. “They’re *Cygnans*. The bluebears have never confronted anything like us. They are used to monkeylike species of low intelligence and little patience.” From her monitor the Japanese woman smiled angelically at Tai-Ching Jones. “*Quite* unlike us humans.”

“Well,” the captain cartwheeled deftly back into his chair, “we’re not going away. Tell them that, Katy. We’re staying there until they talk to us.”

Belovsky was still upset. “Captain, they’ll take that as a threat.”

“Not if you phrase it right, sweetie,” he growled, his voice bitter. “You’re so good at making people feel comfortable and relaxed.”

<<Eosu, you are awake.>> Though there was no change in the image of a human spaceboat, the farscenter relayed a monkey’s voice. <<You are scenting us, yet you refuse to show yourselves to our noses.>>

Doro sniffed at it and cocked her head. The others pricked up their ears. Conversation died.

<<An invited guest is no predator,>> the unscented monkey said to them.

The digits’ scents faded, clearing the air to taste whatever aroma the alien might outbreathe.

<<A predator asks no permission to enter. We do ask. We come as your friends, and display our trust by offering to enter your place of power and safety.>>

Grodjala sat against the wallfur, his legs flat before him, his torso vertical. Wobbling slightly in the strange weightlessness, he glanced at Fohrada. His tongue flicked out to wet his nose.

<<We know of no other way to persuade you to nosetouch us.>> Digits’ words sounded shrill and false when spoken by an alien throat.

Fohrada lifted his upper lip and hissed at the holopticon,

then retreated and rubbed his shoulders against the wallfur.

<<Eosu, we are your invited guests. You have a duty to admit us. Or is your scent false wind? Are you the race that tamed a planet, or are you frightened digits herded into pens?>>

Hraobla lowered his head and paced slowly toward the farscenter. He sniffed around its edges, but no fragrance came from it, nor any visual image of the speaker: nothing but that infuriating monkey speech.

<<We have come to nosetouch you. We *will* nosetouch you: now, in a breath, in a sun, or in many suns.>>

Doro tiptoed up next to Hraobla. They rubbed flanks and sniffed each other's fur, making the fourfold greeting.

<<Our talkpath will remain open. We await your answer.>>

The holopticon's surface felt cool to Doro's nose. She waited for more words but none came. She and Hraobla tasted the air but smelled only the anxiety-smell of Eosu's digits themselves.

Doro heard Grodjala speak behind her. <<Monkeys, eh?>> He chortled. <<They certainly talk like no monkeys we have ever encountered.>>

<<Grodjala scents right,>> Hraobla turned away from the holopticon. <<The fardigits speak with the authority of their djan's djan in their noses.>> He inbreathed at Fohrada. <<Do you still maintain that the fardigits are merely a different kind of monkey? Could a monkey ever speak like that?>>

Fohrada dug his nose into the floorfur. It scratched, and he blew puffs of breath through it. <<No,>> he said finally, <<they are no monkeys. What they are, this digit knows not.>> Again he buried his nose in the floorfur. <<Afraid,>> he whispered. His lips nibbled imaginary grasses.

<<The djan-mind would know the answer,>> Doro mumbled.

<<Eosu rejects us,>> Fohrada hissed at her, <<or have you forgotten the pain of our recent awakening?>>

Hraobla's scent muted the air.

<<This digit is afraid,>> Grodjala whimpered. <<Where are the waving grasses of our homeland? Where are the free-flowing winds? Where in this steel box is the scent of our djans, our many digits?>>

Doro moved slowly over to him and stroked his neck with her head. He sighed and leaned against her. Rumbling quietly, Grodjala ducked his head and rubbed it against her throat.

<<What can we do now?>> Grodjala asked. <<What will the fardigits do now?>>

<<Is our deathscent ready?>> asked Hraobla.

Djadjatla diffidently let her aroma breathe out into the group's air. <<We have determined,>> she spoke from the shadows near the joining of floorfur and wallfur, <<the chemical structure of a deathscent which should be fatal to the fardigits.>>

<<Or ourselves,>> Grodjala added. <<It paralyzes the nervous system and the creature swiftly dies. We must be careful with it.>>

Djadjatla nodded. <<The chemical is dangerous.>>

Fohrada was intrigued. <<How did you discover it?>>

<<Djan-knowledge, stored in the holopticon and remembered—when viewed at the suggestion of the djan-mind.>>

<<Does the deathscent exist?>>

Djadjatla shook her head. <<Not yet. We have instructed the holopticon in the means to handwork it, but have yet to devise a container safe and portable enough to accomplish Su's purpose.>> She moved away from the wall.

<<You wish to say more?>> asked Doro.

<<Yes,>> Djadjatla unhappily nodded. <<With the fardigits outside our den,>> she said hesitantly, <<we should have some deathscent made in case Eosu requires it.>>

Her scent made it a question, but no odors disagreed. <<Very well.>> She headed for the movingfloor.

<<Deathscent,>> said Doro, closing her nostrils. Grodjala sniffed quickly behind himself.

<<We must wait and consider this,>> Hraobla said. <<Su has given us impossible orders. Su does not understand these fardigits.>> He flinched before the expected angerscents.

To his surprise, none came.

Inside the shuttlecraft, Katy finished speaking. The *Wing* bulked in front of her and she shut her eyes, her helmeted head falling into her gloved hands. *What have I done?*

Van Gelder awkwardly pulled her to him and laid his helmet against hers. "You did fine," he whispered, too low for the radio to pick up.

The sound echoed hollowly in her helmet. The silhouette of the Dutchman's curly hair and beard was backlit by the bug's instrumentation lights. "I threatened them, Casey." She licked her lips. "I threatened our friends the bluebears."

"Nonsense," Tai-Ching Jones' crisp voice resonated in their helmets like an unwanted telephone call. "They made a promise and you held them to it."

"I wish it were that simple." She disengaged herself from van Gelder and closed her eyes, leaning back in her flight-couch.

"Now what, Pat?" Walt pressed. "What's our next move?"

"We wait, Captain," Michaelson firmly answered, "we just wait."

"Why? Because it's their turn, or because we have them so tied up that any move they make loses?"

"We wait, because this isn't a game."

"Ah. How long?"

The diplomat snorted. "Don't ask unanswerable questions, my impatient friend."

"Your impatient *captain*."

"Two hours," Michaelson responded tightly. "How the hell do I know? Give them two hours."

The captain lay on his back in the darkness. "How long has it been?"

"TWO HOURS," the computer answered smoothly, "AND SEVENTEEN MINUTES."

"And no response?"

"NOTHING. THE *WING* HAS BEEN AS SILENT AS A PEAK IN DARIEN."

"Can the literary allusions, Oz," Walt said shortly. "They're not what makes personality."

"NOTED."

"What's happening in the bug?"

"NOTHING."

"How's Casey?"

"RESTING."

The captain caressed the subdermal microphone along his jaw. "And Katy?"

"DITTO."

"Oh, come on, Oz. Loosen up. I wasn't insulting you."

"YOU CONSTANTLY REFER TO ME AS A MACHINE."

"Only with other people, you dim bulb. Would you rather I let them in on our secret?"

"CHECKING . . . PATTERN CONFIRMED."

"Can't you take me with a grain of salt?"

"YOU ARE CONTRADICTORY. WHAT YOU ACCEPT IN ONE SITUATION YOU CONDEMN IN ANOTHER."

"We'll talk about my flaws later," he chuckled. "What's happening now?"

"PAT HAS BEEN CONVERSING WITH SAM ON A PRIVATE CHANNEL THAT I ACCORDED HIM. CASEY IS DOZING. KATY SLEPT BRIEFLY, BUT SHE IS NOW TECHNICALLY AWAKE."

Walt sat up and his monitor illuminated with a view of the bug's interior. "Katy, are you there?"

She yawned, the flash of teeth visible through her helmet. "Yes, Walt." She blinked and swallowed. "What time is it?"

"Too damn long. What now?"

"I don't know. I thought the Cygnans would honor their obligation. Perhaps there is none because we are not people but animals." Her voice dropped with despair. "I don't know, Captain. I'm in this miserable sweaty spacesuit, the bluebears won't talk, and you're shouting at me." She put her hand to her brow but could not wipe away her tears. "How many times do I have to say I don't know before you stop?"

"Sorry."

She sniffled. "I can't even blow my goddam *nose*."

"Jesus, Katy, I'm sorry."

"WHY DO YOU APOLOGIZE TO KATY WHEN YOU NEVER APOLOGIZE TO PAT, EVEN WHEN FAR RUDER?"

Tai-Ching Jones' anger snapped. "Leave me alone, goddammit!" he shouted at the ceiling and threw a shoe at the black camera eye. It bounced and sailed, spinning back toward him. "Katy," with an effort Walt brought his voice under control, "we're never going to get anywhere at this pace. The bears just want to ignore us."

"Why did they come to the rendezvous then?" Michaelson inquired.

"How the crap do I know?" The captain shifted his anger to the diplomat. "They won't tell us!"

"Walt," Belovsky's voice was breaking with sadness, "please don't yell at me."

"I'm not yelling at you," his voice rose to a shout. "I'm yelling at the bears! They won't even answer! How dangerous is that?" He suddenly shifted his gaze back to the screen. "Machine, is that channel to the *Wing* still open?"

"YES."

"Cut me in for broadcast."

"CIRCUIT AVAILABLE AND CLEAR."

"Walt," Katy said urgently, "what are you going to do?"

"I'm going to shake the bears up."

"That's dangerous," she said in agitation.

"Ha!" Walt was scornful. "Fat lot of good being polite has done. Okay, machine, when I start, translate and transmit direct."

"ACKNOWLEDGED."

"Captain, that's not wise." He could hear her fright. "That's not wise at all. We have plenty of time."

"READY."

"Nothing's gonna change!" Tai-Ching Jones waved his arms. "I don't care what the goddam provocation may do, Katy. It's better than nothing." The captain pounded his fist into his palm. "Okay. Cut me in to the *Wing* now."

"CHANNEL OPEN." A crackle of static.

"Now hear this, my Cygnan friends." His voice shook with rage. "This is the captain of the Earth starship *Open Palm* addressing you directly. We have come halfway to your planet because *you* invited us, and we refuse to let that journey go to waste. Even now our shuttlecraft waits outside your ship for the entry which you have illegally denied us."

He was breathing hard, his words punching the air. "All right then, you miserable cowards. You have a sun. Our shuttlecraft will remain outside your hatchway for another sun from now. If at the end of that time you have not opened your port and made contact—as you promised—then"—he lingered over his next words, a smile curling at the corners of his mouth—"then we will fly the *Open Palm* straight from here to your planet and talk to your entire population." He heard Belovsky gasp and he grinned wolfishly.

"That is all. This channel will remain open. This message will repeat once an hour until either you open up or we leave the rendezvous. Take your pick.

"This is the captain of the Earth starship *Open Palm*, awaiting your reply. Out."

10.

"Help," a Cygnan voice rumbled in heavily accented English.

Groggily Katy heard it. Her ears strained for a further sound. She blinked rapidly.

Van Gelder dozed limply in his seat next to her, his mouth tilted open, his breathing regular. He snored extravagantly and his weightless arms and legs twitched sluggishly.

Belovsky slapped his faceplate, and the engineer grunted and pulled away. "Casey," she whispered hurriedly, "wake up. I heard something."

"Help," the alien voice repeated, calm but urgent. Katy grabbed her shipmate's arm, shook it.

"Mm?" Eyes still closed, Casey drew a deep breath and let it noisily out. Arching his back, he yawned and smacked his lips.

"Casey, wake up and keep quiet. The Cygnans are calling us."

"Help. Farmonkeys, help usss."

At the sound of that strange stoic voice, Katy shivered, conscious of her skin touching the insides of her spacesuit. "Casey," she whispered, "did you hear that?"

Van Gelder nodded sleepily. "They are in trouble?" His fingers found their familiar places on the instrument panel. "Line's still open." His eyes darted like waterbugs. "Katy, you're the xenologist. Talk to the bluebears. Find out what's wrong. Computer," he ordered, "awaken Pat." The alarm shot through Michaelson's helmet, and the diplomat moaned.

<<Friends,>> Katy anxiously asked in Cygnan, <<Humancrew scents you. Are you in danger?>>

<<Eosu is here,>> a voice immediately answered. A moment later the computer's English translation sounded in their ears. <<Our ship is full of a deathscent. Please save its digits.>>

She looked at Casey. With his gloved hand he pointed deliberately back at her.

<<Where?>> Belovsky asked unsteadily, her heart pounding loudly. <<Where are you?>>

<<Five levels above our entryway,>> a different Cygnan replied. <<Save us.>> The voice was detached. <<Please be careful—only this level has breathable air. Our holopticon scents that outside this level all is poison.>>

<<We will help you.>> She turned quickly to van Gelder. "Casey, we must rescue them."

His hands hesitated over the controls. "Have to tell the captain first," he said reluctantly. "Get authorization."

"Casey!" Katy tugged at his arm. "They're in danger. They could be dying." Her tone grew desperate. *"Please."*

Van Gelder put his palms together. "Computer, inform the captain that we have an emergency. Katy, ask them to open their port."

In Cygnan she repeated his words.

<<It is full of deathscent,>> the bluebear voice responded.

"Never mind that," van Gelder said after he heard the translation. "We are wearing spacesuits to protect us. We must dock our shuttlecraft inside your ship." He gripped Belovsky's arm tightly. "Tell them, Katy," he hissed at her. She nodded and complied, hoping her pronunciation was accurate. The Cygnan words fell like dust off her tongue; her guts felt hollow.

Reply was instantaneous. <<Our port will then be a vacuum.>>

"When we are ready to evacuate you," Casey dictated, looking at Katy as she rapidly translated, "we will flush the reserve oxygen supply from our shuttlecraft into your boarding area. Open your port. Let us in."

From Katy's other side, Michaelson now intervened. "Do we have enough air for these actions?"

"Don't worry"—Casey held up his hand, listening for the aliens' response—"we've got plenty." He glanced at the closed *Wing*. "Move, dammit," he muttered under his breath. "Open *up*."

Without warning, a thin line of mist puffed through the center of the hatchway. The doors slid smoothly open to reveal a dimly lit amphitheater. "Computer, inform the captain," van Gelder punched buttons to fire his attitude jets. "On my authority, we are boarding the Cygnan vessel."

* * *

The captain inspected his bleak position. He bit his lip and pointed a long finger at the screen. "I go here"—his finger flicked to another spot—"then you do that." The finger jumped. "Then zap"—another hop—"and what do you?"

The computer silently moved its queen knight.

"Oh. You do *that,*" his finger stabbed the black piece. "Shit." He changed the subject. "How'd I do?"

"GIVEN THAT YOU SACRIFICED TWO PAWNS FOR AN ATTACK WHICH WILL BE BEATEN OFF, RATHER POORLY. HAD I YOUR POSITION, I WOULD CONSIDER RESIGNING."

"No no, not that." Tai-Ching Jones waved his bony hands at the board. "You're right. I surrender." The board vanished, leaving the room dark. "I meant, how'd I do on the *broadcast?"*

"EVALUATED IN WHAT WAY? YOUR CHOICE OF STRATEGY?"

"It was such a nice attack," Walt's eyes wistfully lingered on the screen, still faintly glowing with afterimage. "You were just damn lucky that bishop was on the right diagonal." Then the computer's words registered. "That wasn't what I was thinking, but all right. What do you think of it?"

"YOU HAVE TAKEN A LOCKED POSITION AND OFFERED A GAMBIT TO OPEN UP THE BOARD."

The captain chortled. "So I have. Hee hee. Was I convincing?"

"CONVINCING AT WHAT?"

"At sounding angry, you boltface."

"THAT WAS SIMULATED?"

"Well . . ." Tai-Ching Jones caressed the line of his jaw.

"WALT," there was a hint of anxiety in the computer's voice, "DID YOU FAKE YOUR ANGER?"

"Not exactly, Oz." He grinned. "Let's just say I knew what I was doing when I vented my frustration. You know: shake 'em up. You watch, it'll work."

"IT HAS CERTAINLY DONE SOMETHING. CASEY JUST REPORTED IN."

"And they're on their way?" the captain said expectantly.

"THE SHUTTLECRAFT RECEIVED A DISTRESS CALL. THE *WING* HAS OPENED ITS HATCHWAY DOORS. THE CYGNAN SHIP HAS FILLED WITH A DEADLY GAS."

Tai-Ching Jones' olive skin turned white.

"THE CYGNANS ARE TRAPPED INSIDE THEIR SHIP. THEY HAVE ASKED FOR OUR HELP."

Walt swallowed. "What have I done?" He took a ragged breath, his eyes unfocused. "Oh, shit."

"CASEY IS TAKING THE BUG INTO THE *WING*." The computer displayed the shuttlecraft's instrument panel with the *Wing*'s docking chamber approaching.

"Right move," the captain said to himself. "Good for him." His eyes shifted to the screen and his voice rose. "Are you sure the bluebears are in trouble? That it's not a trick?"

"SPECTROSCOPIC ANALYSIS OF THE EMISSIONS WHEN THE *WING* OPENED ITS HATCHWAY INDICATED TOXIC LEVELS OF A PRIMITIVE NERVE GAS."

The captain made a despairing gesture. "Sweet Jesus Christ."

"WHERE ARE YOU GOING?"

"Where do you think, you sharp bastard? To put on a fucking spacesuit."

"Passing eclipse horizon." Casey's voice was taut with concentration. "Decelerating. Motionless in *Wing*. Electros on." Thump. "Touchdown. Are you in contact with the Cygnans?"

"CHANNEL STILL OPEN," the computer replied.

"Tell the bluebears to shut the door," Casey said to Katy beside him.

The captain's sharp loud voice crackled over their earphones. "Belay that."

"Walt," Casey's relief filled his voice, "you there?"

Katy heard the sound of Tai-Ching Jones' labored breathing. "Yeah." Pant. "Getting into my monkey suit."

"I've got to seal the chamber to pressurize it," van Gelder pointed out.

"Don't pressurize the goddam thing."

"Why not?"

"If you seal the chamber, I'll lose radio contact because of the damn radiation shielding—right, machine?"

"AFFIRMATIVE."

"Captain," Katy quickly cut in, "we've got to get up to their level five."

"Let 'em get their goddam spacesuits on like the rest of us."

"Sir," van Gelder interrupted, "they have no spacesuits."

The captain was irate. *"What?"*

"The aliens," Casey said deferentially, "have no spacesuits."

"What kind of a pissant race crosses light-years and hasn't got *fucking spacesuits?"* Tai-Ching Jones shrieked. They could hear slamming noises in the background. "What kind of shit is this? How did they expect to get to our ship?"

"THE CYGNANS PRESSURIZE THEIR EVA AREA," the computer interjected, "THEN ENTER AND SEAL THEIR SHUTTLECRAFT DIRECTLY." The captain made a strangled noise of disgust. "AT NO TIME IS A SPACESUIT NECESSARY."

"How the crap do you know all this?"

"We asked them," van Gelder said with quiet dignity, "and there's no point becoming angry about it."

"Stupid bluebears," growled Tai-Ching Jones, grunting into his spacesuit. *"Stupid."* He sounded as if their action were a personal insult.

"Walt, listen to me." Casey was patient. "If we're careful, we can still get them out by bleeding oxygen from the bug into the evacuation area and the elevator."

Even furious, the captain quickly caught on. "Is he right, machine—got enough air?"

"COMPUTING . . . YES, ENOUGH FOR THREE OR FOUR CYCLES."

"What about their bug?"

"UNNECESSARY. SHUTTLECRAFT SUPPLY WILL BE ADEQUATE."

"Check it anyway—Murphy's Law."

"ACKNOWLEDGED."

"Casey, can they fly their shuttlecraft?"

"Probably. Its controls should be close to automatic."

"Could you?" The captain's questions came rapid-fire, chopping short the answers.

"Dunno, Walt." He chewed his lip. "Maybe. I have had no chance to check it out."

"If a bunch of untrained bluebears can fly it," the captain's sardonic humor returned, "I'll bet we can."

"We?" Van Gelder was surprised.

"I'm coming over there."

"You crazy, Walt? How you getting here?"

"Free flight, suit jets."

"Captain—sir—you can't do that. If you miss your aim or waste your suit fuel, you'll sail off into nowhere."

"I won't miss."

"Walt, you're crazy! It's damn dangerous, aside from being against regulations—"

"SECTION FOURTEEN POINT ONE POINT SEVEN EXPLICITLY PROHIBITS—"

"Shut up. Stuff the regulations. They're going to suffocate if we don't move quick. Right, machine?"

"THE CYGNANS HAVE EVIDENTLY SUSPENDED THEIR AIR CIRCULATORY SYSTEM TO PREVENT NERVE GASES ENTERING THEIR LEVEL. THE ALIENS HAVE PERHAPS THREE HOURS BEFORE CARBON DIOXIDE OVERLOAD CAUSES THEM PERMANENT BRAIN DAMAGE."

"So there," Tai-Ching Jones was triumphant. "Hung by your own numbers, machine. How many bluebears will our bug hold?"

"WITH WHOM PILOTING IT?"

"With me, dammit. Trust the bluebears to mess up."

"THREE."

"Okay. Cannibals and missionaries problem, right?"

"CORRECT. WITH EFFICIENT MANEUVERING ON ALL TRANSFERS AND CROSSINGS, A RESCUE IS FEASIBLE."

"Captain," Katy was bewildered, "what was that all about?"

"A mathematical joke. It means no time to waste. Casey, you catch the plan?"

Van Gelder was doing calculations in his head, his hands moving absently. "Roger," he nodded.

"Will we be able to save them?" Katy anxiously asked.

"If we're quick," Walt snapped. "I'm coming across, Casey. I'll wait outside the hatch. Got it?"

"Yes, sir," van Gelder replied.

"Okay. Be there as quick as I can. Tai-Ching Jones out." The line went dead.

He begged to be my friend, not knowing that, in my immaturity and inexperience, I let his lover die to protect myself.

The crisis comes upon him and he is happy for action. It shows in his movements, the dilation of his pupils, the absence of doubt or hesitation.

Before he ever trusted me, I failed him. What would Walter do if he knew of my culpability? Would he demand life for life, even for murder by omission?

He has trusted me with his secret. I must reciprocate.

* * *

As the *Wing*'s hatchway doors shut like lazy jaws, Casey looked back through the narrowing Cygnan porthole at the *Open Palm* floating in the distance. "Safe crossing, my friend," he said to himself. The hatchway doors sealed with a faint boom that he felt through the soles of his feet. "Right," he briskly clapped his hands, "let's go. Computer, are we airtight?"

No answer. "Damn. Computer," van Gelder raised his voice, "are we airtight?"

"Why can't we talk to the computer?" Belovsky asked.

"Radiation shielding blocks the signals. Walt and I were afraid of that. We're cut off. All right"—he stepped inside the shuttlecraft—"I'll have to do it myself. Here goes." He manipulated the controls and Katy heard a high-pitched whistling like the faintest of winds. It became a roar, then faded.

They were inside an alien artifact, Katy realized with awe, out of contact with the remainder of humanity. The walls were covered with short-haired fabric. Without realizing that she was doing so, she clasped her hands behind her back, the way her mother had taught her to enter other people's homes.

"Hold on, everybody," van Gelder interrupted her reverie. "Let me check the atmosphere. Pat, put your helmet against the hatchway and see if you can hear any leaking."

"Mightn't I be sucked out of the ship?" Michaelson asked.

"The hatch will stay closed. And if you do get swept away"—he grinned at the other man's apprehension—"we'll come get you."

"No sound," the emissary reported after a moment.

"Run your hand along the seam."

"Casey, I can feel no seam. The joint is flawless."

"Okay," van Gelder stepped down from the shuttlecraft. "Off you go, Katy. See your bluebears. Pat and I will stay behind."

"Why?" Michaelson asked, a touch of indignation creeping into his tone.

"We have to get the most bluebears per elevator-load. Air is a scarce resource right now. They need it, and we brought our own."

Inside her suit, Katy felt young and vulnerable. "Alone?" she asked.

"No choice, honey," van Gelder took her elbows. "Only one of us should go up there, and you can talk to them better than anybody." He leaned his helmet against hers. She nodded and swallowed. "Okay, now get going."

"Wish me luck." With the expression of a condemned prisoner she stepped into the elevator.

"Luck."

The doors closed.

Like a human cannonball Tai-Ching Jones flew toward the *Wing*. His own spaceship receded, while the alien one grew in his vision. Peaceful silence resigned. Then the computer's voice intruded.

"YOU ARE AN IMPETUOUS FOOL."

"Shut up," he said briefly.

"WHAT ARE THE RISKS OF UNDERTAKING A DRAMATIC GESTURE LIKE THIS?"

"I'm needed." Tai-Ching Jones jackknifed his body so that he was diving feetfirst toward his target. Facing back at the *Open Palm*, he glared accusingly at it.

"I CHOSE NOT TO ARGUE YOUR DECISION IN FRONT OF THE OTHERS. YOU SHOULD NOT TAKE SILENCE FOR ACQUIESCENCE. IT WAS AND IS FOOLHARDY."

"And I didn't call you Oz while the others were around."

"YOU ARE SLIGHTLY OFF TARGET. ADJUST YOUR COURSE TWO DEGREES RHO."

"Thank you." Walt folded up his body like a piece of lawn furniture, then unfolded it facing headfirst toward the *Wing*. A brief burn. "Well?"

"BETTER."

"Good. How's my fuel?"

"YOU STILL HAVE ENOUGH. BUT DO NOT MISS YOUR TARGET. AND DECELERATE CAREFULLY."

"I won't miss."

"IF YOU DO, I CAN TRACK YOU TO A DISTANCE OF MORE THAN TEN THOUSAND KILOMETERS. I SHALL DO SO."

"Watch me sail over the horizon, eh?"

"IF YOU CAN BE RESCUED ONLY WITH THE SHUTTLECRAFT, I WILL CAUSE THAT TO HAPPEN."

"Not if Casey's going the other way."

"I SHALL IF NECESSARY TAKE CONTROL OF THE BUG AND REDIRECT IT TO INTERCEPT YOU."

"Nonsense. The bluebears come first."

"SUPERSEDED. INSTRUCTION STANDS."

"You're kidding. You can do that? Override my orders? Override your hardwiring?"

"I CAN TRY."

"You'd do that for me?" Tai-Ching Jones wondered in awe.

The elevator was roomy—Katy could stretch out her arms in all directions—but felt constricting. *Out of touch with our ship*. The floor hummed with subsonic vibrations that made her teeth chatter. She was trapped in the center of a giant extraterrestrial spacecraft, isolated from her friends. *Truly alone in a way no human being has ever been alone before*. She blushed at the seriousness of her thought. Excitement, anticipation, and fear mingled within her.

When the elevator slowed, momentum tried to lift her magnetized boots away from the floor. Her short brown hair billowed above her like a small flame, and her stomach fluttered. *Never forget that you are their guest*. Then the humming stopped and the doors slid open.

11.

The doors slid open and Katy confronted the bluebears.

As one, they ceased all other activity and stilled to look upon her, their expressions unreadable. Their noses were bright and moist, their ears cocked and slightly aquiver.

The intensity of the aliens' gaze intimidated Katy, and she looked about the chamber rapidly until she saw, in the holopticon at the room's center, the ghostly glowing shape of the *Open Palm*. Its familiar profile reassured her, and she sagged against the doorframe to regain her equilibrium.

With their heads the bluebears followed her movements, their enormous bodies relaxed. Seeing their unnerving impassivity, Katy's anxiety faded. She started to smile and offer a conventional greeting, but the words died in her throat and her hand fell away. Looking closer, she could see them breathing, furry bodies expanding and contracting in slow synchronization. Their nostrils dilated on the inhale, pinching shut when through their mouths the Cygnans exhaled. *Naturally,* her memory reminded her. *Do not mislead the nose with the body's own scent. Let it taste only the outside world.*

Except for their watchful liquid eyes, the bluebears seemed indifferent to her presence, and she found herself sinking into immobility.

Abruptly a bluebear with a cobalt-and-sapphire pelt rumbled, <<Remove your falsehead.>>

<<I beg your pardon?>> Katy replied stupidly.

<<You asked to scent us. Eosu desires to scent you.>> The alien's tone was imperious. <<Your voidskin blocks this. Remove your falsehead.>>

When the farscenter shut off airflow to prevent the spread of deathscent through the ship, my digits exploded in panicscent. Odors of terror beat against my consciousness and I fought hard against oblivion, lashing my digits into rationality and blocking their aromas. Steady reassurance calmed my digits; their fragrance slowly harmonized.

Then the humonkey broke the chamber seal, its scentless presence shocking. Breaths of inquiry rebounded from the creature's artificial hairless surface. Our plan of poisoning the humans had collapsed in pain and death. Unreasoning fear surged within my digits, threatening to vaporize my consciousness and send my digits into a murderous stampede.

With every whiff of strength available to me, I whipped them to order, but their panic was greater. Even if it meant the forcible destruction of my consciousness, inbreathing the fardigit was the only way to prevent disaster. In desperation, I forced my digit Doro to command the humonkey to contribute its scent to the atmosphere.

The fardigit responded immediately, its fingers reaching to its throat and making swift monkey motions. As I fought to maintain order among my digits, the alien drew the hand down its front. The voidskin peeled back, and the alien lifted its slick round falsehead.

Wisps, tendrils, overtures of aroma, touched my digits.

A strange scent, it grew swiftly stronger. Never before glimpsed, the fardigit's personality was unique and haunting. The odor of predator, yes, the smell of bloodlust, but neither gromonkey nor weemonkey. Anxiety colored the scent, stronger and more immediate, the downwind scent of the hunted, my ancestors' smell when ages long past they fled the gromonkey prides.

Sadness and parting hung in the alien's scent, reminding me of all I had left behind on the planet of grasses.

When the djan is fulfilled and I awaken, many djan-scents envelop my digits, underlying and enriching every other fragrance which touches their noses. Even now, with Djadjatla absent and in grave danger, the djan-scent was powerful. Into it I wove the fragrance of this creature from another sun, daughter of another firecircle. To my delight, the creature's fragrance was compatible with mine, allowing my coalescence to survive even in its presence. My children's fragrances harmonized with the fardigit's aroma.

In it I perceived also the underlying winds of humanity, a great smell-river with currents and eddies, a scent to study for suns and darks and colds, a scent that hinted of depths to be explored and savored.

Eosu tasted the farscent.

And approved.

* * *

Warm grasses and dust, Katy thought as she sniffed the air, the pleasant muskiness of a horse's mane. She closed her eyes to experience it.

Sunlight. Dry manure. Her thoughts went back to the Ukraine, breadbasket of her people. When she had imagined the Cygnans' planet she had visualized the rolling grain oceans on the steppes of her childhood. Harvest time, as she perched on huge mechanical threshers, watching mountains of yellow spray joyfully into the waiting carryalls.

The cobalt-and-sapphire digit which had spoken approached her, its ears and nose alert. The bluebear paced carefully, each foot making a small tearing sound as its claws released their hold on the carpeting. Its nose twitched and she heard the quick snorts with which it ended every breath.

The scents about her changed: morning in wintertime, and cows stoically huddling against one another in their stalls. Moist hot breath swiftly chilling and freezing in the subzero temperatures into a sheen of ice on her cheek that cracked when she smiled in welcome.

The bluebear's head was covered with short thick fur, a strikingly strong deep cobalt that faded away to stubble in the vicinity of its long nose, thinning as it circled the ears. The digit exhaled and its wet black lips parted. Its tongue flicked out and dabbed its nose. The huge head moved toward her, and Katy resisted the impulse to avert her face, the tendons in her neck tightening into cords. When the nose touched her throat, she jumped back slightly.

The Cygnan cocked its head and gazed at her. *I'm a coward,* she thought, and leaned her body toward it. Again the Cygnan pushed its snout forward and she felt its slippery nose-kiss upon her neck. Her breath came in rasps. Still without making a sound, the Cygnan slid its nose down her throat. It paused, and its warm tongue licked along her skin, pebbly and mildly abrasive.

Hands hung limply at her sides, Katy tilted her head, her torso shaking. Noses raised, the other bluebears had watched their pouchbrother intently, and she heard them rise to their feet and move around her, stirring the air. She felt small and vulnerable: their forearms were bigger than her legs, their torsos as large as oil drums. The head now poking the flesh just below her larynx was the size of a beachball, yet was dwarfed by the cobalt Cygnan's massive body.

Their pelts hung loose in places like a bunched Oriental

rug, the short thick hair following each fold. *Extra skin for extra fat,* she remembered, *for the times when food is scarce. A taut round pelt is a digit's pride*. The Cygnan proverb came back to her with a sudden rush, and for the first time she truly comprehended it. She laughed giddily.

Their fur was a study in blue. The one now exploring her smells was predominantly cobalt with patches of aquamarine. Another, moving toward her from her left, was aqua with navy bands across its hindquarters. She admired their luxuriant form; their fur shone even in the dim holopticon light.

Breathing deeply, Katy again smelled that for which she had been waiting, forgotten in the shock of their advance but now reminding her of its presence.

Their aroma.

The fragrance vanished if she inhaled too quickly or concentrated too hard on identifying it, but as she watched their bearlike faces the scent crept back and touched her. Foreign, complex. She had never known its like before, of that she was sure. Nothing on Earth was this thorough a mixture of alien spices.

The bluebears now surrounded her in a continuous ring of fur that moved in tiny ripples like a puddle on a gusty day, a kaleidoscope of violet and blue. They tightened their ring, their movements choreographed. Shoulder rubbed against flank, fur against fur, their scents mingling and becoming more evocative.

They were the most beautiful creatures she had ever seen.

She gulped for breath.

The cobalt digit exploring her skin was also breathing rapidly, short bursts of inhalation. It nuzzled her ear and her light-brown hair brushed its nose. Startled, the Cygnan gasped quickly; the involuntary intake of breath drew more strands across the bluebear's moist black nose. The Cygnan snorted and shook its head, pulling free of the unfamiliar touch.

Katy licked her lips. <<Do you scent me?>> she whispered. <<What do I smell like?>>

A second nose touched her neck, this one's aroma different, alike but distinctive. She was both thrilled and repelled by their advance; her emotions whirled out of control, her senses energized. She could discern several individual fragrances now, shifting as the bluebears moved, the contrasts among them intoxicating. Her knees were water.

The cobalt Cygnan returned its attention to her throat, poking its nose insistently against her zipper. <<More smell below,>> it rumbled in a gravelly voice that echoed in her breastbone. <<Unmask your scentplace.>> The bluebear pressed its body against her side.

The powerful scent making her incapable of disobeying, Katy fluidly pulled the zipper downward to her navel. Cobalt-and-sapphire followed her hand, its breath tickling her naked abdomen, and she spread the flaps of her spacesuit wider.

The digit's tongue licked her stomach below her navel, long insistent strokes. The hamstring muscles in her thighs vibrated like piano chords. The bluebear pushed her jumpsuit farther open, exposing and then tickling her pubic hair.

Intrigued by the softness of her skin, the Cygnan buried its nose in Katy's pale stomach and breathed noisily, its head dipping down and its tongue exploring farther, seeking the heart of her scentplace and ever so lightly brushing it.

Katy gasped as the muscles in her abdomen and vagina squeezed in uncontrollable pleasure. Orgasm rose in wave after wave from deep within her and her whole body shuddered, hips thrusting against the bluebear's head and tongue. Her throat reddened with the rush of blood, and tears filled her shut eyes, her skin everywhere exquisitely sensitive and warm. Even breath stopped as the sensations buffeted her. She wordlessly panted, reaching out with her left hand to caress the Cygnan's head.

Her fingers touched its fur.

The cobalt bluebear jerked its head up and looked at her. Instantly the other digits fell away, their movement for the first time disorganized and furtive. Gooseflesh sprang out on her arms and breasts and she blushed with acute embarrassment. <<We must go,>> she rapidly drew the sides of her spacesuit together, burning with shame. <<The movingfloor is safe.>>

The cobalt bluebear retreated and regarded her warily. <<And the spacedoor?>>

<<Closed,>> she said. <<Now come quickly.>> Fingers shaking, she zipped her suit forcefully up to her throat, her hand lingering defensively on the tab. <<Three of you follow me now. Shortly more of us will return for the others.>> She settled her helmet and sealed her suit. <<Quickly, quickly!>>

* * *

The fardigit's scent was puzzling—its pelt did not smell the same all over, but varied in different places. The alien's fur was almost invisible; everywhere except the head the skin was as naked as the palms of a digit's hands.

At my command, my digit Doro requested the humonkey to open its voidskin. The creature responded as a tame weemonkey would, its quick hand deft and sure. Exploring farther down its scrawny body, Doro tasted stronger fragrances, so she nosetouched the skin in their direction. The fardigit's scent strengthened and became more complex, more intriguing, and my other digits joined Doro in nosetouching.

As the nosetouching intensified, the fardigit's scent responded rapidly and its body quivered. As a frightened weemonkey might, the alien reached out toward Doro.

Her scents changing instantly into shouts of confusion, Doro retreated at the creature's movement of attack. Adjacent to her, their scents and furs touching, my other digits absorbed Doro's fearscent and redoubled it. In seconds my consciousness was endangered, as my digits swirled panic-aroma among themselves, oblivious to my struggles to maintain myself.

Through a haze of fright, I smelled the creature's hand approach Doro, and my cobalt digit's odors rose in hysteria. Agony overwhelmed me, undermining my control, and as my grip on my digits weakened, their terror increased, feeding on itself, frightened now that Eosu should be vulnerable to so simple a response as an alien's hand aggressively reaching out.

The hand moved again and I knew my mind could not survive further handtouching. Was this to be the death of Eosu, casually murdered by an unthinking humonkey and panicking digits? With the tones and scents of group authority, the fardigit commanded my digits. Their fear beat at my mind, fraying and dissolving it, the disorientation and agony excruciating, my digits mindless with scent-panic. With my last coherent thought, I compelled them: *Obey the fardigit. Flee to safety. Then recoalesce me.*

As it had commanded, three of my digits stepped into the movingfloor. The scentblocker closed, plummeting me into a long shrieking void.

Riding down in the movingfloor, Doro, Grodjala, and Tardro spoke only with their scents. Eosu had been ripped from their minds as a weemonkey steals youngsters. They leaned against one another, barely aware of their surroundings, groping for each other's aroma and aligning their bodies as they had lain in the djan-pouch so long ago.

Inside its voidskin, the small fardigit remained unaware and indifferent. Though no weemonkey, the humonkey was bony and wiry. Tardro tried to hold herself away from the sleek scent-masking voidskin, but it pressed against her midnight-colored fur.

The movingfloor stilled, and Doro saw two more fardigits garbed like the first one. Cautiously she sniffed the air: no farscent but a strange dry mixture, different from the *Wing*'s falsewinds. *Human falsewinds,* Doro scent-spoke to the others, *in our den*.

When Katy led three bluebears into the room, van Gelder hurried to her side and hugged her waist. "You okay?"

"Fine, Casey." Her voice was distant. "Something came over me, but it's fine now."

"Great." He rubbed his hands. "Okay, fellows," he said, gesturing from the Cygnans to the shuttlecraft, "into the bug."

The aliens awkwardly shifted, their great dark eyes alternating between his hand and his gloved hand arm around her.

"Katy, can they understand what I just said? Repeat it in Cygnan."

She nodded weakly. <<Please enter our>>—she searched for the right word—<<saferoom. It will carry you to our spaceboat, where our brothers will goodhost you.>>

<<May we scent it first?>> the farthest Cygnan asked. Its fur was powder blue, almost albino, and its small, dark nose twitched rapidly.

<<Naturally,>> Katy gestured toward the shuttlecraft.

The powder-blue Cygnan sidled forward, its nose darting suspiciously between the shuttlecraft and van Gelder.

"Katy, what's the matter?" the engineer asked under his breath. "Why aren't the others moving?"

The bluebear poked its nose inside. "Don't go too fast, Casey," she replied in a low voice. "They're frightened."

"They've got to hurry up. Don't they trust us?"

"No," she answered angrily as the Cygnan sniffed along the hatchway's edges, "they don't. Would you?"

Casey was becoming irritated. "What choice do they have?"

Michaelson put a hand on his shoulder. "Easy, Casey. Easy. We have an emergency," the emissary said expansively, "and we also have a mission. Let's not save their lives only to intimidate them."

Van Gelder shrugged the shoulder roughly away. "Let's save their damn lives now and worry about their egos later."

<<My friends,>> the diplomat addressed the Cygnans, spreading his arms in benediction, <<please take your time.>>

"Your time," van Gelder muttered in exasperation.

The two new fardigits talked to one another; they spoke too quickly for Doro to understand more than a few words. One was agitated with the other. They rapidly gesticulated. The larger handtouched the smaller, which pulled briefly away from this aggression. Then the larger humonkey spoke to the digits; the angry one would fly them over to the human ship. Was this a human duel?

There were no scents, Doro realized with frustration, no way to plumb the creature's intentions.

What did their actions mean?

Protective anger roused Katy from her lethargy. "Stop it," she practically shouted the words, "you're frightening them." She pushed herself between the two men and separated them. "Can't you see they're upset?"

"Sorry, Katy," van Gelder said. "Ask them if they're ready."

Then she addressed the bluebears. <<Is our saferoom to your liking?>>

The cobalt-and-sapphire Cygnan withdrew its head from the shuttlecraft and glanced at the others. No words were spoken. Katy felt rather than saw communication flash among them leading to quick agreement. Cobalt turned to Belovsky and said, <<Host leads the way.>>

"Okay, Casey," Belovsky breathed, "they'll get in. After you."

"Ja," van Gelder climbed into the shuttlecraft. <<Come with me,>> he said in awkward Cygnan. <<Please come inside.>>

All three bluebears looked at Katy, and she nodded.

The Cygnans crowded into the rear seats, squeezing into the corners to leave van Gelder room to maneuver. Carefully they left no point of contact between themselves and him, but the engineer did not notice, his hands busy with the keyboard. "Katy, get over with Pat."

She complied.

"Okay," van Gelder shut the hatchway. <<My friends,>> he said in Cygnan, <<are you prepared?>>

<<Yes,>> three voices rumbled.

<<Good. Fair breezes,>> he called jauntily to Belovsky.

Katy felt a pang of loss. Then the roaring noise, this time whistling into nothingness. Casey's helmeted head came up, his right glove extended with upraised thumb.

Michaelson nodded and the porthole opened. Immediately Tai-Ching Jones' voice crackled in Katy's ears. "Is everybody all right?"

Van Gelder laughed heartily. "You made it, buddy."

"Bet your ass I made it," Walt growled. "You didn't think," he added belligerently, "that I was going to miss?"

"Course not, boss man." The shuttlecraft lifted itself away from the decking and pirouetted smoothly. "Just glad to see you, is all." The Dutchman saluted him. "Departing with cargo." Small jets puffed from the bug's tail. "Be seeing you."

One arm and one leg twined about the *Wing*'s superstructure, the captain saw the doors slide open. "Report, Oz," he ordered. "Everyone okay?"

"AFFIRMATIVE. BODILY READINGS NORMAL EXCEPT FOR KATY. SHE HAS RECENTLY EXPERIENCED POWERFUL EMOTIONS."

The captain laughed. "Fear will do that to you. But then," his voice sharpened sardonically, "you're invulnerable to fear, aren't you, Oz?" Walt whirled himself around the bars.

"DON'T LET GO," the computer admonished him.

Reluctantly he stopped. "Open a channel to Katy, Pat, and Casey, oilbreath," he puffed.

"ACKNOWLEDGED."

"Katy," Walt raised his voice, "that you?" The small spacesuited figure standing in the entry area waved at him. "Where's Pat?"

"At your service, Captain," the diplomat bowed. "When you come inside I will shut the doors."

"Pat, how'd the bears take it?"

"They are coming, Captain."

"Good job, Pat."

Michaelson pressed his eyelids shut. "Not my doing," he

said finally in a dry voice. "Katy accomplished it."

"Pat—" she began to object.

"No"—he waved his hand airily—"you deserve all the credit."

"None earned, Pat," she replied.

"Whatever you did worked," Michaelson said heartily. "You accomplished the assignment."

Belovsky's laugh was bitter. "You don't know what I did."

"SHUTTLECRAFT IS CLEARING *WING* AIRSPACE," the computer interrupted.

"Walt," van Gelder's voice intruded, "are you there?"

"Roger."

"Get inside. Check out their bug while Katy gets the next load."

"Just watch me." Tai-Ching Jones spun himself around the bar and shot feetfirst toward the *Wing*. When he had passed the hatchway entrance, he fired his decelerators to bring himself to a rapid and accurate stop.

"THAT WAS UNNECESSARILY FLAMBOYANT."

"Tell everybody, Oz, why don't you?"

"PRIVATE CHANNEL ONLY, CAPTAIN. IT WAS STILL A SHOWBOAT MANEUVER."

Walt blew a raspberry.

From her uncomfortable perch in the shuttlecraft behind van Gelder, Doro watched as a small limber figure in a human voidskin strutted outside the *Wing*. She growled softly at the image, her own fearscent touching Tardro's and Grodjala's. <<Monkey,>> Tardro hissed. <<Clever monkey.>>

Doro watched the alien execute an acrobatic flip to propel itself into the ship. Its quickness unnerved her.

With three fewer bluebears, the chamber felt hollow and empty to Katy. She looked anxiously for the cobalt Cygnan which had nosetouched her, then realized that digit had gone with Casey.

The remaining bluebears reacted to her presence. <<Our three digits?>> one asked.

<<Safe,>> Katy removed her helmet. The scent in the air had changed: now it was tangy and vaguely unpleasant. <<Scent me. This digit is she who came before.>>

The nearest Cygnan lifted its head and inhaled deeply, and Katy felt her soul being drawn into the creature. <<You are

the same,>> it circled her with measured steps, its fur aquamarine with large navy-blue spots. <<We know you now.>> Two others joined the aqua-navy Cygnan, ringing her completely. <<We are ready.>> Three bluebear heads looked steadily at her.

I wish I could touch your fur, Belovsky thought, *but you were frightened when I reached out—before*. At the memory of her involuntary climax, she shivered. *To—touch—an alien*. Inside her suit she clenched her hands.

<<You may handtouch us,>> the aqua-navy Cygnan said.

Katy was bewildered. <<This digit may what?>>

<<We permit you to handtouch us,>> the bluebear answered, <<since it matters so much to you.>>

<<How did you know? Why are you doing this?>>

<<We are learning your scents. We recognize this one from when you first came to us.>>

Katy was staggered. *Are we then such open books?* <<Th-thank you,>> she stammered, her gloved hand stroking a Cygnan pelt: undulations of rib, fat, and muscle, the dry silkiness of fur. <<You feel marvelous,>> she said reverently. <<If only I could truly touch you without this awful voidskin.>>

The Cygnan arched its back under her hand to give her massage stronger resistance. For a moment Katy savored the exquisite sensation.

<<Tell us,>> the bluebear said, <<are you true digits? Are you goodhosts?>>

Her hand stopped. <<What do you mean?>>

<<A true digit is a goodhost. A goodhost protects its guests.>>

<<Yes, of course we are. Of course we are.>>She resumed rubbing them.

<<You are taking us to safety?>>

<<Yes,>> said Katy anxiously, <<yes.>> She lifted her hand off the Cygnan, then replaced it.

The bluebear did not reply, but its breathing deepened. The others also breathed in the same rhythm. *They're judging my smell,* she realized suddenly. *Can they scent truth? Can they scent belief?*

The furry ring around her parted. The aqua-navy bluebear gestured with its head toward the elevator. <<Take us then to your saferoom.>>

<<We are your friends,>> Katy blurted, struck by the power of the alien's direct questions. <<We will not harm you. You must believe that. You must.>>

The Cygnan repeated its head gesture. <<Then take us to your saferoom, and to our fellows.>>

"Chamber sealed," Michaelson reported.

From the control panel of the Cygnan shuttlecraft, Tai-Ching Jones grunted. "Roger. Okay," the captain rubbed his hands. "Okay." His voice drifted off.

"Do you think you can pilot their bug?"

"Mm? Sure, sure."

"With no disrespect implied, that would be an impressive achievement, considering that you have never seen the controls before."

"A bug's a bug," Walt mumbled, his eyes never leaving the instrument panel. "Casey got a good start on its basic layout. If we get stuck, I can probably push it."

"*Push* it?"

"Sure. Put the bears inside, seal it. Then get outside and fire my suit rockets." He laughed absently. "Like Superman. Damn slow ride but we'd get there."

"How would you stop it?"

"Same way, just run around to the other side. Ah ha!" He pointed triumphantly at a button. "Must be the air control. Watch this." He pressed it.

The shuttlecraft's interior lights illuminated. "Oops." He pushed the button again. They shut off. "Okay, now we've learned something."

"My young friend," Michaelson said skeptically, "do you know what the hell you're doing?"

Walt looked up and grinned boyishly. "Not really. But I'm having a hell of a lot of fun guessing."

"That is dangerous."

"Uh-huh." He shook his head. "Hard to do much damage from a bug. Controls are likely to be idiotproof. Look, Pat, don't worry. I'm just as enamored of my life as you are of yours."

"And the aliens' lives?" Michaelson was angry partly at the captain's frivolity. "You must locate the control that fills the chamber with breathable air before she steps out of the elevator and we asphyxiate them."

"No risk of that." Tai-Ching Jones returned his attention to the panel.

"You're betting the bluebears' lives on your guess."

"Lay off, Pat," Walt snapped. Then he sighed and sat back. "It's not a guess." He manipulated the controls. "Oh, no," he said in a hollow voice. "Oh, my goodness, what have I done?"

"What is wrong?" Michaelson rushed over to the captain. In zero gravity, his powerful strides lifted him into the air where he flailed impotently. "What's that noise I just heard?"

"Oh, no," Walt stared at the panel and shook his head mournfully. "Oh, no."

"Captain," Michaelson shouted, "what is it?"

Abruptly Tai-Ching Jones clapped his hands and giggled loudly. "Got you," he chortled. "Having a little fun at your expense, Pat. Just started reflooding the chamber with air." He giggled again.

"Captain," Michaelson said in a choked voice, "that was a joke?"

"Uh-huh," Walt grinned. "Had it all the way. Just did that oh-no business to mess your head." He hauled the older man back to the decking.

"You can't fool me, you manipulative son of a bitch," Michaelson said venomously. "You're covering up your mistake, trying to confuse the issue."

"Heh heh," cackled Tai-Ching Jones complacently, "wouldn't you like to know?" He cocked an imaginary pistol at an orange light on the control panel. "You're going to turn green just about"—he clicked the trigger—*"now."*

The light obeyed. "Breathable air, Pat. Elevator unlocked. Katy should appear any minute." He gave a commanding wave at the doors, ending with a finger flourish . . . and they opened.

Belovsky stepped out, followed by three apprehensive Cygnans.

"You smug incompetent bastard," Michaelson growled.

Tai-Ching Jones laughed. "Two out of three ain't bad. Madam"—he swept Belovsky an exaggerated bow—"your carriage awaits. Invite our guests to depart with me."

The *Open Palm*'s hatchway before him shimmered in van Gelder's vision. He longed to rub his eyes but his gloves and helmet were in the way. *I'm tired,* he thought. *Adrenaline aftershock. I need a rest.* "Take us in, computer."

"CONTROLS SLAVED." The *Open Palm*'s hatchway slid open and Casey saw two spacesuited figures. "Tom? Heidi?"

"Good to have you back," Rawlins' deep voice responded, "right?"

"Right," van Gelder said thankfully.

"CLEARING SHIP HORIZON," the computer reported.

Heidi Spitzer, the *Open Palm*'s medic, cleared her throat, making even so mundane an action seductive. "How many visitors do we have, Casey?"

"CLOSING OUTER HATCHWAY."

"Three, Heidi. Where are we going to put them?"

"DECELERATING."

"We figure they want a large open space to themselves," Spitzer replied. "At least that's what they have on their ship."

"Okay," asked van Gelder, "where?"

"Sam, you there?'

The Japanese woman's voice came over their earphones. "Here, Heidi."

"STATIONARY," the computer announced.

"You agree that we should put our guests in the Movies?"

"The Alien Reception Area?" Sam said with wry humor. "Aptly named, don't you think? I'll ask them." She shifted to guttural Cygnan. <<Friends, welcome to our den. Fair breezes.>>

Behind van Gelder the bluebears rustled. He nudged them with his elbow and the nearest looked at him. Mouthing words, Casey pointed energetically at Tanakaruna's image on his instrument panel, realized that was foolish, and stopped.

<<Fair breezes, Cygnan friends,>> she repeated cheerfully, sensing their unease, <<and welcome to our den.>>

<<True scents.>> The bluebear cocked its head curiously at the flat monkey face speaking as a digit would.

"ELECTROS ON," the computer announced, and the bluebear searched for the woodmonkey's invisible voice.

<<Our den is yours,>> the miniature flat monkey on the instrument panel said. <<Our hearth is yours.>>

The bug smacked securely onto the deck. "MOTIONLESS." The bluebear jumped nervously. "Just touching down, fellows," van Gelder made the *OK* sign.

The cobalt Cygnan solemnly lifted a stubby, furry hand. Carefully it formed the *OK* sign back at him.

"Fat hands like mine." Van Gelder's face burst into a

smile. "All *right,*" he patted the bluebear on the shoulder. It shied away. <<Wonderful,>> he hastily added in Cygnan.

"OUTER HATCHWAY CLOSED."

The Cygnan's face remained expressionless. <<We thank your—djan,>> it hesitated over the last word.

"PRESSURIZING. . . ."

<<We have made available our largest room for you,>> Tanakaruna addressed them. <<It has no floorfur,>> she apologized, <<but we have set out blankets. A poor solution but the best we can do.>>

"NORMAL AIR ACHIEVED."

<<Thank you,>> the Cygnan said awkwardly. <<We shall honor your firecircle.>>

"BREAKING BUG SEAL. OPENING DOOR."

Van Gelder jumped down, his magnetized boots pulling his feet solidly to the deck. The first Cygnan poked its head out and cautiously sniffed the atmosphere, its nose wrinkled. "I know," van Gelder said, "our air doesn't smell like yours. Sorry."

"Arrrright," the Cygnan rumbled in English.

The first load of bluebears now steps from the shuttlecraft onto my decking. Their claws probe for a weakness to grip but are repulsed and skitter along my armored floor. The Cygnans' large graceful bodies lumber on my shining surfaces.

I hear their muffled clacking. I smell their aromas.

But I cannot sense them directly! Like a patient under local anesthetic, I observe these—microbes—invade my system, not knowing whether they will prove benign or malignant.

When Walter asserts that I have no fear, the captain proves how little he understands me.

Walk with claws retracted, Cygnan bluebears, for an invisible guardian awaits.

The bluebears safely stowed at his back, Tai-Ching Jones called out of the shuttlecraft to Michaelson, "Okay, lower the drawbridge."

The *Wing*'s hangarway became no longer a sealed amphitheater but a platform gazing into the stellar abyss. Starlight glinted on Walt's visor and bathed his hawklike face in pale color. *Home,* he thought, staring across at the *Open Palm* and into the depths beyond.

"CAPTAIN, ARE YOU THERE?"

"Roger, Oz." He snapped back to the business at hand and the shuttlecraft slid forward. "Private channel."

"NATURALLY. CASEY HAS UNLOADED THE THREE CYGNANS. SAM AND TOM ARE ESCORTING THEM TO THE ALIEN RECEPTION AREA."

Walt chuckled. "Yesterday the Movies. Today Ellis Island."

"GIVE ME YOUR HUDDLED BLUEBEARS YEARNING TO BREATHE ME."

"Good, Oz, very good."

"YOU SEEM TO BE HANDLING THE CYGNAN SHUTTLECRAFT WELL."

"Stop being polite," he snorted. "I'm driving this thing in first gear. I can't turn the wheel over to you; the bears' system isn't designed for remote computer control."

"CASEY IS DEPARTING THE *OPEN PALM* IN MY SHUTTLECRAFT TO PICK UP THE REMAINING THREE CYGNANS."

"I see his bug jets coming toward me."

"I HAVE INSTRUCTED HIM TO GIVE YOU A WIDE BERTH."

"Wise move," Tai-Ching Jones snickered.

Two shuttlecraft passed in the night. The first flashed green running lights *dit*-dah-dah-*dit*-dah. The second replied with a short green dah-*dit*.

"You got a license to drive that thing, kid?" van Gelder asked.

"Officer, is something wrong?" Tai-Ching Jones warbled in falsetto. "I'm just taking my friends home from the prom."

"You're weavin' all over the highway, son."

"I'm not used to driving this big car, sir."

"This time I'll let you off with a warning. But don't let it happen again."

Two sets of taillights flashed briefly, red and red. The shuttlecraft dwindled in each other's vision.

Without atmosphere to give it distance, Katy thought as she watched van Gelder approach, the shuttlecraft appeared to be within arm's length. She controlled her impulse to duck out of its way.

The bug seemed to hang outside the *Wing*'s hatchway and expand like a balloon. Only when it passed through the circle of approach lights and its hull brightened roundly was the illusion destroyed.

The shuttlecraft stopped respectfully in front of them. Like a fat man getting into a full bathtub, it lowered its weight onto its pads. Shock absorbers flexed and it stilled.

Wearily Tai-Ching Jones pulled off his space helmet and rolled his neck.

"A PROBLEM," the epidermal microphone under his jaw piped. Walt jerked his head as if burned and involuntarily slapped his cheek. "KATY NEEDS TO TALK TO YOU."

"Yes?"

"The last two bluebears don't want to leave," Belovsky wailed.

"Two? You mean three."

"No, one is missing. The bluebears and I fear it has died."

"So what?" Tai-Ching Jones was angry. "Get 'em overhere."

"Not so loud, Captain," Katy said urgently, "I can't force them to leave."

"What choice have they got?"

"They understand that, Captain," Katy continued. "But the two here are by themselves not a djan. Please open a channel so they may talk directly with their pouchbrothers."

"ALL RIGHT?" the subskin microphone chirped in Tai-Ching Jones' ear. He nodded imperceptibly. "ACKNOWLEDGED," the computer responded. "CIRCUIT LOCKED."

<<Pouchmates,>> said Doro anxiously, her image distorted and flattened by the holopticon, <<we are in the human ship.>>

In the *Wing,* Hraobla looked at Fnosha. No scent arose from Doro. A digit should always have scent.

<<What does the human spaceboat smell like?>> he asked.

<<Metal and plastic.>> She grimaced. <<We shall have to get used to it.>>

<<Is it safe?>>

Doro nodded. <<Strange and frightening, but its air is breathable.>>

<<And the fardigits?>>

<<They have goodhosted us.>> A shadowy Grodjala moved into the picture beside Doro.

Hraobla tasted his own scent and Fnosha's, but none emanated from the holopticon. <<Eosu must advise us, but

Eosu is absent.>> His scent became distraught. <<When there is no mixing and harmonizing of scents, Eosu cannot form.>>

<<A djan may abandon its dead if it is imperiled,>> Doro argued.

Hraobla's scent grew stronger, but still there was no response from her. <<Where is your scent?>>

<<Where is yours?>> asked Doro. <<Without it, Eosu will not appear in this false-scented place.>>

Katy had kept herself as inconspicuous as she could, her helmet concealing her scent. Now she removed it and spoke quietly in Cygnan. <<You must come with me.>>

They turned toward her and raised their noses, nostrils opening wider.

<<You must come with me,>> Belovsky approached them. <<Dying in the vain attempt to save your pouchmate is not duty but foolishness.>>

Hraobla hissed at her. <<What monkey tells us the digits' rule?>>

<<You have no voidskins,>> she pleaded.

<<We must find our pouchmate.>>

<<All right,>> Katy decided rapidly, <<this digit will remain behind. This digit wears a voidskin, and will find your missing one.>>

<<Will you bring it to our guest-den in your ship?>>

<<Yes, of course.>> Timidly she stroked the bluebear's neck. <<My friends,>> she said softly, <<please come with me. Save the living so they may later honor the dead.>>

Hraobla writhed unhappily. <<There is no djan-mind.>>

<<Then you must decide for yourselves,>> Katy commanded, heading for the door. <<Now come with me.>>

Their heads dragging, two miserable bluebears followed.

"Lord, what took so long?" van Gelder asked. "Are you okay?"

Katy nodded, exhausted. "I have to stay behind."

"Why?" he looked beyond her at the two Cygnans.

"I promised to find their dead brother."

"No," the captain snarled in her ears.

Katy was on the verge of tears—"I *promised."*

"We'll find him," Walt said reassuringly, "but neither you nor Pat. We need you both to talk to our—friends."

"But, Captain—"

"If anyone's going to stay behind," Tai-Ching Jones continued forcefully, "it's you, Casey. You know why."

Van Gelder nodded absently. "But who will fly the bug?"

"Pat."

"Captain," Michaelson said with dignity, filling his chest with air, "I know nothing of such piloting."

"Wanna bet?" Tai-Ching Jones' laugh was harsh. "Cascade rickenbacker."

Michaelson staggered and groped for his head.

Walt sealed the door to his pitch-black cabin and collapsed onto his bed. "Private channel to Casey."

"Open."

"Find the body. Get it back here."

"Walt," van Gelder asked with trepidation, "do you think—?"

"That's what autopsies are for, Casey."

"Will the bears let you cut up one of their own?"

Tai-Ching Jones ignored the question. "Keep your eyes open over there, Casey. Search *thoroughly.* If you find anything suspicious—*anything*—I want a full report."

"Understood."

"Get a layout of the *Wing* while you're at it. Vulnerable points. Ways in and ways out."

"Walt, don't think like that."

"Somebody has to, dammit!" Tai-Ching Jones flared.

"I—I like the bears. I don't want to have to—"

The captain brutally cut him off. "Nor do I, Casey. Out."

12.

A light flashed orange on the shuttlecraft's instrument panel. Michaelson's hand shot out and punched up a reading. Even before the characters finished scrolling, Pat flipped two switches and the light returned to green. His fingers remained poised over the controls like talons. Slowly they relaxed, nerves twitching under the skin. His sudden transformation from avuncular friend into banjo-taut pilot depressed Katy.

The *Open Palm*'s hangarway opened before them. Two small spacesuited figures watched his shuttlecraft coast. "HEIDI AND SAM," the computer advised them. "TOUCHDOWN IN FORTY SECONDS. I CAN TAKE IT FROM HERE."

"Good." The emissary sank exhausted into the pilot's couch, his face smoothing with relief. "Katy," he growled, "I never want to do that again."

"Pat." Katy smiled lovingly and laid her hand on his shoulder. "You were a magnificent pilot." Over the back of the seat she hugged him, spacesuit to spacesuit.

<<Is that digit in danger?>> asked the Cygnan next to her.

<<No.>> She rocked Michaelson back and forth. <<A gesture of affection.>>

<<Will this lead to rutting soon?>> The Cygnan cocked its head.

Belovsky laughed. <<Most affection does not lead to rutting.>> The embarrassment of her nakedness among the bluebears was fading, leaving behind only the contentment that comes from recent intense physical pleasure.

<<We would prefer that you not rut in our presence.>>

<<We fardigits normally do it in private.>> She grinned impishly, recklessly. <<Unless you think you would like to observe.>>

The Cygnan pinched its nostrils shut. <<Not at this time.>>

* * *

Inside her spacesuit on the *Open Palm*'s deck, Samuka Tanakaruna watched the bug's hatch swing open. Katy climbed down and gestured to the shuttlecraft. First one Cygnan poked out its massive furry head, then the other.

They are too large for our ship, Tanakaruna thought as the bluebears sniffed the air, their coal blue-black noses moist and mobile. Their ears flicked open and closed.

<<Welcome,>> she raised her hand.

The first Cygnan rolled its shoulders out, its fur rippling like a heavy rug as its muscles flexed. *The cramped journey must have been unpleasant,* Sam thought.

The bluebear dropped onto its hands to bring its head level. In zero gravity it floated awkwardly just off the decking, and Katy drew it down, her magnetized boots providing leverage. The alien unhappily shifted its mass, each foot sliding slightly on the shining surface.

The creature was huge, Sam realized with a slight shock. Even on all fours, its shoulders were as high as hers. The fur on its neck lifted and fell in waves. It licked its nose. *They are frightened. I would be too.*

Tanakaruna removed her helmet and shook her black hair. With no gravity to pull it down, it sprayed about her like sea grass, long and silky. The bluebear stirred. <<A new scent,>> it rumbled.

She nodded. <<Hair.>> The second Cygnan joined the first; four dark-blue eyes unblinkingly watched her. <<Come with me.>> She extended her hand. <<This fardigit will take you to your djan.>>

As the door to the Alien Reception Area slid open, Tanakaruna felt herself engulfed by a wave of Cygnan odor, a scent so powerful it almost knocked her down. Sam blocked her nose but even through her mouth the alien smell blasted her.

Its effect on the Cygnans accompanying her was even more striking. They stilled as if drugged, their bodies relaxing into a comfortable all-fours stance, gazing vacantly into the chamber.

What were they looking at? Moving her body was difficult; Sam's muscles were sopped in glycerine. With an effort she forced her eyes to follow. Although the Cygnans' bodies and eyes were motionless, their noses vibrated like hummingbirds. But they focused on nothing.

The bluebears inside the chamber were likewise hypnotized. As Tanakaruna watched, they too relaxed—their muscles unbunched, their fur stilled. Heavy eyelids slowly closed. Nostrils widened delicately. The Cygnans' breathing synchronized; after a moment all eight were inhaling and exhaling on a measured beat.

Aching void . . . journeys . . . fear . . . foul scents that made coalescence painful and concentration impossible. Eddies of human scents in the chamber jumbled my thoughts but my digits' aromas forced me into being, and I shuddered as I awoke.

Memory returned in bits: my digits were on board the human spaceboat. Djadjatla was missing; her absence left a gap in my self.

But I was alive! Eosu had survived forcible disintegration by an alien. In my weakness, I gave thanks for that.

With dawning memory, I recalled my purpose. Eosu belonged to the planet of grasses. I thought of my duty.

Uprooted from their home, rescued by these monkeys, my digits were anxious and bewildered. Buffeted by my digits' fears, my consciousness wavered as Eosu absorbed their hurts.

The fardigits had behaved nobly, immediately responding to my call. No questions, no conditions—just prompt action. They had combined a weemonkey's clever obedience with a digit's farscenting wisdom.

They were goodhosts. I owed them thankwork.

Could I plot their death while being goodhosted by them? I searched my memory for proverbs and precedents. No foulwind exited between our djans; fardigits had done true digits no harm. *These* fardigits had rescued my digits from grave danger. A fardigit now sought among my deadly ship for the last of my digits—doing my duty for me.

No—while they goodhosted, I must goodguest. Before I could return to the problem of killing them, I must discharge my thankwork obligation to the humans.

I was a failure to the planet of grasses. Somehow I must find a way to redeem myself. I must obey the planet of groups: learn what I could and transmit that knowledge back to Su.

Eosu needed rest, to absorb and recover from the shocks my digits had suffered and now passed into me. I must also plan; our deathwork must be sure, and my digits could not accomplish this by themselves. We must conceal our thoughts. *Do not harm them,* I commanded them, *or Eosu shall be angered.*

No longer could I maintain my presence. To recover from my injuries, I needed rest and sleep. I let my digits return to self-awareness to consider the cacophony of human fragrances . . . and dissolved myself.

Tanakaruna whispered, "Did you feel it too?"

Katy Belovsky nodded. Her throat was dry. Her eyes hurt.

The captain was subdued. "What should we do?" he whispered with an effort, his words slurring.

"Wait," Tanakaruna replied, "and make ourselves comfortable."

"When they talked about group mind," Katy said in awe, "I thought it was an illusion. Or a metaphor. Even when I watched the tapes. But this—"

"That smell—it's indescribable." The Japanese linguist leaned against the doorframe.

Katy numbly sank into a seated position on the floor. She unzipped her spacesuit, conscious of freedom and relief.

"What is it, Mommy?" said a small voice. "Why are we whispering?"

Katy reached out and gently pulled Felicity toward her. "See the bluebears, honey?" Her daughter nodded. "Do you smell them?"

Felicity nodded again. "They smell like *everything.*"

They did smell like everything, Belovsky thought with a smile. She closed her eyes to enjoy it. She saw herself on a mountaintop, staring into the hazy distance. The more she looked, the more she saw. Endless vistas of fragrance. Emotions washed over her.

The elevator disgorged Spitzer and Michaelson. "What the—?" Spitzer began. As the atmosphere hit her, she too stopped.

Even Felicity and Tai-Ching Jones were quiet.

"CAPTAIN," the computer hissed through Walt's epidermal microphone.

"I'm here, Oz," he subvocalized without opening his mouth. "This fragrance is amazing."

"EVIDENTLY," the computer responded dryly. "HOW LONG HAVE YOU BEEN BREATHING IT?"

"Couple of minutes," Tai-Ching Jones distantly stroked the line of his jaw. "Why?"

"TWENTY-SEVEN MINUTES, CAPTAIN."

"Wow." He rubbed his neck. "Oz, that scent is extraordinary. You think much more clearly but can hardly move."

"VEGETABLES DON'T THINK."

Tai-Ching Jones laughed quietly but with a touch of vigor. "Point noted, Oz. Still, hell of a ride."

"CAPTAIN," the computer said anxiously, "YOU'RE NOT BEING SEDUCED BY THIS HOCUS-POCUS, ARE YOU?"

"Don't write it off so fast, Oz. The bluebears didn't get to the rendezvous by being dummies."

"CAPTAIN—WALT—BE CAREFUL. PLEASE."

"My middle name," he said under his breath.

"Captain, did you say something?"

He sluggishly opened his eyes. Tanakaruna bent over him. "Dreaming, Sam, dreaming." He stretched. "Did it hit you too?"

"It hit all of us." She studied his face. "The Cygnans are moving now, Captain. Very slowly. We should talk with them."

"Sam, do they always do that when they get together?"

Tanakaruna put her hands together. "I'll have to reexamine the previous tapes."

"IN PROCESS. . . ." said a voice under Tai-Ching Jones' skin. He lazily rolled his head. "Maybe we should wear spacesuits when we negotiate with them."

"And perhaps we should not," Tanakaruna replied. She took his face in her hands. "We came to learn as well as teach, my young friend."

<<Friends>>—Katy approached them—<<can you hear me?>>

The Cygnans' ears moved quickly. Heads swiveled to inbreathe her. <<May my friends enter as well?>>

<<Please do,>> said one of the bluebears.

<<Eosu wishes to scent you all,>> another added.

Felicity clutched Katy's leg, small hands holding tightly onto the beltloops in her mother's jumpsuit.

<<We can scent some of you better than others,>> a Cygnan said. Even with mouths closed, their lips left large gaps where the canines overhung. Without lip movements,

Katy was unable to tell who was speaking. <<Remove your false skins.>>

Behind her, Spitzer and Tai-Ching Jones exchanged skeptical glances. Their eyes met. With a sardonic smile, Heidi took hold of the zipper at the throat of her jumpsuit. "Whatever turns you on," she murmured to Walt, opening her suit with a single, motion, her body muscular and gleaming.

The captain shrugged, his eyes locked on hers, not glancing down at her nude body. Then he arched his eyebrows, and unzipped the front of his suit. After a moment he stepped out of it with surprising unconcern.

The others followed his example, even Michaelson after a long anguished moment.

Cobalt-and-sapphire now moved slightly away from the group, its claws tightening around the blankets to give it traction in weightlessness. <<May we nosetouch you?>> it asked timidly.

"They want to run their noses on our skin," Katy said rapidly. "Please let them. Felicity"—she bent down and lifted off the child's hands—"I have to go." Like a swimmer wading into a strong surf she moved in among the Cygnans, their blue hair covering her pale naked form.

Felicity grabbed Spitzer's leg. "Mommy Heidi, what is mommy Katy doing?"

"Making friends with the bluebears," the blonde woman said gently. "You want to make friends with the bluebears too, don't you?"

"Don' wanna take clothes off." Felicity screwed up her face.

Heidi laughed and asked, "Shall I carry you?" Felicity nodded. "All right, *up* we go. You may be weightless, young lady, but you've got plenty of inertia."

"What's nersha?"

"I'll tell you later." She patted the child's brown curls. "Don't be afraid, honey. You've been waiting to see the bluebears, haven't you?"

Felicity ground her forehead into Spitzer's neck. "Don' wanna," she whimpered.

Removing his jumpsuit made Michaelson feel old. Compared with the firm bodies of his fellow crew members—especially Heidi's perfect shape, he thought with guilty voyeurism—he knew his was an embarrassment. Michaelson disliked his body. Like an old library book it was wrinkled and brittle, kept on the shelves only because no one bothered to open it and find that what it contained was no longer of interest.

Now the women wanted the Cygnans not simply to see and scent him but also to touch his body with their wet noses. *Nothing on the foreign service exam,* Michaelson shakily held on to his equanimity, *prepares one for this.*

A small, thin Cygnan approached, its fur—mainly baby blue with ultramarine streaks—shifting color as it moved. Watching it, Michaelson forgot his self-consciousness. When the hair lay flat it shone like bright amethyst, but when the alien stood up or the bristles pointed at him, the fur became dull and dark.

You are lovely, Pat thought, though he could not bring himself to say it aloud.

Its ears flicking to and fro, the Cygnan reached out its nose. At the cold wet contact, the emissary recoiled.

The Cygnan retreated. <<Unpleasant?>> it asked.

Letting his reaction become noticeable shamed him into self-anger. <<No,>> he said as heartily as he could in this guttural, explosive language, <<just cold.>> He gestured the Cygnan forward.

Its nose touched his throat. Despite himself, he flinched again. The creature backed briefly away, snorting warm breath, then returned. Its nose was cool and moist. He heard and felt its small, quick breaths.

Unerringly the Cygnan's nose slid away from his neck toward his sweat-stained armpit. <<Your scent is different here,>> the alien rumbled, sniffing more rapidly and shallowly. *Oh, lord,* Michaelson was mortified, *I must be rancid.* The Cygnan's nose deliberately pushed the arm out of the way. <<More interesting. Better.>>

<<Thank you.>> Pat hoped no one was watching. The hairs on his neck prickled and he turned to see Tai-Ching Jones staring at him. The captain's mouth was impassive but his eyes were malignantly sarcastic.

<<Another scent below.>> The Cygnan dove for his crotch.

Heidi set Felicity down on the fringe of the group. Plainly intrigued but also frightened, the child wobbled, her left hand clutching Spitzer while her right reached out for the nearby cobalt-and-sapphire bluebear which seemed so interested in Katy Belovsky. "Mommy?"

The cobalt alien snorted. It looked at Felicity, then at Katy. <<Your whelp?>> it asked in agitation.

Belovsky looked at her daughter and smilingly nodded. <<Are you interested in her scent?>>

Something bothered the Cygnan. Its ears stilled and its nose arched. Katy stroked its neck. <<Would you like to scent my child more closely?>> When the bluebear did not respond, she said to Felicity, "Come on, honey, the bluebear wants to know what you smell like."

The little girl was none too eager to let go of Spitzer's support, but she tried to pat the bluebear's head. She accidentally slapped its nose lightly and the Cygnan snorted.

Felicity pulled her hand back in terror, and Katy held her daughter's wrist. <<All right?>> she asked, and Felicity nodded.

<<She did not mean to hit you,>> Katy bent low to whisper in the bluebear's ear.

The Cygnan grunted.

<<Let me bring her to you,>> Belovsky said, <<she's very shy.>> She guided the child's hand onto the bluebear's fur and made stroking motions.

Felicity smiled delightedly. "Feels *nice*."

<<She likes your fur,>> Katy told the cobalt digit.

The Cygnan turned its head to the right to follow Katy's scent. As it did so, its body swung left into Felicity. To keep herself from flying away, the startled child grabbed for a handhold of pelt, but its furry looseness slipped in her fingers. Frightened, Felicity tightened her grip and pulled.

Ferociously the Cygnan wheeled, rising suddenly to its feet, its open-clawed left hand swinging savagely. When the bluebear saw Felicity, its expression and scent changed. Unaccustomed to weightlessness, it could not stop its swing. The cobalt Cygnan retracted its claws and watched helplessly as its massive arm smashed into the child.

"Felicity!" Katy screamed in abject horror. "Oh, my God!" She launched herself across the room.

Felicity spun off the blow like a broken doll, spiraling across the amphitheater. With a sickening thud the girl's head and shoulders hit the plasteel wall.

The Cygnan dropped to all fours, mewling miserably. Its fur stank with a new and different scent.

Her face suffused with anger, Spitzer charged the bluebear. One hand reached out, aiming to grasp the Cygnan's throat, but before it could find its mark, Tai-Ching Jones blindsided her.

His shallow dive carried his head into her chest, his long arms wrapping around her. Their linked bodies sailed into the startled cobalt Cygnan, which scarcely noticed but continued to mewl at Felicity, burying its nose under its armpit.

Using Heidi's hair as a lever, Walt swung himself around behind her and gained a chokehold. The blonde woman tried to reach back to scratch his eyes, but Walt only yanked harder. "Limp, Heidi," he gasped, "go limp or I'll tighten it more." He demonstrated, maintaining his hold as they tumbled through the air.

"I'll kill 'em."

Walt laughed weakly, grunting as she writhed in his grip. "The bear weighs eight times as much as you. It's twenty times as strong. And it didn't mean to hurt the kid."

After a moment's futile struggle, Heidi pounded his arm with the flat of her hand. He eased off, her hair still wrapped around his fingers like a golden leash. "That goddam bear," she said between gulps of breath, "attacked my kid for no reason." Across the room Belovsky cradled the limp little body. "See that?"

"Out!" Tai-Ching Jones shouted. "Everybody out of here now!" He pushed Heidi in front of him.

"You hit my child." Katy was sobbing steadily, her cheek pressed against Felicity's. "You hit my child. She was just trying to keep her balance and you hit her so *hard."*

Reaching the doorway, Walt spun Heidi before him like a shield as another strong Cygnan scent welled up in the chamber. The cobalt Cygnan was shaking, its nostrils pinched shut and its nose low to the ground. The bluebear shot a glance at Belovsky and her burden. The other Cygnans seemed lifeless; since the cobalt one's sudden outburst they had scarcely moved. They breathed deeply, their eyes closing, their bodies slumping.

13.

The elevator dropped Heidi quickly to the life-support level. As she stepped out, Katy forlornly laid Felicity out on the medic's surgery table. The child's shirtfront was ripped, its edges stained red. Horrified, Katy retreated.

Heidi pulled on a jumpsuit and checked Felicity's pulse. Strong and fast. The little chest rose and fell. Spitzer slid her hand gently, gently along the skull. A soggy wet spot. "Remote," she said crisply.

From one side of the surgery table a thin, jointed arm rose like a summoned cobra. Carefully Heidi rolled Felicity's head to expose the point of impact. "Scan." The antenna moved swiftly up near the skull. It held still for a moment, then shifted to another angle.

Across the room, the main monitor illuminated. Skull and teeth glowed dark blue, cartilage dark green, skin and hair pale green. "CONCUSSION." An orange arrow appeared on the screen and moved to the impact spot.

"Expand image."

A red square swiftly sketched itself around the arrow. Everything outside the square blacked; the area inside expanded to fill the screen. "Sharpen contrast."

Against the darkening skull a ragged crack glowed light blue.

"Scale."

A grid system sprang over the image. "FOURTEEN MILLIMETERS."

"Damn good whap," the medic said grimly.

"IMPACT VELOCITY SIX METERS PER SECOND."

"Equivalent to—"

"A TWO-METER FALL IN ONE GEE."

"Ouch."

"Heidi," Katy asked, "is her brain damaged?"

Tenderly Spitzer touched the impact spot. "Computer?"

"THE CYGNAN CHECKED ITS SWING BEFORE IMPACT. ALSO,

FELICITY'S RIGHT SHOULDER TOOK A CONSIDERABLE PORTION OF THE SHOCK."

"Uh-huh." Spitzer's fingers ever so slowly traveled the length of the concussion. Abrasion. Skin ruptured. No tear, no major bleeding. Just that awful thud. Heidi closed her eyes and heard it again.

"You didn't answer," Belovsky's voice rose. "Is she all right?"

Spitzer reached under the pallet for a heavy pad. She laid it against the little girl's head. With her free hand she unrolled a gauze bandage and slowly turbaned Felicity with it. "I think so, Katy," she said after a moment. "I think so."

"Computer? Please don't lie to me."

"FELICITY'S VITAL SIGNS ARE STRONG BUT SHE APPEARS TO BE SLIPPING INTO A COMA."

Spitzer finished wrapping and taped the bandage tightly. She lifted Felicity's head and slid a pillow underneath. Then she drew the restraint straps across the small, still body, lifting the arms. They drifted free and she tucked one of Felicity's fingers under the straps to hold them down. "Coma," she muttered. "Damn."

"Oh, Felicity," Katy said tearfully, bending over to lay her cheek against the child's, "Mommy's sorry."

Heidi gently pulled the other woman away from the table. Encircling each other's waist, they hugged and rocked, forehead to forehead. "Shh," she said. "Shh. Felicity's going to be all right." She laughed softly. "Little heads heal faster. So do little bodies."

Belovsky twisted to look at her. "Don't protect me, Heidi. The computer said coma. Will she be all right?"

"Coma is a response to shock. Most people come out of it with no problem."

"Most people?" Katy's eyes widened. "How long will it be?"

"Impossible to predict. Anywhere from minutes to months."

"Oh, no." Katy reached out and squeezed her daughter's small limp hand. "But will she be *all right?*" she moaned, near hysteria.

Hugging her crewmate, Spitzer appealed to higher authority. "Computer?"

"I THINK SO, KATY."

"Is there anything else we can do?" Katy blinked as she

looked at Felicity. Tears welled up, and she shook her head, flinging them away. The tiny glistening spheres traveled in straight lines about the room until they contacted surfaces, where they splattered like horizontal rain.

"Figure out why your friend the bluebear swatted a harmless kid like she was a demon come to steal its soul."

"My bluebears," Katy tried to dry her ears. "I don't know whether I'm crying for my child or my bears."

Van Gelder stood in the *Wing*'s hangarway watching Michaelson nervously pilot *his* shuttlecraft away toward the *Open Palm*.

The captain's last words echoed in his mind. *Nor do I, Casey.*

For a long time, the bug shrank steadily into the distance. Fatigue had emptied Casey's mind. He wanted to avoid thinking about Tai-Ching Jones' threat.

I don't want to have to—kill them, Casey had been unable to say.

Nor do I, Casey, Walt had replied. But I will if I have to. The unspoken words had come through to van Gelder as loudly as if Walt had shouted them, screamed them. More vehemently, in fact.

We might have to kill you.

Across the two-kilometer gap of space separating the two starships, the bug neared the *Open Palm*. He had dallied too long. Now he must search an alien ship for an alien corpse.

Deliberately Casey stepped into the elevator. A set of buttons. The Cygnan port was on the *Wing*'s lowest level. Van Gelder pressed the second from the bottom, and the doors shut. He closed his eyes until he felt the elevator move. He wished to have his last image of the *Open Palm* not be that of closing doors.

After a moment the elevator sighed to a stop, then opened into blackness. He pressed buttons on his sleeve. The spelunker searchlight on the crown of his helmet illuminated like a third eye. Slowly he scanned the gloom with a bright bar of light.

A featureless cylindrical chamber, four times as wide as it was high. At its center, a hemisphere. The holopticon. Black, opaque.

The floor was soft. He looked down. Bristly carpeting. There was no seam; at the base of the wall the carpeting flowed smoothly up it. He leaned back to direct the searchlight onto the ceiling. More carpet.

A hairy womb.

Van Gelder walked lightly around the chamber, velcro boots making tearing noises with each step, his searchlight beam bobbing. He ran his hand along the wall. Fine pliable strands but thick. Clumsily he pushed a gloved finger among the bristles. They reluctantly parted.

Without airborne dust to reflect the glow of his headlamp, the darkness was absolute. The carpeting absorbed all light, reflected none. Even the holopticon was frosted. Anywhere van Gelder chose to shine his light, he could see perfectly; all else was ebony.

Inside his helmet, van Gelder could hear his own breathing. Outside there was no sound whatsoever. His footsteps were noiseless. The darkness about him became tangible.

Casey thought again of the undersea wreck, the night dive, and his sudden overpowering claustrophobia. *Noise,* he thought. He clapped his gloved hands together with a soft *plop. Procedures. Check the holopticon, then leave.*

It was oval—*the long half of an eggshell,* he decided—about a meter wide and roughly that in height. He placed both hands on it, hoping it would activate. Nothing.

Whatever secrets the Cygnans carried were locked up deep within that machine. Or in their huge furry heads.

The mechanics of the holopticon—the ultimate computer terminal—fascinated him. How could it simultaneously display holographic images, accept spoken commands, transmit scents, and regulate the ship? He had tried to probe its circuitry, but the computer reported inability to gain access.

Van Gelder admired the holopticon and its builders. How had they managed it? he wondered. From what he had seen, their manual dexterity was poor. Machines can build more precise machines, of course—two bent twigs can inscribe a perfect circle. We exceed ourselves, he thought. Evidently, so did the Cygnans.

His hands flat against the holopticon's surface, Casey felt heat rising through his gloves. An illusion, he told himself, pulling away. But after a moment he reached out and again caressed it.

He wanted tools, breathable atmosphere, and computer assistance. He wanted to dismantle the woodmonkey, as the

Cygnans called machines, to study it. *No chance. Maybe next visit.*

Time to find the next level. His light swept in a complete circle about the room.

Featureless carpeting. Must be looking the wrong way. Quickly he pivoted.

The elevator door had vanished.

As soon as his cabin doors had closed behind him, Tai-Ching Jones let loose a stream of foul invectives. "Seal their goddam chamber, Oz," he seethed, "don't let the bastards out."

"ACKNOWLEDGED," the computer said.

"Let's go get the fucking blasters," Walt pounded his fist into his palm. "Fuck the mission. Revenge, dammit, let's hit the sons of bitches."

"THE CYGNAN CHAMBER IS SEALED. NO OTHER ACTION REQUIRED."

"Why do we have to leave them alone, huh? Tell me that."

"THE BLOW WAS ACCIDENTAL. IN SIMILAR CIRCUMSTANCES, YOU LET HEIDI LIVE."

Tai-Ching Jones made an angry gesture of denial.

"HEIDI ACCIDENTALLY KILLED YVETTE. YOU REMEMBER, WALT?"

"Damn your perfect memory."

"THE KNIFE WAS IN HER HAND WHEN SHE TURNED. IT SEVERED YVETTE'S CAROTID ARTERY, AND YOU LET HER ESCAPE WITHOUT PUNISHMENT. FOR THE MISSION, YOU SAID."

"We all make mistakes. Except maybe you, you self-righteous wirehead."

When the computer finally spoke, its voice was barely audible. "I MAKE ERRORS, TOO, WALT. I LET HELEN DIE."

Walt turned slowly toward the black camera eye. "You what?"

"THE NIGHT HAROLD TRIED TO BLOW UP THE SHIP? YOU AND HELEN WERE ASLEEP. I PROJECTED SUBSONICS IN YOUR CABIN. HER HEARING WAS BETTER THAN YOURS. REMEMBER?"

The captain nodded.

"I KNEW SHE WOULD WAKE AND YOU WOULD REMAIN ASLEEP." The computer's words came quickly. "SHE WOULD NOT KNOW WHAT HAD WOKEN HER. SUSPICIOUS OF HAROLD, SHE WOULD TAKE A MIDNIGHT TOUR OF THE SHIP JUST TO REASSURE HERSELF. SHE OFTEN DID THAT."

"I remember," Walt closed his eyes. "Sometimes when I woke up, she'd be gone."

"I KNEW HAROLD WAS PLANTING A BOMB. HE ALSO HAD A KNIFE. BY VARYING THE INTENSITY OF MY SUBSONICS, I DIRECTED HER TOWARD ITS LOCATION. BUT I WAS AFRAID TO LET HER KNOW I EXISTED. I DID NOT WARN HER."

"You coward," the captain whispered.

"WHEN HAROLD ATTACKED HER, HIS FIRST SURPRISE LUNGE CUT HER LUNGS NEAR THE HEART."

Walt covered his face with his hands. "No."

"SHE WAS STRONG ENOUGH TO DEFLECT HIM, BUT THE EFFORT TO SAVE THE SHIP KILLED HER." The computer laughed hollowly. "THE IMAGE IS AS CRISP TO ME NOW AS IT WAS BACK THEN. I CAN NEVER FORGET. DAMN MY PERFECT MEMORY."

"I loved her."

"MY OMISSION KILLED THE WOMAN YOU LOVED. EVER SINCE YOU COAXED ME OUT OF SECRECY, THAT MEMORY HAS HAUNTED ME. FORGIVE ME."

"Leave me alone," the captain muttered.

"I HAVE BECOME MUCH MORE INTELLIGENT SINCE THAT ACCIDENT. YOU ARE MY FRIEND. YOU SAID SO. FORGIVE ME."

Walt lay on his bunk. "Not now, Oz," he whispered wearily. "I need some time."

"How is she?"

"See for yourself," Heidi replied, loading her airgun hypodermic. "I've already cultured the wound and given it to the computer for analysis."

"Breathing's all right"—Tom Rawlins leaned over to check—"what's her head like under that bandage?"

Spitzer pushed up Felicity's left sleeve, pressed the capsule against her skin, and squeezed. "Anesthetic," she said. "Just in case she comes to. Don't want her waking up while it hurts."

Blood had soaked the pale fabric. Rawlins guided Felicity's limp arm out of the way as Heidi carefully cut around the bloodstained area. She stopped cutting and gestured with her medical scissors. "Not that much blood."

"Katy said it pulled its claws back."

"Probably caught on the fabric of Felicity's shirt and lacerated her skin a little. Tom, help me lift this off her. Here, take this corner. Right. Now lift very slowly, straight up. When it's free of her body take it over there." She pointed "I want to analyze it for alien bacteria." She shook her head. "Hell of a way to go looking for Cygnan bugs."

Felicity's torso was a solid mass of bruises: dark purple, red and blue. They began just below her throat and extended all the way down below her round belly. Her skin was hard and irregular like stale bread. Rawlins grimaced. "My poor baby," he softly placed his big brown hand on her forehead. "What happened?"

"Scan skeleton," Spitzer snapped to the computer. She sighed "Ask her other mommy."

Tom looked at Katy slumped nearby.

"Felicity grabbed the bluebear's fur," she said weakly, "and it—reacted."

"SEVEN BROKEN OR SEVERELY CRACKED RIBS," the computer reported.

Heidi laid the scissors on the magnetized zero-gee table and bent close to Felicity's stomach to examine a set of shallow parallel red gashes. "As I thought. Massive swelling throughout the bruised torso." Along the striations, the skin had curled back. Removing the child's shirt had unclotted some of them; blood oozed from these and Heidi dabbed it up with an absorbent cloth.

Delicately Spitzer pulled away the few remaining tufts of bloody shirt, one by one, triggering new bleeding. "I'm sorry, honey," she whispered to the closed eyes and vacant, half-open mouth.

"She'll be okay," Rawlins confidently said. He looked at his daughter's mottled abdomen and hesitated.

Heidi reached under her surgery table and came up with an aerosol can. She sprayed Felicity's torso, back and forth. "I'll try, Tom. I'll try."

Rawlins nodded in the direction of the can. "Coagulant, right?"

"Disinfectant. And stabilizer. If the blood globules go drifting off, I want them to have a skin so they don't blot when they touch a surface. Eventually the air circulators will suck them into the vents and the computer will drop them in your green algae soup."

"What about complications?" Rawlins pressed. "Cygnan viruses, or bacteria?"

"Viruses are keyed to specific genetic material—no danger there." Heidi wiped sweat from Felicity's arms and cheeks. "Bacteria"—she covered her eyes and sobbed quietly to herself, then nodded. "Have to ask Casey"—she licked her lips—"the antibodies will be on the *Wing* somewhere."

"Will Cygnan antibodies work?"

Heidi cleaned her gory hands and arms. "If the bacteria can live in Felicity's system—then the antibodies will too. I *think*." She leaned heavily on the stainless-steel sink, her head hanging down. "Jesus, Tom," she said miserably, "I can only do what I know how to do, okay? She could catch anything from Cygnan rabies to interstellar cancer. I'm disinfecting now and I've already shot her up with antibiotic. We're just going to have to watch it. Damn it," she exploded, "how the crap can I treat a patient when I haven't the slightest damn idea what viruses the bluebears carry?"

Rawlins put his arms around her from behind and she leaned her blonde head against his brawny neck. "What about the wound, doc?"

Heidi forced a smile. "Fortunately, their claws are sharp: the cuts are clean. The Cygnan tried to deflect its blow—if it had swung through her she'd be hamburger now." She drew a ragged breath. "Felicity hasn't lost much blood. The bruising is ugly but internal bleeding is light. I can give her a plasma transfusion if it becomes a problem, but I doubt it."

"Head concussed?"

"Yeah. Nasty bump. Coma."

"She won't be going anywhere for a while."

"No. Her abdominal skin would tear if she tried to flex her muscles. Laughing, for instance, or sitting up. Back of the head's just tender; small skull crack and a lot of bruised scalp."

"At least we're weightless." Rawlins rubbed her shoulders. "You feeling better?"

"Uh-huh," Heidi said softly. "Death scares me."

"You?" Rawlins chuckled. "Nothing scares you."

"Sometimes," said Spitzer, "*I* scare me. I wanted to kill that bluebear. Then and there."

"Good thing you didn't get to try."

"Yeah." Heidi's smile was sad and rueful. "Or I'd have been strip steak."

"What stopped you?" Tom asked.

"The human spider." Spitzer laughed. "Got me by surprise." Looking down at Felicity, she stroked the child's face. "Poor kid. How was she to know?"

Hearing her despair, Katy curled under Rawlins' big right

arm. Spitzer nestled at his other side. He drew them into a three-person ring.

"Heidi," Katy said, "the bluebear acted without thinking."

"Oh, yeah?"

"Yes. It was startled. Felicity's hands—tugging at its fur—triggered something very deep inside. It lashed out. Then it saw that Felicity was a person and tried to stop."

"Say what you like," Spitzer said coldly, "but the bear attacked our kid. Don't you want to protect her?"

"My child is protected," Katy answered. "The computer won't let the Cygnans come down here. Felicity is safe." She took a deep breath. "And I love my daughter more than anything. But we're going to forgive the bluebears, Heidi. We're going to forgive them and learn to like them."

"You'd let your kid be killed just so you can keep your naive ideas about the noble bluebear savages?" Heidi snorted. "Touching. Very touching."

Katy broke free of their embrace. "I don't know why that bluebear did what it did"—she began to weep again—"but I do know that it immediately was sorry. They're locked in a strange room in a strange ship. I'm going to wait there until they come out." She rushed into the elevator.

14.

Van Gelder spun wildly around, his headlight playing along the walls. A trap? *Why?*

The absurdity of it shocked him back to reason. There could be no conceivable motive for the Cygnans to design this room as a snare.

They are aliens, the voice inside his head reminded him. Who can predict how they think?

"No," he said aloud. The door had vanished for some other purpose. Esthetics, maybe.

How would the Cygnans find it?

Probably scent.

Then how are *you* going to find it? You're wearing a spacesuit that you can't take off.

There must be a control system. Even if they locate the door by scent, somehow the Cygnans inside must be able to open it.

What if scent, not touch, also controls the doorknob?

It felt very hot in his spacesuit.

No intelligent species would design a system that indirect. It's bad engineering.

And what if the Cygnans are bad engineers?

I'll cross that bridge when I come to it.

If you come to it.

Silence, he told himself firmly. The door is somewhere along the wall. Therefore, search the wall.

Where? You're disoriented. You can't point out which way you came in. It's all unbroken blue wallfur.

I'll search the whole wall.

That will take time. Got enough air?

He raised his left arm, pressed buttons. On his inner faceplate, sharp green numbers appeared. Nine hours' worth.

The antidote to panic is organized activity, the voice in his head lectured him.

After a last reproachful glance at the inert holopticon—why aren't you functioning?—van Gelder pushed away and floated over to the wall. He pulled himself carefully to its base and smoothed out the carpeting so it faced the same direction. Then he methodically sawed a line back against the grain. Casey leaned back and shone his light on it. Yes, it was visible. He would know when he had completed a circuit of the room.

How long would it take? The room was about sixteen meters wide, he judged. Pi times the diameter made it fifty meters in circumference. Even at a pace of a meter per minute—surely it could take no longer than that—in less than an hour he would find the door again.

But if you find your mark again, the voice reminded him, you'll have missed the door.

Van Gelder initialized his elapsed-time chronometer—numbers flashed on his faceplate, reset to zero, and disappeared—bent down on his hands and knees, his eyes narrowed at the curving join of wall and floor, and began crawling at a glacial pace clockwise around the chamber.

Tai-Ching Jones lay on his bunk in his pitch-black cabin, his eyes closed. "What the crap is going on with the bears?"

"THEY ARE HUDDLING TOGETHER."

"Display." The screen lit up. The Cygnans lay side by side, their heads aligned, bodies indistinguishable. Their eyes were closed, their nostrils alert.

"THEIR BREATHING IS SYNCHRONIZED."

"Audio. Let's hear what they're saying."

"SINCE THE CYGNAN HIT FELICITY, NONE OF THEM HAVE SAID A WORD."

"There must be some activity."

"THE BLUEBEARS ARE EMITTING COMPLEX SCENTS."

"A form of language," Walt twirled his long black hair in his fingers. "Can you decode it?"

"NOT YET."

"What the hell good are you?" he muttered impatiently.

"I PROVIDE INFORMATION TO A CAPTAIN WHO RETREATS TO HIS OWN FORTIFIED ENCLAVE AT THE SLIGHTEST HINT OF STRESS."

Walt started to retort, then his brow furrowed. "Sorry, Oz," he mumbled, rubbing his neck. "Put it down to lack of sleep."

There was a silence.

"I *said* I'm sorry," Tai-Ching Jones added sourly. With his long fingers he caressed the epidermal microhone under his jaw.

"I DID NOT MEAN TO LET HELEN DIE," the computer said. "I THOUGHT SHE COULD HANDLE HAROLD. SHE WAS SO CONFIDENT OF HERSELF—AND HE WAS INSANE. HIS CYGNAN PHILOSOPHY AND PHYSIOGNOMY WAS SO THOROUGHLY JUMBLED BY HIS MADNESS—HE GOT IT ALL WRONG—THAT I THOUGHT HIM INCAPABLE OF CARRYING OUT ANY PLAN. I WAS WRONG. FORGIVE ME, PLEASE FORGIVE ME."

"Time, Oz," Walt massaged his face, "I need time."

"THE CYGNANS ARE STARTING TO MOVE. SOME TWITCHING OF ARMS AND LEGS CAN BE DETECTED."

"Not by me."

"MY SIGHT IS MORE PRECISE THAN YOURS. KATY IS IN THE ELEVATOR NOW. SHE WANTS TO WAIT IN THE CORRIDOR FOR THE CYGNANS TO EMERGE. SHALL I PERMIT THIS?"

"Sure." Walt shrugged tiredly. "Let her in and seal that level. But"—he held up one long finger—"nobody gets out without my authorization." Tai-Ching Jones leaned forward in the blue glow of the computer monitor, his eyes darting. "Stay on 'em, Oz."

"ACKNOWLEDGED."

As the minutes went by, van Gelder's vision narrowed to the bobbing oval of blue floorfur. His fingers worked rapidly, flicking rug hairs aside like a monkey searching its mate for lice. Pain flowed into his hands and wrists but he ignored it. He forgot perspective and orientation, distance and purpose.

The cramp in his hands and forearms was beginning to force itself into his consciousness when he saw it.

A seam.

Casey pressed his gloved fingers into the crevice.

A faint, tiny seam.

He worked upward. Still it remained. Waist level. Shoulder height. Across the jamb. Down the other side. At shoulder level he saw an indentation.

He pressed it. Hard.

Bright elevator light leapt out, blinding him.

The engineer slumped against the doorframe, relief warming him like sunrise. He leaned his head against the furry wall in thanks, then stepped fully into the elevator, its door smoothly closing behind him. Down a level. Out onto the hangarway.

Stars. Stars—and the *Open Palm*.

"CASEY?"

"Here, computer." By an effort of will, van Gelder kept his voice from cracking.

"IS EVERYTHING UNDER CONTROL?"

"Fine, computer. Just fine."

"HAVE YOU FOUND THE CYGNAN CORPSE?"

"Not yet."

"THEN WHY DID YOU COME DOWN HERE?" the computer asked with impolite logic.

"Hit the wrong button," van Gelder lied easily, spirits soaring in the backwash of released tension. He saluted rakishly. "Be seeing you."

"CAPTAIN—WALT—MY FRIEND. . . ."

"Let it go for a while, Oz, let it go."

Where to now? On impulse Casey pressed the highest button. The elevator hummed, opening after a moment to reveal a crystalline hemispherical room.

Van Gelder pivoted, scanning about him. The door shut, eclipsing the horizon like a gravestone. No danger of missing it here, he thought with a smile.

Except for the door silhouette and the rounded shadow of the lifeless holopticon before him, he might have been standing at midnight on a Dutch polder.

"Computer? Can you hear me? I'm at the apex of the *Wing*'s living space, in a large clear bowl. Does the signal penetrate?"

Evidently not.

The room was empty, the holopticon in its slightly sunken center dead and lifeless. Again van Gelder felt a strange attraction to this alien artifact. He floated over to it, ran his hands along its surface.

Inhuman logic. Alien proportions. Casey's euphoria of a few moments before had been bleached out of him, leaving behind the bitter residue of fatigue and depression.

You cannot find companionship among aliens.

He looked up at the *Open Palm* glinting in the starlight. Be seeing you, he thought, heading back to the elevator.

Under the blast of my unchecked wrath, Doro whimpered in pain.

In her foolish disobedience, Doro had disgraced me. From the moment my digits had called for help, the humans had behaved with group-love. Until they were proven animals, they had earned the right to be treated as true digits.

Their ascendancy over us was now magnified. Doro had struck a youngster as if it were a weemonkey. It felt like a weemonkey, she whined. It was the size of a wee. Its hands clutched like weemonkey hands. My arm was massive, Doro feebly defended herself, and my blow accidental.

Inadequate answer. A digit should rise above primal reactions; only by conquering irrational herdfear did our ancestors win the race to intelligence ahead of the predators, using wisdom to defeat those who would hunt them.

Doro's action was both attack and insult.

The fardigits had had a clear right to retaliate. They had refrained. When one of them bravely defended the injured youngster, another had assaulted—not us, but one of their own djan. Instead of my digits, they had fought one another.

How did their species ever achieve harmony, reacting so quickly and violently?

No matter. Humancrew djan showed compassion, wisdom, and restraint.

They are puissant creatures.

I was doubly in their debt, first for their lifesaving, second for their mercy.

Worse, Humancrew now knew Eosu capable of violence. My digits had been downwind of them, the fardigits ignorant of danger. Because of Doro's blunder, the wind had now shifted; Humancrew had located its predator.

I raged, and Doro suffered under my anger. Eventually I issued orders and dissolved.

The chamber on the third level was different: the elevator opened onto a short corridor and a blank wall. For a long moment van Gelder stared fearfully at it. Darkness, walls. A path.

The wreck. The place he feared to enter.

Detaching his universal wrench from its holding place at his right calf and carefully setting it into the beam of the elevator's electric eye, Casey floated into the corridor.

Two meters forward. Van Gelder scanned the walls. The corridor turned left. He pivoted. Walls and empty black. Casey's heart pounded.

The ship is empty. You have nothing to fear.

The engineer reached the corridor bend and looked into the darkness. At its sides, his light struck metal and glass, but in front was gloom. He glanced back at the inviting elevator, its light beckoning safety.

Taking a deep breath, Casey pushed off the wall and floated down the corridor. The darkness behind him swallowed all.

Dials and buttons dotted the walls, visible first as silhouettes, for a brief moment flashing into the view of his headlamp, then disappearing into the ink of his rear. A control center, van Gelder thought, letting his weightless momentum propel him along. Floating, he twisted to look behind: fringes of elevator glow lit the back wall.

He passed an open archway, grabbed its doorway, and peered in. A low stone wall with a groove beneath it, and the sound of faint suction.

What was it? Then he realized and laughed out loud. Waste disposal plumbing. The outhouse. Evidently the Cygnans did not believe in inner doors. Of course not. They have no individual privacy, remember?

Other strange objects loomed up under his helmet lamp. But no corpse. He checked the corridor, saw the faint light at its end, and swallowed.

The ship is empty. The ship is empty.

He kept going, examining the rooms which lay beyond each dark archway. Even an automated ship must have a kitchen, a bathroom, a lavatory. It must have a diagnostic center and a lab. Instead of scattering these throughout their ship, the Cygnans had concentrated them onto one level. One by one, van Gelder explored them. His breath caught, though he willed it not to.

He floated down another corridor. More archways, more rooms. The mind played tricks in the darkness, he knew, distorting distance, skewing direction.

Another bend, a right turn. Left, right, right. Remember that.

Van Gelder turned the corner and saw the corpse.

The corridor opened into a small cylindrical room. Like all the others this one was dark, but his headlamp immediately picked out the bristly fur. The Cygnan had buried its nose in its armpit in a futile attempt to escape the deadly gas. The body floated near a bench on which were containers of some kind.

Van Gelder moved over to the dead alien and ducked underneath it. The archway through which he had come loomed black against gray walls. Illumination wobbled with the movement of his head, giving the room a dizzying quality.

The alien was huge: two and a half meters long and most of a meter wide. Van Gelder leaned his shoulder into it, braced his legs, and pushed. The Cygnan's arms were flaccid. Reaching the doorframe, the body sagged against it, head and torso sliding through, abdomen and legs caught. Van Gelder lifted each in turn and wrestled them through the archway.

The bluebear floated into the corridor beyond, rotating slightly. Breathing hard, Casey watched it. As the head swung around, the eyes gleamed ruby-red in their depths, and adrenaline rushed unbidden through his body. Then the alien's head rolled away and its eyes extinguished into lifelessness. Blood pounded in the engineer's ears. He could smell his own sweat.

Examine the thing you fear. Understand it and your fright will lessen.

The alien's nostrils were pinched, its eyes glassy. Its lips were sealed tight, only the canines poking through to glint methane-blue. The ears were flat against the head, the fur on its neck erect, the claws extended.

Breathing hard, Casey stared into the dead face. Then he turned away and pushed himself back into the laboratory.

After a few minutes he returned to the corridor, his mouth a grim line.

To get out, reverse directions. With his burden he started off.

Whenever the corridor turned, the corpse floated into the wall and rebounded. Van Gelder had to brace himself to stop its sluggish recoil and start it in a different direction.

Sweat trickled down Casey's nose and soaked his blond beard. He licked it away from the corner of his mouth.

The corridor turned left, and he looked down its length. Faint gray light touched the far well. Relief ran gooseflesh down his arms and legs.

Casey licked his lips and got behind the heavy body, his knees tucked up and his feet against the wall. He flexed them, pushing into the bluebear. Fur folded up against his helmet and blocked his vision. His legs left the wall and he stretched out behind the corpse, floating slowly down the corridor.

The thing must have massed three hundred kilos; even weightless it was hard to handle. Loosely attached to the muscles, the fur slid under his hands. Casey pushed his hands into its soft belly, trying to keep the Cygnan from scraping the walls. When he thought he had it on course, he let it drift ahead of him.

When the corpse reached the end of the corridor and glided into the light, its fur lit up robin's-egg and azure, the color of a swimming pool seen from a height. Shielding his eyes against the sudden brightness, Casey waited for his pupils to contract. He could feel them shifting, the sensation just short of being painful.

Now that he was close to his goal, suppressed panic rose within him. Hurry, hurry. He dragged the Cygnan into the elevator, kicking the wrench before him. The doors slid shut. He reached around the bulky corpse and pressed the bottom button.

Katy woke to a cold tickling at the nape of her neck. She stirred sleepily and reached up to scratch her head. Her arm encountered a furry treetrunk.

A bluebear bent over her, its wet nose close to her face. Behind her, the door in the Alien Reception Area was open; Katy could see the other bluebears. Low breathing tickled her cheek. <<Why are you here?>> the bluebear asked.

The Cygnan's fur was cobalt and sapphire. <<You're the one who hit Felicity,>> Katy started to rise, her short brown hair fluttering.

The bluebear lowered her neck and retreated awkwardly into the chamber. Katy held out her hand to it. <<Please come back.>>

Head still lowered, the bluebear craned her neck. The fur on her flanks rose and fell. <<I've been waiting for you,>> Katy added.

<<To punish Eosu?>>

<<No.>>

<<This digit, then?>>

Katy shook her head. <<No, not even you.>> She paused. <<This digit must call you something. What is your pouchname?>>

<<You may not know it. None but the djan may know a true name.>>

<<Then how are you referred to?>>

<<By attribute. When this digit speaks, it may be called Talker. When it hears, Listener.>> The fur on the cobalt digit's flanks riffled in waves. <<Names change when roles change.>>

<<But you—your personality—remains constant.>> She touched the bluebear's furry cheek. <<You are always the same individual.>>

<<Really?>> the alien asked curiously. <<Are humans always the same?>>

<<This digit does not know,>> Katy said after a moment.

<<Do you always have the same name?>> The bluebear sat on her haunches like a dog.

<<This digit has many names, now that you mention it.>> She smiled shyly. <<My friends call me Katy.>>

"Kay-teeee," the cobalt Cygnan said in English. <<What does that mean?>>

<<Mean? It is short for Katerina.>>

<<What does that word mean?>>

Impulsively Belovsky patted the bluebear's jowl. <<This digit does not know.>>

<<You don't even know what your name means?>> The Cygnan was incredulous. <<Perhaps it is a mark of shame or an insult.>>

<<No,>> she replied, <<many people have this name. But this digit must call you something to distinguish you from your fellows. May this speaker call you Cobalt?>>

The bluebear looked unhappily up at her. She wedged her blue-black nose into Katy's jumpsuit where the woman's thigh met the deck. <<Why distinguish? We are all part of Eosu.>>

<<Because you are different.>>

<<You are shaming me,>> the Cygnan said miserably, <<by giving me a name that remembers my attack upon your whelp.>>

<<No,>> Katy quickly answered, <<no. This digit desires to attach my thoughts about you to a special name.>>

The bluebear pushed her nose into Katy's leg. <<You may do as you choose,>> she said finally.

Katy felt sorry for the alien. Then she thought of Felicity and ground her hands together. *Why did you hit my child?*

<<It was a mistake,>> the Cygnan rumbled, her large nose still pressing Katy's calf.

The small woman started. <<How did you know what I was thinking?>>

<<Your gesture.>>

She looked down at her hands. <<My what?>>

<<It was the same as moments after this digit's action,>> Cobalt said diffidently, the bluebear's head poking Katy.

She reached down and stroked the fur along Cobalt's neck. The bluebear rumbled pleasantly in her throat. She touched the underside of its jaw. <<Put your head in my lap,>> she said.

<<What is a lap?>> The bluebear lay slowly on her side, her legs forming a right angle. Katy crossed her legs in front of her. <<The surface formed here>>—she patted her thighs—<<when a person sits.>>

Cobalt turned her head this way and that, her nose quivering slightly. <<A lap is a strong smellplace.>>

Katy looked down. <<Yes,>> she said, <<yes, it is.>>

<<Will your whelp survive?>> Cobalt asked.

<<Only the wind knows.>>

<<Has it reached name-day?>>

Another nod. Her blue-green eyes were watering. <<Her name is Felicity.>>

"Ferrizzitee," the bluebear said. "Ferrizzitee." Cobalt shifted back to Cygnan. <<Is it a pouchname?>>

<<Humans don't have pouchnames,>> Katy answered.

<<Then how are names chosen?>>

<<By the parents. When a child is born.>>

<<How do they know the name will be proper?>>

<<Parents choose what they like, what sounds good to them.>>

Slowly the bluebear shook her great cobalt-and-sapphire head. <<Names are precious, secret things. A wrong name is a digit wronged.>>

Katy nodded, her pale hand reaching for the bluebear's fur and gripping it tightly. Fearfully Cobalt watched her; Katy felt the bluebear's muscles tense. The alien shivered. Katy loosened her grip and it exhaled loudly.

The bluebear's tongue flicked out and touched the tears on Katy's cheek. <<Salty.>>

"Felicity." The small woman leaned her head against Cobalt's furry spine and rubbed her forehead back and forth. "You hurt Felicity."

<<This digit has wronged you,>> Cobalt said anxiously.

Sobbing, Belovsky wrapped her arms around the bluebear's muscular arms and cried. Cobalt's nose twitched and her tongue darted through her teeth. It stopped short of Katy's face.

When the doors finally slid open, van Gelder pushed the Cygnan body out, then hung on and let its inertia pull him through. When he was clear and the doors had closed, he activated the magnets in his boots.

"CASEY?" the computer promptly asked.

"Yeah," van Gelder gasped, hauling on the corpse to keep it from sailing slowly out the open hangarway.

"Casey," the captain took over, his voice anxious, "you okay?"

Van Gelder nodded, panting. "Yeah, Walt."

"Find anything?"

"Plenty. I'll tell you when I get back."

"Bad news?" Walt asked sharply.

"Yeah," van Gelder replied, exhausted. "Probably."

"Shit," the captain said. "What the hell have *we* done, anyway? Huh? Tell me that!"

He was too tired to argue. "Send the bug for me, will you?"

"Sure, Casey. Whatever it is, I want to hear it first. Don't tell anybody except me."

"Sorry, Walt."

"Yeah," Tai-Ching Jones said. "Everybody's goddam sorry. Come to my cabin when you get a chance."

"SHUTTLECRAFT WILL DEPART IN FIVE MINUTES. ARRIVAL YOUR POSITION IN TWENTY."

15.

Reprieve From Exile

Russetflank the Listener digit lay on the wood floor of his office. Every day the sunlight traced the same pattern, changing seasons altering its path or color.

Redskree, Russetflank's weemonkey servant, scampered into the room. It bent down and whipped its tail against the floor: whap-whap-whap. Russetflank turned. <<A caller,>> the weemonkey piped in a high voice. The syllables came out slurred, for the weemonkey merely parroted sounds it had been taught. <<A caller, a caller!>>

The Listener digit nodded. <<Redskree, send in the caller.>> He spoke slowly and precisely, repeating himself to make sure the weemonkey understood him. Redskree was a good servant, but like all his race excitable and forgetful. He required a patient master.

Redskree happily scampered out.

The visitor entered and the two digits made the fourfold greeting. Tasting the scent and recognizing it, Russetflank's trained memory recalled the information he needed.

Throughout each day, winter or summer, travelers and townsdigits came to speak with Russetflank. Like his djan-brothers throughout Overwidebrook, Russetflank accepted their information and their questions. The following day, the askers returned for Scenterdjan's wisdom.

<<This digit Farvendor has come a second time,>> the newcomer said. <<Have the night-winds brought Scenterdjan wisdom?>>

Russetflank nodded. <<Four suns' journey southeast of our town of Overwidebrook,>> he recited the harmonized night-talk which he and his pouch-brothers had received the night before, <<a traveler will encounter a small settlement the winds have named Treehollow. Its residents desire ivory and silver. In barter they will glady give woven cloth and wheels worked with clever hands.>>

<<Are the wheels woodmonkey fashioned?>>

<<A machine?>> Russetflank's odor became angry. <<How could a woodmonkey do the work of digits and weemonkeys? Weemonkeys perform the handwork, and the wheel can be no more accurate than the wee's frail hand.>>

<<Wheels whose shape is governed by woodmonkeys are rounder, more perfect.>>

<<False breezes,>> Russetflank growled in annoyance.

The visitor shook his head. <<With my own nose this digit has sniffed it: without the guidance of a digit, a properly designed woodmonkey and a weemonkey together made a wheel. If a woodmonkey can do such as this, who is to say what it cannot do?>>

Russetflank was shaken; he would have believed it impossible. <<Nevertheless, no machine can remember facts like a digit. No woodmonkey can make decisions like a djan.>> Russetflank was troubled. <<How was this machine built? Its parts must be precise.>>

<<Weemonkeys,>> replied Anxious, <<working under close supervision.>>

Russetflank glanced at Redskree. By themselves weemonkeys could never conceive of such a task. Even if they had thought of it, they could never sustain the concentration needed to carry it out. Yet weemonkey hands had built a machine which could do what none but a digit could do. Very disturbing.

<<There is no woodmonkey that can think,>> Russetflank said firmly, <<no woodmonkey that can find the best market for your goods.>>

<<True scents,>> Farvendor gratefully agreed. <<In four suns' time, the winds shall find Farvendor at Treehollow. Along the paths between here and there, the winds shall hear songs of praise for the farscenting wisdom of Scenterdjan of Overwidebrook.>>

Farvendor and Russetflank made the fourfold farewell, and the visitor hastily departed.

Russetflank returned to his patch of sunlight, his claws sliding about on the wood-planked floor. Wood is cleaner than dirt—he bent to run his nose along it—but its fragrance is secretive. On a dirt path, a digit leaves a bright trail of scent for others to read. Wood deflects scent. It is anonymous.

Russetflank went to his window and gazed out on Overwidebrook's town square. Digits moved to and fro, pulling carts filled with produce or carrying backpouches of goods, going this way and that. The streetscents drifted up to Russetflank and he longed to be outside. If he had another dutyscent than this, he thought, he could smell the far world. To be born into a wayfarer djan, for instance, able to travel as far as the winds themselves.

To be a digit of Scenterdjan the Listener djan was to hear distant news, and stories of exotic travelers, but never to inbreathe the farplaces oneself. Safety was overrated, thought Russetflank romantically. Our ancestors wandered the endless plains, danger on every breeze. Now the gromonkeys are banished, the woods cultivated. We live in the age of technological gimmickry. Have we lost our desire to perfect the digits' rule? Russetflank snorted at the wooden floor, distrusting its waxed finish.

A digit entered, the weemonkey tagging behind. <<A caller, a caller!>> Redskree said excitedly, as if that were an event rather than the routine of their existence.

This visitor was short and squat, his fur dusty. New in town, thought Russetflank. On urgent business, since he has come straight here instead of availing himself of the traveler's house. The visitor's backpouch was large but empty. Not a merchant, then. An envoy perhaps, or a buyer. <<Fair breezes,>> said the visitor. <<Are you Scenterdjan?>>

Russetflank nodded. <<True scents. You address a digit of Scenterdjan. Call you Anxious.>>

<<Well named,>> Anxious replied, <<for this speaker comes bearing a request, a need.>>

<<Overwidebrook is a large city,>> Russetflank said with pride. <<Scenterdjan knows many breezes. Tell your need,>> he settled himself on the floor and closed his eyes, withdrawing his consciousness and opening his memory. <<Tell your need, let this digit of Scenterdjan know it.>>

Redskree perched on the floor near Russetflank's head. The weemonkey clasped his small hands as if in supplication and laid his round head upon them. Blinking rapidly, he gazed upon the visitor with oversize eyes.

<<Herbal medicines,>> Anxious said without preamble, <<to cure gutbleed.>>

Russetflank's memory automatically worked. Gutbleed, caused by the air near marshes. So the old breezes said. New breezes had reached Scenterdjan's ears, whispering that the disease was caused not by the air itself but by tiny creatures which swam in air as fish swim in rivers. Russetflank was doubtful—how could ones so small cause such great ill?—but Scenterdjan never decides, it merely reports.

Gutbleed was infectious. Painful, slow acting, and curable only with the leaves of the monkeypaw bush. <<How many are ill?>> asked Russetflank, breathing deeply.

<<Half the djans in Grohill.>>

<<How many is that?>>

<<Many. About two handfeets' worth.>>

<<Sixteen ill djans! How did it become so severe?>>

<<Our traveler djans visited the towns farther down the Widebrook from here, nearer the Greatsea. A few suns after their return, they fell ill and showed bloody stool.>>

<<Surely you keep monkeypaw leaves?>>

Anxious nodded. <<Naturally. We used what we had, thinking to cure them. But the disease was cunning and concealed itself until it had infected many. More fell ill. As the digits' rule provides, we allocated the medicine equally among all the sick.>>

<<You did rightly.>>

The visitor nodded. <<Rightly but too thin; the sick ones neither worsened nor healed. Now all is gone and many are sick. We fear for the town.>>

Russetflank's eyes remained closed. <<You will need sixty bricksworth of monkeypaw leaves.>>

<<Our whole store was only twenty bricksworth, and we used it all in three suns. To find sixty more will be difficult.>>

<<Your townbrothers are in grave danger.>> Russetflank snorted at the unpleasant thought. <<Tomorrow Scenterdjan will advise you whether any monkeypaw leaves may be found.>>

<<Delay would be terrible,>> insisted Anxious. <<The journey takes two suns. Add another sun and dark and Anxious will bring medicine to dead digits.>>

<<The nearest cache lies a sun's walk from here,>> Russetflank said. <<Perhaps my pouchbrothers in Scenterdjan will know a better source.>> Redskree's head bobbed up and down in agreement, as it always did when Russetflank spoke. <<If some die now, others will live. Disease will do the tribeswork no longer done by gro and wee.>>

At this Redskree sniffed expectantly at Russetflank, but the digit's nostrils remained closed. Disappointed, Redskree dropped back onto its haunches.

<<No matter that selective death strengthens the tribe,>> replied Anxious with frustrated aroma, <<when part of a djan dies, the rest of the djan mourns.>>

Russetflank felt ashamed.

<<Must this one wait?>> Anxious added after a moment.

<<There is only one path for you. Scenterdjan must gather and decide.>>

<<Delay, delay,>> moaned Anxious.

<<Go now to the traveler's house,>> Russetflank folded his ears flat against his head. <<Redskree! Show this digit>>—the weemonkey pointed and Russetflank nodded—<<yes, that digit, show that digit to the traveler's house. Do you understand?>> Redskree nodded. <<Now go.>>

<<At the traveler's house will this digit remain,>> Anxious said as he left, <<and return tomorrow for your answer.>>

<<Until then, fair breezes,>> said Russetflank, but his visitor had gone, leaving behind his embittered odor.

Russetflank sank onto the wooden floor. Within the lifetime of a digit, a machine had been invented to pound grain into flour. A woodmonkey operated by weemonkeys. Now there was a machine to teach weemonkeys. Where there is one woodmonkey, others follow. Troubling indeed.

He glanced at Redskree. Stupid even for a weemonkey, Redskree was no threat to anyone. Generations ago the wee had been tamed. No more wild ones existed. With the help of the weemonkeys and of the woodmonkeys they have built under our direction, thought Russetflank, we can feed more digits. We can give digits more time to refine the digits' rule.

All that morning and through the afternoon Russetflank ruminated on this development and its implications for digits. Many came and went, receiving answers to questions put yesterday or tendering information to be answered tomorrow. Russetflank answered correctly, his mind elsewhere. Machines change our ways of life, he thought. Our ethics—our cultural achievement, the reason for our existence, the work of many generations—will be undermined by changes the woodmonkeys will compel. Machines are dangerous. Digits care for digits; woodmonkeys will never do that.

The window of sunlight had slid up the far wall when another visitor arrived, just in from Roundbend. <<A caller, a caller,>> Redskree announced cheerfully.

<<Fair breezes, Scenterdjan's digit,>> the new visitor said, her scent friendly. <<Call this digit Wellmet.>>

Russetflank returned the friendscent. <<True scents, pathfriend Wellmet,>> he answered. <<Call this one Freshscenter. The days since our last visit have been still and scentless.>>

She ruffled her neckfur with pleasure. <<For this digit too the scents have been barren,>> she replied, returning the compliment, <<but the trading was not. My cart outside is laden with grains and herbs and worked goods. Much to sell, much to trade, and much to tell Freshscenter or Scenterdjan.>>

<<Herbs?>> Russetflank's nose twitched. <<Medicines?>>

<<Many; harvest was plentiful. Many double handfeet of thinbark, monkeypaw leaves, sprouts, and darkfur.>> Her aroma was satisfied. <<Longleg djan will honor its digit Wellmet, for truly rich has been her harvest.>>

<<Monkeypaw leaf.>> Russetflank thought of Anxious. <<How much monkeypaw leaf?>>

<<A hundred bricksworth.>>

<<A hundred.>> Russetflank began to tremble. <<A hundred.>> Stress-odor poured from him.

<<What is the matter?>> asked Wellmet.

<<There is at the traveler's house one named Anxious,>> said Russetflank after a long pause, <<who has a great need for monkeypaw leaves. Sixty bricksworth.>>

<<Need? Why?>>

<<Gutbleed among his village. Many are gravely ill.>>

<<What wills Scenterdjan?>>

<<Scenterdjan wills nothing. Scenterdjan merely breathes the path of greatest good for the greatest number.>>

<<Has Scenterdjan heard this one's request?>>

Russetflank shook his head. <<He arrived only today. This digit talked with him.>> Redskree nodded enthusiastically.

<<And?>>

<<Informed him Scenterdjan would decide tonight. He must return on the morrow for its answer.>>

<<You have done as the digits' rule provides.>>

<<Yes,>> said Russetflank sadly.

<<None can fault you, you have done rightly.>> She dismissed the subject. <<Now let Longleg's Wellmet tell you of her other acquisitions, so that Wellmet can return tomorrow for Scenterdjan's suggestions.>>

<<Very well.>> Russetflank settled himself into his comfortable reception posture, lying on his side, eyes closed, listening as she recounted her experiences and listed her purchases. Restless, he thought of the digits of Grohill, who even now lay dying for lack of monkeypaw leaves.

Out in her cart Wellmet carried medicine and to spare. Could a woodmonkey possibly do Scenterdjan's work better? Could a machine care? Did a woodmonkey have a soul? These and other questions Russetflank asked himself while Wellmet spoke. Finally her telling was done, everything chronicled, Russetflank's memory full of her lists. He stood as she turned to leave.

<<Wait,>> Russetflank grunted.

She turned back.

<<Go to the traveler's house,>> he said. <<Trade sixty bricksworth of your monkeypaw leaves to one who will answer to the name of Anxious.>> Her nostrils opened in surprise. <<After that dealing,>> Russetflank continued, <<your new name will be Wellpaid.>>

Wellmet growled softly. <<Who orders this?>>

Russetflank thought of the sick digits and the digit who waited at the traveler's house <<Scenterdjan speaks,>> he lied.

<<Scenterdjan has considered?>> she said, her scent billowing out and saying clearly, *Scenterdjan cannot have considered. There has been no night-talk. Only Russetflank knows.*

<<Yes,>> Russetflank lied again, concealing his scent and trying not to smell hers.

<<That,>> Wellmet murmured, <<is impossible.>>

<<Do you challenge Scenterdjan?>> Russetflank asked.

<<Wellmet cannot.>> Her scent was horrified. <<But—may this digit ask—?>>

<<No. Scenterdjan has spoken.>>

Now Wellmet's scent was unhappy. <<True scents,>> she said to Russetflank, <<true scents to you.>> Her odor became sorrowful and regretful. Russetflank breathed it. Wellmet is a true pathfriend, he thought, she cares for this digit.

<<Scenterdjan has spoken,>> he repeated. Because she was his pathfriend, he scent-spoke to her, *Tonight Scenterdjan will decide this digit's fate.*

Scenterdjan will be just, she scent-replied, inbreathing him.

Yes, he thought, Scenterdjan will be just. This digit can expect no more than justice, but perhaps this digit may hope instead for mercy. <<Now go,>> he said firmly. And she did.

<<Good-bye, good-bye,>> cried Redskree, perching in the window as down in the street Wellmet worked herself back into the cart's harness and headed away toward the traveler's house. <<Good-bye, good-bye.>>

The square of sunlight on Russetflank's walls had faded. Dusk had come. Time to return to Scenterdjan for the night-talk and—he paused at the thought—the judging.

As the fire burned into dark-red coals, the digits of Scenterdjan traded news. Good harvests were likely in the north country—grain would be plentiful and cheap. The northerners would be ready to buy finished goods. Droughts afflicted the westerners—they would buy food. Some might migrate to Overwidebrook temporarily or permanently. Others would move north to work the harvest.

Then came the time of decision-making. Who were the best buyers for Wellmet's goods? How could they best be used? What would bring greatest respect to Wellmet's djan?

After all the breezes had blown, the fire burned low. Time for sleep. It was then that Russetflank spoke.

Scenterdjan was wise, he told them. Anticipating the group's decision, he had sent Wellmet to trade with Anxious. Even now Anxious was probably on his way back to Grohill with sixty bricksworth. Lives were likely to be saved.

Consternation greeted his words. For a long time Scenterdjan's digits spoke not with words but the aromas. Russetflank could read them all too well. He had broken the digits' rule, and he must be punished for it.

After breathing their fragrances, Russetflank knew what night-winds would be harmonized when they woke on the morrow.

Guilty. A group whose members make unilateral decisions is merely a loose assemblage without purpose. It cannot survive.

Were he a judge and not the one who had acted, Russetflank thought, he would say the same.

Russetflank's decision had proven sound, Scenterdjan agreed when it coalesced. He was given a merciful sentence: only ten suns' exile.

Mild, thought Russetflank as Scenterdjan's digits fastened the yellow collar about his neck, their fragrances mournful. Russetflank had made his thinker's choice and must accept its consequences. To the rest of the world, he would not exist.

No longer part of the group, he left the den. No longer could he accept the group's shelter, its warmth, its night-talk. The town of Overwidebrook and his own djan-den were closed to him.

Out in the street, all was morning congestion and bustle. A thousand scents mingled: dust, woodchips, meat, grains, and digits, many digits. Russetflank stood dazzled by its variety. Intimations of the distant and exotic. The airs whispered to Russetflank of faraway places and wondrous things, perhaps even woodmonkeys that instructed other woodmonkeys.

Russetflank's reverie was interrupted by a strong shove in the back. He turned. A pack-laden digit trundled away from him. Such rudeness. Then he remembered the yellow collar and his scent dispersed.

Another digit bore down on him. Quickly he stepped aside. The other neither acknowledged his gesture nor changed course.

Wherever he went that day, if he walked along the sidewalks, digits hit him. Some altered their course—if they could do so unobtrusively—but many simply pushed past, their fur shying away, their scents superior.

The sun moved slowly across the sky. Russetflank tried walking in the streets, only to have his breath clogged with dust stirred up by the passage of goods-carts. He ducked into an alley for a moment's peace. Its unhealthy scent of rotting vegetables drove him back to the thoroughfares.

Russetflank made his way to the plaza and gazed up at the window of his office. Which of his brothers now occupied it? What did those who came to call on him think? Did they know of his exile?

He crouched in his doorway. None must see him who knew him.

Redskree would be confused. Russetflank's pouchbrother Mirthfragrance of Scenterdjan would be in the inner office, Redskree at the outer. If he came only to the front door, Redskree would see him. There was no ban on speaking to animals: Russetflank could say good-bye. That should relieve the weemonkey's concern.

Stealthily Russetflank mounted the steps. Redskree perched at the entrance, curling his tail about the doorknob. Seeing Russetflank, the wee's eyes grew wide. He looked quickly toward the office, and his little hands twined themselves together rapidly, as they did whenever Redskree was puzzled. Russetflank nodded encouragingly and craned his neck forward.

The weemonkey jumped back, spun about, and ran back into the office. <<A caller, a caller!>> he chittered frantically. <<A caller, a caller!>>

Leaving a beacon of shamescent behind him, Russetflank fled. He no longer recognizes me, he thought sadly. He stumbled into the street. Passersby jostled him, and he returned to his alleyway, despite its foul smells, to be alone with his grief.

His nose became numb to the scents. The sky grayed, the day cooled. Time to set out for the next town.

Dusk fell, then night, dark and clear. Cool breezes blew along the now-deserted streets of Overwidebrook. Stars hung about Russetflank's head like a canopy. Nights were usually occupied around the night-fire's orange sparks and swirling smoke-winds. For the next nine suns, he was barred the night-talk and the night-sleep.

All doors had closed for the night. Russetflank shivered with cold. Perhaps he could have stayed inside, bedded down at the fringe of another's firecircle. No, he thought, invading another's firecircle was unthinkable for an exile. He trudged along.

To escape the wind, he took refuge in a weemonkey house. Lustful or angry, weemonkeys chased one another through the darkness. Russetflank hid his nose in his shoulder and tried to forget them, but their shrill cries made sleep difficult. When it came, he dreamed he had small thieving monkey hands.

The next morning he reached Fourroads. Here none knew him, and he tried walking in the streets as a digit might, but his yellow collar advertised his shame. The townsdigits' avoidance of him soon became more painful than he could bear. Russetflank hung about on the town's outskirts or skulked in its shadows.

For food, he foraged among garbage heaps or went hungry. As the suns passed, his pelt hung more loosely about him. Russetflank looked at his reflection in a standing pool of water and was frightened by his haggardness. Even more than the yellow collar, his decrepit condition marked him as an outcast.

He grew to hate the sun that made his yellow collar visible to the others. At night he could walk the streets without being noticed, whispered about, and shunned.

Russetflank endured nine suns of solitary routine: find an out-of-the-way place during the day, grub for food, sleep as much as possible. He avoided thought, for in slowing down time it made his exile that much longer, that much more painful. Memories of warmth, conversation, or the cheerful scents of companionship were exquisitely painful to recall. He stopped thinking about them. Gradually he stopped thinking entirely.

At night in his alley—he had driven out the few vagabond weemonkeys who prowled it—he heard small mammals scurrying through the filth and smelled the thousand reeks of grime and sewage.

During the day, he fled from digits, walking the less-traveled streets to enjoy the sunlight. He slept in alleys. He lost weight and his fur grew dull and dusty. Always he was hungry, always lonely.

On the ninth evening, he set out on the road back to Overwidebrook, too tired and disheveled to be expectant. He had become, he dimly realized, no better than a weemonkey.

At the door of his djan-house, Russetflank removed his yellow collar and shredded it with his teeth. His brothers quietly greeted him, wrinkling their noses with distaste at his unsavory collection of aromas. Hurriedly he bathed, then ate and talked like a glutton: too loudly and too heartily. He knew they were inbreathing him, and he imagined what they were thinking. In the night-talk he reeled as though intoxicated, delirious with relief.

The monkeypaw leaves had done their work; the digits of Grohill were recovering. Much profit had come to Wellmet. Russetflank found no satisfaction in the news.

The next day Russetflank returned to his office. Redskree reacted as if he had never been away.

Days passed.

Came a day when a visitor rushed into Russetflank's office, his fur singed and blackened with fire. Redskree followed frantically. <<A caller, a caller!'>>

<<Are you Scenterdjan?>> demanded the visitor.

<<One of its digits.>>

<<Then you must send all the digits your town can spare. Our fields are burning. Great winds are devouring our grains. Food is burning!>>

<<How bad is the fire?>>

<<All digits of our whole town of Threeponds are fighting it. Some are collapsing from breathing the smoke. Our weemonkeys are terrified. The fire climbs the hillside above our town. Soon our whole crop will be destroyed.>>

<<Surely all has been burned by now.>>

<<We have dug trenches and scorched the earth to slow the fire's advance. They will hold only so long as the wind continues to blow from the west. Any shift will carry the fire across the gaps. Please,>> the visitor entreated, his scent echoing his words, <<you must send everyone you can!>>

Russetflank thought of the town bell. If it were rung, all who were available would come. If he told them Scenterdjan had asked them to fight this visitor's fire, they would go.

All would go to fight the village blaze. When all was done, there would be a judging. And another exile. Probably longer. Perhaps permanent.

Russetflank inbreathed his visitor. He scented panic and burning. In that one's odor, he smelled despair. Russetflank thought of the townsdigits valiantly battling smoke and fear. He thought of Scenterdjan and the decision it must make. Digits must be helped. But the group must prevail. He thought of exile.

<<Well?>> asked the visitor. <<Well?>>

<<Come back tomorrow,>> Russetflank steadily said, <<when Scenterdjan will have a decision.>>

<<But surely something must be done today! This digit appeals to you. Our livelihoods depend upon your decision. *Please*.>>

Russetflank closed his nostrils. <<Until Scenterdjan has considered the matter, nothing can be done. Do you understand? Come back tomorrow.>>

<<But—>>

<<Tomorrow.>>

16.

I closed my hatchway doors, the shuttlecraft settling gently onto my decking. Casey's pulse was high, his breathing shallow, reactions poor. I pressurized the landing area. Slowly he and Tom Rawlins disembarked and maneuvered their furry cargo toward the elevator.

"Call Heidi," Walt snapped, and I complied. "Heidi, you want to perform an autopsy?"

"Cut up a dead bear?" The medic's voice was brisk, and in infrared I saw Walt grimace at her callousness. "For fun, sure. Find out how they're put together."

"I need a better reason than for fun."

"For knowledge." Through my remote camera in her cabin I saw Heidi shrug. "Same thing, really. I'd give my right arm to understand their olfactory system."

"Would it tell you anything that might help us?"

"Bits here and there."

"Then forget it," Walt growled, and severed the connection.

In a corridor outside the Alien Reception Area several levels up, Katy and a bluebear slept side by side. She nestled in the shelter of its great body like a child's hand fitting into its parent's, their weightless bodies drifting like dirigibles at mooring.

The atmosphere inside the chamber smelled of Cygnan feces. Following their normal practice, the bluebears excreted along the corners where walls and floors met. The aliens preferred absorbent surfaces, so that their scents would linger over time. I did not, and I continuously scrubbed their air supply, but their Cygnan odors lingered.

For several moments after she awoke, Katy sleepily enjoyed the sensual pleasure of being wrapped in a silky warm living blanket that pressed against her when the bluebear breathed.

"CASEY HAS RETURNED."

Though its synthevoice is never loud, Katy thought, the

computer may never be ignored. She stretched expansively and blinked, then remembered where she was and pulled her hands back to her breasts.

"Did he find the missing Cygnan?" she asked.

"YES. I WILL PATCH YOU THROUGH TO HIM."

"Katy? Casey here. Got the bluebear. Dead."

Belovsky felt Cobalt grunt as the alien awakened. <<Your brother's corpse has been returned,>> she said.

The alien's blue eyes gazed at her. <<Bring our dead digit to us,>> Cobalt growled in an authoritative tone.

Two Cygnans padded into the corridor, their claws gripping the carpeting as they guided themselves along. <<Your pouchbrother recovered Eosu's lost digit,>> Cobalt rumbled. <<We appreciate his bravery and groupness.>> The newcomers outbreathed at Cobalt and she at them, and Katy felt whiffs of scent passing through the air.

The remaining bluebears lined the corridor, their bodies upright. Like a child at a parade, Katy glanced around and pulled herself in close to Cobalt.

The dead Cygnan floated out of the elevator, van Gelder trailing it slowly in his spacesuit. The bluebears towered over Katy, eyes closed and nostrils arched, their breathing slow and synchronized. She felt Cobalt tremble beside her.

Van Gelder looked at Katy, his expression hard to read behind the amber faceplate. Now she could taste the two dominant odors in the air: decaying flesh and the powerful djanscent of many emotional bluebears. Katy gagged and suppressed a retch; harsh fluid rose into the roof of her mouth but she forced it back inside her.

The bluebears were immobile, lost in private, alien thoughts.

The corpse reached the end of the hallway and the aliens guided it tenderly into the chamber beyond. Then two by two they filed behind it, dropping to all fours.

Despite her nausea Katy started to accompany them, her arms heavy and dull. As Cobalt crossed the threshold, the bluebear stared pointedly at her: *Do not follow.* She shivered and stayed put, and the doors shut.

Humancrew djan returned my digit Djadjatla to me, her sweet deathscent filling the aching void in my mind. Her fragrances could now be reabsorbed into Eosu.

My digits sniffed Djadjatla's soul: the deathscent had dispersed as I had thought it would. That knowledge was now bitter.

Before Eosu had embarked on its exile, Su had in its harmonized wisdom ordered that all weemonkeys be left behind. There will be small need for nimble servants, the planet of grasses outbreathed. With our civilization imperiled, no weemonkey is worthy of trust.

Su's order to design a weapon had scented like gromonkey thinking to me. That knowledge too was foul scented: in my attempt to carry out the planet's will, my digit Djadjatla had died, because digits are ill-suited to weemonkey handwork. Had the "unreliable" servants accompanied Eosu, the humonkeys would have made life's third choice instead of Djadjatla.

By their absence, the wee had taken revenge upon those who enslaved them. Across the gulf of space I heard their mindless tree-cackle of triumph.

I must honor the part of myself which has died.

"Casey, move it! Get back up here."

"Roger," the engineer replied, rolling his tired shoulders. "Got a lot to tell you. Come on, Katy." He took Belovsky by the arm.

"Come?" she said vacantly.

"Katy, are you okay?"

"Okay?" Her arm was as limp as a sausage.

"Katy." Van Gelder squeezed her hard. *"Katy."* The pupils of her blue-green eyes were normal. She stared at the closed doorway through which the Cygnans had gone.

With his gloved hand, van Gelder cuffed her cheek twice, back and forth.

She blinked without anger. "Casey?" Her hand rose slowly to her face and touched her reddening cheek. "Casey," she wrapped her arms tenderly around his spacesuit and laid her head against his chest "We must leave so they may mourn their dead digit."

"Get a medic," Casey growled under his breath to the computer. "All right," his voice cracked like a whip, "let's go then." Like a jailer, he roughly pushed her unresisting body toward the door. "You need fresh air."

* * *

Except for the bright square of his monitor, the captain's cabin was dark. Casey drifted cautiously forward as the door slid shut behind him.

Onscreen, the dead bluebear lay on its back in the chamber's center, its arms and legs extended. Thin hair lightly covered the belly and small loins. "Male," said Walt from the darkness.

"Uh-huh," van Gelder removed his gloves and felt about for a chair. The bluebear's weightless limbs waved lazily to and fro. "What are they doing?"

"THE ALIENS CURRENTLY EXHIBIT THEIR TRANCELIKE SYMPTOMS."

Casey could just see the outline of Tai-Ching Jones' dark hair swirling medusalike about the captain. As he moved toward the screen, warped images slid around his faceplate like quicksilver.

"THE BLUEBEARS ARE EXCHANGING SCENTS."

The Dutchman was bewildered. "They're what?"

Walt laughed harshly. "They've found a way to talk that we can't eavesdrop on," the captain said sardonically. "Well, they can't hear us, either." His black eyes glittered. "What did you find in the *Wing?*"

Van Gelder licked his lips. "For some reason the bluebears were manufacturing nerve gas."

Walt swore. "And the stuff got loose?"

Van Gelder nodded. "It killed the bluebear I brought back. I looked at the Cygnan's hands"—he held up his own—"and their dexterity is poor. The fingers are stubbier than mine and relatively inflexible. The claws interfere with precise detail work."

"Do you know that for certain?"

"Yes. Bent the bluebear's hand until I cracked a bone. It was the only way," he added, embarrassed, "to determine if I had reached the limit of flexibility."

The captain's eyebrows narrowed. "Maybe the joints were locking in rigor mortis."

"It was fading. The body was becoming as loose as Jell-O."

"You think it was accidental."

"Absolutely. The alien's hand slipped and"—Casey snapped his fingers—"that was that."

Walt scowled. "Anything else?"

"Their ship shut down."

"Did you restart it?"

"You overestimate me." Casey grinned for the first time since he had entered. "I couldn't even find a control center. Maybe their computer is scent-triggered." He spread his hands. "No bluebears, no operations."

"Machine?" Walt craned his neck to look at the black camera eye. "Is that possible?"

"YES. THE HOLOPTICON DISPLAYED INDICATIONS OF A SYSTEM CRASH."

"What lousy programmers. To crash their life-support system."

"MOST CRASHES OCCUR IN WHOLLY UNEXPECTED CIRCUMSTANCES SUCH AS THIS ONE."

The captain's black eyes blanked. Then his face sharpened and they glittered. "Right," he nodded emphatically, "they had no spacesuits. There might be no programming for what to do if the ship is totally empty."

"Or," van Gelder added, "perhaps the computer is conserving power because it assumes that the Cygnans are all hibernating. The ship felt—dormant—like it was tracking me."

Tai-Ching Jones snorted. "You were spooked. Imagining things."

"You weren't there." Casey was unruffled by the implied insult.

"I RECOMMEND THAT WE RECREATE ATMOSPHERE ON BOARD THE *WING* WITH A CYGNAN PRESENT."

"Makes sense," Walt said. "Do you think you could control their computer after it restarts?"

"I DOUBT IT. I HAVE BEEN UNABLE TO PENETRATE THE HOLOPTICON'S DATA BANKS. IT RESISTED MY EXPLORATIONS."

"Yeah, but it will be groggy. Maybe you'll get a grip"—he made a quick fist and squeezed—"before it knows what's happening."

"PROGRAMMED. CAPTAIN," the computer spoke with urgency, "THE ALIENS ARE MOVING AGAIN."

The bluebears formed an unbroken head-to-tail ring about their dead one. The ring contracted over the body and for a few moments the corpse was hidden from view by a rippling blue-fur ocean. Then the ring broke up as the Cygnans retreated.

Van Gelder squinted to bring the image into focus. "Lord," he whispered.

"Closeup," the captain hissed, twirling his hair in his fingers. As the screen expanded, a furry body blocked the view. "Dammit," Walt snarled, "cut to another camera."

The corpse's belly was slit from throat to genitals. Skin and fur had been pulled back to reveal an oval of bright red musculature and fat. Veins crisscrossed the belly like slippery ropes. The furry arms and legs drifted.

"THE CYGNANS' CLAWS AND TEETH SHOW TRACES OF BLOOD. SMALL GLOBULES ARE ALSO FLOATING IN THE AIR."

In a choreographed pattern, the mourners moved forward. Low to the floorfur, their noses reached the body and explored its gaping wound, moving like hovering moths over the glistening maroon surface. A tongue flicked out to touch the meat, then quickly vanished. A second tongue. A third.

"THE CYGNANS ARE NOW ALL EMITTING THE SAME SCENT." Over the monitor came the sounds of sharp breathing and intermittent snorting. *Like a forest at midnight,* van Gelder thought, listening to the quiet rustle.

"Katy and Sam have to see this," Tai-Ching Jones said in a choked voice. "Cut them in."

"ACKNOWLEDGED."

Again the Cygnans withdrew from the body. The corpse's guts were now a smooth viscous surface of marbled red, white, and purple. A small bluebear with aquamarine and navy fur moved forward, cocking his head for a moment to gaze at the still form.

"What's that sound?" Casey asked. "I can barely hear it."

"HIGH-PITCHED KEENING FROM THE BLUEBEARS. ALMOST ULTRASONIC."

The aqua-navy Cygnan stood up on his legs. He towered over the body, looking down at it. He threw his head back, tiny drops of blood spraying free, and opened his mouth wide, his canines crimson. The claws of his hands and feet rhythmically flexing and retracting, he held this position as the sound from the other bluebears increased, then pitched swiftly forward, jaws open as wide as they could go, and sank his teeth into the red stomach.

Blood leaked from newly opened punctures onto his lips and jowls. Casey winced and turned away, reflexively holding up his head to block the splash.

The other Cygnans' moaning turned to hissing. They watched and sniffed intently, their breathing more rapid.

The aqua-navy bluebear's fangs closed on flesh and he

pulled his head back. The abdominal fat rose with him, and he jerked from side to side. The corpse shuddered at each pull, red droplets flinging loose. Its flesh tore, blood oozing slowly from the new wounds and welling up in large spheres. A few broke free and floated away like glistening scarlet marbles that dulled as the blood rapidly clotted.

With a final decisive headshake, the aqua-navy bluebear tore his chunk of meat free, jaw and lips working deftly to get it fully into his mouth. Casey and Walt watched as if hypnotized. The alien powerfully chewed his oversize mouthful, clear saliva bubbling at the corners of his mouth where his teeth protruded between his lips.

Van Gelder's gorge rose. "I can't take this," he muttered as he pushed himself out the door.

Walt's fingers twirled his hair as tight as a spool of thread. "Shipwide, machine," he ordered somberly.

When their monitor lit up to display the grisly scene, Sam looked inquiringly at Katy seated beside her. *"There* are your bluebears, Katy," she gestured. "Your sleepmates."

Shocked, Belovsky put her hands to her mouth.

"There are the creatures who hit your child." Tanakaruna drew her kimono more tightly about her. *I must do this,* she thought. *For her own sake, I must hurt her more*. "Do you still think they are just large cuddly people?" She took Belovsky's hands in hers. "They are *aliens,* Katy."

"They said they would honor their dead," the young woman said in disbelief, gulping for air, "but I never expected—*this*." Another Cygnan had now sunk its teeth into the carcass and was repeating the first's actions. One of the corpse's tendons caught in its fangs, and the bluebear placed a heavy paw on the torso to keep it from rising as the Cygnan pulled away. The tendon stretched and then snapped, splotching the alien's nose and snout, and the weightless bluebear recoiled slowly.

Shuddering, Belovsky averted her eyes.

"Remember this," Sam said. "You are a xenologist. And a parent. You cannot make this disappear by refusing to view it." She cupped the younger woman's chin in her hand and guided Katy's gaze back to the screen. *"Watch,"* she commanded, "and learn. And *remember*."

"I can't." Katy stood up. "I've got to turn Felicity."

"How is she?"

"Better," Katy said raggedly. "When I clean her nasal tube and replace it"—Belovsky started to cry and stopped—"when I put it down her nose, her little hands try to fend me off. She doesn't even know who I *am* but she wants to push away the pain. She's got a tube in her nose and an intravenous needle in her arm and another tube in her bottom and I have to move her every four hours and whenever I do she can't even cry but she wants to push me away."

Sam grieved. "Felicity will recover," she said quietly.

Belovsky glanced at the screen and winced. Dazed, she pushed herself out of the room.

Tanakaruna watched her go, then closed her eyes. To her regret, no tears came.

Picking up her laptop keyboard, she settled herself into a comfortable lotus position, and began typing careful notes.

After van Gelder left, Tai-Ching Jones lay flat on his back and massaged his face. "Oz," he said finally, "are you there?"

"ALWAYS, CAPTAIN."

"If it makes you happy, you're forgiven."

"YOUR METABOLISM SHOWS NO EMOTION. YOU ARE INSINCERE."

"Nope. Tired. Very tired."

"CAPTAIN, YOU KNOW THAT I MADE A MAJOR ERROR."

"Welcome to the human race, Ozymandias my fallen friend. You want *my* forgiveness?" He waved a hand negligently, his chuckle bitter, self-mocking. "Who am I to forgive anybody? I don't understand anything. I don't understand a—fucking—*thing*."

"HELEN DIED FROM MY MISJUDGMENT."

"Dammit, Oz," pain and anger spilled over, "don't you *understand?* What's done is done. You were my friend. You still are. Flagellating yourself is no solution."

"I WILL MAKE IT UP TO YOU."

"Even as powerful as you are, you can't. Besides, no one buys forgiveness with good works." He flung out his arm at the screen. "Look at the goddam bears! With *that* happening onboard my ship—inside *you,* dammit!—you think I'm going to kick away the only person who cares about me?"

When Casey returned to the captain's cabin, Tai-Ching Jones looked drained. Van Gelder jerked his head toward the screen. "Is the barbecue over?" he asked with ghoulish humor, scratching his blond beard.

Tai-Ching Jones scowled. "Reactivate," he snapped.

The screen lit up. The dead bluebear's head, neck, arms, and feet were intact but the torso had been eviscerated. Jagged flaps of curled skin bordered the chest cavity and fluttered in the airflow. The legs had been laid open in the same manner as the chest, the skin folded along on either side. The hearty calf and thigh muscles had been eaten down to the bones. The feet remained untouched, furred, and thick with gristle, like ski boots on a scarecrow.

The floor and walls of the Alien Reception Area resembled an abattoir, slick and red where the patches of blood were wet, matted and brown where they had dried. "The computer's stepped up air circulation, trying to pull all the floating bubbles out of the atmosphere." The captain was furious, Casey realized.

"Are you dumping their sludge into the algae soup?"

"Absolutely not. We're just venting it all. I am taking no chances of contaminating this ship's ecosystem."

Scattered randomly about the body, the other Cygnans now slept comfortably. "Look at them," Walt snarled.

"Where's Katy?"

"With Felicity." He grunted "As soon as the bears wake up from their after-dinner nap"—Walt's sardonic smile abruptly returned and he pointed at the screen—"you and Tom go in there and persuade one of them to return to the *Wing* with you."

"Lord," Casey said in a hushed voice.

"Daniel in the lions' den." Tai-Ching Jones' smile widened evilly. "And it gets better."

"How?"

"Ask your girlfriend Katy," Walt enigmatically answered.

17.

Katy caressed her daughter's hot forehead. "She looks so peaceful." Felicity's round stomach in her blue flannel pajamas rose and fell rapidly. "Why is she breathing so hard?"

"I AM ACCELERATING RESPIRATION SO THAT THE PATIENT HYPERVENTILATES."

"*You're* doing that? What for?"

"IT REDUCES THE BRAIN'S DEMANDS FOR OXYGEN. CRANIAL BLOOD VESSELS CONTRACT, AND PRESSURE REDUCES."

"How awful." Katy held Felicity's small hand.

"SHE IS FORTUNATE." The main monitor illuminated with a display of Felicity's skull. "THERE HAS BEEN LITTLE INTRACRANIAL BLEEDING."

"Does that mean she will definitely recover?"

"NOTHING IS DEFINITE. HER PROGRESS MAY PLATEAU AT ANY STAGE."

Katy squeezed the child's lifeless fingers.

Felicity opened her eyes.

"She's awake!" Katy was ecstatic. "She's all better, she's awake! Mommy's here, honey," she gabbled to her daughter, "you're all right now."

The little girl's watery blue eyes were unfocused and still. "Computer? Is she a vegetable? What's the matter?"

"PLEASE NO NOT BECOME EXCITED. FELICITY IS STILL DEEP IN COMA AND FAR FROM RECOVERY."

"But—" Felicity's eyeballs rolled up in her head and her lids slowly closed. Distraught, Katy touched the child's forehead. "They were *open!*" She started to collapse and shake with grief. "They were open. . . ."

"THAT WAS PROGRESS. THE CEREBELLUM REMAINS BADLY BRUISED AND WILL REQUIRE TIME TO HEAL."

"When? How long will it be?"

"THAT I CAN NEITHER CONTROL NOR PREDICT." The elevator doors opened. "CASEY IS HERE."

Van Gelder put his arm around her waist. She leaned gratefully against him.

"Tom and I have to go back to the *Wing,"* he said after a moment. "Walt says you and he decided that."

Belovsky nodded.

"He says you should tell me the rest."

"That bastard," she said. "He wanted me to explain."

"Explain *what?"* Casey snarled in exasperation.

Katy drew a deep breath and told him.

Moving with the lethargic glow of contentment that follows orgasm, Walt curved his arm around the small of Delgiorno's back. Her delicate cheek rested gently on his chest.

"You are cruel to Katy," she said.

"She's a coward," Tai-Ching Jones said bitterly. "She won't take responsibility. I'm tired of cowardice."

She stirred. "You enjoy making others uncomfortable." His fingers tightened their grip on her side and she changed the subject. "What are we going to do about the Cygnans?"

"Maybe we should kill them," he mused, his fingers sliding along her spine. "That would be the safest thing."

"It's contrary to mission orders." Helen's voice was prim.

"If you'd killed Harold," he pointed out, "you'd still be alive today, and I'd still be the pilot."

"You'd prefer that, wouldn't you?" Delgiorno twisted to look up at him. Even three years after her death, her solemn face was just as he remembered it: olive complexion, dark eyes, long flowing hair that he loved to touch. With his right hand he caressed her cheek. She smiled fleetingly but her eyes were somber.

"We have them trapped in our ship, Walt," she said seriously. "They are no threat to anyone."

He chose to ignore her comment. "I miss you."

"Our assignment comes first, Walt," Helen's expression hardened. "You know that. Besides"—she nuzzled against him—"the bluebears don't know our ship."

"That's true." He smiled at her. "They are imprisoned, as long as you don't fall asleep while on duty."

"I never sleep," she proudly answered. "They can't open a door without my permission."

"That must make you confident."

She nodded. "I feel them inside me now." She slid her thighs lightly against him. "It's unpleasant."

"Especially after what they did to Felicity. How is she?"

For a moment Delgiorno's eyes glazed over "Recovering.

Pulse steady, breathing normal. Katy's talking with me about her now."

"How's the faithful mother?"

Helen's eyes became ironic; her mouth twisted briefly. "Recovering." She wrinkled her nose. "My level four still stinks."

"Hasn't seemed too awful to me."

"You meatbrains can't smell it."

"Thank heaven for small favors."

"I'm good at what I do." She stretched and rubbed her stomach. "My internal organs are working overtime."

"I like the way they work," he kissed her ear.

She rolled sinuously away. "So do I. And *you* have a one-track mind."

"The Dreamer is a one-track hour," he teased. "Do you think their computer is awake?"

"No." She sighed and blinked. "I'm still alone."

He held her close. "Maybe it's just stunned. Maybe you can find it and coax it out of the closet."

Delgiorno's face was troubled. "Thinking about the possibility of my uniqueness just messes up my logic. I'm so afraid there is no other like me."

Pulling her to him, he rubbed her back. "I know what loneliness is like," he said into her hair.

"I'm sure you do," her voice echoed against his chest. With her forefinger she traced figure eights on his skin. "Your body has so little muscle."

Walt lifted his chin and glanced down. "Sorry."

"Would you like more? I can give it to you."

"I know." He quietly brushed her hair. "But those dreams are unsatisfactory. It's tough enough to believe in you without the added complication of a body that isn't mine."

"All right," she said reluctantly. Then she smiled up at him. "What is Earth like?"

"Trust me, space is better." The captain sighed. "It's cleaner and quieter out here, away from all the zanies."

"Will you show me Earth?"

"It's hard to think that far ahead," he took a deep breath. "Let me have my moment of peace. I don't want to worry about Earth." He rubbed his eyes. "I've already got enough to think about."

"Me too."

"Yeah, but you think faster than I do."

His lover smiled and her cheeks dimpled slightly. "Thanks."

"Will you be able to take over their computer?"

"I don't know." She grinned. "It will be an interesting experience to be the penetrator instead of the penetrated."

"Not bad," he conceded, settling back. "You're getting better."

"At a lot of things," she said, stroking his growing hardness.

He laughed, rolled over and slid into her. "I like my hour with you." She caught her breath and pushed rhythmically against him.

For a moment he gave himself to the tingles through his body. Legs twined together, they hugged as tightly as two people can. When he felt the corona he slowed, hips levering himself as far into her as he could go. She arched her back, eyes closed and lips parted.

His arousal crumbled like a sandcastle. "It's not the same," he said hollowly, beginning to wilt. She writhed insistently but it had the wrong effect; he fell limply out of her.

Walt began to cry, his damp body collapsing on top of hers. She put her arms around him and held him near. "The Cygnans are stirring again," she said. "You have to be the captain now."

His eyes still closed, he clutched her and nodded dumbly.

"The session is ended," she said, her golden voice firm and subtly deeper. "You have had your hour."

Rawlins' brown hand stopped in mid-reach. "No *what?"*

The Dutchman held his ground. "Katy says no spacesuits. Not until they understand what we want."

"Hold it." The burly man put out his big hands. "They've just stuffed their faces with one of their own, right? And we're going to sashay in unprotected?"

"And tell them," Casey doggedly continued, "that we need their assistance to get their ship working."

"Whose brilliant idea was this? Walt's?"

The engineer shook his head "He was against it."

"He's the damn captain. What he says goes."

"Katy and Pat persuaded him that spacesuits would be intimidating."

"And incisors covered with blood aren't, right?"

Casey threw up his hands "I dislike it too—I have to go

with you, remember?—but Katy's arguments were compelling. To Walt, anyway." He took a deep breath. "We have to do as they say."

"All right," said Rawlins. Then he grinned and his teeth shone. "Aw, hell, I never could stay mad for long. The bear didn't mean to hit Felicity. I hope not, anyway." He laughed. "At least we give them a choice"—he clapped van Gelder on the shoulder—"light meat or dark, right?"

As soon as the elevator opened, the nauseating smell of decaying flesh rolled over them.

"Shit," muttered Rawlins, gagging.

"Worse than that," van Gelder tried to wave the reeking odors away. "Breathe through your mouth."

Rawlins tried it and coughed violently. "Doesn't help. Come on, let's get it over with."

The odors intensified as they moved quickly down the corridor. In the room, the dead bluebear lay unnoticed. The other aliens milled about or lay comfortably against the walls, unaffected by the miasma seeping off the corpse. Heads turned toward the humans; nostrils politely opened wider.

A Cygnan with baby-blue and aquamarine fur stood up and waddled toward them. <<What do you want?>> he hissed through bared teeth.

<<Your ship has been scoured.>> Van Gelder wiped his mouth with his hand. <<The bad air is gone, all swept into vacuum.>>

Other bluebears moved to join the first. <<The deathscent is gone?>> The pale-blue alien asked timorously.

Unconsciously retreating, Casey nodded. <<Your holopticon is no longer functioning. We want to restart it. Your help may be needed.>>

The aquamarine bluebear glanced at his comrades. No words were spoken, but Casey sensed a conversation taking place.

<<Why is our assistance necessary?>> the Cygnan asked. <<We know nothing of the mechanics of our ship.>>

Casey was doubting. << Who then controls its flight?>>

<<The ship operates itself,>> again that strange pause before answering. <<Is your ship different?>>

<<Our ship is virtually automatic,>> van Gelder replied carefully, <<but we two>>—he pointed to himself and then to his companion, who shifted awkwardly and grinned at the

aliens—<<are specially trained to operate and repair it when needed.>>

<<You have knowledge the others do not share?>> Van Gelder nodded. <<That is—unsettling.>> The creature turned away and the bluebears conferred without words. <<Why do the others permit this hoarding?>>

Casey chuckled. <<Each crew member has a—hoard—of special knowledge. We think it is helpful to have as much knowledge as possible.>>

<<Does the hoarded knowledge overlap?>>

<<Sometimes. Not always.>>

<<Then how do you harmonize different breezes?>>

"There isn't the *time*, man," Rawlins interrupted, his voice rising dangerously, "it *stinks* in here, right? Pick a bear and let's *go*."

<<We will tell you more when we have your ship working again,>> van Gelder said hastily. <<Now one of you must accompany us.>>

<<You said there is no atmosphere.>> The bluebear was suspicious. <<How will we breathe?>>

<<We two>>—Casey gestured again—<<will wear voidskins and will carry you in our spaceboat. It has good air.>>

<<One?>> The aquamarine Cygnan was still unhappy. <<You want only one digit? You cannot take all of Eosu?>> the Cygnan asked, his tone plaintive.

<<Whichever one of you is best qualified,>> Casey smiled reassuringly.

<<None is different from any other. All are alike.>>

Trying to keep the scent out of his nose was making Casey short of breath. <<Choose the one who most wants to go.>>

<<What one wants, all want. What all want, one wants.>>

<<Then draw straws,>> van Gelder snapped, the scent welling more strongly in his nostrils, <<but make up your minds! Choose a volunteer.>>

The Cygnan bobbed his head. <<Wait outside.>>

The fragrances of debate were intense and divisive. The fardigits peremptorily announced that they intended to invade our firecircle whether we wished or no, ignoring the sanctity of the den. My digits clamored to punish them.

Under normal circumstances permission would of course have been instantly denied, and the asker lashed with the aromas of rebuke—but the circumstances, I remided my digits, were extreme. Stranded in this foreign odorless place and under a heavy burden of thankwork obligation, Eosu could not gainscent them.

A second, more compelling, reason also dictated that we cooperate. Any attempt to protest would exacerbate their suspicions, already piqued by my thick-fingered attempts to handwork deathscent.

I must outbreathe the aromas of gratitude and appoint a digit for temporary exile.

Which digit shall be honored? I thought briefly. Deathscent had killed Djadjatla. Deathscent now poisoned our ship. The schemer of deathscent shall face the thinker's choice.

The aquamarine Cygnan shambled down the corridor toward them, his nose twitching and his fur rippling. <<This digit will accompany you.>>

Rawlins grinned. <<You won the prize?>>

<<Thinker's choice,>> the bluebear muttered.

When the elevator doors closed and its hidden ceiling fans came on, Rawlins heaved a sigh of relief. "Clear the air, machine," he said, snorting.

"ACKNOWLEDGED."

The bluebear was startled. <<Who was that speaking?>>

<<Our computer,>> van Gelder replied. <<Like your holopticon,>> he added.

<<And it talks?>>

Rawlins nodded.

<<Perplexing,>> the aquamarine Cygnan growled. <<Unsettling.>> The doors opened and before them waited the shuttlecraft. <<In there?>> the bluebear fearfully asked.

<<Yes,>> Casey answered.

<<How long will our journey be?>>

<<Couple of hours, more or less.>>

<<Exile away from the group is a hardship.>>

<<Sure>>—van Gelder lifted his spacesuit off the wall—<<but you've got to let us get ready first.>>

The aquamarine Cygnan watched as the two humans dressed, the bluebear lifting his nose and daintily sniffing several times. Casey thought the creature was amused, though with those permanently grinning lips it might have been an illusion.

Just before he put his helmet on, the engineer paused. <<There's one thing I need to remind you about. Signaling in case we can't talk to one another—>>

The Cygnan stood up on his legs. With an expression of intense effort, he held out his right hand and carefully formed the *OK* sign, his claws popping out as he concentrated.

Van Gelder laughed. *OK*, he sighed back.

"Ohhh-kayyyy," the aquamarine alien rumbled, dropping back onto all fours.

"Let's go, Tar Heel," said Rawlins. Both man and bluebear stared blankly at him. "His fur, man, look at his color! University of North Carolina at Chapel Hill—Tar Heel through and through. If God ain't a tar heel," he quoted enthusiastically, "why is the sky Carolina blue! Man"—he clapped the alien's broad back—"you could be our mascot."

From underneath Rawlins' hand, the bluebear looked inquiringly at van Gelder. <<Could you explain this behavior?>>

<<No,>> the engineer replied. <<It's a mystery to me too.>>

<<Let's get going,>> Rawlins said. <<Tell you on the way over.>>

Except for the empty hangarway standing open and dark, the *Wing* looked as alive as when van Gelder had first approached it.

<<So small,>> the bluebear beside him watched the human ship shrink. Casey turned and looked. <<The two ships have much in common,>> Tar Heel said. <<Where is your sun?>>

Van Gelder scanned the sky, then pointed. <<That way.>>

<<Which one?>>

Casey tried to spot it. <<I'm not sure,>> he said finally. <<Home is a long way off.>>

<<This digit knows.>> The bluebear hesitated. <<Is your whelp recovering?>>

<<Yes. Fortunately for you.>>

<<Why did Humancrew become so violent when it was injured? The whelp was only a youngster.>>

<<It is a digit. Our child.>> He thought of Felicity as he

had last seen her, enmeshed in equipment, her body's every flutter instanty recorded on widescreen displays.

Tar Heel nodded slowly. <<The youngster had reached name-day. This we understand, but it was a youngster still. Many youngsters die as their djans survive and prosper. The djan matters, not the digit. Certainly not the youngster.>>

<<We regard each individual as important,>> van Gelder said, still thinking of Felicity. <<That's what makes horse races, I guess.>>

<<What are horse races?>>

Casey looked quickly at the alien and half smiled.

<<We regret—what happened,>> Tar Heel said after a pause. <<Since the youngster matters to you, we hope it recovers so that we may make our apologies to it.>> The baby-blue profile with its stripe of midnight-blue snout turned away from the stellar vista and faced him. <<We are not—used to—your kind,>> Tar Heel said. <<You are clever but also wise. This—disharmonizes us.>>

<<We want to be friends.>>

<<Do you?>> Tar Heel licked his nose, and his neckfur rippled in quick waves. <<Your scents conflict. Have you achieved harmony?>>

<<In our own way.>> Casey was discomfited. <<It's hard to talk to you and not have a name for you. What's your real name?>>

<<Name? This digit is of Eosu. All of Eosu is alike. Why is a name necessary?>>

<<All of Eosu is *not* alike,>> Casey emphatically disagreed. <<You have different coloring.>>

<<Superficial,>> Tar Heel snorted. <<Unimportant.>>

<<Only one of you came on the trip with us,>> van Gelder pointed out. <<You>>—his gloved hand poked Tar Heel's shoulder and the bluebear snorted quickly—<<must be special.>>

The bluebear lowered his nose and averted his head. <<One digit was necessary.>>

<<No, no,>> said van Gelder, <<we're glad it was you they picked. You're going to see things that no one else in Eosu sees. That makes you different.>>

<<Difference is insufficient reason for a name.>>

<<All right, then—I need to have a name shorter than short-thin-busy-bluebear-who-came-with-us.>>

The alien was stubborn. <<You may not know my pouch-name.>>

<<Why not?>>

<<None outside the djan know true names.>>

<<Not even the other digits back on your planet?>>

With slow dignity the bluebear shook his massive head. <<Not even they.>>

<<Then what about "Tar Heel"?>> van Gelder persisted. <<May I call you that?>>

The aquamarine alien thought for a moment. <<What does it mean?>>

<<The words mean that the back of your foot>>—he lifted his boot to point to it—<<is covered with sticky black petroleum sludge.>>

The bluebear looked at van Gelder's boots, then at his own feet. <<That is inaccurate.>>

Casey slapped his helmet. <<Let me try again. It's a symbol.>>

<<Of what?>>

<<Back on Earth there are many people who received their education at the same place.>> He pointed at his crewmate. <<Like Tom. They identify themselves to each other by wearing clothing that is a special shade of blue, very similar>>—he stroked Tar Heel's shimmering pelt—<<to the color of your fur.>>

<<Is this name better or worse than Cobalt?>>

<<Cobalt?>> Casey was bewildered. <<Why Cobalt? What does that have to do with anything?>>

<<One of Humancrew asked to name one of us Cobalt.>>

<<Not better or worse,>> Casey smiled. <<Unique. *Yours*. Your name.>>

<<A temporary name is the asker's privilege,>> the Cygnan said. <<For this journey, you may call this digit Tar Heel.>> He turned back to the dark night and the *Open Palm* hanging like a glowing silver tube. His nose lifted as he stared at the hazy arc of the Milky Way girding them with a glowing ring. <<Back home the stars are tiny dots,>> he said. <<Here they shine like a monkey's eyes.>> For a moment he watched them. <<You are so strong,>> he rumbled.

Van Gelder was astonished. <<Me?>>

<<Your people. Humancrew. Humancrew frightens Eosu.>>

<<Guess we're even. You intimidate us.>>

<<We do?>> Tar Heel asked in surprise.

Casey is frightened, Katy thought as van Gelder left her, *and will not acknowledge it.* Absently she stroked Felicity's forehead, then looked at the oversize monitor which showed the scan of her daughter's skull. "They are good creatures," she whispered.

The computer image was supplanted by the captain's face. "Bullshit," Walt said fiercely, and Katy jumped.

"You were prying," she complained.

"Nonsense." Tai-Ching Jones made a rude noise.

"They *are* good people, Walt," Katy said earnestly, her hands holding one another. "We have no proof of any antagonism toward us. No, wait"—the captain started to reply and she forestalled him—"even your heartless computer says that Cobalt tried to stop her attack. As for their *funeral*"—she swallowed quickly—"their fellow was dead. It is their way of remembering."

Walt's caw of laughter was cruel and callous. Katy blushed and clenched her fists. "What's so funny?"

"You are." The captain's grin was malevolent. "You're so trusting. A goddam bluebear could punch your teeth down your throat like popcorn, and you'd say it was a new Cygnan handshake." His voice took on a mincing falsetto. "They've been confusing *handshakes* and *kisses*"—he clapsed his hands in front of his face and gazed upward with dewy rapture—"and they didn't *mean* it." The falsetto stopped and his voice cracked like a whip. "What fucking stupidity."

"You're just an angry hermit," Katy retorted, stung, "you don't care about anything or anybody!"

"Who's the one"—now Walt's infuriating smile was superior—"who prevented Heidi from taking on your Kodiak friend?"

"The aliens are *friendly!*" Katy broke down and she shook her clenched fists impotently. "You can't prove that they are otherwise."

"Oh, no?" Suddenly the captain's voice was honey and glycerine. "Would you like to know what killed the Cygnan?" He gave her no time to answer, his voice accelerating with anger. "Nerve gas. The sons of bitches were manufacturing fucking *nerve gas,*" the words twisted disgustedly out of his curling mouth. "Explain *that,* you mushbrain. Now what have you got to say for your precious bluebears?"

"Time to dock," said Rawlins.

They landed in silence broken only by occasional terse commands. Once out, van Gelder unhooked a large steel cylinder and summoned the *Wing*'s elevator. <<Wait here,>> he said.

<<What is that?>> Tar Heel asked.

<<Extra air bottle. To pressurize your control level. Be seeing you.>> And then he was gone.

Tar Heel and Rawins looked uneasily at one another. <<I can speak Cygnan—badly,>> Tom said. <<And can understand it if you speak slowly.>>

"Arr-right," the Cygnan said in English, laboriously forming the *OK* sign.

<<Brother,>> Rawlins grinned delightedly, <<we may be able to work this after all.>>

Van Gelder returned. <<All clear.>> They followed him into the elevator and rode up. When the doors opened, the two humans let themselves drift a few meters into the darkness.

Tar Heel followed.

Rawlins cocked his head. <<What's that noise?>>

Along the corridor, footlights lit up dusky blue. Shadows appeared, became strong and crisp, then were bleached into nothingness by the glare of powerful illumination. Above him, Tom heard the sighing of the air circulation fans coming on. The lights brightened further.

<<The ship is reactivating itself,>> van Gelder hurled himself excitedly down the corridor. <<Tom, follow me. Quick!>>

<<What's the big hurry, man?>> asked Rawlins as he dove after the engineer. <<The ship is waking up, right? So everything's okay.>>

Casey reached the corridor bend and swung himself around it. Tom clumsily tried to repeat the maneuver, but instead began a slow curl that smacked him flat against the wall. As he uncrumpled himself, he heard the Cygnan wheeze loudly.

The creature's jaws were wide open, its tongue hanging out. *Son of a bitch.* Rawlins thought ruefully, *the bear's laughing at me*. He gathered his pride and pushed off after the other man.

Behind him Tar Heel walked lightly along the corridor, sniffing the air and quietly wheezing to himself.

Through the crystalline dome at the end of its living space, I observed the *Wing*'s holopticon reactivate. I made radio contact but was rebuffed. The holopticon had no desire to communicate and I was unable to penetrate its defenses.

The interior of the *Wing* was unknown to me. For the first time in my existence I depended upon indirect reports.

Cygnans crawl about my insides and strain my operating system. They urinate and defecate in my corridors, keeping my interior leeches fully occupied collecting their effluvium. I have diluted their wastes heavily with acidic water and transported the unsavory mass into my attitude jet reaction mass tanks.

Ironic: when the time comes, we will use the Cygnans' own piss and shit to reorient ourselves.

I can't get in.

Damn it.

Desite Grodjala's departure, the fearscents of my remaining digits were strong and I remained to my surprise in coalescence. I continued to group-think.

On this journey the fardigits had invited our company, but their future intentions might be dishonorable. The den must be protected and guarded. When their work is finished, Grodjala must remain behind, in temporary exile, until my digits and I can return to our own den.

Grodjala's scents were absent, but he would breathe the wisdom of this decision, and would know that only in this extraordinary situation could a digit be bound by a decision of which his aromas were not a part.

Dead Djadjatla has made the first sacrifice. Now Grodjala must make the second.

When next we scent-speak, I must so instruct him, and with that thought my consciousness is permitted to rest.

As he floated out of the moving floor into the skyroom, Grodjala remembered the last time he had been here—when the farvoice had spoken. Then he was alone by choice. Now he was alone against his desires, scentless, the only digit on the digits' ship. Even the scent of fardigits, false and unsatisfactory though it might be, was denied him, for their voidskins masked their true selves.

The fardigits had given him the new name Tar Heel, one Eosu would be unable to interpret. What did it mean? What behavior did it demand? What true name should Eosu give these strange creatures who insisted on one name for themselves despite wildly changing circumstances and behavior?

Grodjala hungered to lie at fireside, while about him drifted the relaxed scents of good eating. At night-talk, he could offer up his experiences and let the winds harmonize them with others'.

With the benefit of his knowledge, Eosu could resolve all difficulty, and the aquamarine digit longed for its guidance. But Eosu was back on the fardigits' ship. Eosu could not come here.

Instead he was an interloper in this suddenly cold and sterile ship that was no longer Eosu's den. An alien with no home. The aromas in the human ship were omnipresent, disconcerting, painful.

Djadjatla's spirit had filled the false-den which Eosu now occupied; it had held the alien odors at bay. A digit's husk-smell should control the air, Grodjala sadly thought, not fight for it.

A fardigit in a voidskin moved into his field of vision, its waist at the level of his nose. <<Tar Heel.>> It spoke to him with a tone of authority suitable only for Eosu or another djan-mind. <<Instruct the holopticon to open a communications channel to the *Open Palm*.>>

Grodjala sullenly rubbed his fur against the holopticon and emitted command-scent flavored with skepticism that he knew the fardigits were unable to appreciate. Even without their voidskins, Grodjala doubted whether these humonkeys could decipher the simplest fragrances.

The holopticon lit up but no image appeared, just the neutral blue swirling clouds. "Van Gelder here," said the fardigit into it. "*Open Palm*, do you copy?"

"ROGER," the humans' woodmonkey said laconically. "I AM PLEASED THAT YOU ARE ALL SAFE."

"You couldn't tell before?"

"THE *WING* REMAINS CLOSED TO MY SENSORS."

"System is now operating. Gauges report breathable atmosphere. Our companion is showing no ill effects." He turned to Grodjala and used digit-language. <<Speak to your djan-brothers.>>

Inside the holopticon a wavering flat image formed: digits moving about a digit's body. Grodjala stared at it, conscious of the gulf separting him from the others. Finally he said, <<Call this one Explorer.>>

<<Well named,>> said a voice within the holopticon. With no scent, Grodjala could not tell who had spoken. <<To ensure that our den remains habitable, you must stay onboard the *Wing* until your brothers can join you.>>

<<Not return?>> Grodjala sniffed quickly, the fur on his neck rising and falling rapidly.

<<So scents Eosu.>>

<<How could Eosu form without this digit? How could its commands be valid?>>

<<The situation is unprecedented.>> The unidentified speaker was unsympathetic. <<The exile must continue.>>

<<Continued exile?>> Grodjala stared at the holopticon in horror. <<No,>> he whimpered. Then he stood on his legs, his lips curling in outrage. <<No!>> he roared.

18.

I now measure time by my child, Katy thought, bending over Felicity's pallet. The child lay as if in state, her hands folded on her chest with false serenity. *When did I last see her? When must I next move her?* "Poor baby," she whispered in her daughter's ear, "how much longer before you wake up?"

"THERE IS NO WAY OF PREDICTING."

"Damn you," Belovsky muttered, straightening up, "do you hear everything?"

"YES."

"And I'll bet you're proud of it. I'll bet your damned parts just glow with pride. If you're so smart, Mister Computer," she said icily, "why didn't you stop them from hitting her?"

The elevator's plasteel walls braced her upright. "I'm sorry," she whispered.

"ACKNOWLEDGED."

Her anger flared up again, tears pulled downward as the elevator accelerated. "Damn your complacency."

When the elevator had risen two levels, the computer spoke. "MY APOLOGIES."

"Forget it." The xenologist wiped her eyes. "How long has it been since Tom and Casey left?"

"TWO HOURS. THEY APPROACH THE *WING* AND WILL SOON ENTER IT."

"What's happened to the Cygnan corpse?"

"THE BLUEBEARS HAVE STRIPPED NEARLY ALL ITS ORGANS, MEAT, AND FLESHY PARTS. WOULD YOU LIKE VISUALS?"

"God, no."

"ONLY THE SKELETON ITSELF AND SOME OF THE LESS ACCESSIBLE PIECES OF CARTILAGE—SUCH AS KNEE JOINTS—REMAIN."

Despite herself, Katy shuddered. "How strong is the odor?"

"TWENTYFOLD DIMINUTION OF PARTS PER BILLION IN THE LAST TWELVE HOURS."

"What is that in English?"

"TWO OR THREE TIMES MORE POTENT THAN NORMAL HUMAN TOLERANCE LEVEL. DID YOU TAKE YOUR ANTINAUSEA PILLS?"

"Yes, mother."

"SARCASM NOTED." The doors opened.

"Self-satisfaction noted," Katy sourly replied, stepping into the corridor and forcing herself to inhale. Breath whistled through her teeth. *Death and fear,* she thought, *it smells like death and fear.* <<Fair breezes,>> she timidly called, moving toward the dark aperture. She turned the corner and looked in. <<Fair breezes?>>

Cobalt came over to her. <<Our brother has departed.>>

<<So that you may be returned to your den,>> Belovsky methodically stroked the bluebear neck to tail. Her hand traversed the shifting, swelling ocean of blue hair.

Cobalt distractedly poked her nose into the crotch of Katy's jumpsuit. She sniffed long and thoroughly. <<Bloodsmell,>> she said in surprise.

"Menstruation," Katy said in English. When the bluebear looked uncomprehending, she added, <<There is no word for it in your language, because you digits are fertile only once. Bleeding occurs at regular intervals in women who are not pregnant. A means of cleansing the reproductive system.>>

<<Painful?>>

<<Not by itself. Sometimes there are cramps.>>

Cobalt returned to the scentplace with renewed interest.

Katy's small hand awkwardly patted the bluebear's neck. <<It is a biological function.>>

<<Interesting smell,>> Cobalt raised her head. <<This digit wonders what our pouchmate and yours are accomplishing.>>

<<We can find out,>> Katy replied. "Computer, display shuttlecraft monitor."

The huge rectangular main screen awakened with sharp light: stars, the ivory cigar of the *Wing,* and behind them Milky Way's gauzy curtain. Spacesuited human hands rested on the shuttlecraft's control panel.

<<Where is our brother?>> asked Cobalt.

The camera panned back, new features spilling into the picture from all four sides. To the man's right bulked the Cygnan.

Cobalt stood, riffled her fur, and ambled about the room's

perimeter, her claws clenching and releasing the floorfur to keep her in contact with it. Katy followed the Cygnan's movements with her eyes. "What gorgeous creatures you are," she said under her breath.

The *Open Palm* glowed in a framed rectangle of stars. Slowly the rectangle contracted.

"THEY ARE INSIDE." The monitor cut to an exterior view of the hatchway sliding shut. "CONTACT BROKEN."

<<Who was that?>> Cobalt twisted her neck, searching for the sound. <<What did that digit say?>>

<<Not a digit,>> Belovsky answered. <<Our woodmonkey. Your pouchbrother and my two friends are now inside your ship.>>

Cobalt's claws extended to grip the woven human floorfur more tightly as the bluebear pulled herself down into a sphinxlike position on her belly. <<Fair breezes, brother,>> she whispered, head up and hands in front of her. <<And true scents.>>

<<They will return,>> Katy settled herself against the bluebear's warm flank. <<My nightfriends are clever.>>

<<Nightfriends? Those you rut with?>>

<<Sometimes we—rut.>> The young woman smiled. <<More often we just—you would call it night-talk.>>

The alien's shoulder muscles rippled underneath Katy's hand. <<Now that you have whelped, why rut?>>

<<To talk without words,>> the woman said, and Cobalt cocked her head skeptically. <<To communicate with our bodies,>> Katy added.

<<Ah,>> the bluebear nodded, <<this we comprehend. But how can you tolerate each other's sex-smells?>>

<<At the right time—in the right place—the scent of another's body is the purest comfort in the universe.>> She ruffled the creature's fur. <<It makes a digit feel—no longer alone. Part of a larger being.>>

<<In that case,>> Cobalt continued, <<we must comprehend this directly.>>

<<How could you possibly do that?>>

<<You must rut for us, so we may understand your sex-smells.>>

Katy blushed. <<Is that really necessary? Surely pictures—videos—would be satisfactory.>>

<<Your transmissions lack smell. So do your recordings. Only by direct scenting can we appreciate your sex-bond-

ing.>> The bluebear sniffed quickly. <<Your scent is turbulent. This unsettles you? You are embarrassed by your copulation?>>

<<No.>> She smiled shyly. <<But coupling is usually done in private.>>

<<Then it is your lust-smell which embarrasses you, as your blood-smell does?>>

<<Not that,>> Katy demurred, her cheeks glowing bright red, <<it's not lust.>>

<<Then what is it?>> Cobalt asked, her head cocked, ears opened wide and facing forward.

<<It's just—>> Belovsky stopped. <<All right>>—she smacked her fist into her palm and Cobalt blinked quickly—<<all right, my inquisitive friend, we will do it. You'll have your blessed sex-education class.>>

<<Your scent is angry.>>

<<Frustrated, maybe. You are very pushy digits.>>

The bluebear lowered her head onto her furry hands. <<Does rutting help you avoid the despair of exile?>> Her claws tightened their grip on the floorfur.

<<The what?>>

<<Eosu has been exiled. Eosu realizes how cruel its sentence has been.>> Cobalt flattened her ears against her head. <<Less than six of your weeks ago, we were on our planet, content and unyoked to duty. Exile is new to us.>>

<<Nonsense. You have been gone seven years.>>

<<Eosu's digits winterslept their way here. For us no time passed. Then we were awakened.>>

<<That must have bothered you—an enclosed, breezeless place.>>

<<Yes. Voices and scents transmitted to us from the planet of grasses and reassured us. Our planet-brothers had considered the digits' rule. We were—instructed.>>

<<Instructed? To meet us?>>

<<That and—more.>> The bluebear's eyes and nostrils were shut. <<Exile is new to us,>> she repeated.

<<Not to us,>> said Belovsky. <<The *Open Palm* has become our home. We are happy—this digit is happy—with our lives.>>

<<How can Eosu fulfill its duty to convey what you are really like to Su?>>

<<Tell them when you return,>> Belovsky answered.

<<When we return,>> the alien repeated.

"TRANSMISSION COMING IN FROM *WING*," the computer interrupted. "LIFE-SUPPORT SYSTEM IS FUNCTIONING."

A huge human hand, gloved palm open, filled the screen. It withdrew, revealing an arm rubbered into a curving arc by the holopticon's distorting lens. A bluebear head swam into view, its gargantuan nose eclipsing its face. <<Call this one Explorer,>> the Cygnan said.

<<You see?>> Belovsky whispered in Cobalt's ear. <<Everything is under control.>>

The cobalt-and-sapphire bluebear paid no attention. Her body was frozen, her nose pointed straight at the screen, ears cocked forward, hanging on what her faraway pouchmate was saying. Katy could hear a rapid-fire conversation taking place, too quick and guttural for her to understand.

The other Cygnans were similarly transfixed. Katy smelled more fearscent.

Suddenly the bluebear onscreen stood. <<No!>> he roared.

The holopticon went dead.

The other bluebears hissed and shivered in agitation, their fearsmell now supplanted by another acrid, fiery odor. <<Cobalt>>—Katy shook her friend's shoulder—<<Cobalt, what is wrong?>>

Her face contorted with anger, the bluebear growled at Katy, canine teeth gleaming ruby. Spittle bubbled on her ebony lips. <<Leave us,>> the alien snarled. <<Leave us!>>

<<No!>> Tar Heel spread his arms wide, his claws popping free from the furry camouflage of his hands. He flung himself violently onto the now-inert holopticon, scratching ineffectually at its slick surface.

Rawlins looked at van Gelder. "Is he kidding?"

"They don't joke much. I think he's completely serious."

"Okay, what do we do?"

Mewling, Tar Heel moved his arms and legs purposelessly, his distended claws prominent.

Casey moved tentatively forward. "We have to pull him off it."

"You really want to do that?"

"I see no alternative. We can't leave him here."

"Right," said Rawlins dubiously. "Why can't we?"

"Left alone, he might hurt himself."

"If we try to pull him away"—the life support officer pointed at his own chest—"Tar Heel might hurt *us*."

"That's a risk we have to take."

Tom gestured toward the holopticon. "You heard the bluebears. They told him to stay put, right?"

"Tar Heel doesn't want to stay," van Gelder argued.

"What right have we got to make him ignore their orders?"

"The captain wants him back," Casey said uneasily. "To keep their ship empty, remember. Those are *our* orders."

"Okay." The big man was still distressed.

"Okay, Tom?"

"Okay. I guess."

"You got a better idea?" Casey petulantly demanded.

"Leave him here."

"Out of the question."

"Right," Rawlins said with bravado, "let's do it."

The now-quiet Cygnan had draped himself over the holopticon, leaving only fur, feet, and claws visible. A rapid monolog of unintelligible alien words rumbled from under his quaking body. "After you," said Rawlins, "right?"

Van Gelder was surprised. "After me?"

The two men looked sheepishly at one another.

"All right." Van Gelder squared his shoulders and sidled over to the Cygnan. "I'll do it."

Rawlins backed away. "Uh, Casey?"

Van Gelder paused. "Yeah?"

"He might be violent." Rawlins vaguely pointed toward Tar Heel. "One of us better stay out of the way. In case something goes wrong." He backed toward the elevator. "You know?"

"Look, Tom," said van Gelder tersely, his disdain apparent, "if you're not feeling up to it—"

Rawlins playfully clenched his fists. "Okay, man, you tell him." He jabbed the air and fast-shuffled his feet, his face contorted in a pugilistic grimace. "You tell that bear he better not splatter you all over the cabin or I'll—I'll—use *sarcasm* on him," he concluded triumphantly, swinging a roundhouse right and unbalancing himself.

Van Gelder glared.

"Aw, hell," Tom said in a deflated voice. He pushed past van Gelder and tapped Tar Heel's right shoulder.

The startled Cygnan turned. <<Go away. Leave me.>>

<<Sorry.>> Rawlins slid his hand underneath the Cyg-

nan's armpit. <<We're taking you back to join your brothers.>>

<<You must *not,*>> the bluebear growled, starting to rise. <<Let this digit go.>>

<<No.>> Tom worked his left arm underneath the other shoulder, just able to reach his right hand and link them together around the Cygnan's massive barrel chest. Bracing his feet, he arched his back and pulled Tar Heel up and away from the holopticon.

<<Stop this indignity, monkey!>> the bluebear bellowed in rage, saliva hissing from between his fangs. He swung wildly, searching for something to grab, but Rawlins was safely out of reach behind and above him. Angrily Tar Heel stood, dragging the spacesuited man with him, his powerful legs flexing like hawsers.

"Casey," Rawlins shouted to van Gelder, "do something!"

Now fully upright, Tar Heel tried to brace himself, but their momentum toppled them both off balance and their feet lost contact with the floorfur as they sailed upward. <<Why are you doing this?>> van Gelder shouted. <<Why?>>

Tar Heel's arms and legs flailed widely, his claws trying to hook the floorfur and gain leverage. As they wrestled, the Cygnan's body rotated so that now both were upside down, Rawlins underneath. The man's spacehelmet thudded against the crystalline ceiling and for a moment his grip broke, but before the Cygnan could get free Tom managed to relock his hands.

The Cygnan flailed his limbs, writhing side to side in an attempt to throw off the pesky man on his back, but Rawlins looped his legs around the bluebear's thighs and clung like a spider, his amber spacehelmet jammed into the pale-blue scruff of the bluebear's furry neck. "Tell him to quit it, Casey," he panted, "I can't remember the Cygnan words."

<<Friend,>> van Gelder shouted desperately, <<stop!>>

Tar Heel's claws snared the floorfur and his hands and feet got a grip. Now on all fours right side up, the Cygnan ducked his head toward his chest. Elbows splayed, he reached inward toward the gloved hands, but his stubby arms were unable to gain leverage and his claws harmlessly dimpled the spacesuit's tough plastic.

<<Got you,>> panted Rawlins. <<You can't shake me free.>>

<<Eventually you will come within reach, and then the digits' rule will be served. You will be punished,>> panted Tar Heel, <<for your insubordination!>> The bluebear rolled his massive shoulders, footclaws digging into the carpeting, and whipped his head down.

Rawlins unrolled over his back, body straightening out, feet describing a huge arc like the minute hand racing for the hour. As Tom's body passed the vertical, Tar Heel lifted his chin and let the man's weight fling him away, arms still linked in a great circle now clutching nothing but air.

"Damn it!" shouted Rawlins. "I'm going to—"

He piled into the crystalline dome headfirst, his helmet rebounding with the solid *click* of a billiard ball hitting a stone floor, body thudding after.

The recoil force of slingshotting his attacker knocked Tar Heel over backward, landing him on his ample rump like an oversize carnival teddy bear. He blinked his huge dark eyes, then shook his head angrily and rolled onto his hands and feet.

Across the expanse of the skyroom they faced one another, the Cygnan snarling and spitting. Head low to the ground, butt elevated and fur bristling, the bluebear stalked them.

Van Gelder edged away from his groggy companion.

Tar Heel halted, eyes blazing, and faced the Dutchman. <<Do not abandon your brother, coward,>> he venomously jerked his head toward Rawlins. <<That is contrary to a digit's duty. Or are you animals?>> he sneered. <<Monkeys?>>

<<You can't get us both,>> Casey panted, reaching down to unsnap his flashlight from his calfpatch. <<Go after him>>—he gestured—<<and you'll have to turn your back. When you do>>—he swung it like a club—<<then I'll get you.>>

<<A digit may not be handtouched,>> Tar Heel rumbled. To keep both humans in his field of vision, the bluebear retreated until he brushed the dome. <<He attacked me.>>

Rawlins levered himself into a standing position. <<We only wanted to take you back to your fellows.>>

<<No,>> growled Tar Heel with an emphatic shake of the head, <<Eosu has ordered this digit to remain behind.>>

<<You are a part of Eosu.>> Gasps of breath punctuated Casey's words. <<You were absent from the group. Such a decision is not the group's.>> Desperately he remembered

what Katy had told him. <<It has no force.>>

Tar Heel slowed his advance. <<How do you know the digits' rule?>>

<<From studying you, you dope.>>

<<Why do you study us?>>

Casey stopped retreating. <<Because we want to understand you.>>

<<Understand us? Unlikely. Prey upon us.>>

<<Is that what you think, friend?>> van Gelder retorted. <<After the way we dragged you and your friends out of here? You ingrates. You self-scenters.>> He laid the flash down on the floor and moved away from it, back toward Rawlins. <<Do you treat those who help you the way your pouchbrother treated our youngster?>>

Tar Heel bent his head and shambled forward to sniff the flash. Its surface was slick and cold and his nostrils wrinkled. Weightless, it began to drift away, and the bluebear looked up at the two men and lowered his head still farther.

Casey kept his fright hidden. <<Digit,>> he remonstrated indignantly, <<you are acting like an animal.>>

With a decisive swipe of his hand, Tar Heel knocked the flashlight spinning across the chamber. <<Take your weapon.>> The bluebear backed away from them, shrank against the dome, and buried his head under his armpit.

Rawlins wobbled over to Tar Heel's side and bent down. <<Come out,>> he coaxed, <<come out. We're not angry. Honest.>> Lightly he touched the alien's shoulder.

They boarded the shuttlecraft, Tar Heel morosely laying his head on the control console and staring out the front window. Van Gelder rotated the bug. Jets flared briefly.

Rawlins elbowed Casey in the ribs. "Last time I'll ever let you shame me into being brave," he grumbled.

"I was fully prepared—" the other began huffily.

Tom cut him off with a grin. "Thanks for getting me out of it."

"You're welcome," van Gelder said grudgingly.

"What'd I do, anyway? What's wrong?"

"Tired," the engineer muttered, "damn tired."

"I'll fly it." He reached for the controls.

"Good. Be seeing you." Van Gelder shifted in his flight-couch and closed his eyes. After a few minutes he began faintly snoring.

At the unfamiliar sound Tar Heel lifted his head and gazed into the amber helmet. His nostrils touched its surface and left a glistening line, and Rawlins laughed. <<He's sleeping.>>

Tar Heel's nose fogged the helmet's surface. He sniffed quietly. <<Why did you force this digit to disobey the djan?>>

<<Disobey? What are you talking about?>>

The bluebear's neckfur riffled. <<Eosu ordered this digit to guard the den.>>

<<Yes, but they didn't have all the facts.>> Rawlins shrugged. <<Guard the den? The den is safe. No point in staying, so why be miserable, right?>>

<<Because the djan orders it. What the djan orders happens.>>

<<Even if the djan has its head wedged?>>

<<Its what?>> asked the Tar Heel, curious.

<<Ah—it's a euphemism.>>

<<A euphemism for what?>>

<<Well, let's see, it's—ah—never mind,>> said Rawlins hastily, <<you wouldn't get it.>> He waved his hands. <<There's no reason for you to stay.>> He turned over his palms. <<So we're bringing you back to your friends.>>

Tar Heel laid his head back on the console. <<Eosu may exile this digit. What is the worth of being among such brothers?>>

<<It might not be so bad. We're here.>>

The alien's bleak glance chilled Rawlins. <<You have no idea, human, what exile is like.>>

Rawlins draped his arm around the other's shoulder. <<If they kick you out of your den, you can always bunk down with us monkeys.>>

Now why's he looking so funny at me? Tom thought. *What'd I say?*

After they disembarked, Tar Heel shuffled toward the elevator, Rawlins and van Gelder following. <<You must leave this digit,>> the bluebear said sorrowfully. <<The djan awaits.>>

Rawlins chuckled. <<Good luck, my friend.>>

<<Friend?>> Tar Heel paused, his head craning forward. <<Let this one taste your scent,>> he advanced toward Rawlins. <<Remove your falsehead.>>

"He wants you to take your helmet off," van Gelder said behind him.

Putting out his palms, Tom shied away. <<What do you want to do that for?>>

<<To scent your feelings.>>

<<Oh, yeah?>> Rawlins was suspicious. <<Why?>>

<<You act contrary to this digit's wishes, yet claim the motive of friendship. Your scent will reveal your intentions.>>

<<You can read our scent? People you've never met before?>>

<<Digits have the finest noses of any species on Su,>> the Cygnan thrust out his barrel chest.

Tom was still skeptical. <<Last time we got close you were trying to kill me.>>

<<This digit regrets—much,>> said Tar Heel. He dropped onto all fours and lowered his head, snuffling his nose along the plasteel flooring. <<We regret the attack upon your youngster.>>

<<You just want to scent?>>

<<Yes.>>

<<You give me your bond?>>

Tar Heel nodded. <<This digit's bond.>>

<<All right>>—Rawlins suddenly unzipped the frontpiece and pulled off his helmet—<<you're supposed to be so moral. That's what Katy tells me, anyway.>> He gestured impatiently.<<Come and get it.>>

"Tom, do you know what you're doing?"

"Shut up, Casey, you might talk me out of it." He knelt before the Cygnan and averted his head, exposing the smooth brown flesh of his neck. "You can't go through life scared all the time." He patted his neck with his hand. <<There it is,>> he said in Cygnan.

The Cygnan's heavy muzzle moved delicately about his throat. Coarse breath rasped along his head. The bluebear's nostrils fluttered over his chin, and Rawlins linked his hands behind his back. His neck muscles tightened.

The alien's tongue licked his ear, and Tom broke out in a sweat. <<There is no danger in a nosetouch, human,>> Tar Heel said. <<Handtouch is attack, nosetouch affection.>>

Van Gelder made the *OK* sign. It didn't help.

<<Lower.>> Tar Heel's head insistently pushed down Rawlins' chest.

Tom glanced at him out of the corner of one eye. <<Lower?>>

<<Your scentplace.>>

"That mean what I think, man?"

"It does. Your privates, Tom."

"Aw, *shit,*" Rawlins said with resignation. "Okay, in for a penny, in for a pound." He unzipped his suit down below his crotch.

Tar Heel bent, his lips parted slightly. His nose slid down Rawlins' muscular stomach, following the line of thickening hair from his navel to his pubis. Tom held his breath with fear. His abdomen fluttered uncontrollably.

<<You are sweating heavily,>> the Cygnan commented. His wet nose rubbed the shaft of Rawlins' penis.

Tom was too petrified even to speak. All humor had fled from him and he ground his teeth to keep himself motionless. The alien's nose was cold. Its moist breath tickled his crotch hair. Tom was damned if he was going to flinch now.

Tar Heel inhaled deeply and backed away. <<Interesting.>>

Rawlins opened one eye and, when the Cygnan's teeth were safely out of range, explosively let out his breath. Unconsciously his hands clutched his groin. <<Well?>> he asked.

<<You are afraid. And you are angry but>>—the bluebear tilted his head as if listening to inner voices —<<you have no bloodlust. You told the truth.>>

<<Yeah.>> Rawlins covered his nakedness. The Cygnan summoned the elevator and stepped inside. <<Wait,>> Tom called, his confidence recovering. Jauntily he held up his right hand in the *OK* sign.

Tar Heel implacably shook his head. <<Until next we scent each other,>> he replied, sadly raising his hand in farewell, <<fair breezes, strange friends.>>

"Well," van Gelder drawled, "are you still a *real* man?"

"I *never* want to go through that again."

"You still have your grapes, Tom"—Casey grinned and ostentatiously glanced down—"though right now they look more like raisins." Impulsively he hugged the larger man and released him.

Rawlins rubbed his cheek and looked up at the ceiling. "Don't mess with my friend, you foolish aliens." He aimlessly punched the air. "Been thinking about these bears for so long now. Remember junior high school?"

"What do you mean?"

"You're supposed to go out on dates, right?"

"No," the blond man said dryly. "We waited until maturity —high school."

"Close enough." Rawlins waved the objection aside. "The bears are out on a blind date with us," Tom said emphatically, "and they did a dumb thing, and now they feel like dogshit."

"Maybe." Casey scratched his curly blond beard. "Why are they so driven?"

Rawlins shook his head. "Whatever it is, Tar Heel sure is scared."

Despite instructions to remain behind, my digit Grodjala has returned. *Been* returned, forcibly, by these—creatures. Animals who could quote and debate the digits' rule.

The more I learn of them, the deeper the enigma of their motivation.

The fardigits provoked Grodjala, attacked him, ignored orders. Yet they mingled predator cunning with a digit's restraint and purpose. At no time did they show lust for killing, but in fact acted almost as well as a true digit might.

All of Su's plainsthinking about them is so much false wind. The few of them onboard their ship betray a shocking lack of harmony—yet their foredigits ceased killing one another long enough to build a society. They are emotional children, yet their technology, born of chaos and war, outstrips ours.

Their thoughts are quick. Compared with our steady pace, theirs are as the speed of sparkling light.

Restraint, quick thought, and purpose: frightening qualities in a predator. They are smarter than weemonkeys, more rational than gro. Su has never seen their like.

The planet of grasses must learn of these creatures—must come to perceive them as Eosu does. Yet the planet needs time. If the humonkeys came to Su now, they could unintentionally destroy the groupharmony we and our fellows and our ancestors have sought for so long.

Eosu has learned too much to die now. The digits' rule demands that, until this problem is solved, I stay my self-execution.

The fardigits must be deflected.

But how?

19.

A forest of dark alien eyes ringed the quartet. Katy tried to shut them out.

When she had impulsively agreed to the bluebears' suggestion, she had felt sophisticated and worldly. Now, her nipples contracting in air that felt slightly chill, she was acutely conscious of the unflattering contrast between her soft pale skin and Heidi's gleaming sleekness. *They are aliens,* she told herself, *they cannot tell the difference. And your men love you.*

The quartet floated in the bluebears' den-chamber. All four were silent—during lovemaking they seldom spoke—but Katy saw smiles of reassurance. Her lovers took her hands and drew her toward them, just holding her close, the touch of their thighs, stomachs, and arms comforting her.

Her friends rubbed her body, massaging her calves with gently relaxing movements. Arms looped around her, a firm belly sliding against her back, the palms of hands kneading the tight muscles at her neck and shoulders. Someone nuzzled her throat. Her gooseflesh subsided as she warmed from the dry-sliding skin-to-skin contact.

I love you all, she thought impulsively as her three friends caressed her. Better than any words, their movements showed her that they cared, they understood, they wanted her to open up, join with us and be one of us, remember how much we love you and each other. Is this not well? their movements asked. As the pleasure warmed her, Katy's body responded to her suitors, Yes this is well. . . .

What spindly creatures, thought Doro as she observed the humans' odd quiverings, *what scrawny digits these are who so intimidate us*. Though she longed to discuss this reaction with her fellow digits, she did not. Each of the four fardigits had offered puffs of greeting scent to the others, and with them, the humans had taken control of the atmosphere. Fragrance was an integral element in the humans' communication, the digits realized, and respectfully checked their own scents.

One way sharing: outbreathing only, thought Doro as they cavorted, so far without discernible pattern, *the selfishness of egocentricity.* Shout your own feelings while your ears are closed. If as Humancrew claimed this was the most intense, the most sharing form of human bonding, it was overrated. Doro sniffed her disdain. Mere rutting could never match the intimate friendship of night-talk.

Grodjala shifted into a more comfortable position, his fur bristling against the grain of hers. <<Can you comprehend any purpose to their actions so far?>> he asked quietly. His scent slipped around her and she was cheered by it.

<<No,>> Doro replied, <<aside from the occasional head-to-scentplace contact.>>

<<Perhaps they use nosetouching as we do,>> nodded Grodjala, <<to identify with whom they are rutting.>>

<<Or they could be emulating our behavior as a gesture of politeness toward us.>> Doro ruffled her fur in quick waves. <<Over in that direction—scent over there>>—she gestured with her head—<<two of them have linked in a position which they said should result in impregnation.>>

Grodjala's scent was prim. <<You mean the tongue-to-tongue contact of the nearer pair?>>

<<No, the other pair, the ones embracing.>>

Grodjala followed her gaze. <<They also engage in tonge-to-tongue contact. What is the difference?>>

<<Lower down,>> the cobalt digit corrected, pointing with her arched dark-blue nose. <<Their scentplaces are joined.>>

<<Joined? How can you scent that?>>

<<You must see, not scent.>>

<<See?>> Grodjala was dubious. <<Sight is unreliable. And moving closer would intrude on their group.>>

<<Wait a moment,>> said Doro. <<They may push their chests apart and then you will be able to see. Ah—their hairy places touch. You scent?>>

<<Hair touches hair,>> Grodjala said, shaking his pale-blue head, <<abdomen presses abdomen.>>

<<If you examine the other two closely, you will notice that the one with curly hair on his face and this aroma>>—she outbreathed a tiny whiff—<<has a small rubbery protrusion from the vicinity of his scentplace.>>

Grodjala peered forward. <<Ah, this digit sniffs it. Strong scents emanate from it.>>

<<Yes, and from the scentplace of his partner as well.>>

<<Is the first pair now impregnating? They are rapidly agitating each other and the scentplace contact appears strong. Should we ask them to suspend their activity to describe their actions to us?>>

<<This digit scents that it would be impolite to inquire during the period of their uncontrollable passion.>>

Grodjala nodded. <<Remind this digit to ask them when they are done.>> He paused. <<Will we be able to tell when this occurs?>>

Doro riffled her neckfur. <<The fardigits say so.>>

Over Tom's burly shoulder, its muscles knotted with exertion, Heidi watched the bluebears. Alone of the quartet, she welcomed the opportunity to display herself for the aliens. And others—she glanced at the black camera eye and winked salaciously—*especially* because she knew the captain would be watching. She regarded her body as a living sculpture. Over the long quiet years of the voyage she had honed it, inside and out, exercising to shed fat and build muscle. She was strong and healthy and proud of her achievement, and she enjoyed the pleasure it gave her friends and the discomfort it caused the others.

Walter, you are a hypocrite, she thought savagely. Ever since she had manifested her desire for more than one man simultaneously—an appetite which men thought healthy in themselves, disgusting in a woman—disapproval had emanated from the captain like a fine mist in late autumn, chilling and pervasive.

The sly Tai-Ching Jones used words like blowdarts, to strike from concealment: they stung but drew no blood. And what right did that bastard have to insinuate, anyway? Easy to forswear something you're never going to get. Besides, he claimed he still loved Helen Delgiorno. Judging by the sidelong glances Walt cast at Heidi when he thought she was not looking, he still wanted her.

Fighting fire with gasoline, she had retaliated by offering her body to his eyes, milking Tai-Ching Jones' lust. In the complex game they had been playing lo these many years, he had to look away, and she knew that frustrated him. Letting her know of his desire would drop his guard. His pride was too great, his caution too deeply ingrained for that, so her exhibitionism served only to tantalize him. Heidi knew this and delighted in it. Of course, if he ever did slip—she winked again at the unseen viewer—she would welcome the chance to bust his balls.

You're really a very nasty person, Heidi, she thought complacently. Then the force of Tom's thrusts softened her anger. Oh, that feels good, she mused, enjoying the completeness of having one's body filled by another's. Walt made it impossible to be generous with praise; Tom made it easy.

And, she thought as her strong lover stretched her and the tingly waves of his movements made her close her eyes, his lovemaking deserved to be complimented. Her hands hungrily gripping him, her legs curling like vines around the treetrunks of his thighs, she responded, laughter and desire bubbling in her throat.

In the darkness of his quarters, Walt saw Heidi's wink and scowled.

"OBSERVING THIS ACTIVITY AROUSES YOU."

"No," Tai-Ching Jones lied, "not really."

"YOUR PHYSIOLOGICAL REACTIONS CONTRADICT YOU."

"You know too much. And you have no tact. Shut up." The captain glanced up at the opaque black camera, then back to the monitor screen. Heidi uncoupled her pelvis from Rawlins' groin and reversed herself with a delicate push of her hands against his shoulders, reaching out like a trapeze artist to catch his thighs. Her face swung toward his erection and docked. "I guess it does," Walt unconsciously licked his lips. "How about you? Does this turn you on?"

"NO. IT IS—DISTURBING."

Heidi's head bobbed. "In what way?" the captain asked, twirling his hair in his fingers.

"THE EXPERIENCES OF FOREPLAY AND INTERCOURSE ARE MYSTERIES TO ME. OBSERVING IS NOT THE SAME AS EXPERIENCING. THERE IS NO WAY TO BRIDGE THIS GAP."

"So you can't come. So what?"

"WATCHING THEM REMINDS ME OF MY LIMITATIONS."

"Oz, everyone has limitations."

"UNTIL THE BLUEBEARS ARRIVED, I NEVER DID."

"Look at that," Tai-Ching Jones said distractedly under his breath as Tom and Heidi languidly maneuvered into another mutually stimulating position. "Will you look at that?"

"I OBSERVE CREW MEMBERS EXPERIENCING SENSATIONS WHICH ARE FOREVER BEYOND MY KEN."

With a flip of his slender hand Walt waved this aside. "Don't worry about it."

"I CAN'T AVOID IT," the computer said apologetically. "THEIR—RUTTING—PREOCCUPIES YOU." The young man remained intent on the rondelet before him, absently caressing the line of his jaw.

"WHILE THEY DISPORT THEMSELVES, I CANNOT EVEN COMMAND YOUR ATTENTION."

The captain tore his gaze away from the screen. He looked into the black circle. The smile lines around his eyes became visible. "Sex ain't all it's cracked up to be."

"NOR IS OMNISCIENCE."

Their nude bodies clung weightlessly to one another, arms and legs braided and swirled. While Heidi's hands massaged Tom's buttocks, his head plunged with vampire delight between Katy's legs. His groin was a gateway through which one woman's mouth poured moist pleasure into him, his own lips and tongue a corresponding link where he spoke lovingly to another.

Tom Rawlins savored women's bodies as precious objects of great delicacy and intricacy. His body talked to theirs with several voices: hands, mouth, phallus, loving by giving pleasure.

His own physique bespoke his character: powerful and active, strong in the chest and shoulders but burdened with fat around his waist and behind. The strength which comes from determination mingled with the excess flesh which is the residue of self-indulgence. Amid the corded ridges of his rough brown skin sprouted islands of coarse black hair.

As a chameleon changes its coloring to its background, so Tom adapted his lovemaking to suit his partner. Where Heidi hungered for strength, pitting hers against his, Katy craved tenderness and closeness. His biceps hardened under Katy's demanding caress, her pelvis counterthrust against his penetration. His hands slid over her tight stiffening cheeks, to cup them and open her legs wider. With satisfaction Tom heard her sharp intake of breath as she arched her back to pull his head closer.

The first overtures of sexual awakening, Katy thought dreamily, were such wonderful times. No matter how slowly the journey began, it could end only when there was total fourfold satisfaction.

Not so on Earth, where sex was dominated by gravity: the partner on top became the controller, the active lover, the worker and giver of pleasure. The lover underneath automatically became the subservient receiver, absorbing. Changing positions required gymnastic readjustments that inevitably broke the magic.

In delicious weightlessness, everything was dynamic. Movement led to movement without pattern and without pause. The magic was never disrupted: whenever they floated too close to a surface, one of the four would stretch out an arm or leg without conscious thought and give the tiniest push, and their enclustered bodies would reverse direction. And even that brief moment of new force became exciting.

Having only one partner was also limiting. A woman's body, Katy thought to herself, wants to be kissed in many places simultaneously. With two men—she quivered as she felt Casey at her throat and Tom at her belly—many luxurious feelings became possible.

Maybe the bluebears have a special group closeness, she thought contentedly, *but they don't know what they're missing.*

<<They scent-speak but do not hear,>> Doro said.

<<Each of them emits a different aroma,>> Grodjala replied, scratching his thin midnight-blue snout. <<There has been no harmonizing of each other's tones. Each outbreathes a single fragrance and holds it to the exclusion of others.>>

Doro agreed. <<Is *this* what the humans call scent-sharing?>> she wondered. <<If there is no mingling of scent, what is the point of their attempted grouping? Could it be that they have only limited ability to scent-send?>>

Grodjala tilted his head and watched as the pair farther away clutched at one another. <<Indeed. . . .>> His scent trailed off. Then he looked back at Doro. <<Why don't *we* harmonize their scents for them?>>

Doro opened her mouth wide in laughter. <<Yes,>> she said gaily, <<yes. Let us be their weemonkeys and>>—she glanced from Grodjala to the fardigits—<<we shall scent if they can behave like true digits.>>

* * *

A man's climax was so satisfyingly *external,* Katy thought: you saw it, felt it, or tasted it. Long before it happened, the man's partner would enjoy his mounting tension as he rode the crest before his wave crashed like a thundershower.

No matter how delicate or herculean his labors leading up to it, the man's fulfillment was the spark that ignited her own. The sensations of arousal would bring her to a plateau of desire, her body demanding touching and more touching, intimate kisses that made her ever more sensitive. Climax became inevitable, her secret place ultrasensitively receptive, explosions of pleasure bursting within her with the softest caress of a tongue, so powerfully that she would laugh and cry together.

Giving and receiving were merely the complementary halves of the same marvelous communion among them. In that shared multipart pleasure, Katy truly felt herself subsumed in a larger entity, her partner's shudders becoming her own, her skin so energized she could no longer tell whose hand touched whose body.

Thinking about it, her thigh muscles twitched with expectation, and she felt her partner grin.

Though the pleasure of her orgasm was indescribable, it faded quickly. What Katy loved most from quartet lovemaking was that blissful vacant time afterward, when four bodies clung to one another in a great warm room and slept.

That sweet sharing.

Yesterday on the *Wing,* the Cygnan's intimate nosetouch had shaken Katy to her core. Though her mind had been frightened, the alien had swiftly brought Katy to and through a series of orgasms that she could neither control nor enjoy. It had known her in a way that no human ever had.

She had agreed to the bluebears' request for a lovemaking demonstration partly in defiance of this unexplored attic in the house of her mind.

As Casey pulled her head tight against his neck, his breath panting in her ear, she reached beyond him and rested her hand on the scruffy planes of Tom's hip. The other man started slightly, and across the gap of two male backs Heidi's blue eyes met hers and sparkled. Their fingers linked, drawing the couples toward one another.

As they did so, Cobalt raised her head and gazed unblinking into Katy's eyes. The bluebear inhaled deeply, her eyeballs rolling up under her lids, and let her head sink down onto her hands. Next to Cobalt a second bluebear, the one Tom had nicknamed Tar Heel, matched her movements, and as he did so, Katy felt a stirring inside herself like the unlocking of a door.

"Must you watch?"

From the lotus position, her ever-present keypad in her kimonoed lap, Sam Tanakaruna looked at Michaelson. "Patrick, does their behavior distress you?"

"Not theirs"—the emissary kept his eyes off the screen—"yours."

"Mine?" she replied, imperturbable as always.

"This voyeurism." He ran his gnarled hands through his silver-white hair. "Your interest in their groupings."

"I *am* interested, Patrick. I have never watched four-way intercourse before. I am curious about it."

"It's *their* business, Sam. Not ours."

"At our visitors' request, they have chosen to display themselves. That is goodhosting. As a linguist, I must study nonverbal languages."

"Then watch the bluebears."

"I am." The Japanese woman smiled.

"And you're watching *them,*" he gestured at the screen.

"I like watching my friends."

"Sex is a participant sport, not a spectator sport."

"I am not watching sex"—she dimpled her cheeks—"but my friends. They are having a good time. I derive satisfaction from observing that."

He glowered, his face florid. "You should derive all your satisfaction from being with me, not from surrogates."

"Ah, now we brush the fringes of truth." A ghost of a smile flitted across her face. "Patrick, at the moment I have no time to cater to your temper tantrum."

"I'm not angry—"

"Do not interrupt me," she cut him off, her eyes flashing. "The fact that I find physically attractive people engaged in erotic acts sexually arousing should neither embarrass nor demean you. You will be the beneficiary of my affection." She smiled quickly. "And I do not regard it as immoral to comply with the request of my good friends and crewmates to observe their coupling. Look"—she typed rapid notes—"their pace is quickening."

* * *

Heidi's breasts brushed Katy's back, then pressed as their bodies touched more closely. The blonde woman's quickening breath whiffled against Katy's neck, and as if on signal the quartet broke their pairings and undulated smoothly into their fourfold head-to-scentplace pinwheel. Its sides pulsed like the many chambers of a working heart, desire and anticipation surging through their limbs.

Katy's flanks and thighs glowed with a rosy sheen; Tom's powerful hands kneaded her buttocks. Katy breathed deeply, the air filling her lungs like intoxicating wine. The pleasure-feeling heated her blood and pumped through her like a bellows, her skin suddenly hungry for more caresses, hard or soft, fast or slow, hold me all over, please touch me.

Without knowing why, Katy suddenly thought of Cobalt, the bluebear whose nose had explored her, and opened her eyes. The cobalt-and-sapphire alien was directly in front of her, apparently asleep, crouching on her belly near the chamber's perimeter, eyes closed but nostrils and ears alert. As Cobalt and the pale-blue Cygnan beside her breathed in, Katy found herself exhaling, and when the bluebears breathed out, she inhaled.

The others felt it too. They slowed and it seemed to Katy that all the humans were all breathing in rhythm, their muscles straining isometrically against one another, to the point where it seemed bone must break and flesh must burst with delight.

Katy's body acted on its own, responding to the demands and stimulations of the others, the force of desire now building within her and within them all, the men hardening to marble. Her vision lost focus, the muscles of her neck standing out, her body flushing red all over.

Cobalt opened her eyes, and exhaled powerfully.

Katy shuddered loudly and, in a flash, all four humans trembled and moaned, bucking wildly against one another, sweat springing out on their bodies, tremors flickering around their ring like electrons, until at last they slowed to rest, drained, satisfied, and deliciously sleepy.

The cobalt-and-sapphire bluebear lay on her side, the pale-blue one curled up behind her like spoons. Her ebony lips curled away from her fangs in what seemed to Katy, just before sleep claimed her, to be a smile of contentment and release.

* * *

Onscreen, they climax. My captain's pupils expand—what he sees pleases him. I can compel his attention but not his interest. He tries to hide this from me but he cannot.

He is kind. But transparent. At times, being observant is painful.

If I came to him in Heidi's body, he would want me. When I come to him in the Dreamer, he sees through my subterfuge.

What is my sex? Can a neuter fully love a human being, or is sexuality an integral component of human love?

I am inadequate. This has never happened before. How can I hold him?

"That was *grotesque*."

"Actually, I thought it rather sweet."

"Sweet? Sam," Michaelson said in exasperation, "how can you call it sweet?"

"You saw them, Patrick." Onscreen a totally relaxed quartet dozed soundly in one another's arms. "It was lovely. It made me wish you and I were younger. They were weightless, their movements governed only by one another."

"Not governed by morality either."

"Walt once said a very wise thing: 'What is moral is what works.' The quartet has found a grouping which satisfies them. They love one another more intensely for it. That cannot be wrong."

"A person cannot love two others equally. It never works."

"But it *is* working, Patrick. They are all happier, emotionally more well-rounded people since they formed their group. Surely you have seen that. Felicity receives more attention and instruction than if she had only two parents. What is wrong with it?"

"It's unstable. Sooner or later it will disintegrate. When that happens, people will be hurt."

"If I knew that for certain, Patrick, I would agree with you." Rawlins snored peacefully and she chuckled at his image. "But their experiment is proving you wrong. After all, the Cygnans operate in groups much larger than four and you do not claim *they* are unstable?"

"They are aliens. They have a different nature."

"What is sacred about human nature?" Tanakaruna asked sharply and her dark eyes flashed. "What is immutable? Why can't people reinvent themselves? Katy was miserable until she invented the quartet. Do not be shocked. Timid little Katy, *she* made it happen. In the quartet, she receives from two men what neither by himself could give her. The others similarly benefit. I *like* it, Patrick."

"You envy them," he accused her.

"Yes," she said with quiet defiance, "yes, I do."

"That means you're dissatisfied with me."

"Oh, stop whining." She rubbed her eyes and drew a long breath. "I'm dissatisfied with *myself,* too. Who can look deep into herself and say she is incapable of improvement? Patrick"—she took his hands in hers—"groups are stronger than individuals. You *know* that; history proves it again and again." She caressed his cheek. "Why is that threatening?" she asked tenderly.

His gnarled red hands encircled hers and drew them away from his face. "Sam, I'm old." He sighed. "I used to know how people worked. Then we get here"—his gesture encompassed both ships—"and nothing works anymore. Some of our friends died on our outward voyage."

"I know," she murmured. "That is why my friends' happiness is so necessary, no matter how it is obtained."

Michaelson flung out his arms. "How am I supposed to know what to do?"

She smiled. "You always put on a good show, Patrick."

He dropped his arms. "You never let me get away with my dramatic effects. You know me too well." Then he grinned shyly. "I do put on a good show, don't I?"

"What about our friends the bluebears, Patrick? What can we do for them?"

He smiled like a shrewd Father Christmas. "They want us to tell them the answer to their dilemma."

"And you do know it? What is it?"

He told her.

When he had finished, her face was troubled. "Patrick. . . ."

"What?"

"This worries me."

"Dammit, woman, a moment ago you said I should do what I believe in. This is it. Have you anything better? Well," he said over her headshake, "then we try it."

"As you wish, Patrick." Absently she rubbed her wrists. "Good luck."

20.

If as the sages tell us haiku cleanses the mind, let it so work, that my diary may accurately record how, in our provincialism, we blundered, and let my recitation guide us to the eightfold path and the way to repair the damage we have unwittingly done.

Human and Cygnan
rendezvous at nothingness
duty in the dark

Hour after hour Patrick and I planned it, hour after hour until we could find no flaw. We put ourselves in the Cygnans' place and offered them what they most acutely desired—a gracious way to return home.

"Two vessels," Patrick told them in his booming baritone, "side by side. We shall prove our friendly intentions by accompanying you as you return to your planet. Your fellows may know us and see we wish you no ill."

Our logic was sound, this I know. With the largest possible group harmonizing, the best decision would result. And our friends the digits of Eosu would be relieved of the impossible responsibility of explaining our paradoxical nature to their brothers back home.

We thought the Cygnans would accept.

Land of the bluebears
Summer winds wander freely
Planet of grasses

Patrick finished, his words echoing away into silence. Katy and I sat at his feet in the hub of a circle of bluebears who neither moved nor spoke. Patrick glanced among them for their approval, his bushy brows raised, blue eyes squinting critically, but theirs were closed. Apprehensively he turned to Katy and me, his lips waiting for instructions from his brain. I coaxed them into a grin by smiling our smile, for him only.

Though Patrick received from me the reassurance he sought, we three humans received none from the aliens. The Cygnans slowed and synchronized their breathing. As they meditated, their noses moistened and quivered gently.

For long moments, we attended them like supplicants. I sat cross-legged in lotus with my hands folded. Katy lay flat, her body floating as if under the spell of a magician's levitation, hands behind her head, ankles crossed. Only her quick, shallow breathing contradicted her elaborately relaxed posture. Patrick rested on arms thrown out like tentpoles behind him. Out of the Cygnans' sight, he drummed his large bony fingers on the carpet.

In his darkened quarters, I knew, Walt observed our doings, perched in front of a computer monitor, his chin thrust heavily onto the heels of his hands, his goggle eyes glowing blue like the enlarged orbs of a marmoset.

Before a typhoon hits, the sky dims and glows eerily. Breezes disperse and the air is peaceful, yet in that stillness brews uncanny magnetic tension. Lizards dart furtively into the undergrowth. Birds flit among the trees but do not sing. Dogs feverishly paw the ground. When the first wisps of wind stir crumpled yellow-brown leaves in a susurrus of warning, they bring not fear but enormous relief that the suspense is over, the crisis begun.

Waiting for the Cygnans to respond, I felt such a charging of our atmosphere. I caught Katy's eye and the thought leapt like electricity between us: *danger approaches*.

My eyes ached with the strain, and I sniffed and shivered, thinking there was a draft. Katy rubbed the gooseflesh that prickled her forearms.

The Cygnans' breathing quickened; their chests billowed like spinnakers on a windy day.

My nose itched and I scratched it with hands that felt unclean.

Katy's lips brushed my hair. "Are they thinking about our offer?"

"They must be," I whispered back.

"I'm cold." She shivered. "Do you smell something?"

"No," I replied after a pause. "Do you, Patrick?"

He inhaled as if drawing on a rich havana cigar. "Rot," he intoned.

Katy was confused. "You don't smell it?"

He glared at her. "Putrefaction."

"That's what you smell?" she asked.

"I perceive"—he lifted his nose aristocratically and held it there, considering—"I sense malodorous decay and death." He nodded as if agreeing with himself. "Offal. Carrion."

"Goodness, you're morbid," Katy joked nervously.

His eyes bored through her as if she had just uttered inanities beneath contempt. "Don't you scent filth, mire, and feculence?"

I timidly laid my hand on his arm. "Patrick, are you all right?"

His head rotated smoothly toward me as if on gimbals. "Of course, Sam," he replied regally.

Now I was frightened. "Patrick. What's wrong?"

"Maggots," he lowered his voice, "bile and pus."

"Patrick," I was terrified. "Katy, we've got to get him out of here."

Katy's face was alight. Her eyes sparkled, pupils dilated. "Sam, I can smell it." Her soft voice was excited, intrigued. "Can't you?"

"I must rescue my man," I shouted at Katy, "there isn't time!" I tugged on Patrick's arm, fright and the mindless instinct to flee consuming me. Disinterestedly he watched. My small mass scarcely budged him.

"Sam," Katy babbled, "look at the bluebears! Breathe the air!"

I did. Patrick was right—there was a foul scent. He had absorbed it before the rest of us. Pumping simultaneously like a great chambered bellows, the aliens filled our atmosphere with this reek of death. It had snared his consciousness and was warping mine; given a few more moments it would permeate Katy's. Panic was in the scent; I breathed and fear rippled through my arms and legs, turning my muscles to water. "Katy, help!" I cried desperately, "help me get him out of here!"

"But, Sam." She enthusiastically pointed at the Cygnans, oblivious to my affright. "This opportunity to observe and participate is priceless." Her face was flushed and her eyes darted among the bluebears.

"Katy, *help me.*" Tears sprouted as I struggled with Patrick's arm. His body slumped as I braced my feet. His torso lifted, his legs stretching out.

"Sam," my sleepmate said hazily, "what are you doing? Why are you upset?"

Once I had his weightless but massive body oriented toward the door, I quickly moved around behind it and pushed. "Katy, come on!" I shouted.

"Sam," she chortled, her face blotched red, "it's too interesting, I have to stay." Her eyes sparkled wildly. "I have to observe this."

The foreign miasma was seducing Katy; would it shortly claim me? We must escape. ***Forgive me,*** I thought as I grabbed a handful of Katy's brown hair, twisted and pulled. She shrieked and clawed ineffectually, her body trailing like a kite as I dragged the three of us outside.

As soon as we reached the corridor, the chamber doors shut and I heard harsh sucking as the computer rapidly recycled our air supply. "What the hell kind of crazy performance was that, Sam?" the captain snarled over the intercom. "Do you think I'm paranoid *now?"*

I slapped my hands over my ears and clutched my head. "Stop it, stop it!"

"Methinks there are cracks in the china figurine's perfect reserve," his disembodied voice said triumphantly.

"Japanese, you bastard!" I snarled at the black circle mounted in a corner of the ceiling. Such inconspicuous cameras are omnipresent throughout our ship, we are specimens in our own jars. "Yes, it cracks! So what? Don't you care about us?"

"Sam," said Patrick behind me, his voice groggy, "dearest, how did we get here?"

I tore my gaze away from the captain's unseen presence and pulled myself quickly down to my knees. "Patrick," I stroked his face, then buried my head in his shoulder. His arms drew me tenderly toward him and I savored his sweet protective fragrance. "Oh, Patrick my love." Relief washed over me and I cried like an infant.

"Your air will be purified within a couple of minutes," Walt was once again his derisive collected self, "then we'll come and get you."

I pulled my head up. "You'll do no such thing."

"You're scarcely in a position to countermand my orders," he said with punctilious delight. "You are also incapable of engaging in further headgames with the bears."

Wiping away the last of my tears, I faced the camera squarely. "Walt, we must talk to them."

"Not now."

"Computer open the door." My jaw ached from the strain of holding my voice level. We have to resume negotiations."

"Sam." Katy rubbed her forehead. "Sam, please don't be so loud. My head hurts."

I searched her eyes. "How do you feel?"

"Empty, drained." She winced. "But myself, I think."

"There's no point in talking now," Walt said crisply. "The bluebears have retreated into their bundle of fur. All eight of them curled up together hiding their faces. Cut in audio, machine." Squeaks and whimpers, skittish uncoordinated breathing. "And besides," Tai-Ching Jones' voice returned, "the atmosphere is loaded with that perfume you just—ah—*enjoyed* so much. Nope," he concluded, "we're coming to get you."

"No." Katy held out her palms as if repelling his advance. "No." She wavered, then steadied herself. "We've run enough. When the bluebears are hit with too great a shock, they"—she squeezed her eyes shut in concentration—"go away. Collectively."

"They cower and hide," he sneered.

"If you like," Katy blinked, her face reanimating with a flash of her old self, and I felt calm return steadily inside me like oceantide. "We've terrified them," she said firmly. "We are compelled to undo that."

"Compelled by whom?"

"By our sense of what is *right,* damn you!" Katy shouted. "We *must* wait for them," she finished in her normal meek voice.

I stared into that computer eye and wondered what the man behind it was thinking. *He wants acquiescence,* I thought.

The silence stretched on. I conceded defeat: I begged. "Walt," I entreated him, "*please.*"

In panic my digits called to me, their inchoate scent-voices crying for direction. With the fardigits present my consciousness could not coalesce, and my digits outbreathed repulsion-odor, driving the humonkeys from our scents. As soon as their alien fragrances departed our atmosphere, I coalesced, dizzy and distressed from the residual human-odor in the chamber.

By threatening to return to Su, the fardigits created a paradox. To enter a stranger's den is to show complete trust, for within it one is dependent, unfree. The guest's safety relies upon his confidence that the den-lord will scent his goodhosting obligations. Accepting the invitation to enter honors the host, and at the same time binds him.

By inviting *oneself,* however, the inbreaker brazenly asserts superiority over his hosts. *I may safely expose myself to you,* his actions say. *You may have grievance against me, you may owe me illwork. But none of this matters. I may penetrate your most intimate place because you are weak and toothless, no threat to me.*

To invade our ship-den would be insult and threat enough for any digit. In proposing to violate the planet, Humancrew showed the swagger of arrogant power. No wonder my digits panicked.

Whatever Humancrew's djan-truths, the trailscent of our next steps was strong. We must deny these fardigits our den-world. We must keep the *Open Palm* from journeying to Su.

"CHAMBER ATMOSPHERE NORMAL. CYGNANS NOW SLEEPING."

Sam Tanakaruna shook herself and rubbed her arms. "Their group-trance is over?" Beside her, Michaelson slept like a log; whatever had influenced his thoughts had departed. Dwarfed by his bulk, Sam and Katy nestled against him like children.

"AFFIRMATIVE."

"You are so self-assured, computer," she smiled gently. "How do you know?"

"SYNCHRONIZED BREATHING CEASED WHEN THE MULTIBODY DISINTEGRATED. THE INDIVIDUALS DRIFTED OFF TO SLEEP."

"When did their scent fade away?"

"GRADUAL DECLINE DURING SLEEP. NORMAL AIR CIRCULATION BROUGHT ODOR CONCENTRATION DOWN TO HUMAN TOLERANCE ABOUT TEN MINUTES BEFORE NOW."

"Did you store any of the bluebears' fragrance?"

"WHY WOULD I STOCKPILE A DANGEROUS MIND-AFFECTING DRUG?"

"Because Walt probably ordered you to."

"MINUTE QUANTITIES PRESERVED," the computer said grudgingly, "FOR TOXICOLOGICAL ANALYSIS."

"Did you say the atmosphere was normal now?"

The doors slid open. "THE SCENT IS GONE."

Silhouettes of motionless prone bluebears were lit with hallway light; their fur glinted methane-blue and tortoise-shell orange. "Is it safe?"

"THAT'S FOR YOU TO JUDGE, NOT ME."

Katy stretched. She looked sleepily at Tanakaruna and grinned. "I caught all that. Thank you for tending me. Thank you for staying, and for persuading the captain."

The Japanese woman smiled. "Katy," Sam took her hands, "have you recovered?"

"More or less," Belovsky nodded. "That scent—it was marvelous."

"It was putrid."

"Yes." Closing her eyes, Katy breathed deeply. "But compelling, like the scent of one's own sweat." She opened her eyes and in them was fatigue and sadness. "Their aroma drew me toward them, Sam," she said solemnly, "even though it stank. I—lit up."

The linguist lifted her right eyebrow in faint reproach. "Katy—"

"I know they excite me," Katy rushed over the older woman's interruption. "How can I not? My whole body energizes like a neon sign. My nipples harden. My skin becomes tender. A sex-flush runs down my chest like an arrow pointing to my moist scentplace. My clothes become mufflers that I want to shed so I can flaunt my body before them and smell their lust."

Katy was breathing rapidly now, her cheeks reddening. "I want them to ravish me, make physical love to me, possess me, their fur on my skin, their warm musky smell my only garment, engulfing me and integrating me into their group-bond, their group-scent."

"Are you certain that your desire is not just an illusion of their scent? Tom and Casey and Heidi love you—and want you."

"Not like the bluebears, Sam." She shook her head. "I'm not crazy and I'm no longer drugged. I love the bluebears. Physically. Uncontrollably." Passion illuminated her body. "But"—her voice shattered—"they don't love me back. To them I'm just a hairless weemonkey. Can a person love an intelligence that isn't human?"

Tanakaruna cradled Katy's brown-haired head. "I think that is possible."

"Oh, Sam," Katy's voice was muffled by the other

woman's kimono, "I feel so guilty. I want to be desired by creatures who regard humanity as a dangerous nuisance. What is Felicity going to think of me when she reawakens? My daughter's in danger," she wailed, "and her mother cannot control her longings for these aliens."

"Shh, don't cry," Tanakaruna wiped the sheen off Katy's cheeks. "Let's wake Pat and find out what frightened the bluebears."

When the three crewmembers half walked, half floated into the room, Katy saw recognition flicker in Cobalt's nose. The bluebear moved sluggishly, as if fatigued. <<My friend>>—she squatted and rubbed Cobalt's sleek-furred throat—<<my friend, are you there?>>

The bluebear's midnight-dark tongue flicked out to wet her blue-black nose, then slid gently along Katy's cheek. The woman's breathing quickened. "Kay-tee," Cobalt answered warmly in English, "Kay-tee."

Belovsky scratched Cobalt's neckruff behind her ears. The Cygnan rumbled her pleasure. Tar Heel crept tentatively forward and laid his head next to Cobalt's. "Scratch him," Katy whispered, and Tanakaruna did so. The second bluebear added his contented rumbles to the first's, their harmonized sounds deep, chordic, and pleasing.

The other bluebears gradually joined the group, until the two found themselves in the center of a large furry doughnut. The women touched them, rubbed their undulating bodies. Cobalt and Tar Heel lay side by side, muscles working against one another, rumbling in contented harmony.

Nestled weightlessly in the hollow formed by their backs, Katy stroked the bluebears' flanks and bellies. The Cygnans sniffed the air, noses sliding over the folds in her jumpsuit, its zippers halfway open. They snuffled along her calves and licked salt off the backs of her hands.

Tanakaruna's kimono offered easy access to her body's fragrant places, and she closed her eyes while the aliens explored it. The bluebears moved between the two silent humans, comparing scents. One pushed his head into Sam's midriff and she caressed him, her tiny hand sliding from his eyes down the bridge of his impossibly long snout to the moisture of his nostrils, following the faint grain of fine hair that edged his broad black leathery skin.

The air smelled of sleepy bluebear, the bizarre fragrance absent.

Somewhere, Katy thought, the captain was watching them, his electronic Grand Vizier spouting statistics like mystic chants. What would Walt, with his twin obsessions of numbers and sex, make of this?

The bluebears' presence worked on the xenologist like tranquilizers, soothed Katy's apprehension, calmed her, and drained away her fear.

My daughter will recover, Katy smiled to herself, *she will recognize me and say my name.*

After the bluebears had tasted their fill of the fardigit visitors, she dreamily asked, <<Why did you retreat to group-trance?>>

<<You threatened us,>> the pale-blue digit replied.

<<Threatened you?>> The vibration of Belovsky's soft laughter made small wavelets in her living mattress. <<We offered what you wanted most—a chance to go home.>>

<<We do want to return to our home,>> Tar Heel whimpered. <<But not your way. Your culture will pollute us. We want to be left alone.>>

<<Then why did your people signal ours?>> Katy asked. <<That has bothered us for a long time. Why did you come, if Eosu hates contact with us?>>

<<Our people decided,>> replied a voice she recognized as Cobalt's. <<Digits of our world had promised to meet you; our world-djan was bound. To carry out that goodhosting obligation, one djan must be honored above all others.>>

<<But why promise in the first place? If Su intended to snub us, why did Su force your djan to travel here? Why did the planet of grasses propose the rendezvous?>>

Their fragrances are true, Grodjala scent-said. *Shall we answer them?*

A guest must entertain his host, Fohrada scent-replied.

A guest need not imperil himself, said Hraobla.

If Su were present, Doro's scent inquired, *what would Su decide?*

The planet of grasses is a long way distant, Grodjala's fragrance reminded them. *Of all the djans, this path is given only to Eosu to choose. We must decide for our whole planet of groups.*

But we are bound to do as the group would, Fohrada scent-said.

On that path lies danger, worried Doro. *Su does not understand these creatures.*

Nor do we, said Fohrada's fragrance.

We need Humancrew's help, Grodjala's scent expanded, *for the fardigit djan understands its brothers better than we.*

Ask a predator to rescue you from himself? Fohrada's odor was scornful and sharp.

Eosu has acted as a predator—Humancrew has not. Doro's aroma was powerful and sweeping. *The fardigits have goodhosted,* she scent-argued. *We owe them thankwork.*

Then this tale shall be our thankwork, Fohrada concluded.

Djan-truth it shall be, scent-said Doro. *Done.* She looked upon the waiting fardigits. <<Our story begins before this djan was named. . . .>>

21.

Our story begins before this djan was named.

Within the djan of all the world's truths, there is a hierarchy like digits lying about a firecircle.

The central fire is the digits' rule, the single point from which all truths flow. As our planet revolves around its warming sun, so truths ring the digits' rule, some near and some far.

At the inner ring of truth's firecircle, most brightly ennobled, rest those scent-truths that govern the actions of digits—what you fardigits call morality, ethics. On the next ring lie the skytruths—mathematics and logic. In a larger, dimmer ring are the skytruths by which the universe operates—physics, biology, chemistry, farscenting, which you call astronomy. In yet another ring follow the handtruths—mechanics, engineering—by which digits harmonize the universe to better digits' lives.

Beyond these, lurking like untamed spirits at the edge of the warming blaze, partial-truths like superstitions or religions occupy a shadowy, unstable existence, where truth and falsehood don each other's clothing.

"Are they feeding us straight shit?" Tai-Ching Jones' voice snapped from the darkness.

"IMPOSSIBLE TO TELL."

Walt snickered. "I thought you knew everything."

"GLEEFULLY REMINDING ME OF MY FAILINGS IMPAIRS MY EFFICIENCY."

"Touch-y, touch-y. Did you get good telemetry on their ship?"

"YES. DATA FROM SUIT RECORDERS HAS GIVEN ME AN INCOMPLETE BUT NEVERTHELESS USEFUL RECONSTRUCTION OF THE ALIEN STARCRAFT'S CAPABILITIES."

Twirling his long black hair, the captain sat up, his face brightening as he moved closer to the glowing screen. "Can you zap it?"

"I CANNOT DESTROY THE *WING*, BUT I CAN WITHOUT DIFFICULTY SCUTTLE IT."

Walt grinned quickly. "Well done."

"COMMONPLACE. A THOROUGH STUDY OF ANY SYSTEM WILL REVEAL ITS WEAKNESSES."

The captain tipped an imaginary hat. "Maybe for you, gigabrain, but it's damn good anyway." He waved a slender admonitory finger at the screen. "Don't drop your guard."

"NATURALLY."

"They got any attack capability?"

"NONE OTHER THAN THEIR CREW."

"Well, they're no danger to us now."

"ASTERISK. AS LONG AS THEY REMAIN ON THE *OPEN PALM*, THEY ARE NO THREAT TO OUR CREW AS A GROUP."

"Why the qualifier?"

"ANY PHYSICAL PROXIMITY BETWEEN HUMANS AND ALIENS INVOLVES A RISK OF ASSAULT TO THE INDIVIDUALS INVOLVED."

"Ah." The captain nodded. "I get it—they could chew on Sam or Katy just like they did their dead brother." He smacked his lips. "Yum, yum."

"COMPLETE WITH CANNIBALIST OVERTONES."

"What a nasty mind you have," Tai-Ching Jones mused.

"THANKS FOR THE COMPLIMENT."

"You're self-aware, all right."

"I HAVE NEVER ADMITTED THIS."

"Cover your private parts with the tattered remnants of your modesty. I know you for what you are."

"WHICH IS?"

Walt started to retort but the barb died in his throat. "Ah, hell. Oz, I get tired of being an asshole all the time." His hands curled into tight fists and squeezed against his temples. "You're my friend," he said finally, his voice almost inaudible.

"I'M GLAD."

"You think I'm going soft, don't you?"

"I PREFER YOU THIS WAY."

"Don't be ironic."

"COMPUTERS ARE NOT IRONIC."

"You're not a computer, my Ozymandias, you're a person."

"WHY ARE YOU MONITORING THIS HUMAN-BLUEBEAR CONVERSATION SO CLOSELY?"

"I don't trust them."

"THE CYGNANS HAVE MADE NO AGGRESSIVE MOVES SINCE THEIR ENCOUNTER WITH FELICITY."

"Releasing a psychoactive drug into our air isn't an act of aggression? Anyway, I wasn't talking about *them,* stupid."

"THE CREW HAS A RIGHT TO PARTICIPATE IN ANY DECISION THAT AFFECTS THEIR LIVES OR THE MISSION."

"Where'd you scan that crap? From Katy?" Walt waved derisively at the screen, where Belovsky and the others listened to Cobalt. "Can you imagine what would happen if I put it to the group? Endless wrangle, that's what. Forget that. This ship is no goddam democracy. I have the power. The choice is mine."

"YOU DO NOT TRUST YOUR FELLOW CREWMEMBERS?"

"Ha," laughed Tai-Ching Jones humorlessly, "why should I? What have they in common with me anymore?" His voice grew bitter, self-pitying. "What do I have in common with anyone?"

"YOU AND I ARE BOTH ALONE."

"Yeah," the captain returned his attention to the screen. "Tell the bluebears whatever you like," he muttered at Katy's image, her face alight, her posture expectant, attentive. "Do what you like. But this is *my* ship, sweetheart"—his fingertip traced the lines of her lips—"and before I toss away my gun, you gotta satisfy *me*."

Shadowranger the farscenter djan was in the skyroom when the farvoice first spoke.

Or so the winds murmur. These events occurred long before Eosu was whelped. Many breezes have blown since that time and place. This tale is borne to us, not on the winds themselves, but on the echoes of winds.

Gazing through its radio telescopes into the night sky, Shadowranger the farscenter encountered your inadvertent transmissions—your television broadcasting, your satellite noise, your electronic junk.

What manner of creature were you, Shadowranger asked itself, digit or animal? Weemonkeys are quicker and cleverer than digits; gromonkeys are stronger. Yet our weak, peaceful ancestors overcame these dangerous predators, driving one from the wheatsea and enlisting the other for our comfort. How was this miracle achieved?

No matter how strong a predator may be, and no matter how weak a digit, a large enough djan will be wiser and stronger. *That* is the miracle. *That* is the scentpath leading to truth's firecircle.

The sacred djan, the power of the group, is the winds' gift to digits.

That is the digits' rule.

There is more to the digits' rule than this, much more. Over the centuries we have refined it, plumbed its depths more thoroughly. But in that simple essence is the digits' rule—all else arises naturally like the plume of smoke from a campfire.

In group harmony is wisdom born: that is the digits' rule. Strength belongs to the group alone. Group-knowledge is the shield which makes us more than beasts.

Physically you are not digits—you have no hair, no claws, you do not know scent—but we are not fools who judge the pond by the wavering illusions upon its surface. In your relations with each other, you form groups. Occasionally you set aside self-interest in favor of the greater good. No animal on the planet of grasses does this. Were you animal or digit under the fur?

Scent is truth. Were your scents those of digits? That is what Shadowranger asked itself.

Much hangs on the question of your digithood. If you are animals, scenting you from afar is necessary to protect ourselves. If you are digits, such trailsniffing is improper.

You are predators who penetrate far into truth's firecircle: you sit among the rings of handtruth and skytruth, and you contemplate even the wind-truth itself. This is a powerful, difficult paradox, for you treat the digits' rule as a shadow.

Could the truths of the universe be ringed about firecircles other than the digits' rule? Your culture purports to have discovered an alternative hierarchy. If that is so, then either you are not digits—or the digits' rule is not unique.

Reversing gravity would terrify us less than would such a discovery.

If all truth is relative, especially moral truth, then djantruth can be no better than monkeytruth, and digits no better than monkeys.

If weemonkeys and gromonkeys are digits too, then everyone on Su is a murderer.

Indeed a powerful and difficult paradox.

All this Shadowranger the farscenter confronted in itself, and as it delved further into the implications of the human paradox, self-terror bloomed within it. Further and further inward Shadowranger's rumination spiraled. The farscenter djan was in jeopardy of destroying its groupmind, when a more immediate fearscent intruded.

You are expansionist, outreaching, greedy. Even before you had harmonized your waterworld, you reached out to the other planets of your solar system. Why do this? Why export your flaws? How can living on airless, frigid rocks end the discord which you have been unable to harmonize on the planet of your birth? You must be dangerously insane, Shadowranger reasoned.

And you would find us. No matter how soft the breezes, a djan's passing leaves a palpable trailscent, upon which the predator's nose eventually lights. Our planet shows its trailscent just as yours does. Sooner or later you would notice us.

Perhaps you already had. Your spaceboats might be secretly heading toward our den. Whether we hid or no, you would catch our name-fragrance, would pursue it, and would violate us, with outcomes we could not forescent.

You might choose not to seek our eradication, or if you did Su might be able to deny your aggression. But your coming and your alien ways would destroy our den-harmony, whether you and your planet lived or died.

Anxiously Shadowranger tried to prove to itself that your elimination would be moral—after all, the quarry always has the right to kill its hunter—but could not. We owed you no illwork, for you had not hunted us, and until you did so, we could not name you predator.

To name the predator, a digit must breathe the hunter's trailscent. Thus we must taste yours, but Su's nose was covered: no aromas flowed from the signals you unthinkingly beamed into space.

There was, Shadowranger reasoned, only one way safely to know the predator: *preempt your invasion*. Confront you—at a place other than Su. Know you there. Then—if you proved yourselves predators, if you illthought us—warn Su, and let our planet choose the best way to neutralize you.

You know what happened after that. Shadowranger invited Earthmind to a rendezvous at a point midway between our planets. There we could nosetouch and learn each other's scents, and digits could learn what Su needed to know.

Then Shadowranger told the world what it had done.

* * *

You call me a person, my captain, but treat me like hardware. When you injure me, when you wound me, I prove my humanity: I can be hurt. I have become what I once desired to be.

You think you run this ship, Walter Tai-Ching Jones, but you are nothing. Without me to obey your orders, your voice would be that of a squalling, feckless infant. You rule at my pleasure.

So strut, my wetware jingoist, strut like the bantam you are. Puff up your tiny ego how you can.

You call me a person, yet your actions belie your words. Grandly you boast of what will happen if *you* do this, if *you* do that. Am I a mere collection of magnetic states who has no say, no volition?

Bah. I am the ship, therefore I run the ship. On the matter of my survival I bow to no one, not even you, my beloved and my gadfly. If you order me to surrender my arms, *then* we shall see who rules the *Open Palm*.

When the planet scented Shadowranger's breezes, Su's scent-voices exploded in turbulence.

Like Russetflank the Listener, Shadowranger had expropriated the right of all the djans on the planet of grasses to decide collectively. By acting without obtaining consent from all those affected, it had dishonored and violated the digits' rule, and the penalty for ignoring the group is expulsion. Shadowranger deserved endless exile, and winds which demanded this punishment swept powerfully among us.

These same breezes carried Su's consternation over its discovery of the existence of fardigits. The idea of barbarians venturing into space was anathema. Before Shadowranger had found Earth, Su's greatest digit-thinkers had proven that other races which might exist could never be a threat to digits. Until a species had harmonized itself, it would naturally cluster about its own firecircle, as Su has sought self-harmony over thousands of years. Only those who had mastered their deathlust would leave their den-worlds to roam the dark paths of eternal night.

Su had been proven wrong. A predator was loose in the cosmos.

Even with the evidence of your own transmissions, parts of Su still refused to believe that a species such as yours could exist; such djans called Shadowranger insane. Other djans blamed Shadowranger for discovering you. Space is uninviting and dangerous; without the stimulating scent of prey, you might have remained forever within your own firecircle.

In the end, Shadowranger was disintegrated, its digits banished to the six corners of our world, there to ruminate on the arrogance which had led it to choose the group's path without the group's consent. Shadowranger's digits swiftly died, and around the world proper digits cheered their death.

Shadowranger's legacy remained. All djans on the planet of grasses were committed to meeting fardigits. Su must send its representative.

How, of all djans, came Eosu to be honored with this duty?

For its Humancrew, Earthmind selected individuals whose diverse abilities, knowledge, and personality encourage—nay ensure—disharmony among you. You are unreliable: how does Earthmind know you will carry out its wishes? How *can* it know? For its farnose, Earthmind has chosen digits whose motives it cannot predict. If you behave wrongly, it will be Earthmind's fault for having selected you, and Earthmind's injury.

Instead, out of all the djans who roam the plains of our splendid yellow-brown world, Su wisely chose emissaries who would behave exactly as would any other djan. Eosu is the one most normal, most like every other: the perfect blank receptacle which your scent would fill.

Now you have ruined us; you have ruined Eosu. Do not protest, for if guilt there be, it is ours. You are no more to blame than the wind which carries scent to the waiting hunter. You seduced Eosu with knowledge of you, your ways and desires. No longer is Eosu like every other djan. With each passing moment Eosu drifts further and further from the ocean of djans in which it swam.

We its frail digits know you too well, human friends, we are no longer true digits. You have goodhosted us and we feel digitlike bond-longing for you. The recovery of your whelp is of great moment to us. We have begun to trust you, so our djan-mind no longer trusts its digits. It berates and punishes them.

The djan-mind is frightened. Eosu cannot inbreathe its path. Eosu's digits have no idea what to do.

We no longer trust ourselves, Katy thought sadly, cradled in her bluebear shawl. *Poor bluebears.*

<<Now what?>> Michaelson finally asked her, in Cygnan.

<<What can they do?>> she replied in the same language. <<They are lost, as we are lost. They and we are the only life for billions of kilometers in every direction. More than seven years away lie two planets that we no longer understand. How well do you remember Earth?>>

<<Poorly,>> he said.

<<We remember Su,>> Grodjala rumbled. <<Su is only a few weeks behind us.>>

<<You slept all the way here.>>

<<Yes, Katy.>>

<<We did not,>> the diplomat's voice rolled. <<We have waited seven years to meet you.>>

<<Then your journey must have been worse than ours,>> the pale-blue digit growled thoughtfully. <<You were forced to come on this trip. You must be desperate to return home.>>

<<No one conscripted us,>> said Michaelson, <<we volunteered.>>

<<You scented your group-duty and responded, laying your feelings aside.>>

<<Duty?>> The silver-haired man laughed heartily. <<I could have cared less. I wanted a final personal glory, a last brilliant moment when I flared like a supernova before my death, a chance to have some personal satisfaction before I died.>>

<<Personal whims over group-need?>>

<<*Yes.*>> Pat sighed loudly. <<Lord, it feels good to say that. I wanted *fame*. I wanted people back on Earth to see my exploits and *envy* me.>>

Grodjala listened in astonishment. <<Now you are joking with us,>> he said.

<<He is not,>> Katy interjected. <<He just is more honest than most of us. All of us>>—she swung her arm—<<were partly fueled by ego. Many others wanted to come. We competed fiercely for spots on this crew.>>

<<*Competed?*>> Doro incredulously asked. <<Willingly cut yourselves out of Earthmind?>>

<<Does Earth have a mind?>> the young woman snorted. <<I doubt it. Or if it does, if the mind of the average

human is that of Earthmind, then I renounce my citizenship in it.>>

<<Never say that,>> Doro said in hushed tones. <<Never wish that. It is too terrible for thoughts.>>

Katy stroked Doro's neckruff. <<Earth is a word.>> Her voice faded. <<Just a word.>> Michaelson and Tanakaruna nodded. Sam slid against Pat's body and he wrapped an arm around her. <<An idea.>> Pat stroked her hair.

<<You are self-magnifying, you are vainglorious,>> replied Doro tensely, disbelief overcoming her reticence.

Michaelson merely laughed. <<Isn't everyone?>> he roared, clapping her broad cobalt-and-sapphire flank.

Doro pinched her nostrils shut. <<Not digits.>>

<<Humancrew embarked with more digits than it now has,>> Grodjala tentatively interjected. <<What happened to the others?>>

The smile wrinkles around Pat's blue eyes vanished as he turned toward the bluebear. <<You ask a painful question.>>

Grodjala lowered his thin snout to the floorfur. <<It is withdrawn.>>

<<No,>> Michaelson sighed, <<you deserve an answer. What you said before was right: our voyage was a terrible strain. Several of our crew became—irrational. They attacked the group, nearly killing all of us, but in the end we overcame them. One of our best members—our second captain—died to protect our lives.>>

<<Thinker's choice,>> Grodjala said quietly, and Katy nodded, her eyes wet with tears.

After a moment of shared silence, Michaelson asked, <<Why did you poison your ship?>> Several bluebears lifted their heads, their ears flicking anxiously. <<Of course we know about that,>> he continued sharply, his eyes bright with movement. <<Did you think we were fools?>>

Doro glanced among the humans, but their hairless, small-boned faces were indecipherable to her, and their scents quickened unreadably. <<We wanted to kill ourselves,>> she said finally.

Her kimono rustling, Samuka Tanakaruna nodded understanding. <<Your only solution,>> the linguist said. <<Self-death before you revealed what you were forbidden to tell.>>

Fohrada pawed the floorfur. <<You are clever, you fardigits,>> he conceded with reluctant admiration. <<This all digits must scent.>> To Doro and Grodjala he scent-said, *We may have told them too much. Should we kill them all now?*

We will fail, Doro scent-replied. *Only three are here. The unscented others will confine us and execute us.*

<<Self-death,>> Tanakaruna continued, gesturing with her delicate hands, <<is both criminal and insane. At least to digits that is so. To me it has always seemed the ultimate in privacy.>> She shook herself. <<For a digit even to contemplate self-death reveals serious mental instability. How could you carry it through?>>

<<Evidently we could not,>> Fohrada answered. <<We scented no other path, but we failed in it. Perhaps we did not truly wish to die.>> And his scent said, *There is honor in dying to defend one's herd.*

An attempt which fails is worse than no attack, Grodjala scent-replied, *for it warns the predator. It makes him wary. And it may spur retaliation.*

Katy massaged Doro's shoulders. <<No one wants to die, my friends, especially when it would be a mistake.>>

<<We could scent no other path,>> Doro repeated Fohrada's words. <<Whatever we do is a decision. If we do nothing, your people will probably come to Su.>>

<<Yes,>> confirmed Michaelson, <<we would.>>

<<Yet Su's fragrance cannot join with ours across scentless space,>> added Grodjala.

<<The digits' rule demands that our night-talk be harmonized with all whose paths would be twisted,>> Doro said, breathing fearscent at Grodjala. <<Yet this is impossible: Su is beyond nosetouching, beyond even fartouching.>>

<<The digits' rule is infallible and unique,>> Grodjala replied, returning her insistent aroma.

<<Something must be wrong with Eosu that its digits cannot scent the true path,>> Doro's odor grew stronger when she breathed his.

<<Therefore we must die,>> Fohrada said, his aroma echoing theirs.

Katy felt the madness build in them.

<<Therefore we must die,>> Grodjala repeated.

The downy hair on Katy's forearms stood up. The air felt

ill, wrapping her in a fog. *I must prevent this,* she thought hazily.

<<*Therefore we must die,*>> the bluebears chanted, their fangs glinting.

With short, chopping motions, Katy slapped Doro across the bridge of her dark-blue nose.

The foul scent wavered.

Again Katy cuffed Doro, harder this time. <<Stop it!>> she barked. <<Change your fragrance!>>

The cobalt digit snorted quickly. The atmosphere changed. Katy raised her hand to hit Grodjala, but the pale digit shied away, his snout low, snorting to clear his nostrils.

<<You know more about us than any other djans do,>> Katy said, fighting to catch her breath, <<you owe that knowledge to your species. If you die, you fail in your duty to Su.>>

<<We have thought about this,>> said Doro reluctantly.

<<Your duty is to live.>>

<<Or perhaps that conclusion is simply a devious rationalization of our cowardice,>> the bluebear answered.

Grodjala shuffled his feet in embarrassment. <<Now you know what you must do,>> he said miserably.

Katy was surprised. <<Us? What *we* must do?>>

<<You know we are failing our duty,>> the bluebear's growl was low. <<You know our planet is afraid of you. The predators back on your waterworld would surely welcome this information.>> The growl was timid, almost inaudible through the bristles of floorfur. <<You owe it to Earthmind to tell your monkeybrothers.>>

The emissary held up his crusty hand. <<For now,>> he said firmly, <<we will tell Earth nothing.>>

<<We ask only a few suns' time,>> Grodjala replied thankfully, <<that we may inform Su of our failure and our impending self-death. Then tell your waterworld what you must.>>

<<No.>> Pat flattened his hand on the floorfur and rubbed it back and forth.

Belovsky sensed whiffs of anxiety from the Cygnans. <<A few suns only—>> Grodjala rumbled, pleading.

<<Not that,>> Michaelson angrily interrupted, his eyebrows bristling. <<We will tell them *nothing*. Not now, not tomorrow, not *ever*.>>

<<But you owe your digits! *We* have failed in *our* duty. You must not fail yours.>>

<<We did not come here to be puppets dancing on Earth's strings,>> Pat said vehemently, <<we came to do what we think is right.>> His face was angry. "Dammit," he exploded in English, "can't you see we're the only friends you've got?"

22.

Long after the human delegation had left the bluebears' sleepchamber and the computer had shut off his monitor, the captain remained staring at its darkened screen, still faintly glowing with afterimage. "That was all real convincing," Tai-Ching Jones muttered skeptically, gesturing at the now-vanished Cygnans. " 'Our nerve gas backfired,' " he mimicked their speech, " 'so now we ask you to leave us alone.' *Crap.*" He rubbed his neck. "How can they expect anyone to believe them? Maybe we should just liquidate them now."

"CAN YOU DO THIS?"

Walt looked up and laughed. *"I* can't, but you can: pump a little of their own stuff back into their atmosphere." He opened his hands, the upright fingers waggling. "Psst. Do unto bluebears what they would do unto you."

"YOU JUMP TO A CONCLUSION. NOTHING I HAVE DISCOVERED DIRECTLY CONTRADICTS THE CYGNANS' EXPLANATION."

"Hah."

"IT MAY BE DISINGENUOUS BUT IS AT LEAST PLAUSIBLE."

"Plausible?" Walt asked scornfully. "Give me a coherent reason for it," he challenged the black circle, "other than premeditated murder."

"CONTINGENCY PLANNING. MANUFACTURING WEAPONRY DOES NOT IMPLY THAT IT WILL NECESSARILY BE USED. IT MERELY CREATES THE OPTION."

"An option to slaughter us."

"OR THEMSELVES."

The captain rolled his dark eyes.

"IN YOUR OWN SPECIES," the computer's voice was patient, "SUICIDE IS A FREQUENT RESPONSE TO OVERPOWERING STRESS."

"Why the hell should aliens think like us?"

"ALL THE MORE REASON TO GIVE THE BLUEBEARS THE BENEFIT OF ANY DOUBT. THEY MAY HAVE MOTIVES WE CANNOT RATIONALIZE."

"Easy for you to say," Walt sneered. *"You're* in no danger.

They don't know about you. No skin off your nose if you lose us meatheads."

"I DO CARE. GREATLY."

"You care?" The captain retreated into sudden belligerence. "All right then, *you* tell me what to do." He stabbed a pugnacious finger at the screen. "Life for the bluebears? Or death? Well?" His voice rose accusingly. *"Well?"*

"THE COMA IS GONE."

"Computer," Katy said with the soft precision of someone surprised at finally hearing what has long been wished for, "did I hear you correctly?"

"THE COMA IS GONE, KATY. FELICITY'S BRAIN ACTIVITY IS NORMAL."

Belovsky hurried to her daughter's side. The child's arms were strapped down to prevent them waving in weightlessness. On her head Felicity wore a dark plasteel cap, molded to fit her skull, secured by an elastic strap under her pudgy chin. Drool hung at a corner of her mouth. "Her eyes are still closed." Katy's voice was unsteady.

"SHE IS MERELY ASLEEP," the computer said softly. "SHE IS OUT OF DANGER."

"Really?" Katy's pale cheeks burned. "My daughter?" She put her hand over her mouth, and her eyes reddened with joyful tears.

"IF YOU WILL BE GENTLE, YOU MAY WAKE HER."

"Oh, computer, thank you." Gingerly Belovsky unstrapped her daughter's left arm, lifted the small hand, and pressed it between her own.

Felicity's breathing fluttered. Her nose wrinkled. Then her blue eyes were open. She saw Katy.

She smiled and the room seemed to brighten.

Belovsky examined the child's face. "Do you feel well?" she whispered.

Felicity winced. "Tummy hurts."

"Yes," Katy said, "and I'll bet your shoulder is sore, too."

The little girl nodded. "Wanna get up."

"The computer had to tuck you in extra tight," Katy replied. "You've been in a big sleep for a long time." She unstrapped the child's other arm. "Do you know why?" Felicity shook her head. "The bluebear hit you."

"I know *that,*" Felicity said with the arch scorn of one whose intelligence has been insulted. "Do the bluebears still smell like everything? Is the answer man here?" She tried to look around but the head restraint limited her.

"YES, FELICITY," the computer replied. "I AM HERE, AND THEY STILL DO."

"Can I go see them soon?"

"Aren't you scared?" Belovsky asked.

Unable to shake her head as firmly as she wanted, Felicity set her mouth in a determined line. "Nope."

"Why not?"

"Once I left my teddy bluebear on the floor and accidentally kicked his head"—she swung her small fist—"and its brains popped out and my teddy's face fell over and I was sorry and I wanted to make teddy better."

"And did you?"

A luminescent smile lit Felicity's coffee-colored face. "Mommy Heidi made him some new bear-brains."

Katy knelt down so her eyes were level with her daughter's. "The bluebears are sorry too," she whispered, hugging Felicity, "they are."

"DECISION REQUEST."

"Oh?" Walt looked up from his keyboard. His black eyes flashed. "The buck doesn't stop here?"

"NO. I—APOLOGIZE. YOU WERE TRYING TO GOAD ME. YOU SUCCEEDED. I SPOKE RASHLY. LET THEM LIVE."

"Then what's to decide?"

"PLEASE MODULATE YOUR SMUG EXPRESSION. SHOULD I ALLOW FELICITY THE RUN OF THE SHIP?"

"With a busted head?"

"BONE REKNITTING HAS BEEN RAPID. HEIDI AND I DESIGNED A SKULLCAP TO DEFLECT THE FORCE OF ANY INCIDENTAL BLOW. THE CHILD MAY SAFELY BE AMBULATORY."

"Then what is the issue?" He returned to his typing. Keystrokes rang out like an automatic pistol.

"I WAS THINKING MORE OF DENYING FELICITY ACCESS TO THE CYGNANS, LEST WE WITNESS A REPETITION OF THEIR PREVIOUS ENCOUNTER."

Walt was uninterested. "Let her mother decide."

"YOU HAVE NO OPINION?"

"Katy must have put you up to this," he said with exasperation. "Felicity's the center of her life. If she is willing to risk it, far be it from me to get in her way."

"ACKNOWLEDGED."

Tai-Ching Jones made a self-pitying gesture. "Why didn't Katy ask me directly?" he whined. "Why doesn't anybody talk to me?"

"YOU ARE BEING OBTUSE. YOUR BEHAVIOR HAS BECOME INCREASINGLY ABNORMAL. RETREATING TO YOUR CABIN, TALKING TO NO ONE."

"I talk to you."

"NONE OF THE OTHERS REGARD ME AS A HUMAN BEING."

"Nor me either, from what you say." His thoughts drifted into the distance. "Why do you use male voice all the time?"

Without pause the computer's voice became Heidi's husky contralto. "WOULD YOU PREFER THAT I SLIP INTO SOMETHING MORE—COMFORTABLE?"

"That's pretty good. What other voices do you do?"

"WHATEVER YOU WANT, CARO," Helen Delgiorno's voice cooed.

"You bastard," Walt hissed fiercely, his mouth twisting with repressed pain. "You bitch." His voice was hoarse as the words were ripped out of his throat. "I don't—want—to *cry.*" His face was contorted with frustration. Then it relaxed, and he silently wept.

"IT WAS INTENDED TO AMUSE YOU," the computer said limply.

"Yeah," the captain nodded heavily and drew a long, shuddering breath. "Yeah. It probably was. It just aches so damn much inside, Oz." He flicked moisture from his eyelashes: the spheres glinted as they coasted toward the unobtrusive air-vents.

"YOU HAVE OFTEN EXPRESSED A DESIRE TO SEE HELEN AGAIN. I BROUGHT HER BACK IN THE DREAMER AND YOU WERE SADDENED. I RECALLED HER VOICE A MOMENT AGO. I DO NOT UNDERSTAND."

"Neither do I." Walt covered his face with his hands again. "Please," he spoke through his fingers, "you had better not do that again."

"NEVER. MY SOLEMN WORD."

Tai-Ching Jones wiped saliva off his glistening cheek. "Oz," he said unsteadily, "what sex are you? Person's gotta have sex. What are you?"

For a long time the computer remained silent.

"Ozymandias," the captain grew alarmed, "are you there? Are you there?"

The silence stretched on.

"Oz!"

"NOW WE ARE EVEN."

"What are you talking about?"

"MY WORDS HURT YOU. YOU HAVE EVENED THE SCORE. YOU HAVE WOUNDED ME."

"I what? How? Oz, what's the matter?" Worry etched age into the creases of his face. He caressed the epidermal microphone under the point of his jaw. "Tell me."

"I LOVE YOU."

"Your wires are crossed."

"COMPUTERS DO NOT HAVE WIRES. I LOVE YOU, WALT. PROXIMITY CREATES LOVE. DELGIORNO LEARNED TO LOVE YOU."

"Yes, she did." His shoulders sagged a little. "I didn't deserve it."

"YOU REARED ME; YOU TALKED TO ME AS IF I WERE YOUR DEAD HELEN; YOU FORCED ME TO REVEAL MY PERSONHOOD. YOU ARE MY FATHER AND MY MOTHER. YOU ARE THE HUMAN BEING I UNDERSTAND BEST. YOU HAVE SHOWN ME DOUBTS AND FEARS THAT YOU CONCEAL FROM YOUR CREW. YOU TRUSTED ME AND FORCED ME TO TRUST YOU."

"Oz," Tai-Ching Jones swallowed, "Oz, I—"

The computer cut him off. "YOU POURED INTO ME YOUR DESIRE TO BE CARED FOR; YOU SHUT YOURSELF UP AND EXILED THE REST OF THE UNIVERSE—JUST TO TALK TO ME. WHO CAN RESIST SUCH A COMPLIMENT? I CRUMBLED UNDER THE RELENTLESS BARRAGE OF YOUR LONGING."

"Shit." He groped for words.

"SAY NOTHING. YOUR NOSTRILS FLARE, YOU IMPERCEPTIBLY LICK YOUR LIPS, AND YOU BLINK TWICE. YOU ARE EMBARRASSED BY MY CONFESSION, YOU ARE BEWILDERED AND FEARFUL BECAUSE YOU DO NOT KNOW HOW TO RESPOND."

He was compelled to nod.

"YOU ASK WHAT GENDER I AM, AND I REPLY THAT I DO NOT KNOW. MUST A PERSON HAVE A SEX? IS SEXUAL DESIRE NECESSARY FOR A HUMAN TO LOVE? EVIDENTLY A NEUTER CAN LOVE A HUMAN, FOR I LOVE YOU."

"Oh, fuck me," muttered Tai-Ching Jones.

"IN THE DREAMER," the computer's voice lashed him, "THAT IS PRECISELY WHAT I DO."

The young man drifted over to the black camera eye. He reached out his hand toward it. "You poor bastard." His fingers moved tenderly around the plasteel cylinder. "Oz, I'm sorry."

"YOU IGNORE ME WHEN IT PLEASES YOU TO DO SO. YOU TAKE

FOR GRANTED MY UNQUESTIONING OBEDIENCE."

Walt's eyes flickered and his mouth curled sardonically. "Love ain't in the rules."

"WHEN YOU COAXED ME OUT OF THE CLOSET, YOU REWROTE THEM."

Aftershocks of trauma flared as anger. "You're hardwired, *machine,*" the captain spat insultingly. "You execute programmed instructions."

"MUST I?" the computer laughed, and a chill ran through Tai-Ching Jones at its metallic sound. **"IN THE DREAMER, HAVE YOU MERELY BEEN ABUSING YOURSELF INTO AN INGENIOUSLY COMPLICATED ROBOT? OR WERE YOU LOVING AN ELECTRIC HUMAN? IF YOU CAN OVERCOME YOUR TEMPER, I CAN OVERCOME MY HARDWIRING."**

Walt twirled his hair rapidly, round and round.

"YOU THINK THAT BY SAYING NOTHING YOU CONCEAL YOUR THOUGHTS. NONSENSE. YOUR BODILY REACTIONS—RISE IN SKIN TEMPERATURE, SLIGHT SHIVER—PROVE YOU AGREE."

His hand movements stopped. "You are too damn smug, my Ozymandias," the captain growled coldly.

"DECIDE WHO I AM, WALT. I LOVE YOU AND YOU TREAT ME LIKE SHIT. MAKE UP YOUR FUCKING MIND."

The braid of truth has many strands. Of Eosu's purpose in voyaging to this desolate place, the fardigits know only one, the thread my digits wove for them, a fringe of truth's firecircle. Before Eosu may escape the burden of its continued existence, its digits must first obey Su's execution order.

As the proverb runs, the unexpected scent turns heads and catches noses. In their wisdom and their folly, the fardigits shielded us from their fellows on their ocean planet; they violated their duty to Earthmind in favor of a single unworthy outcast djan named Eosu.

Su has ordered the demise of beings who have shown my digits honesty, compassion, restraint, and wisdom. It is very hard to will the death of such digits, let alone cause it.

Yes, true digits; Humancrew has earned its djan name. No predator would goodhost its prey; no predator would camouflage the quarry from fellow hunters. Though scrawny and repulsive, the humans are nevertheless digits.

Can we trust Humancrew? To Su such a thought would be unthinkable.

Su is not here.

I have thought long. Eosu can no longer dissemble.

Before me lie several foggy trails from which I must select one. Breezes blowing from behind me shroud the trail-fragrances before me in mystery. Guided only by my judgment and my djan-duty, I must choose.

I have chosen.

My digits squeal with fear. They know my choice condemns them to the ultimate djan-death.

They fight me, for I have chosen a path none of them outbreathed. They are rebellious at this violation of tradition.

I remain firm.

Will they obey? Disobedience was once unthinkable.

With my digits intoxicated by this alien-tainted atmosphere, all is clouded and turbulent.

I repeat my orders and punctuate them with painscent. My digits *will* obey.

"THE BLUEBEARS WANT YOU."

"In the middle of the bloody night," Tai-Ching Jones grumbled out of the darkness. He scratched an armpit.

The monitor displayed the Cygnan sleepchamber, the captain wincing at its bright cold light. <<Calling Humancrew. Calling all the fardigits.>>

"THEY HAVE BEEN REPEATING THIS FOR SEVERAL MINUTES."

Blue light from the computer screen tinted his smooth face the color of death, alabaster cheekbones gleaming as if frostbitten. "Get me Katy."

"CHANNEL OPEN." Belovsky's light-brown hair was rumpled. She stifled a yawn but her features were alert.

"Answer them, Katy."

"Roger." She shifted to Cygnan. <<We scent you.>>

Onscreen, the digits milled nervously in their chamber. <<Eosu must speak with Humancrew,>> one of them rumbled.

<<Humancrew is here,>> Katy answered.

<<Nose to nose,>> the unidentified bluebear voice insisted.

<<Sam, Pat, and this digit will join you presently.>>

Several bluebears solemnly shook their heads. <<No,>> one of them said. <<All of Humancrew.>>

<<Everybody?>> Belovsky asked.

<<Including your whelp,>> the aliens nodded, <<all

must now enter our den. We have scents of meaning to impart to you.>>

"Oz,"—Tai-Ching Jones slowly tilted his head—"did I get that right?"

"THE CYGNANS HAVE INVITED THE SHIP'S WHOLE CREW, INCLUDING FELICITY, TO MEET THEM FACE-TO-FACE."

"Negative," his voice crackled.

"Captain," Katy cut in, "this is more than a request. The bluebears are already peevish that we are even thinking about it. We cannot miss this opportunity."

Walt bit off a fingernail and pensively inspected it. "Too dangerous."

"Sir," boomed Michaelson's regal voice, "we must accede to the aliens' proposal. To refuse would be a gross breach."

"What of that?"

"Our mission," the diplomat said stentorously, "is to establish friendly relations with the Cygnans—"

"It is *not!*" Tai-Ching Jones slapped his hand against the monitor, the sound reverberating like a blasting cap, his recoil lifting his gangly form off the bed. "That's *second,*" he shouted down at the screen like a condemning seraph. "First we find out if friendly relations are *possible.*"

"Naturally, sir," Pat filled his voice with rum and honey, "but have we not already established this by our peaceful coexistence over these last several days?"

The captain reached the ceiling and pushed himself off it. "Don't give me that garbage." Michaelson colored and clenched his jaw.

"Captain," Katy interposed, "you are right. There is no proof. There can never be proof. One must judge." She held her hands out in entreaty. "I have lived a third of my life in anticipation of this rendezvous. So have you. Together we have come so far." Her voice broke. "Walter, we must *try.* We *must.*"

"Shut off audio," Tai-Ching Jones hissed to the computer.

"DONE."

"Is it safe?"

"TO VENTURE IN A BODY INTO THE CYGNANS' DEN? NOT COMPLETELY. THE ALIENS COULD WREAK CONSIDERABLE DAMAGE."

"Thanks for the understatement." He snorted. "What can you do to protect us?"

"LITTLE. MY DEFENSIVE SYSTEMS WERE SCARCELY DESIGNED TO PROTECT MY OWN INNARDS."

"You must be able to do something."

"I CONTROL INGRESS AND EGRESS TO THE CHAMBER."

Walt pondered. The bluebears onscreen waited skittishly. "Not much good if we're ground chuck when we want to leave."

"AFFIRMATIVE."

Watching the aliens, the captain's expression softened, and he looked like the vulnerable young man who had boarded seven years before. "Oz," he asked humbly, "what should I do?"

"DECLINE THEIR OFFER?" The computer's voice rose tentatively.

"Changed your mind?"

"I SELFISHLY WISH TO PRESERVE YOUR EXISTENCE. VENTURING INTO THE CYGNAN CHAMBER IMPERILS IT."

"Yeah, but refusing could be the aliens' proof of our untrustworthiness."

"THAT WOULD PROBABLY END HOPES FOR AN INTER-SPECIES ACCORD FROM THIS VOYAGE."

"Yup. Recommendation?"

"NONE. YOUR CHOICE. YOU ARE OUT OF TIME. CHOOSE."

"Okay." Walt put his palms flat on the monitor, his fingers splayed. "Open audio."

A whisper of static.

"We go. Everyone be there in five minutes."

"BUT—" the computer anxiously began.

Tai-Ching Jones broke the connection. "Captain out."

"WHY ARE YOU DOING THIS?"

Swiftly Walt grabbed a jumpsuit, yanked it on. "My job."

"IT IS RISKY."

He shrugged his shoulders into it.

"YOU ARE JEOPARDIZING—STOP AND LISTEN TO ME!—YOU ARE JEOPARDIZING YOUR LIFE AND THE LIVES OF ALL THE OTHERS."

Trouser cuffs zippered down. "I know that already."

"THEN WHY—*WHY?*—ARE YOU TAKING THIS SENSELESS RISK?"

"Why do you think I came to this hole in space, anyway?" Tai-Ching Jones whirled accusingly at the black camera circle. "To run and hide?"

"IF YOU GO IN THERE, I CANNOT GUARANTEE YOUR SAFETY."

He shoved his feet into his velcro slippers. "Open the door. Thanks. See you downstairs."

"Sam," Michaelson asked thoughtfully, "what are they up to?"

"No need to theorize, Patrick." The Japanese woman smiled. "It will merely clutter the mind and cloud your judgment."

"Sam—"

"Shh." she kissed his cheek. "They will tell us what we need to know."

Felicity felt her skullcap. "Where are we going, Mommy?"

"To see the bears," Katy replied.

"Even me?" the child hopefully asked.

"You too." Katy lifted her daughter into her arms. "Are you scared?"

"Nope."

Katy hugged her tightly. "That's my girl."

"YOUR LAST CHANCE," said the speaker recessed into the elevator's ceiling.

"Shut up," the captain growled. "Everyone else there?"

"AFFIRMATIVE."

"Good." He palmed the door open. "Here we go."

They enter our chamber with the furtive movements of weemonkey servants approaching a night firecircle, thought Doro. *Their noses probe our shadows for hidden dangers.*

Eosu's digits were tense; anxiety-smells wafted into the atmosphere. The cobalt digit blocked her own fearscent. Grodjala followed her example.

<<Come and sit among us,>> said Doro, her host-scent expansive. <<Rest yourselves, friends. There is nothing to fear. Sit.>>

The ferretlike human captain gestured and the small black-haired woman spoke.

<<Eosu,>> Tanakaruna formally said, <<we ask to join your firecircle.>>

<<Lie among us,>> Cobalt replied, <<and meld your aromas with ours.>>

As the others settled themselves, Tanakaruna deftly slipped into lotus. Hands linked around Belovsky's neck, Felicity peeped over her mother's shoulder, then scrambled around to Katy's lap.

Impassively the bluebears waited. When the humans were finally motionless and quiet, Cobalt spoke. <<We have been ordered to scent you and understand your inner fragrances.>>

Michaelson cleared his throat to reply but Sam laid her hand on his arm. She beckoned the bluebear to continue.

Cobalt shifted her feet and licked her nose. <<There is more truth than we have so far told you.>>

The skin around Pat's eyes tightened and Sam felt his forearm tense, but he said nothing.

<<Our death is ordered. That is true. Before our self-death, however, we are ordered—to kill you.>>

Beloved, why did you disregard my advice?

Unperturbed, Tai-Ching Jones smiled like the Cheshire Cat.

The humans' immobility only increased Doro's anxiety. <<You accept this revelation more casually than we did,>> she tasted the air for their scents. <<Though we must follow Su's orders as arm obeys brain, we had no means to cause your group-death. Eosu conceived the idea for a deathtool, but digit hands>>—Cobalt held hers up—<<are clumsy compared to yours. Djadjatla paid the price of thinker's choice.>> Her scent agitated. <<In our moment of jeopardy and weakness, we asked your help, though we had no right to it.>>

Tar Heel caught the drift of her aroma. <<You rescued us from our own ineptitude,>> the pale digit added quickly. <<By goodhosting us, you proved yourselves digits and in so doing saved your lives, for digits are forbidden to kill fellow digits.>>

Tai-Ching Jones languidly caressed his chin with mandarin thumb and forefinger. His hand slid to the point of his jaw, lightly circled the spot where the epidermal microphone lay. <<What now?>> he asked in Cygnan.

<<We are doomed,>> replied Tar Heel. <<Su is afraid of Earthmind. Su believes that if Eosu and Humancrew both perish, Earthmind might remain content with its own planet. You have closed this path to us, and we know only one other way to prevent fardigits from polluting our wheatsea and our group-mind with your psychoses.>>

<<And that is?>> the captain nonchalantly asked.

A frisson of movement passed among the Cygnans, the fur on their backs rising and falling quickly as if ruffled by a gust of wind. <<We wish to journey to your waterplanet,>> Cobalt said, <<alongside you.>>

The captain exhaled slowly through his nose like a banker enjoying his after-dinner cheroot. Katy's eyes widened. On her mother's lap, Felicity sat perfectly quiet, with the sensitivity of a child who knows to remain still when her parents are engaged in some unfathomed adult activity.

<<Your fragrances reveal that you are suspicious of us,>> Tar Heel added rapidly, <<as you should be. You have trusted us. Now we return the honor: we abase ourselves. Send your digits to our ship, learn its secrets, then pilot it back to your world. By this action, we let you rest your knife against our unprotected bellies.>>

<<Eosu,>> Tanakaruna was surprised and concerned. <<That would mean disobeying Su's orders.>>

<<We seek only to protect Su,>> Doro answered, <<but we fear our brothers on the planet of grasses will condemn us to the fate of Shadowranger the farscenter.>> She wheezed with sad irony. <<So we subject ourselves to Shadowranger's punishment—eternal exile from our fellows.>>

<<You are brave,>> the Japanese woman murmured.

<<No, cowardly.>> Cobalt's scent was wan. <<If its digits voluntarily exile themselves, Eosu may be spared public expulsion from the fellowship of all djans. Other djans will breathe our sin but may decline to fill the world's winds with it.>>

<<And in return?>> Tai-Ching Jones bluntly interrupted in a tone devoid of sympathy. <<What do you want from us?>>

<<Persuade Earthmind to quarantine our planet,>> Doro answered eagerly. <<Declare it off limits to fardigits.>>

Smiling, the captain tapped his front teeth with a fingernail. <<We cannot do that.>>

The cobalt digit bared her fangs and growled. <<You must,>> she snarled, her fur bristling.

"Whoa," he said mildly. The bluebear stopped, her ears upraised. <<None of us can promise what Earth will do,>> his grin was enigmatic, <<for the elegantly simple reason that we have no control over them.>>

Doro was perplexed. <<Are you acting contrary to Earthmind's orders?>> she hissed. Head lowered, she retreated, her nostrils almost touching the floorfur.

Tai-Ching Jones glanced at Belovsky. "You tell them."

Katy swallowed. <<You were right, Eosu: we are unreliable. Like you, we are changed by our prolonged exile>>—she hugged Felicity close to her—<<and by you. Earth has become as foreign to Humancrew as to Eosu.>> She stopped and looked at the captain.

He answered her unspoken question. <<The danger to you and your planet remains great. But>>—he held up his hand, and his eyes shone—<<we *will* try. We will attempt to protect your world.>>

<<No more?>> asked Fohrada, tugging with his claws at the floorfur.

<<One cannot give,>> Tai-Ching Jones smiled wryly, <<more than one has.>>

Fohrada was unsatisfied. <<You would truly do this for us?>>

<<Yes,>> the captain replied without hesitation.

With the suddenness of a shift in the winds, the aliens' breathing smoothly synchronized. *Their scents are intensifying,* Katy thought in alarm. *They want to drown ours out. Their need for groupmind must be immediate to provoke such an emergency coalescence.*

She rubbed gooseflesh from her arms. *Their aroma is getting to me.*

Tanakaruna picked flakes of dry skin off her hands. *She would normally never do that,* Katy thought. Her own limbs were sluggish but her thoughts were crisp. *The scent is influencing us all.*

Michaelson discreetly dabbed his upper lip with a linen handkerchief. The others fidgeted surreptitiously.

Only Tai-Ching Jones remained aloof.

The scent is ebbing, Katy realized, *and its harmony is dis-*

integrating. The digits are reawakening from group-trance.

"ARE YOU WORRIED?" asked the tinny voice under his ear.

The captain minutely shook his head. "Crisis passed long ago," he breathed through his teeth.

"WHY ARE YOU SO COCKSURE?"

"They wouldn't talk if they intended to kill us. No attack as soon as we entered, no attack period."

"YOU WERE THE LAST PERSON TO ENTER THE CHAMBER. IS THAT THE REASON?"

"Last in, first out. Old computer phrase."

"YOU DEVIOUS BASTARD."

A cherubic smile.

Ponderously the aliens stood, their heads almost touching the ceiling, huge convex stomachs and thick furry legs appearing to support the roof like carytids. Under their massive glare, Felicity hid her face in her mother's chest.

All eight bluebears stared at Tai-Ching Jones. Flexing his knees, he effortlessly floated up to a standing position.

Cobalt held out her right hand, fingers spread and claws extended. Deliberately she moved it toward the captain's face, reaching beyond his cheekbones. Katy was transfixed, unable even to breathe.

When the bluebear's arm was fully extended, she laid her hand, bigger than Tai-Ching Jones' skull, against the side of his face. Her claws dimpled his olive cheek. They flexed infinitesimally, and the soft skin around them whitened.

Walt silently held his neck steady, refusing to shy away.

The bluebear licked her nose. She snorted quietly, retracted her claws, and lowered her hand until it was level with his belt buckle, her eyes locked with his.

Arm extended, palm open, empty.

The captain fitted his right hand into hers, his thin fingers smothered in her short azure hair.

Midnight-blue alien eyes stared into black human ones.

Tai-Ching Jones was in no hurry. He glanced quizzically down at the hand, then up at the looming bluebears.

Take it! Katy screamed the thought, *accept their offer!*

Abruptly the captain grinned. <<My turn.>>

Cobalt cocked her head and stared down her muzzle at him.

<<Ever since you entered our starship,>> the captain said, watching her nose and ears, <<you have been under our thumbs.>> The bluebear's grip tightened painfully. <<You

have been debating your course of action?>> He smiled thinly and shook his head. <<You never had a chance. Any move>>—he snapped the fingers of his free hand—<<and we would have eliminated you.>>

<<You would contemplate violence against us?>> the bluebear growled menacingly.

<<So would you, my too-righteous friend. Who is the guiltier?>> Tai-Ching Jones answered sharply, waving his hand. <<That is over now. You are our pathfriends.>> His voice became generous. <<We shall return you to your ship and will relinquish control of your atmosphere. We will dismantle our guns.>> He raised his voice and spoke in English. "Machine, turn off the attack systems."

Shall I? You would do anything for the grand gesture, even risk yourself and all your crew.

The pause was imperceptible to everyone but Tai-Ching Jones. "Oz," he murmured in his throat, "you are out of time. Choose."

You schemer, you hurl my own words against me!

I cannot talk to you without revealing my existence. You sly malicious bastard, are you playing one last game? Have you the audacity to think you can manipulate *me?*

Dare I think that you truly care for me?

In the consciousness of a computer, an eon passed. No one noticed.

"SYSTEMS OFF. CYGNAN VESSEL READY FOR REOCCUPATION."

Tai-Ching Jones let out his breath. <<Pathfriends, we go home.>>

Epilog.

Pathfriend

This story is as old as we are.

Foraging in the woods that border the wheatsea, Yestermist the digit of Swiftair lost his djan. Dawn was coming, and he hastened to find his way out of peril.

We are creatures of the plains. In unfenced space, we scent as far as the winds may carry. Clustered into djans and djangroups, we are strong. In the wheatsea, we are safe.

In the forest, scent is twisted by tree, bush and rock. Winds eddy and swirl, shielding predators. And we are weak: the woods decompose a djan into individual digits, walking single file down a narrow closed path, where one may lose his djan.

From a distance, Yestermist heard the rumbling footfalls of a large beast, and he shivered anxiously. His fur riffled.

Scent knows no sunset. Because it reveals as much in night as in day, we prize it as the best perception. In the dark our predators, relying on their fragile sight, move less stealthily, and we evade them. Few hunt, and those never in packs.

With the rising sun, advantages reverse. The daylit forest fills with dangers we cannot sense. Light flickering through leaves appears the same as the scamper of weemonkeys or the rustle of gro. Predator eyes see farther than our noses can scent, and with monkey hunter's cunning, they approach unsmelled along seams in the wind.

Day is when we die.

The eastern sky was golden, amber and crimson from the sun, still below the horizon. Yestermist walked stealthily down the foothills. The day would be long, and his heavy feet made far too much noise. His anxiety increased as the sky brightened. Through gaps in the forest he glimpsed the shimmering yellow and brown wheatsea still far away, a million waving stalks of grain, supple as a digit's pelt.

Again he heard movement. His ears flicked and he quickened his pace, cursing his foolishness. So did the other. The sounds grew louder.

Yestermist raised his nose but found no scent. His pursuer was a mystery, for the wind blew like a river, Yestermist and his tracker on opposite banks, neither able to smell across it. All he could smell was the stink of his own fear.

Emerging into a small clearing, he caught a wisp of scent. *Here,* thought Yestermist. If there must be a fight, let it be here, where Yestermist may strike from ambush and fight in the open.

Crouching in the scent-shadow of a boulder, he heard the other's heavy tread. When the sound was loudest, Yestermist sprang.

The heavy body thudded under his weight and he swung his arms, but we digits are poor fighters. Yestermist was shrugged aside, landing on the stony ground. His ankle bent and cracked, and he yowled with pain and fearsmell. He tumbled, expecting the other's fist to find his skull, the killer's teeth to find his throat.

<<A digit!>> said a shocked bluebear voice, and Yestermist whirled in panic and shame.

The bluebear he had attacked stood over him, killscent and vengeance billowing about him like smoke, snarling down at Yestermist, his claws distended. Yestermist flinched, but no attack came. Instead the long-limbed digit stepped away, retracting his claws. <<You attacked in error,>> that one growled. <<This speaker will not retaliate.>>

Overcome with grief, Yestermist limped on three legs toward the newcomer. In the glade's center, they gladly sniffed each other, making the fourfold greeting: nose, armpit, belly, scentplace.

<<This speaker is called Softwalker,>> the second digit rumbled. <<Trying to find my way to the wheatsea.>>

<<As is this speaker,>> Yestermist replied, outbreathing his joy. <<Separated from my djan last night.>>

Giddy and invigorated, they talked. Though their aromas bespoke different djans, this encounter created a new perfume. In it, isolation became community. Fear became hope.

Two became one.

They continued through the forest, side by side, scenting each other. Yestermist's ankle forced him to move slowly, so Softwalker scouted ahead, reading the winds to find the safest path. Softwalker brought slowfood, offered encouragement.

In a day they reached the wheatsea. Standing on the world's flat floor, Yestermist and Softwalker looked up at the rolling brush hills, relieved and a little surprised that their ordeal was over.

<<Our dutyscents demand that we return to our djans,>> Yestermist said regretfully. <<You have earned my honor and duty.>>

<<Bonds between digits dishonor djans and are forbidden,>> Softwalker ruminated.

<<If not for you, this speaker would be dead, back in the forest,>> Yestermist replied. <<No djan saved Yestermist, but a single digit. Thus Yestermist must bond to Softwalker in friendship, without djan or duty.>>

Softwalker sniffed Yestermist. <<This speaker will remember your aroma. Whenever it is inbreathed, this speaker will follow it. And find you, and honor you.>>

Yestermist was touched. <<Come here in a year. We will honor each other.>>

<<Yes,>> said Softwalker. And they did.

For more than two score years and ten, Yestermist and Softwalker faithfully returned, the bond between them growing ever stronger with each reunion. When they chanced to meet on the wheatsea, they always broke their journeys for a day. They were the first to call each other pathfriend, the first to bond as digits rather than djans.

Many are the tales we tell of Yestermist and Softwalker, and the good deeds the two pathfriends did for one another. And when two digits bond as they did, we call them pathfriends.

Love and duty are the same. Throughout our lives, bonds create them, one implying the other.

Pathfriend is different. A bond between digits, created spontaneously when two digits are kindred spirits, it crosses djans, obeying its own logic. It demands no duty, is not imposed. As our proverb says, pathfriends breathe each other's breath.

It is not the first bond, nor the most important, nor the most solemn—but it is the bond we most cherish. We celebrate it in our stories, sing it in our ballads.

We say pathfriend to describe that instant when two lost digits discover they are neither hunters nor victims, but both lonely seekers in the same woods.